# No Warning Shot

## An Isaac Stompski novel of fiction

Written by: *Paul J. Provencio*

ISBN
Hardcover: 978-1-966565-84-0
Paperback: 978-1-966565-83-3

# Dedication

The dedication for my first novel took no thought at all. I owe all that I am to our loving mother of three, Beryl Arnold, and her deceased husband, Robert Arnold. Without their love and support through Life, these books might never have been written. I Love You Mom!

# Special Thanks

A special thanks to Tom Berg. A tattoo shop owner in San Pedro, CA, and his work created the portrayal of Issac Stompski in front of the "No Warning Shot" sign with wings unfurled. Tom, I look forward to meeting you in person in the near future.

A special thanks to Kenny Woods, who introduced me to this very talented artist.

A special thanks to the NYBP team of professional editors, artists, consulters, and administrators who, without their help, this publication may not have materialized.

# About the Author

Paul J Provencio was born and raised a Native to San Diego. He began his educational journey at St. Vincent de Paul Catholic School. His family later relocated to Del Mar, California, where he attended Earl Warren Jr. High in Solana Beach. His life took an intriguing turn when he found himself living abroad as a Diplomat, following his father's career as a DEA agent in Bogotá, Colombia. Amidst the challenges, Paul graduated from high school at Colegio Nueva Granada in Bogotá. Returning to his roots in Del Mar, he continued his education while building a successful career as an Electrical Contractor. Today, Paul pours his rich and varied experiences into his work as an Author, crafting fictional novels that celebrate the vibrant spirit of his native San Diego. Enjoy your reading adventure, and be sure to watch for his upcoming book, "Yard Down."

# Prologue

The helicopter lifts off from Montgomery Field in Kearney Mesa, thirty miles from Tijuana, Mexico, the "Gateway to the South." It is the Witching Hour, 2:30 in the morning. The many bars in San Diego have just closed their doors to patrons. These same patrons are now pilots of several-ton-missiles heading towards home, unaware of the dangers they pose and unaware of the "interceptors" waiting to prevent death caused by these patrons. "San Diego's Finest," The San Diego Police Department, and "Chips," the California Highway Patrol, are those "interceptors."

The pilot of the Channel 8 Helicopter is on a risky flight mission, high above the risks of the road, but he could be targeted as hostile, nonetheless. The "hot shot" reporter riding shotgun has solid information on which she intends to get coverage of this clear August summer flight to the south. Her reliable source, a transport deputy for the San Diego Sheriff's Department, has leaked information about a "special transport" of a high-profile serial child killer. After two years of a heavily reported media-circus trial, "The Monster Within" is sentenced to death.

The reporter's source lets her know that mainline transports leave George Bailey County Jail at 4:00-5:00 am; however, a "special transport" will leave at 10:00 am with one passenger aboard, Mark Sutter. Although Mr. Sutter committed heinous crimes, killing exclusively the children of sheriff's deputies, his isolated transport is for his protection, deserved or not. His appeal was filed by his attorney, possibly putting off his execution for decades, all at the expense of the taxpayers and reinforced by pacifist sympathizers.

Kristy Lyons, reporter for KSDN News, plans on filming both transports to R.J. Donovan Prison, about one and one-quarter miles from George Bailey County Jail. Any aircraft over the prison violates several laws and breaches all security measures. Her informer knows this, is adamant about anonymity and was paid a high sum of dollars and "special favors" only known to him and Kristy. She plans on following the second transport all the way to the front gate of R.J.D. Prison, then panning over the Level 4 reception yard, then over the Level 3 lifer yard where Sutter will be housed until his permanent housing is determined, at which time he will "trans-pack" to that prison.

The pilot of the helicopter is only 22 years old, hired that same year by KSDN News. He will claim to be ignorant of the laws concerning the no-flight zone. No seasoned pilot would risk his license but a naive youngster may get off with a hand slap, no guarantees. Don Ellis, the pilot, is dressed casually in blue Levi 501s and an Iron Maiden Concert shirt depicting Eddie, a 30-foot-tall inflatable likeness of the storyline character. Kristy is wearing black, skin-tight Levi 505s, tactical Navy boots, a black Squadron 54 bombardier jacket with fleece lining, and a pair of Ray Ban Aviator sunglasses. At this hour in August, the temperature is 69 degrees, and sunrise is hours away. The Ray Bans are of no protection; however, Kristy, only six months after giving birth to her first child, looks 100% edible.

As they rise above the tarmac, Don calls in his flight pattern consistent with a freeway traffic helicopter: Flight over Highway 52, which is relatively short at 21 miles and travels west to east from La Jolla to Santee, a very congested stretch for east-county commuters traveling to Sorento Valley and cities; from there south, past Pacific Beach, Mission Bay, Lindberg Field International Airport (named after Charles Lindberg made famous by his flight aboard the Spirit of St. Louis), through the "S" turn downtown and Sea Port Village, east up Highway 94, then south on I-15 towards "nasty city and the "Mile of Cars" to Broadway in Chula Vista, east up H Street (at the mall); then all the way to East Lake, south over the Olympic Training Center; from there to the East Mesa Juvenile Facility, East Mesa Re-entry Facility, George Bailey

Detention Facility 8 (nonpolitical housing, formerly ICE) and the "grandpappy" of all....R.J. Donovan Prison.

Donovan is more like a fenced-in city. Go any farther south, and you'll be at La Mesa Prison in Mexico.

Kristy Lyons planned to fly over the Sheriff's shooting range after getting the call that the mainliners were loaded up and then come up over Alta Road just as the bus was in the canyon dip. Don Ellis would then bank the helicopter into a 180-degree turn and fly backward as the bus approached the turn west into the gates at R.J. Donovan. Videography at its finest! After which they would fly over the "new car and truck" overfill yards and auction yards, landing for fuel at Brown Field Airport. While fueling, they would have breakfast at the coffee shop, sending the footage via encrypted broadband to the KSDN news station in Kearny Mesa. There will be plenty of time to edit and refine the video before this evening's news. When Kristy's source at Bailey Detention lets them know that they've pulled Sutter from High Power 6, cell living, they would read the news helicopter and fly the same route back. If timing went according to plan, they should reach the turn-off to R.J. Donovan at the same time as the transport.

GPS is a wonderful advance in technology for auto pilot. Just like a drone, a helicopter can follow a recent flight path in the opposite direction, which is exactly what Don Ellis used to return to the entrance drive to R.J. Donovan Prison.

Kristy's ringer was the song "No Rest for the Wicked" by Cage the Elephant. Don Ellis fired up the rotor and they lifted off the tarmac. The helicopter intercepted the bus as it was turning west into R.J.D. Prison. They banked left and were a mere 40 feet above the bus. They could not turn back now. Cameras were rolling as Kristy began her reporting.

"Kristy Lyons here, once again hovering over an R.J. Donovan Prison special-transport bus. On board is the high-profile child serial killer Mark Sutter. After two years of trial litigation, he refused to inform the District Attorney of the whereabouts of his remaining four victims, all children, ranging in age from 6 to 11 years; all born to San Diego Sheriff Deputies." The bus began to slow its approach to the highly fortified gate entrance.

"It may be decades before the appeal process ticks down in this state, all costing the taxpayers millions to house, transport, feed, and protect. For fifteen years Tookie Williams in San Quentin Prison dragged out his appeal. The process is slow, and so is eternity being prodded by Satan's pitchfork. Pure evil is this multiple-personality killer. Satan may have met his match!". Kristy Lyons was adamant in this statement's delivery.

As Don Ellis passes over the gate with only 40 feet of clearance, the sharpshooters take aim but are told to stand down. Guy wires crisscross over the Level 4 yard, there to deter any helicopter escapes, but that only happens in Hollywood. "We're over the fence into the lifer yard now," Don says into the Bose headset.

Kristy pans the camera below the sharpshooter tower, focusing on a very weathered plywood sign that reads "No Warning Shot," easily visible even from this far away.

"What do you suppose that means?" Says Kristy.

Don Ellis says, "That means it's time to 'exit stage left' immediately!".

All of a sudden, alarms sound off, and a voice comes over the huge speaker below the tower, "Yard down. Everyone hit the track!"

Three sharpshooter rifles appear; red dots fill the canopy of the helicopter; all three sharpshooters get the same voice order over their Bose headsets, "Stand down. Stand down until a skid hits the track, and then take it down. Wait for the order!"

The entire yard has become a sea of inert bodies with hands crossed behind their heads. All except for one convict who seems unfazed by all the excitement, one Isaac Stompski. Hanging from the high bar by his knees, his glistening muscles ripple as he continues his abdominal crunches. Kristy can't help but notice this perfect male

specimen. She says to young Don Ellis, "Now that is what I'm talking about, an Adonis Alpha Male! He has a six-pack on top of his six-pack! Why, oh why, do they keep him caged up in here, away from the female gender? That is the real injustice!"

Don's sense of jealousy kicks in, and he says, "If I had 365 days a year, 24 hours a day, to work out, I'd have that physique as well, Kristy!"

The voice from the guard-tower speaker repeats, "Yard down. That means you, too, Stompski!" Isaac does a backflip and lands in a crouch, landing in a perfect form that would earn a 10 by any judge in gymnastics. Grinning up to the tower, Isaac stays crouched and motionless.

From the guard tower once again, "Well, I guess that is good enough. Thank you, Stompski!" Isaac simply grins wider and thinks back on his recent events, which got him here, remembering...

# PART 1:
# "I. STOMP"

# Chapter 1:

Four years earlier... Isaac and his very beautiful wife of less than a year, Hannah, lived high atop Mt. Helix in a west-facing home overlooking Casa De Oro with spectacular scenic views to the west. On a clear day, the Pacific Ocean can be seen. The purchase of this multi-million-dollar home was a partial wedding gift from both Isaac's and Hannah's families. The fact that these two had been betrothed to each other, arranged since youth by their parents, was of no importance.

Isaac and Hannah have been in love for their entire lives, both virgins until their honeymoon night. Hannah has not known another man's penis, except for her brother's, accidentally.

Hannah is aware that Isaac is exceptionally large. Since Junior High School, then through High School, followed by College, gossip got around among the young ladies. Told to them by their brothers, who shared a P.E. class with Isaac. Hannah heard the gossip, and many a skank tried to sway Isaac from his devoted love for Hannah, but all were unsuccessful. Hannah worried about the honeymoon night that whether her petite physique could handle her man or not. Isaac was also gentle, allowing her to ease onto him and into her orgasmic bliss.

That night, they would be celebrating an anniversary, their first year in marriage. Dinner at the Brigantine at Severin Avenue and I-8 after she picks up Isaac at the La Mesa-Spring Street trolley station. This is not the best part of the evening, however. She has filled the hot tub at home with champagne the night before, and the aroma from it already has her sensuality peaking.

Hannah gives Isaac a sweet, sensual kiss as he awakens. She says, "Good morning, my Isaac." Then she gives his penis a shake and says, "And good morning to you, Mr. Stomp! Happy anniversary to both of you and especially to me!" She then starts covering his chest with kisses, stroking Mr. Stomp until it's as big as her forearm.

She starts kissing Mr. Stomp's very bulbous head, "Amazing, amazing, just scrumptiously amazing! Oh Isaac, how I love you so... I am the luckiest woman on earth!" As she straddles Isaac.

Isaac looks up into the beautiful eyes and angelic face of his wife as she lowers herself slowly onto his manhood. She squeals just as he enters her. Gasping, her face making that 'Oh' face that he loves so much. "Oh Hannah, it is I who has been blessed with a wife and a life so lovely!'

"Make love to me, Isaac. Please, please give me a little son, a little Isaac, just like his father. That would only double my desire in life!" He then fills her up with his hot love.

"Remember, Hannah, I will be at the trolley station at 6:30 instead of 5:00 tonight. We have reservations at 7:00 at your favorite restaurant." Isaac reminds her.

"Isaac, let me remind you... You are my favorite restaurant!" She eases off of Isaac, still pulsating, and pads off to the bathroom to wipe off her inner thighs. Hannah comes back into the bedroom holding a red jelly bean and drops it into the 2-gallon Sparklets water bottle that sits on top of the nightstand.

"Red for romance. Oh, Isaac, this bottle is over half filled in our first year! While you are at work, I plan on counting these for a total count. I, for one, plan on showing your grandfather that he is wrong! Not only will we remove all the jelly beans in the rest of our years together, but my goal is to get it done before our second anniversary!" Hannah says confidently.

Isaac hops into the shower and begins his morning ritual, preparing for work. Hannah has the bottle of beans dumped out on the bedspread, running her hands through them all. Each bean represents an orgasm that she has had with Isaac, her wonderful man, her husband. Isaac walks out of the bathroom in his sports briefs and wife-beater T-shirt, and his wife's jaw drops, gazing at the outline of his manhood down his left thigh.

Isaac loves Hannah so much; she is like an angel, his angel. He has created a nympho-angel woman.

"Oh honey, all these beans are my beans of unadulterated happiness and bliss! When I pick them up and feel them in my hand, I get aroused all over again. They are magic beans!" Hannah beams.

Isaac loves Hannah with all his heart. God has blessed them both since childhood. "Life is very wonderful, Hannah. I do not doubt that we will prove my grandfather wrong!" Not only will Isaac's grandfather be right... but today's bean will be the last bean to go into that bottle in this home for that year.

# Chapter 2:

It took Isaac extra time to get ready. He spilled coffee down his shirt while eating his bagel and cream cheese for breakfast. His clumsiness always made Hannah chuckle, saying, "You're so clumsy because your center of gravity is always in motion. Your gyro is off kilter!" a private joke between the two.

Hannah drops off Isaac at the Spring Street trolley station in her Audi A-6 Quatro Turbo Adelante, still wearing her sheer nightgown under her SDSU oversized hoody sweatshirt. Of course, she pulls it off as very sexy, and Isaac has to think thoughts of tax law just to keep his erection in check. Hannah is of little help, allowing her gown to rise to her cleft and purposely trying to shift gears with Isaac's penis rather than the shift knob.

"Oh, Isaac, our first year, and you can't take a day off? You know Daddy would let you! You really should have requested it!" Hannah pouts, her puffy lips even more sexy than ever.

"Hannah, pouting is making it harder. I can't walk up that ramp while thinking about you. You know that! My angel has turned into an incubus in a mere year!" He sets the cold pack that he brought for this reason on his lap until the trolley comes into view. He opens the passenger door, and his lunch tumbles to the ground along with his travel coffee mug. "See what you do to me!"

Hannah giggles. Isaac's best friend, Samuel, claps at the scene from the elevated platform as Hannah gives a honk and a wave. "My clumsy 'stallion stud."

La Mesa, the 'jewel of the hills' and one of the finest parks in San Diego, Harry Griffins Park, makes a living in this section of San Diego County fun. Canine Corner Dog Park is another claim to fame for La Mesa. The Spring Street trolley is usually uncrowded, and most patrons are very friendly and familiar. Samuel and Isaac have been

friends since childhood. Both work at Hannah's family law firm, Levi and Levi: Probate and Tax Law. Samuel lives on top of Lee Avenue between El Cajon Boulevard and University Avenue. His house is known for the huge American flagpole, always lit up at night. Two smaller poles are on each side with the California-State flag and the Star of David, denoting his Jewish roots. Both Samuel and Isaac have been competitive in work, life, and all sports, as well as in boxing; both are members of City Boxing Gym just south of City College.

Inseparable since the 3rd grade and often mistaken for brothers, both claim to have two sets of parents from each other's families. Isaac, Hannah, and Samuel are shining examples of living a blessed life in God's favor to all the Jewish youth in San Diego; all are active in their church near the Scripps Genesee Hospital and UCSD College east of La Jolla.

Isaac walks up the ramp to meet Samuel, both smiling. Samuel reaches to help carry the lunch basket lovingly prepared by Hannah for the both of them, as she does each day. Samuel has not married, prefers a bachelor's life, and claims to have been spoiled by Hannah. When asked his reason for remaining a bachelor, his answer is, "God only blessed our world with one Hannah, and He favored Isaac before me."

Hannah has given up trying to play Cupid for their lifelong friend. All share the same love for one another, a bond that can't be broken. Samuel says to Isaac, "Our one-year anniversary is today, Isaac. Hannah will be getting my dozen long-stem red roses at lunchtime today."

Isaac smiles at his best friend and says, "Samuel, Hannah, and I both love you with all of our hearts. We really do... but when she gets home this morning, she will hit the garage door remote, and the door will open to 365 long-stem red roses, one for each day of our marriage. I am surprised that you were able to find a dozen roses left in San Diego for sale."

Samuel's laugh is so boisterous that everyone turns to see what is so funny. He says, "Isaac, you are the man! The reason the roses can't get here before noon is that they have to come from Carlsbad Growers....direct!'

Isaac unzips the lunch basket to put away his coffee thermos and laughs even louder than Samuel. The entire platform erupts into laughter as Isaac showers Samuel with red rose petals that fill the basket to the brim. The day is already one of the best days in life for the both of them, shaping to be an epic memory, a memory they will be forced to hold onto as one of their last.

# Chapter 3:

The Orange Line trolley pulls up while Isaac is being congratulated and backslapped by fellow "O-Line" commuters. May weather in the eastern part of the county is gorgeous, with 70-degree daytime and 65-degree nighttime temperatures, blue skies, and star-filled nights. Downtown is a different story, like a different planet entirely, complete with a society of aliens – the homeless.

The homeless are everywhere in San Diego, mostly due to the climate and partially due to the people of San Diego having compassion. Just like any of God's creatures, to thrive is to have not only a safe habitat but also sources to feed upon. Food banks, soup lines, churches, homeless centers, and county-provided EBT cards ($240.00 food debit cards) are the food sources that provide for the homeless. Proximity to these sources is the main reason that downtown has become a 'tent city' for the homeless, especially around Petco Park, where the Padres play. This is the same stop that Isaac and Samuel commute to daily.

The commute is only 20 minutes by trolley and up to an hour or more by car. For car owners, the area of downtown could be a nightmare, with the cost of secure parking up to $20.00 per day. Isaac and Samuel have experienced many commute methods. One year they spent almost $10,000.00 between them by purchasing high-end Cannondale road bikes and apparel. That was short-lived due to the apparel of Isaac. Isaac's bike shorts had caused too many near accidents by female and some male commuters.

Hannah, the good sport always, had put an end to it, not out of jealousy, but she did not want to lose either of her two best men in one fell swoop. She had her younger brother, Jonah, chop up the bikes with Sawzall and Lennox blades. There was no argument to be had; she made hers loud and clear: this mode of transportation was too dangerous for her clumsy husband.

Leaving La Mesa and entering Lemon Grove's quaint downtown district, the trolley comes to a stop in front of an icon sculpture of a huge lemon. Isaac's grandfather purchased 100 acres of land when he first came to San Diego, right here in Lemon Grove. For $1000.00. Paying $10.00 per acre of land covered with indigenous lemon trees, perfect shade trees for the cows in his dairy. Isaac's roots are deep in San Diego, as are Samuel's and Hannah's.

Professionals, construction workers, college students, and county employees load into the trolley. Lemon Grove Avenue stop then runs into Imperial Avenue; the next stop is on Massachusetts Avenue. This stretch of road is notorious for racing among motor-heads. Floral wreaths and saint candles are memorials to those who lost their lives chasing their adrenaline addictions. Elderly Hispanic women genuflect with the 'sign of the cross' at these. Some use this stretch to pray with their rosary beads cradled lovingly in a lace handkerchief in their hands. They are avid Catholics praying for all their loved ones and grandchildren.

Gangs riddle the areas throughout San Diego today. Work is plentiful and available to all who thrive. Not so much for the youth of today in these gang communities. Bullying throughout all schools, from K-5 to high school, necessitates protection through groups of friends.

Today, these gangs have created nicknames for their groups, usually naming them after their communities or 'barrios,' thus forming 'lil gangs.' A son's father, nicknamed Monster, will continue his father's handle as Lil Monster from 4-Corners, and so on. Lil Monster's son will become Baby Monster.

Babies having babies is very common in poverty areas; home-girls getting impregnated by home-boys of the gangs. The more babies, the larger the digits on their welfare checks...

# Chapter 4:

From Encanto's 60th Street stop all the way into downtown, the trolley fills to standing-room-only status. Although Isaac and Samuel share a window seat facing each other so they can share a conversation, they seem to be the only ones.

Samuel tells Isaac, "I am so thankful, Isaac, that you and I have made a pact to each other never to use our cell phones while commuting. Take a look around us. All these people, all mixed cultures, all capable of sharing experiences, making friends, and finding the loves of their lives... All choosing to pass on society and opt for a 'cyber society' through cell phones."

"Freedom and technology, Samuel. Progress can't be slowed. Protectionism has proven to backfire on economies that enforce it. I have full faith that we two are not alone in understanding the problems with too much freedom floated by 'cyber technology.' I must admit and agree with you that it took us restraint to do so. I do have hope that good is contagious, just as is temptation. Wisdom lies in which path we choose." Isaac is forever positive.

Samuel, after 25 years of friendship, still amazed by Isaac's conversations, says, "A perfect example right there... Simply stated, two intelligent friends commuting and choosing to converse have clearly stated a problem with society and also the solution. This is why our friendship complements us both!"

"Ah, says Isaac, "....and still the wisdom comes forth and is never-ending!" Isaac looks at all the silence from all around them. All heads are downcast, all immersed in their own cyber cell phones, no interaction socially, conversation a lost art. "Such a waste, I admit, my friend. Some are learning. I am sure of it. Some are only wasting time as the clock of life goes tick-tock, passing us all by. I sit with my grandfather. My greatest passion since childhood is his stories and adventures and his friendships made in passing or continuing; in a way, passing on his experiences to me. That is his treasure given to me." Isaac looks around to make his point and says, "What could possibly be shared by society with youth with what they are all immersed in?" Isaac only shakes his head, looks over at his best friend, and again thanks God for his many blessings.

The trolley parallels Imperial Avenue until Euclid Avenue, nicknamed 'the 4 corners of death', aptly named by the locals. Years back, gang-style shootings resulted in a death on each of the four corners. There are two elderly English ladies, who are sisters, on their way to St. Vincent De Paul's Village, volunteering their time as cooks,

feeding the homeless; Doris and Viola, two of the finest and tiniest ladies you'll ever meet and grow to love, this is how Samuel and Isaac explained these two to Hannah.

"Oh, Isaac, please invite them over someday for me to meet!', Hannah asked almost a year ago. What Hannah wants, Hannah gets. Doris and Viola have been guests every Saturday for luncheon ever since.

Doris and Viola are treated as queens at this notoriously gangster/homeless station. They fear no one. Anyone who even looks cross at these two gets disciplined harshly. They are true angels in the barrio, always with a smile and a kind word. A ruffian pushes the open button for these ladies, his face unrecognizable from all of the tattoos covering his entire head.

He beams as Doris reaches up to his face and says, "What a beautiful face, walking art. Thank you."

The crowd parts for these two as they make their way to Isaac and Samuel, who both rise in unison and say, "Good morning, Aunt Vi, Aunt Doris!" Offering their seats as they do each day.

Aunt Viola, mischief in her sparkling eyes, sees the lunch basket with rose petals on the seat and on Samuel's shoulders and says to Isaac, "What a glorious and special day it is for all of us. Hannah and all of us, for that matter, celebrate our first year together in marriage." Isaac chuckles.

"Yes, Aunt Vi, our marriage of friendship extends to all of us: Samuel since childhood; you two since my first week being married to Hannah, who, I don't have to remind you both, sends her love!" Isaac reminds them, anyway.

Doris, always playful, says, "Well, we'll have to have you demonstrate our love to her." As if the two had rehearsed this, they both kissed Isaac, then Samuel, on each cheek, purposely leaving two lipstick kisses on each of them.

Neither Isaac nor Samuel attempt to wipe the lipstick from their cheeks. It is well known at Levi and Levi that both Isaac and Samuel wear these as badges of honor throughout the day. When Isaac meets Hannah after being brought home by Samuel, she retrieves these kisses from them both. The aunts love this and pile on the lipstick just for Hannah.

The aunts take their seats while Isaac and Samuel protectively stand around them. They produce a Hallmark card and give it to Isaac, "This is for Hannah and you, Isaac. We love you both and wish your celebration to be memorable always." He turns the envelope and sees that the seal has two identical kiss prints. He gently opens his lunch basket and lays the envelope upon the rose petals.

Viola nudges Doris and says, "So there's our answer as to why Samuel is covered with rose petals. We were hoping that someone would be able to tame this young lion!"

They laugh and mock Samuel with cat-like claws, raking his chest. All the young girls near them giggle and begin to blush, their crushes on Samuel transparent.

Doris sees this and says, "Yes. We thought the Orange Line's most sought-after bachelor had finally met his match!"

From the rear, a seductive young female voice is heard saying, "I'm up for the challenge!" Samuel feels a pinch on his derriere and a phone number being slipped into his front pocket, his first of many on today's commute. Isaac eyes his best friend and winks at him. The entire trolley is receiving valentine sweet texts from the aunts commemorating Isaac's and Hannah's first anniversary.

The trolley is meandering through the Greenwood Cemetery, one of the oldest cemeteries, other than Old Town, in San Diego. Cabrillo Memorial Cemetery is also one of the most visited by military families. Greenwood's rolling hills, reflecting ponds and mausoleum, with its blue, star-flecked dome, which borders Highway 94, is where San Diego's past citizens are laid to rest. UC San Diego in Linda Vista has a similar dome, which is visible from Mission Bay and Presidio Park. UCSD is one of two Christian colleges here; Nazarene of Point Loma being the other.

# Chapter 5:

Although the trolley is standing room only, the remaining stops, all the way to the Imperial Avenue station, Petco Park and the San Diego Library, will load up with mostly high school kids. San Diego High School sits amid the City College campus buildings and the ancient Balboa Stadium complex. This complex had once seen football greats such as Lance Alworth and "Bambi" and fans filled the concrete stands. Musician icons such as Jimi Hendrix and Janis Joplin have also played here. Today, the high school uses it for football, soccer, and track.

Along this route down Commercial Avenue, remnants of auto-salvage yards are still present but dwindling. Most are now turning into recycling yards to provide income for can-collecting homeless entrepreneurs. Eight cans equal one dollar in the conversion rate. This will provide meals, shelter, and a little comfort where there is none to be found downtown. Competition is tough. Those who compete for cans are very territorial, which leads to bullying any newcomer.

Smart collectors frequent events at stadium and sports arena venues. Beach areas are also good sources but new laws prohibiting alcohol there make it less productive for the can collectors. Some, with small trucks or other vehicles, are found on recycle days in neighborhoods gathering recyclables into their vehicles before bin recyclers, who provide the receptacles, arrive. Homeowners usually don't complain, sometimes even separating the cans from the rest to help avoid a mess being left. Most collectors will not leave a mess; instead, becoming friends with residents at the same time, ensuring that no complaints will be called in.

San Diego has been compassionate regarding the plight of its homeless until recently when the population became more visible. This is very apparent from here to the end of the Orange Line in Old Town. Commercial Avenue from the 25th

Avenue Police Station onto Imperial Station is a literal tent city for the homeless. Similar to Skid Row in Los Angeles, these areas are where the homeless congregate.

There are problems with human waste, garbage, drug use, and the mentally disabled, as well as very prominent health problems. Stripped bicycle frames left over from thefts around the downtown area make it almost impossible to identify a bicycle once parts are removed. Parts are then sold or used to build sellable bikes that have high-end components on mediocre frames with the decals removed.

It is illegal for a person or family to sleep in a vehicle in San Diego; however, it is legal to sleep on the sidewalk or under the threshold of an edifice or business. Sprawls of homeless habitats, which resemble small towns, pop up throughout San Diego.

River bottom from Old Town to Grantsville, just below the beautiful SDSU Campus.

In El Cajon City, underground drainage systems are running its entire length. In these, there are homeless cities. The homeless-built rooms have wooden pallets as foundations for structures supporting beds, couches, cabinets for kitchens, and even vanities and makeshift toilets. There are generators for power to cook and heat. Cooking fires are not allowed, as they bring the fire and police departments to their camps.

Encampments under bridge overpasses are very common, providing shelter from sun and rain. The winter season, which causes flooding here, also turns the Pacific Ocean beaches into septic disasters. Human waste is everywhere. Hepatitis A is rampant where the homeless congregate.

It's a never-ending battle with no winners. No clear solution has been worked out anywhere where the homeless are present. There are safe parking lots and tent-city areas where climate permits. Even private Walmart parking lots have allowed overnight use. They fill up quickly, get abused, and then shut down. The life is nomadic in nature with a gypsy lifestyle.

Red Skelton portrayed a hobo in humorous skits, but there are few smiles present, even in a beautiful city such as San Diego. Isaac and Samuel love their hometown. They love its people and all their cultures. They have compassion for the homeless, yet at night, the homeless have little compassion for other homeless. It is a "dog-eat-dog" lifestyle on these mean streets. The homeless band together for protection at night.

Some choose not to sleep, only doing so in daylight. Safety is still not guaranteed during daytime hours. Angry young vigilantes roam homeless river bottoms, victimizing violently. There have been instances of gasoline being poured on the homeless and then lighting them on fire in store parking lots. There have been other instances of beating the homeless with bats and garden tools while they slept. It's no wonder they choose to draw back from society and exist away from humanity. Who can they trust? The mean streets of San Diego at night, for these people, can be a nightmare of exploitation.

# Chapter 6:

"Here we are, young ladies." Samuel says to the aunts. His charm is noticed by all the swooning females who hear his warm voice. "May Isaac and I escort you to your final destination today?" St. Vincent De Paul Center is only two blocks east of their office, and Isaac and Samuel have incorporated it into their daily routine.

Aunt Viola beams, "Samuel, you are such a hunk of a gentleman! I, for the life of me, do not understand why all these beautiful ladies on the O-Line have not succeeded in scooping you up by now!"

Samuel laughs, and many females join in. He says, "I have saved today's 'scoop' for my two favorites." as he offers his arm to Viola. "May I?" As he escorts Viola off of the trolley, she playfully fans her blush with her handkerchief.

Not to be outdone, Isaac offers his arm to Doris and says, "My lady, our carriage has arrived. Fetch your glass slippers, or we shall miss our dance!"

Doris flutters her eyelashes, attaches herself to Isaac's arm, and says, "My Prince Charming!"

# Chapter 7:

The mass exodus is the best description of the O-Line's debarkation at Imperial Plaza. All trolleys juncture here: the Blue Line to the American Plaza, north to San Ysidro International Port of Entry; the Green Line from Petco Park to Old Town, connecting to the Coaster (for north-county commuters), then on to El Cajon City by way of Mission Valley and SDSU College.

Everyone is in a hurry, bumping into one or the other by not paying attention, faces still intent on their phones; everyone, that is, except for Isaac, Samuel, and the aunts. Their exit is leisurely, all the O-Line commuters wishing these four a great day, single women blowing kisses and winks to Samuel. Viola says to the pretty girls, "Sorry ladies, today he's all mine. Perhaps if you get up a little earlier..."

Samuel says, "Viola, I pray you haven't outdone your use for me?"

"Heavens no, Samuel. Are you blind? Can't you see for yourself all the pretty women and your effect on them? I've not seen so many wagging tails since...well...yesterday!" They all burst out in laughter as the trolleys pull away, clearing their path towards St. Vincent De Paul Village.

The walk went past the Indoor Skydiving Sports Complex, dodging all the cigarette street vendors (made in Mexico or duty-free) selling cigarettes for three dollars a pack. In a liquor or convenience store, a pack of smokes goes for anywhere from eight to ten dollars. All the homeless here know the aunts, and for the entire two blocks, the aunts are kind and give a sincere smile to each one they pass. They remember everyone's name. In front of the Village Isaac and Samuel bid their farewells and hand the aunts off to Father Joe, the Patriarch of the Village.

Retracing their steps back towards Imperial Plaza, salutations are given to Isaac and Samuel, "Good morning,

Isaac. Good morning, Samuel."; "Have a great day, guys."; "Happy anniversary, Isaac. I want an anniversary with you, Sammy!" These two are regulars and loved by all downtown. They walk around the plaza, then between it and the parking structure, to the start of the G-Line, which is just pulling in from Old Town. They scan their Compass card passes at the pedestal, enter, and take their seats.

Isaac reminds Samuel before their stop at Levi and Levi, "Remember, after work, we'll meet at Carl Strauss for a toast, on me, then I have to go shop at Horton Plaza for Hannah."

Samuel says, "Yes. I'd ask what your gift is, but I know your thought process, like mine and Hannah's, and I'm pretty sure that it entails lace and silk and will most likely be sheer!"

Isaac laughs and verifies Samuel's guess with a resounding Austin Powers, "Yeah, Baby! Get shaggy with it! I love Hannah in my SDSU sweatshirt over her nightgown in the morning. I really do, but I think a sexy robe for the drive is in order; you know, business above the waistline, pleasure below it!"

Samuel mimics Hannah's voice, "Oh, Isaac, how I love you so!" and he jumps into Isaac's lap and showers his cheeks with kisses. The entire trolley car goes quiet. The occupants all look in their direction. Samuel continues, "It's our first-year anniversary! Can I get a Whoop-Whoop?"

"Whoop-Whoop-Whoop-Whoop all the way home," the passengers sing along.

# Chapter 8:

San Diego caters to exercise enthusiasts and is frequented by riders on electric scooters of many varieties, riders of bicycles of many varieties, skateboarders, rollerbladers, roller skaters, runners, speed walkers, people pushing strollers with infants, other people pushing carts containing their life's belongings, tourists, lovers hand in hand, families together, families displaced, street entertainers, street artists; the list is endless.

Throughout San Diego, especially paralleling the trolley tracks south to north and west to east, along the San Diego River and its harbor, walkways for pedestrians make it simple to exercise or commute to work. Carpooling and use of the transit system (MTS) should be the responsibility of everyone who commutes. Planet Earth is our petri dish, and we have only one. It is up to all of us to treat her better. Isaac, Hannah, and Samuel have been advocates of planet conservation since their youth.

They not only preach about it, they are about it! Isaac's home has its south-facing roof entirely covered by solar panels for power, additional solar for heating the spa, a retractable cover to heat the pool, gray-water collection, and rain-gutter barrels for yard irrigation. Irrigation is only needed for the fruit trees and ice plants on the bordering banks around the home for fire protection. Hannah is adamant about the landscape, "All vegetation will be indigenous to the region, complete with Vizcaino cactus, with fruit mixed in with the succulents on the banks. Home and fire protection. I can make jam with the cactus apples! Any tree requiring water must produce fruit for the same reason!" Her loving touch is golden.

Plants seem to come alive for her. She speaks to her yard as she cares for it, her joy besides her husband and her Samuel. Isaac makes no move to remove Samuel from his lap. He is comfortable with the intimacy. The other riders have lost interest, shock value is now gone. Samuel, now sitting across from Isaac, says, "Wait for it, wait for it, right about... Now!" They look out to see a gorgeous woman in a coffee cart with the most beautiful smile waving at their trolley car. Both wave back but it's Samuel who is lost for words.

"You simply mystify me, Sam! All day long, beautiful women go out of their way...I mean... They drop phone numbers into your pockets! Never are you shy, always with the 1000-watt smile, the most charming smile... hell, Sam, it almost melts me! Professional women pulling in 6-figure salaries with homes in La Jolla or Del Mar do not affect you at all, but this girl here, this 'coffee cart barista' who makes probably a minimum wage, living off her tips, is the one who catches your eye?" Isaac says with amusement.

"Isaac, you are my brother, more than that. This felt like a slap that woke me up! Do you remember that feeling you had for Hannah the moment you fell in love?" Samuel is serious now.

Isaac gives Samuel his most serious, no-bullshit look and says, "Samuel, I can never forget that feeling, ever! Every time I look at her, I feel that exact same feeling, even after all these years, more so today!"

Samuel gets up quickly, gathers up his briefcase and musses his hair just so. He places his sunglasses on the bridge of his nose and squirts Binaca in his mouth. He shouts over his shoulder as the trolley comes to the next stop, "I'll meet you at your office for lunch!" He runs out the door, and Isaac loses sight of his best friend, who is at full sprint heading back to his lady barista.

"Go get her, Sammy!" He yells, while the whole car's riders start chanting, "Sammy, Sammy, Sammy!" Isaac runs to that side to look for Samuel, but his friend is so far gone that he is only a speck on the trolley walkway. Isaac continues the remaining few blocks on his own, still chanting, "Sammy, Sammy, Sammy, go get her, brother!"

# Chapter 9:

Samuel slows his pace a block away to catch his breath and slow his heart rate before it blows, and his sweat glands open like a firehose valve. From a block away, she feels his gaze; her stomach tightens, then flutters. She lays a hand on her abdomen to settle it. She then turns 180 degrees to make eye contact. Samuel freezes in place, as does she. Then Samuel produces his 'Got ya!' smile and shy hue. She lip-syncs,

"Coffee...or Me...?" and they both laugh hysterically. Samuel holds up four fingers as if ordering four coffees, and he lip-syncs, "Four...ever...You...!" Her hand moves up from her abdomen to the center of her chest, and she flutters her hand to the beat of her heart.

The feelings are mutual. They have never met before, but destiny has been waiting for this day in both their lives. She meets Samuel halfway across the courtyard. They stand close, eyes searching each other's, smiling from ear to ear.

She says to Samuel, "Thank God. At first, I thought I was having a tummy ache, but it was you. Uhm, by the way, my name is Gabriella. My family calls me Gabby. You are...?"

"Uhm, oh uh, oh, that's right, Samuel. My friends call me Sammy. I think... No, I definitely know...that I have fallen in love with you!" Samuel barely gets the words out of his mouth.

Gabriella's contagious laugh is adorable. "Does that line work for you? Because most of my friends would make a run for it if used on them!"

Gabriella's fantastic green eyes never leave Samuel. To this day, he will claim that these eyes are all he can remember. Her fire-red hair with slight green highlights is done in a French braid down to the middle of her back. She wears a light-cream cashmere sweater and a black barista mini skirt over a one-piece fishnet from plunging neckline to her toes. To top it off, her toenails and fingernails are painted the color of her eyes with sparkles to match; truly a vision.

Not one to be put off by Gabriella's frankness, Samuel says, "I'm sure a man's aggressive attraction would take them aback, but you, I have no doubt in my mind, get this line all day long. Am I wrong? See, the real deal here is... This is not a line when I say it!"

Just to be fair, Gabriella returns, "I've got to be honest with you, too. I have named you Mr. Wonderful because until now I haven't known your name. Even still, I have asked women who smile and wave at you, 'Who is your friend there?' and all I hear is, 'O-Line's most wonderful bachelor, that's who!' hence my nickname for you is Mr. Wonderful. Do you know why they call you this, Samuel?"

"This is the first I've heard of it...to my face anyway. I've always thought it was the high school girls with crushes who ride the 'Orange' with Isaac and me. The only importance to me is that you have that impression of me!"

Gabriella touches his arm, sending shock waves, as if he had been tased, up his arm to his brain. She says to Samuel, "Whew! I felt that too; maybe it's static in the air?" She greets a passerby, whom she has served before, with a "Good morning, Sarah. I'll be right there to make your latte. Ok? Oh, while you're here, may I experiment on you?" She touches Sarah's arm but feels nothing.

Samuel cocks an eyebrow with a questioning look and says, "Well?" Gabriella shakes her head and answers, "No, nothing, no static. Be right there, Sarah."

Sarah says to them both, "No worries, no hurries at all, Gabby. Please take your time, and don't worry about me." Sarah walks away humming an old Grand Funk Railroad tune, 'Some Kind of Wonderful,' then turns to emphasize, "Yes, he is some kind of wonderful. Yes, he is now..." and continues to hum, then giggles.

Gabriella touches Samuel on the arm and, again, that electricity that spark is evident. "How do you do that, Samuel? Is there a battery with a coil of wire taped to your wrist? I don't know how...but I like the effect."

Samuel says, "Gabriella, ah, your name flows off my tongue like opera flows out of Sarah Brightman's. You, please call me Sammy. There is no trickery, at least none that I am using. Maybe those fishnets of yours are able to store up static energy like some sort of capacitor."

"My wonderful Sammy," Gabriella says, her voice was playful. "My name never sounded so magical as it does come from your lips. I can't help but wonder what other sparks your tongue could create against my, well, you know." She leans in and kisses his cheek, leaving two bright lipstick marks behind.

With a mischievous smile, she slips her hand into his pocket and pulls out a crumbled piece of paper with another woman's phone number on it. She replaces it with her own, raises an eyebrow, and teases, "So what I heard is true? Are there any other numbers that I need to remove from your pockets?"

Samuel laughs and pleads innocence, "Believe me, and you can. I have no idea where that came from. I mean it! However, from now on, you can check all my pockets to replace numbers with your own. My pants only have openings for your hands, but don't be surprised if I plant my own slips to ensure that the searches continue."

Gabriella's effect has become evident by the rise in Samuel's inseam as she slips her card into each pocket, producing yet another phone number. She coos, "Mmmmm, uh-huh, I suppose you have no knowledge of..." she reads the slip "...your future wife, Celia. The number is '1-800-fuck-me2'. Really, what kind of crazed co-ed would actually have a number like that? Sammy, I think we will have to sew your pockets closed!" She throws her head back in laughter. Even her neck is sensual.

Samuel will not be able to run back to his office. As he limps away, Gabriella returns to her work, her tail swaying playfully with each step. Sarah watches and playfully mimics her, the two girls sharing a high-five. Gabriella turns back to see Samuel's mouth open. She winks and waves. Samuel puts his hand to his chest and flutters it in rhythm with his heart and lip syncs.

"Wow!" He tries to adjust himself but is unsuccessful; obviously, his penis is not done or ready to leave yet. Samuel is now late for work and says, "Down, boy! Down, I mean it, so I can run instead of pogo to the office!" As he limps away with a smile a mile wide.

# Chapter 10:

The Green-Line-North passes by the always-busy San Diego Convention Center, paralleling the Pacific Coast Highway. Just like El Camino Real, it has been a California historical and scenic route for centuries, akin to Route 66 from St. Louis to California.

Adventures along these routes are rich in history. Restaurants, fueling stations, campgrounds, tourist centers, auto wreckers, and lodgings are all throwbacks to yesteryears gone by. Parades of historical vehicles and runs with historical Harley Davidson motorcycles traverse these highways. All of this so we all can revisit the way things were...back in the day. These sections are dwindling. Old Highway 80, for instance, is now I-8. Remnants of the old road through the sand dunes and desert before reaching Yuma can still be seen. Maybe these parts should be protected, but progress moves faster than we can preserve until our history is long lost, covered by our desire for growth and our desire to be entertained, exactly like society's loss of being social. Stories of history being passed down have been traded for phone/video games and substituted for a stimulating conversation with an elderly gentleman willing to share experiences.

The San Diego Convention Center caters to a multitude of conventions throughout the year. Probably the most popular and most entertaining convention held here in San Diego is 'Comicon.' Isaac, Samuel, Hannah, and Jonah always go as 'The Fantastic Four' comic characters: Isaac as Mr. Fantastic, Samuel as The Thing, Hannah as The Invisible Woman, and Jonah as The Human Torch. Their costumes, which they've had since high school, all still fit perfectly even to this day. Isaac has always had the uncanny ability to portray Richard Reed's superhero identity, Mr. Fantastic. Mr. Fantastic was exposed to an atomic blast, along with his three researchers, which gave all of them superhuman abilities. Mr. Fantastic has the incredible ability to stretch his limbs to extraordinary lengths. Clad in skin-tight spandex featuring the iconic large four on his chest, Isaac stands confidently with his fists planted on his hips. He stares off into the stars and concentrates, not on the stars however, but on his wife, Hannah. He remembers them making love in the doggy position as she backs up onto his manhood. His thoughts stir his libido, and his penis begins to grow down his left thigh to about the size of Hannah's forearm. The 'Comicon' crowd erupts in laughter and applause.

Hannah, as Susan Storm, The Invisible Woman, has had her costume made to mimic Isaac's in proportion. Hers has a discreet hoody, and when she covers her head with the spandex material and positions her stance to mimic Isaac's, she becomes a chameleon of sorts, creating the illusion of disappearance. Again, the 'Comicon' crowd erupts in applause and grows larger because of the sight. Jonah, Hannah's brother, as Johnny Storm, The Human Torch, is next. His costume has a built-in butane torch with three high-output tips built into the seat of his pants. Prepared professionally by a costume designer, the seat and crotch area uses welding-glove material. The rechargeable tank is strapped to his back. His left thigh has the igniter button built into the fabric. He raises his right arm in a fist, and as he says, "Flame On," he pushes the igniter to switch on his left thigh, and three blasts of a torched flame erupt from the seat of his costume. The applause erupts even louder than from Isaac's feat of stretching, although some women's jaws are still wide open.

Samuel's costume is probably the most inventive of all four. His hoody resembles a red stone; his face is made up in the same manner. He is Ben Grimm, The Thing. His costume has exaggerated padding throughout and, as he posed for a highly talented 3-D artist, was airbrushed with amazing effect. Each thigh houses a sub-woofer, which is activated by a heel switch in each boot. Each step reverberates through these T.L. Audio high-output, sub-woofer speakers. Each step is felt by the crowd in the same manner as in a virtual movie theater like the one near UCSD, La Jolla Village Theaters. He begins with a lumbering walk. Boom...Boom...Boom... Then he quickens his pace. BOOM! Boom, Boom, Boom. Finally, he runs up the ramp to above the stage and jumps. BOOM, landing amongst his three best friends. BOOM!

"Comicon' officials love these guys. Many producers have approached them to appear before the public in other venues; venues such as rock concerts, conventions, Halloween hotels, private parties, and so on. 'Comicon' loves these guys because they have made it clear to all that their only appearance will be at 'Comicon' once a year as long as 'Comicon' continues to stay in San Diego and doesn't move to Los Angeles, a stand these friends will honor after their Chargers, traitors to San Diego, moved to Los Angeles, breaking the hearts of fans once again!

# Chapter 11:

The Convention Center stop also has the Children's Wading Pool and Park alongside the station. This is Isaac's final stop. Levi and Levi is located on Fifth Avenue and Market, just on the other side of the Spaghetti Factory, a favorite lunch spot for employees of the firm.

Although the park is intended as a place for the children to play, the locals call it a 'homeless park' because the homeless frequent it more than the children. Visible measures to 'help' the plight of the homeless are everywhere. Metal-caged and locked recycle bins containing recyclable cans keep the cans from being collected. Donation receptacles are asking for the compassionate to donate here in these receptacles rather than give handouts to panhandlers. Records are now being logged as to who is using services, who returns to incarceration, who is able to transition into temporary housing, and, finally, who transitions from these services into permanent housing. Alpha Project, in conjunction with a high-school student, Kevin Barber, along with donations from his mother, his grandmother (as a surprise graduation present), Una Davis, SDGE, and the Lucky Duck Foundation, has begun a program called Wheels of Change. This program employs 20 homeless from the Alpha Project Bridge shelter and pays them the minimum wage of $12.00 per hour to pick up trash, trash that would most likely be picked up by city workers who make three to four times that amount in wages and benefits.

It has taken two years of clean-up since a hepatitis A scare to wake up the politicians of San Diego to initiate a change. As usual, preventative measures were not taken, and 54 people died from hepatitis A in 2017. This staggering number could have been prevented. Local politicians, being chastised for allowing problems with the homeless to spiral down to this level, began spraying to sterilize the streets. Two years later there are still city crews cleaning up the San Diego River bottom. Putting the homeless to work cleaning up debris and human waste created by the homeless, is what is needed today. Hopefully, a homeless person who is involved here would think twice before littering the streets. To be fair, anyone who has ever volunteered to assist in a San Diego clean-up crew will tell you...cigarette butts are the highest percentage of litter on our beaches and streets.

At this hour of the morning there is not a heavy police presence. Some homeless take advantage of the water park as personal showers. Not all homeless walk the streets in a state of filth. Most would love to be able to shower, wash their faces and hands, and have the advantage of public restrooms without being chased away by security guards at colleges and private establishments. After all, would a cat lover keep a cat, feed the cat, and not provide a suitable litter box for the cat? The cat would be considered feral if not cared for, wouldn't it? If a city is willing to provide services for a homeless population, Isaac believes it should provide sanitary means as well, protecting its citizens from viruses and diseases that human waste creates. After all, we all share the same petri dish, another reason that Isaac, Hannah, Samuel, and Jonah are active volunteers for Clean-Up San Diego.

It's a short walk up Fifth Avenue in the early morning hours. The streets of San Diego are still slumbering. Restaurants, bars, and entertainment establishments are all busy cleaning up after an all-night street party as patrons fill the streets. After the last call at 2:00 am, congregations of inebriated patrons gather outside to form plans for after-hour parties. There are still places to go. Some are legal establishments, and some are illegal. Casinos, which are legal, are located way out in the country on Indian land: Viejas in Alpine, Sycuan in Harbison Canyon, Hollywood in Campo, Barona near Ramona, and Golden Acorn in Jacumba. All offer 24/7 entertainment.

In San Diego City, there are moving establishments that aren't legal. Gaming houses are very popular with those in the know, all within the city limits, with bouncers at the door and roving the inside. There are slot machines, game tables, poker rooms, prostitutes, and drug dealers peddling their illegal products. There is no 2:00 am last call and the action never stops. All sorts of illegal activity go hand-in-hand with these establishments. Black-market sales of stolen merchandise can be made, along with any number of planned conspiracies.

Those congregating on the sidewalks of San Diego at closing hour are making plans to follow up their evening of entertainment with the next day's entertainment, so long as their money can last. Some are so drunk that they can't keep their meals down, or they forget to use the restroom, and they have an instant urge to purge or urinate. These odors permeate the streets, and they have to be cleaned in order to attract the day's patrons. Some people power-wash with bleach and cleaners; some have to scrub and rinse; all must sterilize away the prior night's sour odors.

Isaac walks past the Spaghetti Factory and eyes the Cost Plus, a wholesale wine distributor across the street. He reminds himself to stop in on his way home to pick up a special champagne, Crystal, at $500.00 per bottle. Isaac knows from experience that if you want a memorable palate-pleaser, Crystal is the only champagne to buy. Hannah deserves this. She is the love of his life. Without her, life isn't worth living. Like all else in life, however, that may be tested sooner than he thinks!

# **Chapter 12:**

The firm of Levi and Levi: Probate and Tax Law has been lawyers for most successful businesses in San Diego. Started by Hannah's grandfather and her father, it will soon be Levi, Levi, and Levi; once Jonah passes the bar, interns for the firm prove he can represent as a partner and produce another Levi son. Tradition and roots are very important to the firm, and nepotism is part of its success. The Levi's believe that if the family works amongst family, any problems can be solved in-house. Everyone who works here is either family or lifelong friends of family; very tight-knit and a great place to thrive.

Isaac walks into the newly renovated lobby. Hannah's niece, Isabella, greets Isaac, "Good morning, Uncle Isaac...uhm...is Samuel not well today?"

Isaac smiles and says, "Good morning to you, Isa. You just keep getting more and more beautiful each day! No, sweetheart, I think Samuel is doing very well. He should be right along at a jog, I would think, and if he's as smart as I think he is, he should be bringing bagels and coffee for us!"

Isa hands Isaac his messages and last week's meeting minutes and says, "Mr. Charming, as usual, flattery has gotten you far, so far. Uncle, Happy First Anniversary!"

She hands Isaac a wrapped gift. "This is for your desk. You can open it now. Hannah has already seen it."

Isaac opens his gift from his niece. It's a photo of Isa and Hannah, both dressed as St. Pauli Girl, maiden servers from the year's La Mesa October Fest; both spitting images of each other, both jaw-dropping beauties. Isaac says, "I love this, Isa. I am, because of Hannah and all her family, the most blessed man on Earth." His eyes begin welling up from happiness.

Isa stands up and kisses Isaac on his lips. She has always done this. The family all kiss each other on the lips, except the men, of course. Isa says, "No, Isaac, we are all blessed together to have each other. Our love is truly unconditional. You have been the mortar in our foundation of trust and love! There is a switch on the back of the frame, Isaac. Push it to the side."

Isaac does so to find this– one hour – or daily. "Clever girl, Isa. I think I'll switch to daily once I see all the photos you loaded up on it. I love this gift, thank you!"

"There are a few of Hannah and me as babies sharing the bathtub. You can forward through them by pushing in on the switch instead of sliding it. We may be toddlers, but Hannah wanted to include the pictures. I just don't want Sam to see me naked!" Isa says seriously. Isaac laughs uncontrollably. "I mean it, Isaac. Please keep that private. He can only see me naked when he marries me, hopefully one day!"

As if on cue, Samuel comes jogging into the lobby with a take-out box from Einstein's Bagels. Isa grabs the photo frame and flicks it off. Her face is beet red, and Samuel notices her demeanor. "What?" Samuel says, "Did I miss something here? Isa, I got your favorite cinnamon raisin with cream cheese and bacon. Oh, and these..." He reaches into the picnic basket and showers her with rose petals.

Isa's love for Samuel is transparent. Her smile is electric and contagious. Her complexion returns to her beautiful hue as she says, "Isaac, always the thoughtful one...but you are both late now...both of you get going...so I can enjoy the view from here. Get now!" She giggles.

As soon as Isaac and Samuel head up the restored oak and marble staircase into the mezzanine loft, she gets up, grabs one of the security guards, and goes out the glass revolving doors. She needs no security. The guard is there just to be safe. She has to clear the homeless from the front of the building before her grandfather shows up. "All right, Mary, Grandpa will be here in 15 minutes. I have bagels here for you, so help me clear everyone out." Mary lets out a sharp whistle to the half-dozen tents with occupants still sleeping within. She takes her tennis racket (no strings left) and walks down the line, slapping canvas and nylon. Mary whistles again. "Let's go, people. Isa is good to us. Her Gramps is on the way. It's time to move on!' She continues until satisfied.

# Chapter 13:

Isaac and Samuel climb to Isaac's office on the third-floor mezzanine. Samuel is well aware of Isa's attraction to him. Isa is the spitting image of her very beautiful Aunt Hannah. Isaac gives Samuel a sideways glance and says, "Well?"

Samuel says, "Well, what?" and begins to blush, something rarely witnessed by Isaac.

Isaac finishes, "Well, was she as intelligent as you expected? Was her voice like music, or was it obnoxiously twangy? Was her laugh contagious, or was it like listening to a mule braying? What did she do and say when you ran back to her like a well-trained Chocolate Labrador with her tennis ball, panting and drooling?" Isaac roars in laughter.

"Panting and drooling? Is that how you picture the scene of me meeting the woman I intend to marry? That woman, unbeknownst to herself, held my heart in her grasp and gently caressed it. I had to restart it after it seized from her touch. She was simply amazing, Isaac! You have always described to me the love you and Hannah have shared for as long as you've known each other; how you could feel her eyes upon you before you could even see her! Isaac, you should have seen her. I stopped jogging over one hundred yards away from her cart to allow my breathing to settle..."

"Yeah, sure, Samuel...' to allow my breathing to settle...'? You stopped because you were about to turn back and chicken out, not wanting to be, once again, disappointed by what you were going to feel! Sam, I am so happy you took the risk..." Isaac slaps Samuel on the back.

"...because without risk...yeah, yeah, I know, there are no real rewards. Isaac, I finally felt what you find so difficult to explain. Thank God, I finally understand this morning what I have been searching for when I ask, "How will I know when I fall in love?" and everyone but your grandfather finds it so hard to answer. Everyone says, 'Oh, Sam, you'll know it when it finds you! Well, Cupid hit his mark today, Isaac. What a shot...right through the heart! I feel like shouting it out from the rooftops. As a matter of fact, I am going to the roof right now!" Samuel picks up his pace heading to the roof, Isaac right behind his pal. Samuel raises his arms to God and spins in a circle; at the top of his lungs, he yells, "Thank you, God, for answering my prayers at last! Gabriella, I love you; my patience in love is finally rewarded. I love you, Gabriella. Hear my roar. I LOVE YOU, GABRIELLA!"

Five blocks away, Gabriella and Sarah pause in conversation. Gabriella says, "I thought I heard my name called from somewhere."

Sarah says, "Yes. I swear I heard your name called, too!"

They both turn around, looking for the source of the call. Then they both hear, loud and clear, the roar of Samuel's, "I LOVE YOU, GABRIELLA!" Tears of joy pour from the eyes of these two friends as Gabby says, "Sarah, I've heard it said, never one to believe it, but answer me this...Do you believe in love at first sight?"

Sarah pulls back from their embrace, looks her friend, Gabby, directly in the eye, and says, "Gabby, I have never believed anything so utterly ridiculous, that is...until today! I now believe this because I have witnessed it for myself. God has favored you both, and his soldier of love and fate, Cupid, has hit his mark; aim true and straight!"

Samuel's roar is not the only sound coming from this century-old edifice owned by Levi and Levi; a heartbreaking in two, the heart of the lovely Isa can also be heard. The only man she has ever loved, ever thought about being married to, has fallen for another. Her Samuel.

# Chapter 14:

Isaac's emotions were two-fold. Everyone in the family, it seems, is aware of Isa's feelings for Samuel. He is very happy for Samuel, while at the same time, he has to be equally heartbroken for Isa. Isaac was, in the past, so positively sure that Samuel would one day fall in love with Isa. Everyone was, it seems, but Samuel was too respectful of Isaac's family to take advantage of Isa's attraction to him. He had to be sure that he was in love before any intimate advance with her, knowing that the relationship would take off like a SpaceX rocket once ignited.

Isaac says, "I know of one caring and loving person who must have heard you, whose heart is probably broken right now."

Samuel returns Isaac's heartfelt statement with, "Oh, my God, Isa. I was so happy to have finally fallen in love that I wasn't thinking clearly, Isaac!"

"Yes, I understand. Clear thinking seems to always escape people when love enters the scene. I get clumsy around Hannah, even today, after knowing that we've loved each other for over a decade. She still affects me this way, and she knows it, too!" Isaac smiles to himself.

"I'd better go talk to her, Isaac. The love I feel for her is, well, like the love I feel for you and Hannah. I feel that this type of love is as everlasting as our friendship. I hope so is the love I feel for Gabriella. I'm not even sure she feels the same way but I do feel that she does. I really do! I am no stranger to infatuation from others, and it doesn't last. The love I feel for Isa will last until the end of my time on Earth! She needs to know that!" As Samuel says this, Isaac knows it to be true.

Isaac says to his best friend, "This is why we all love you, my friend; now...how to say this to Isa so she understands this? However, Hannah's grandfather should be here any minute now. We must get to our desks and start work. I will already be in trouble for being here instead of with Hannah but we are taking these next four days to stay in Avalon on Catalina Island together. He still will have trouble with it. Isa needs a little time to get back her composure, Sam. Her emotions are worn on her sleeve. Women are emotional, not practical. Oh, how true that is!"

"I used to think so, Isaac, until today! I was a fumbling and mumbling school kid on the K-5 playground in front of Gabriella! Me! I have never been that way, ever! Her eyes, like jade, are the most beautiful green that I have ever seen! She must be used to that effect on men, don't you think?"

Isaac hurries off to his desk in song, "...I only have eyes...for...you..." then into an old Guess-Who song, "these eyes...have never ever seen...these eyes...will never ever see..." and he thinks to himself, 'Oh, I will have fun with this all day long!' He roars with laughter, and Samuel knows that today will be epic, one never to forget, no matter how much he'd like to. After all, ask anyone. All will agree on one thing: who says life is fair?

"Timing is everything, no matter what the endeavor; without timing, there is chaos." Amos Levi's voice is authoritative and penetrating. Dressed impeccably and always groomed with not an eyebrow hair out of place, he is the patriarch of the Levi and Levi law firm. He likes to think that this is a surprise visit, but his wife, the matriarch of all that is 'Levi,' has called her favorite granddaughter, Isa, so she can get everyone and everything 'Levi' the way Amos prefers. To Amos, however, Isa can do no wrong. Although her official salaried position is 'Receptionist,' to Amos, she is the one who conducts his orchestra. She really knows how to caress the strings of her grandfather, not to be manipulative; that is not her style. For that matter, that is not the style of anyone who is Levi or works for Levi and Levi, which is the reason that the firm has been so successful.

"Please hold. Thank you." Isa says into her headset. Then she skips across the lobby, giving Amos a hug and a kiss on his lips. She then takes his arm and guides him to the conference room, where the over-stuffed leather couch and matching chairs are Amos' favorites. "I'll be right back, Grandpa. Don't you move now! Promise me?"

"Deal!..." Amos promises, "...for another one of those strawberry-flavored kisses!" He is amused by today's generation with flavored this and flavored that. Isa, blessed with her grandmother's beauty, aesthetically surrounds him, as do all the females of 'Levi' who are so very beautiful.

"Grandpa, this office isn't run by my affection for you. If so, we'd be ten times more successful!" Isa kisses her grandfather and returns to the caller she put on hold. "I apologize for having you wait...oh, thank you...and good morning to you as well. How may I direct your call?" She looks up at her grandfather and gives him a wink. "Sure. He's been expecting your call. Please hold, and I'll connect you." Then, "Hi, Daddy. I have Mr. Emmanuelle on line 2 for you. Oh, and Grandpa just arrived. He is next to your office in his favorite chair. I'm about to bring him his bagel and lochs with coffee, black and strong." Then, she connects the client to her father. The day has officially begun.

# Chapter 15:

"Salutations and good morning, Grandfather!" Isaac says as he enters the conference room to visit Amos. "Your wisdom and advice are always in demand. I need more from you today, sir...your secret. I know you've found what everyone has searched for since Ponce DeLeon. I know you have succeeded where he has failed. That doesn't surprise me. What does surprise me...is your persistence not to share it with your family."

"Ah, yes, Isaac, my favorite historian. You must be referring to Mr. DeLeon's search for the Fountain of Youth." Amos' eyes sparkle.

"Grandfather, I would swear that you are like that movie with Brad Pitt, 'Benjamin Button'! Each time I see you, you grow wiser and, it seems, younger!" Isaac is amazed by Levi's genes.

"Isaac, I so hope you use that same charm on my wife because it is working. So far as it is kept a secret..." Amos reaches back into his cerebral file cabinet, full of life's memories, and says, "If I have to tell you when you already know the secret to a youthful life, that which puts a spring in your step...then how can I expect you to make it through a second year of bliss? Happy first anniversary, Isaac! I am sorely disappointed in you for leaving my granddaughter alone today, left to her own devices. You are surely asking for it when you get back to your house!"

Isaac thinks to himself that Hannah's creativity cannot be harnessed by anyone, and there is no place he'd rather be than at home with her. Isaac reassures Amos, "I am here, Amos because I was ordered here by your granddaughter, my love, and, as you suggest, my fountain-of-youth pursuit through joy and happiness. She needed space to follow through with her surprise. I am taking the next two days off and the weekend for a little isolated getaway. We will be relaxing in Avalon and dancing the night away!"

Amos gives Isaac a wink and a sideways glance. "So, dancing is what they are calling it now! Well, call it whatever you want, Isaac, my boy...so long as the result is the conception of a Levi great-grandson for us to spoil! I've been wanting to hear the pitter-patter of a new 'Levi boy' running around these offices for this last year. What, pray to tell, has been taking you two so long?"

Isaac wants to say to Hannah's grandfather that this is absolutely none of his business but, instead, tells him, "Amos, for starters...Hannah and I were virgins when we married. It has been a year, yes, but even today, we are still exploring each other's bodies, our desires, and even the limits of our stamina. Amos..." Here Isaac leans in close as if he is about to share some unknown secret between the two of them, "...do you want to know some of the wondrous things we've explored?"

"Um...uh...well...let's see...maybe we better not discuss..." Amos stammers.

"I'm only yanking your chain, Amos. Funny, though, how your eloquence goes out the window as soon as your granddaughter's virtue comes into the conversation! I can promise you, Amos, that we have been discussing having not only a great-grandson for you but a great-granddaughter as well. Hannah wants a little Isaac, and I want a little version of Hannah. We want to get right on it, in a manner of speaking." Isaac promised Amos.

"Wonderful, Isaac, my boy...why don't you leave early today and get busy at it...er...I mean, get right on it...er...I mean...well...you know what I'm getting at, my boy!" Amos is still trying to regain his composure.

"I will, Amos, as soon as I get caught up here. As I said, we'll be out of town, and cells will be turned off until Monday. We will be busy consummating our first year and planning a family for the future of Levi and Levi with even more little

Levi's." They both laugh in that hearty Levi way. "I plan on leaving early to do some shopping for Hannah

at her favorite...no, our favorite boutique at Horton Plaza."

"Very good, very good, Isaac! I will call Hannah before I leave here, and I promise she won't be able to drag your plans out of me!" Amos could never keep anything from Hannah. Amos denies it but Hannah wears her grandfather on her pinky finger like her favorite jewelry.

Isa kept up her appearance as a perfect lady, poised and proper, although she was heartbroken. Seeing Amos gave her joy and injected much-needed love back into her aching heart. Samuel badly wants to go speak to her to explain to her how he loves her and always will; an everlasting and unconditional love, just not in the way she's desired since she was a teenager being raised around Isaac and Samuel. Before then, Samuel has a call to make.

"Hello and good morning. Carlsbad Growers here; how may we help you?" asks the voice over the phone.

"Yes, good morning. I have an order being delivered at noon today to the Casa De Oro area." Samuel asks, "Has the driver left for that area yet?"

"I'll check. What is the name of the order? To whom are we delivering?" the florist inquires.

"The recipient is Hannah. My name is Samuel. Do you need my card number or order number?" Samuel pulls out his wallet, just in case.

"No, that's all right. Actually, I am preparing your order myself. Do you wish to change some part of it?" She needs to make sure.

"No, thanks. What we discussed will remain the same. I would just like to add another delivery to a separate recipient in the downtown San Diego area. I have no address...except the Hyatt Hotel Plaza courtyard. It is a coffee cart run by the Hyatt. Would this be a problem?"

"Of course not, sir. Our deliveries can be very inventive and... uhm...discreet as well. Two separate recipients in one day, sir? Maybe we should begin an account for you. We have an app for your phone which makes ordering as quick as 1-2-3. Sounds like this is what you need." she hints.

"You flatter me, surely. The app sounds good, though. I have just fallen in love for the first time, you see...and I certainly may need more of your services. As much as I'd like to toot my own horn, no pun intended, the first order is for my best friend's wife on their first-year anniversary." Samuel tries to explain.

"What a wonderful friend you are...uhm...are you accepting any more applications for friends? I would love to be your friend, Mr. Leighman. Really, is that a fictitious name, or is it real?" she hums.

"Lovely sense of wit you have, my dear. At this early hour, it is refreshing. Please call me Samuel. Now..." he laughs, "...back to business. Gabriella, the barista at Hyatt's coffee cart, has the most beautiful green eyes, like jade. What would complement them? Any ideas?" Samuel likes these things left to professionals.

"Can you describe what she was wearing with those beautiful green eyes; hair color, blouse, skirt, something to contrast with the jade color?" The florist intends to use her craft for this customer to impress his new love.

Samuel closes his eyes and remembers, "Her sweater was cream color, her lips a rosy red color, black hair with green highlights, green eyes that sparkled brilliantly even though the sun wasn't yet visible, and black fishnet bodysuit."

She says dreamily, "I wish my man were as detailed in my description. I could call him right now, and I'd bet that he has no clue what color my eyes are, let alone the color of my apparel. Samuel...uh...Lay-man, you have impressed the right florist! How does this sound? I have light green roses. I can highlight the petals in a lime green, then lightly sprinkle them with silver specks; a total of eight of these and four black roses with green ferns around the bouquet, wrapped in cream-color paper with black-mesh webbing, all in a real crystal vase. If you want glass instead of lead crystal, I can deliver for $85.00. Love requires crystal. She will melt at a cost of $175.00 for you only, today only, because you impressed me!"

Samuel could care less about the cost. She could have said twice that, and he would have agreed. "Please, send me your app to this number...what is your name?"

"Bella" she says.

"Ah, I could have guessed that...true beauty of your craft! Crystal, please. Use your words on the card, 'You only, only you, can impress me! Yours always, Sammy!'. Oh...and please use the name 'Gabby'. No need to use my last name either, please."

"Done! Now I have work to do, Mr. Lay-man...uhm...Mr. Samuel, I mean..." Bella giggles as she hangs up the phone and gets to her craft.

# Chapter 16:

Amos Levi lounges until about 10:00 a.m. or so. His partners and associates, professional terms he uses loosely, are actually all family or connected by family. Levi and Levi: Probate and Tax Law's edifice is an older textile building with four stories of mezzanine lofts, with only the first floor converted to conference and office suites. Even the interior partition walls are brick and mortar to match the exterior. Glass block and glass entry doors lead to office spaces, and the floor-pad-actuated rotary glass door is large enough to accommodate a motorized wheelchair. The large freight elevator, which used to accommodate pallets and a pallet jack, has been restored in a retro fashion to keep the history of the building intact. The stairwell, once enclosed, runs alongside the elevator shaft and uses retrofitted candlestick holders bought from Gas Lamps from the San Diego Hotel when it was demolished. These holders were then retrofitted for electricity. Aesthetic Electric, also a family-friendly contractor, has been taking care of the Levi homes and businesses for the last 20 years or more. Nothing is impossible electrically in specializing in office automation.

Samuel comes down the stairwell with two cups of coffee, black for him, French vanilla with raw sugar, and whipped cream for Isa. Isa senses his nearness and gives him her heartfelt smile, trying to play off her hurt. She says to Samuel, "Thank you, Sammy. You make me the best coffee. What is this...caramel swirled over the whipped cream? Are we expanding our palates this morning, going for new experiences, or finally succumbing to those young college harlots in pursuit of your charm?

"Ahh...touché, Isa. Are you angry with me? Or do you need to say something emotional and feel that you need to be sarcastic as a defense mechanism? Isa, your feelings are very important to me. We have always been there for each other and

I, for one, will always be here for you. You can be straight with me, always. I'll never judge you or treat you any differently. I've known you since you were in pre-school. Remember when your father brought you that first day, when he said to you, 'I'll pick you up at lunchtime,' and you couldn't understand why he left? You started crying nonstop! Remember?" Samuel reminds her.

"Sammy, are you trying to make me cry again? I was devastated that day. I had never been left on my own without my parents. My whole world felt like it evaporated beneath my feet!" Isa's feelings are no longer masked.

"Do you remember how I made you stop crying that day, the bond created by the two of us? Then and now, still today, I am your protector, your unconditional friend. I love you, Isa, and that love will never end!" Samuel puts a protective arm around Isa.

Isa leans into his familiar embrace, eyes welling up, and says, "Sammy, this embrace is my comfort. I do feel protected. Not only that, I feel understood by you. Since we were young, I've known your comfort. Do you remember? That day, just like today, you turned my tears to laughter" she chuckles. "you said my name, 'Isa, look. I am your Uncle Samuel'. Then you walked into a wall! I thought that you actually hit your head. You acted dazed and tripped over your own two feet. Falling down, you took out the building blocks you were working on, just like my uncle!" They roared in laughter together. "Then you told me, 'See...family is still here with you, Isa.' You were always there unconditionally to comfort me while others called me a baby."

"And look at now, Isa. For miles in each direction, you are the most beautiful woman in San Diego's downtown commerce, hands down. You are confident and kind, compassionate and non-judgmental. You are blossoming still. Every day, your growth continues to impress all of us. Understand, this is how we all see you: an amazing young woman who is most definitely destined for greatness. Never limit yourself, remain unharnessed, and continue to flourish until that attracts the person who can complement your growth and grow with you. Believe me, that will happen one day. Unexpectedly, it will catch you unawares, and most likely, you'll feel tongue-tied, maybe even foolish. It's hard to explain; love is not explainable, but the love we share, all of us, is unending for eternity. I love you, Isa, and always will, and that day, when it comes, will make me very happy to witness your happiness and share in your joy." Samuel explains to Isa how their lives are forever intertwined.

"So..." Isa understands, "...here we are, back in pre-school, and, once again, here you are comforting me as if it was just yesterday! Yes, I've loved you all my life, as you say, because you have loved me as my brother, as my entire family does. Today you have stumbled, as Uncle Isaac stumbled..." they both chuckled, "...upon this love, you've been faithfully awaiting, and I am happy for you now when ten minutes ago I felt like I did on the day my father left me at pre-school. I do love you, Sammy, and I, too, always will!" Then Isa stood on her tip-toes and kissed her infatuation goodbye.

# Chapter 17:

Isaac has been watching their conversation from the third-floor mezzanine. Samuel's off-the-cuff approach oozes sincerity. Isa has always known that Samuel would protect her in all ways while at the same time allowing her to grow in character to the point where she needed no one to protect her. As Samuel returns to work, Isaac awaits him to share with him how he cheered up his niece. Isaac asks, as Samuel pretends not to offer, "Well?"

Samuel feigns indifference, "Well, what?"

Isaac asks frustratedly, "Oh, come on, Samuel. Don't leave me hanging here! Is Isa OK? What concerns me the most are her feelings."

Samuel has to assure Isaac, "My friend, Isa, has grown into a mature woman, fully in control of her mind as well as her emotions. Your niece needs no protection from big, bad male genders. I am so proud to be a part of her life. She understands much more than you, and I have given her credit for it. She is happy for me, and with that, she can reach her full potential as a woman now."

Isaac laughs at his best friend. He says to him, "Sammy turned Dr. Ruth now? You fall in love, and all of a sudden, you are a mentor in the emotional well-being of women. I like it, Sammy, and it's obvious that you removed the burden of heartache from her shoulders! I can actually see her transform into a more confident woman with self-respect instead of one who feels she needs a man to complete her."

Samuel has to admit to Isaac, "Isaac, this is not a one-way learning curve. Isa has helped in my development into a man, as I have helped her in her womanhood. My being surrounded by the love of my friends, all of us together, has enabled me to know love when it hit me across the chin this morning. I see it as plain as day. Life has, in a moment, become obvious to me! It only took me longer than it took you, but it's just as rewarding. I merely shared this with Isa. She is so in tune that she understands it."

Isaac is not surprised by his niece's perception. She has demonstrated maturity beyond her years, way sooner than he can remember any others whom he knows doing so. Isaac does not doubt that it has everything to do with Hannah's closeness to her. Usually, the two are inseparable, just as Isaac and Samuel are.

Isaac returns to his desk to complete his client's portfolio and plan for the next year's tax advantages. Isaac is happy about what he has put together for their retired client who, in the past, had to pay too much tax each year. Setting up a Money Market account as a retirement fund uses their hard-saved cash as a retirement-funded investment with the accumulated interest paid out each quarter. All the couple has to pay tax on is monies made over 40K each year. At the rate they were paying, Federal tax would have whittled away at their slush savings each year. Now they will pay not a dime unless their low-risk investment hits high, which is a lottery win at best. Isaac just saved them over 100K on taxes for their remaining 'golden years,' making him very happy. This, no doubt, will bring more clients into Levi and Levi. These seniors spread the word faster than wildfire while playing bocce ball in Balboa Park.

Isaac sends Samuel an interoffice email, "Sammy, I am done here for the day; ready to enjoy Hannah's lunch? Roast-beef sandwiches, cheddar, and avocado with sprouts; my mouth has been watering all day in anticipation!"

Samuel replies, "Be right up...lunch on the roof? I'll bring the O'Douls. See you up there." Before meeting Isaac, Samuel calls the phone number on Gabriella's business card, which reads, Hyatt Hotel Barista: Courtyard Service Hostess; Gabriella Angela De Santo, extension 0707. On the back of the card is her cellphone number in her handwriting...'If you are reading this, please call me, Gabby, at (619) 251-1111'.

The phone rings. Gabriella picks up..." Samuel, is this you?"

Samuel's heart flutters, "Hi, Gabby, how did you know it was me?"

"What type of girl do you think I am? You are the only one I've given my phone number to this week! Plus, I had a feeling in my stomach, the same as I had when I met you this morning. It's sort of an intuition we women have..." she giggles. "Hi, how is your day so far? I thought I heard your voice yell my name after you jogged to work. Isn't that strange? I think that Sarah heard it, too!"

"Oh, Gabby, I'm sure that you hear your name yelled from many rooftops downtown. How can you assume that my voice was the one you heard? Samuel giggles back at her.

"My Mr. Charming, I hope you never change. Sammy, I really do. What a gorgeous day this has turned out to be. I'll never forget it." Gabriella says.

"I know it's only been hours since we met, and I hope I'm not disturbing your work, but to me, the wait to call you seemed like days, not mere hours!" said Samuel.

"To me, Sammy, the wait to hear from you after I heard you scream my name from the rooftops was an eternity! Sammy, I've been waiting my entire life for this call, it seems." Gabriella's throaty sexuality is evident.

"Gabby, please forgive my candor if I say..." Samuel parries with his best return, "...let's not keep our destiny on hold any longer... Dinner tonight after work?"

"A girl's gotta eat!" Gabby laughs, and she continues, "I'll be done here by 5:00 tonight. I live here at the hotel, 26th floor, suite B. I'll be ready by six-ish. Can you suffer until then?"

"I've been suffering until now. I'll manage until 6:00! I hope the rest of your day is filled with more pleasant surprises! Looking forward to this evening with you; until then?" Samuel seems to have found his tongue again.

Gabriella is watching a delivery driver talking to a hotel employee, pointing in her direction. "I am excited to be seeing you once again tonight, Sammy. If you have any problem finding my room, anyone here can direct you. Have a great day, and see you later tonight. Ciao, Sweetie!"

"Bye, Doll!, Samuel replies.

"Hello, are you Gabriella?" the delivery person asks.

"Yes, I am she." She sees the most beautiful floral arrangement she has ever seen. "They are beautiful!"

"I see that your gentleman-caller's description was on point. These roses definitely match your eyes, complete with flecked sparkles. Even the wrapping matches your eyes." he says. "Very rare eye color."

"Let's put credit where credit is due. My very observant gentleman caller's description of my eyes and accessories was perfect! Now, that is rare indeed! He even remembered the color of my eyes?" Gabriella is amazed! "What a gorgeous vase. Is this real lead crystal?"

"It sure is! The vase alone cost over $100 I am not sure what she charged for it. I do know that she was impressed by Mr. Leighman's order. I was the lucky driver to pull this one all the way down from Carlsbad. It seems that someone had already purchased all the roses in the San Diego area. It must be something in the air...or...it could be in the coffee!" He winks at Gabriella, whose smile is beaming.

# Chapter 18:

Isaac and Samuel enjoy Hannah's sandwiches wrapped in pita-bread pockets. Fresh fruit for Isaac: banana, pineapple and tangerine in agave juice, used as a sweetener. Her boys love her tuna pitas or her specialty, King salmon pitas. She has salmon shipped to her each month from Pike-Street-Market fishmongers whom she and Isaac met in Seattle, Washington. These mongers and their family-oriented market have been highlighted on many travel and cooking shows. Mongers throw entire fish across the market to be weighed and wrapped.

Isaac says to Samuel, "I am done here for the day. Are we gonna work out after lunch?" The two are members of City Boxing Gym next to City College off C-Street, where College Plaza caters to the O-Line and the B-Line.

Samuel returns his best friend's question with, "Is a duck's ass watertight? I can't wait to hit the heavy bag, maybe a little sparring if I have time. What about you, care to spar today?"

Isaac laughs, "Well, see, I'm not sure if I want to show up in Avalon with black eyes or bruised cheeks. Sam, you've really got your focus on the last time we sparred."

"Come on, Isaac, you dished out as much as you received. I may be heavy-handed, but your hand speed and combinations score twice as often." Added Samuel.

"And... they inflict less damage! My ribs are still tender from Monday's sparring, and I was wearing my rib pads! You are a monster!" Isaac accuses. "I may just concentrate on speed bags and timing first and see how I feel after that. Sound good?"

"Yeah. Deal! Besides, I'm staying here at the office after we celebrate at Carl's. I have a dinner date tonight at 6:00 with Gabriella. Probably be best not to show up all bruised. Don't want her to think I'm a brawling ruffian on the first date!"

Isaac looks at Samuel's ears. "I'm afraid to let you in on what all of us at City Boxing know...your cauliflower ears are a tell-tale of the sport; a little lumpy, my friend. If she hasn't noticed yet, she will."

They finish their O'Doul's non-alcoholic beer and head for the lobby. Isaac leaves the picnic basket until Monday, not wanting to drag it around Horton Plaza while shopping. They wave goodbye to Isa, who is busy on the phone speaking to clients, as she winks back at her men. Actually, she shares them with her Aunt Hannah. Isaac has already sent her an interoffice email to let her know that he "is leaving until Monday. Any calls should be directed to his voicemail. He turns off his cell phone as he walks out of the building. Hannah's orders."

Isa puts her call on "Please wait, thank you." and calls out to Isaac, "Uncle...wait." and she runs through the lobby to embrace her uncle. "I wanted to hug you and wish you and Hannah a Happy Anniversary and a Bon Voyage to Catalina. I love you, Uncle. Be safe, and see you Monday!" She looks at Samuel and says, "Go easy on him, Sam. Please don't send him home with more bruises than he accumulates on his own. See you after your work-out. We have you until 5:00!" as her petite, cute figure makes its way back to her phone bank.

# Chapter 19:

Although his family well knows Isaac as 'accident-prone' or a 'klutz' or 'clumsy' and even dancing with 'two left feet'. In the boxing ring he has the footwork of Fred Astaire. He can move in any direction and an instant, plant, and jab with precision, and feint the opponent out of his shoes. Both he and Samuel have received high-school, prestigious Golden Glove boxer trophies. Both are extremely competitive with each other, City Boxing's claim-to-fame celebrities. Rarely a day is missed in the gym managed by Jim Holtz, who has trained them both since San Diego High School.

Holtz has the focus pads on in Ring #2 when Isaac and Samuel come in. He's working with another young San Diego High School up-and-comer, Jesse Ortiz. Jesse and his grandmother live in Logan Heights. Her cooking is known city-wide, especially around the shipyards. Tres Milpas translated means '3 Palms', after the Palm trees out front on the sidewalk. It is famous for authentic Mexican food, and corn tortillas are made right in front. Lunch-crowd lines reach around the block. It's well worth the wait.

Jesse lost his father for life at Pelican Bay Prison near the Oregon border. 'Capone,' Jesse's father's street handle, was recruited by the Mexican cartel as a hitman. Logan Heights has been a regular recruitment barrio for years, a poor section under the shadow of the Coronado Bridge, where the youth are reeled in by promised fast money and glory. Usually, the money is too fast and too short; time in prison is much more lengthy.

Chicano Park and its residents who live close by have a plethora of talented artists and car enthusiasts. The underside of the bridge is a mural created by local artists, all cultural to their heritage. The parking lot, visible from the I-5 freeway, is usually totally filled with gorgeous classic cars, all modified in low-rider style, with expensive and technical hydraulic shock and sound systems in each ride. The most desirable is the '64 Impala convertible or 2-door post, and many can be seen on any day here at Chicano Park.

Capone, recruited by the cartel, was found parked at Logan's Chicano Park, passed out in the driver's seat. He had a bag of crystal meth on the floor, a glass pipe, and a Glock 9mm in his lap. As the cops patted him down, they found something revolting and gruesome. In his left front pocket, they found a human eyeball! The trophy would have been used to prove that the hit on the person was complete. That person owed the cartel a load of heroin that he had brought across the Mexico-USA border weeks before and never delivered. That 'mule,' as he was called, was found in a dumpster behind a Filippi's Pizza restaurant in Chula Vista on Broadway Street. Capone was only six blocks from his mother's house when he pulled over for a pick-me-up due to his falling asleep behind the wheel.

Jesse was only eight years old then. His grandmother and he were walking to school by way of the park when they saw his father in the back of a police cruiser. Instead of following in his father's footsteps, Jesse excelled in school and the pugilistic sport of boxing. The local gangs don't mess with him, not just due to his skills with his hands but also his father's reputation. Quick hands, still today, are no match for a 38 Special, which can be bought for $50 on any street corner. Jesse was representing the barrio-Logan community and training for the U.S. Olympics.

Jim Holtz is just the trainer to help Jesse get the job done, too. Jim says to Isaac, "I am surprised to see you...isn't today yours and Hannah's first-year anniversary? Don't you think you'd better reserve your energy for a different arena later this evening?" Jim laughs at his own wit and receives a right-cross from Jesse as he drops the focus pads.

"Nice heavy hand, son, nice! O.K., Jesse, cool down with the speed bag and I'll try to find a volunteer to spar with you. Great job!" Jesse backs up from Holtz and shadowboxes until Jim slips under the ropes and brings up a bucket and towel. He

wraps up his Olympic hopeful and holds the bucket for Jesse
to spit out his mouthguard.

"What do you say, Sammy? Can you spar with our boy for
half an hour today?" Jim asks.

"I can't today; I have to get back to the sweatshop, I mean
work, and I have a serious date tonight with my future wife.
Her name is Gabriella De Santo." Samuel returns the offer,
"Isaac has the rest of the day off. Maybe he'd be willing to help
train Jesse." Qualifications begin in three months and it is
really getting difficult to find sparring partners for Jesse, who
needs to train with boxers beyond his abilities. The problem is
that they are proving to be harder and harder to find. "What do
you say, Isaac? Can you help me out here? We could really use
your help. Not many possess the skill set to stay in the ring
with Jesse at this amateur level. Can you spare an hour with
us?"

"Of course, Jim. How can I say 'no' to you after all you do
for troubled youth in our city? It's the least I can do for you.
Just to warn you though, Jesse,...send me home with too much
bruising...and you'll have to go four rounds with Hannah!"
Isaac warns Jesse, who instantly drops into a defensive posture,
covering up his head with both gloves. All join in laughter, all
but Jesse. He has seen Hannah's box.

# Chapter 20:

Samuel and Isaac get suited and booted. Isaac helps Samuel with his tape and then gloves, lacing them and taping them again over the laces. Isaac needs a lot more protection, however. Jesse may be a 'featherweight' class, but he is fast, very fast. Isaac is quick but twice the kid's age. He must rely on experience and, of course, padding. Lots of padding!

Isaac starts with a spandex tube for his midsection, taped in place to avoid its 'traveling' under the padding; then the hard shell over the ribs; more tape to hold that in place; then the Spaulding rib, kidney, and core pads. A final layer of tape completes the midsection. The throat guard, mouth guard, ear guards, and safety brow shields (like glasses without lenses) are covered with a spandex hood to keep them all in place. Finally, the head padding is added for cranium protection.

Holtz says, "'Brain Bucket' done, that is, assuming there is anything to protect. After all, that is questionable, stepping into the ring with Jesse Jump Ochoa! His choice of names...Like it?" as Holtz laces up Isaac's gloves, then tapes the laces.

"I feel like a crash dummy where it counts, but don't get it messed up, Jump. They call me Stomp because of these." Isaac slams his gloves together. "O.K., Jump, let's see what you've learned this week, youngster! Bring it in."

The two come together in the center of the ring and slap gloves. Isaac instantly begins to move, head down, elbows in, gloves in front. The kid moves back from Isaac out of respect.

Holtz says, "Come on, Jesse, bring it in. We are sparring here with no clock and no bell. Take it to him, and no more backing up!"

Jesse comes back in, catches a left jab in the face but continues to charge into Isaac, steps inside, and sends three consecutive baby shots. Isaac catches them all with his elbows in tight; no score in that flurry. Isaac comes up with an uppercut, driving between both gloves, which slows the power but still connects on the chin and scores. Isaac follows with a cross, but to Jesse's credit, Jesse gets his head back down as it skips off the top of his head pad.

Holtz says, "It's O.K., Jesse. Isaac is no slouch. You won't learn from a slouch. You'll have to use your hand speed and quickness. Come in. Isaac has a beautiful wife waiting to celebrate an anniversary. Bring it back in!"

Jesse brings it back in... instead of a direct attack he changes to more legwork on a lateral attack. Isaac also adapts to the youngster's change of offense. Isaac hasn't even begun an offensive yet. He'll wait until Jim signals for him to go in that direction. Right now, he's merely a crash dummy with a defensive posture. Isaac dances with Jesse, keeping his shoulders squarely in front of his moves, body shots effectively blocked by elbows. In a real bout, this could wear down an opponent who is older, but Isaac is only older by eight to ten years and is still in his prime.

Jim Holtz now says to Isaac, "All right, Stomp, start to go at him, open up on him. Jesse, I want you to gauge his openings, take advantage where you can if you can find an opening anyway."

Isaac lowers his head and moves in. This time, Jesse dances to the side rather than back, lands a jab, and tries a cross follow-through. Isaac anticipates this perfectly, ducks under the cross and gives a midsection shot to the ribs hard enough to move Jesse sideways upon impact, then drops his elbows back down. Isaac's next jab is sidestepped, and Jesse returns the favor to Isaac. They both nod and smile, respect given, respect earned. They are both feeling good, both confident, and the entire purpose of boxing.

Isaac comes in with combos, and Jesse blocks, feints, and lands two to the head pad. Isaac moves in taking and blocking, giving body shots that are landing on elbows, mostly. During this flurry of exchange Isaac has backed his opponent into a corner of the ring, all intentional. Isaac's bulk, due to his heavy padding, gives the appearance of having to box a man twice

Jesse's size. Intimidation can quickly turn to devastation in the ring. Momentum in any sport needs to be turned around. Jesse covers up as Isaac brings it to him, body, head, body, head. Then Jesse snaps Isaac's head up with a head butt, effectively providing enough space between Isaac's gloves to land a quick but powerful uppercut. While his arm is locked between Isaac's defense, Jesse spins, and now it is Isaac pinned against the ropes.

"Good boy, Jump, you've effectively changed the advantage to you. Now what you gotta do...is score more points than he scored until he fights his way out of that." Jim encourages. "Now, let's see how quick you really are!

Isaac knows he is in a bad position here. The padding, although he is glad he has it all, will work against him. The extra size effectively keeps Isaac jammed against the ropes. Although his defense is good, staying covered up, elbows low and tight, he is getting 'rained on'. It's something like being in a lateral hail storm with a baseball-size hail. It comes from every angle and, it seems, all at once! The sight causes all the gym members to stop their routines, Samuel as well and turn their attention to Ring #2.

Holtz says to Jump, "Precision, son. Quantity keeps him there, but not for long. Quality in target selection is what brings them to their knees. Right now, your opponent is waiting you out, knowing your pace can't continue at this rate, blocking 80% of your throws, expending the same of your stamina, gaging your blows as they weaken and tire until just...the...right...time!"

That is the keyword that Isaac has been waiting for. He explodes from the corner, driving Jump back, back again, into the center ring. Jesse's arms are tired, really tired but Isaac was conserving energy by covering up in the corner. Jesse is basically defenseless against the onslaught of this Golden Glove recipient. Even with all the encumbrance of the padding, Isaac's precision is 70% accurate, scoring point after point. There is no bell to save the kid in a sparring match, only a curve to learning. Bells are ringing, but only between his ears. Flashes are still coming as Isaac lands head-shot after head-shot.

Holtz says, "Great job, both of you. I am standing here like a proud parent." He turns to the entire gym and says, "Stamina is the real winner in the ring. This is why we work out, run, work out, train until we can't train anymore! Then we dig down to that deep, deep inner self and keep training. Those who can't find that spot are the ones on their backs at the end. Not these two! These two are winners! Thank you, gentlemen! Thanks to you especially, Isaac, for sharing your wisdom with Jesse here today."

Jesse Jump rapidly nodded his head in thanks to Isaac. Isaac put his arm around the kid and walked him to his corner to Jim Holtz, his mentor, as well.

# Chapter 21:

On this day, the bond between Jump and Stomp became as strong as a stainless-steel weld; respect for each other is, as always, insurmountable. Holtz reiterates to the entire gym at this point, "This is why City Boxing is respected nationwide. We are a family of fine, pugilistic values. We are what boxing is all about! These two fine athletes, I have to say, are equally talented. Their strengths come from two entirely different cores within their souls. A fine display." He gives them both their rewards from him, the Holtz look of approval. "Today, I can feel it as they do, too, as all of you should." Holtz holds up both of their fists, both winners in his ring, "Truly, two champions stand here before you. Not only that, a bond between champions has been achieved here today. I have no doubt in my mind... I have seen this many times... that these two will remain supportive of each other for the rest of their lives... from ten minutes together in a boxing ring... here at City Boxing. Thank you, boys, for yet another lifelong memory I'll never forget! Isaac hit the showers. Jesse, we still have the training to do. Bring it in, gentlemen!" They both celebrate each other. Isaac has no idea yet how many times Jesse's friendship will come into play in the near future.

"So much for sending you home to Hannah bruise-free!" Samuel laughs as the trainer removes Isaac's headgear. Although Isaac is skilled in the sport, the beatings at this level of competition usually require long periods of healing. It sometimes takes years for the scarring to heal properly and still reopen after repetitive strikes. Cauliflower ears are tears and scars opened and closed, over and over. "I appreciate your standing in on that one. Gabriella would definitely be put off seeing my face altered in such a way!"

Isaac says, "Sammy, shut the hell up, please. I gave as much as I got! I'm glad Jim asked Jesse to stay suit. We felt like equals until the gear came off. It seems ten years ago I could spar all day long and not come out of it with this much damage!"

Samuel laughs and says, "Isaac, don't be so hard on yourself." He shakes his head. "You stayed upright and righteous for ten minutes with USA's future Gold Medalist. You gained his respect for crying out loud. These..." he pokes at Isaac's cheek "... should be worn as badges of honor!" Samuel takes out his phone and snaps a photo of the trainer unwrapping Isaac's midsection.

"Owww, Sammy, don't touch my honor badge, please, and there are rules against taking photos in the locker room, pal!" Isaac playfully covers up his groin area with a sweat towel, then says, "Where you going now? You should be getting into the shower. Karl's is the next stop for us, then I won't be seeing you until Monday morning at the trolley for work."

"Be right back...gotta get a shot of Jesse as he's still...fresh?" He cracks up as he heads out of the locker room.

"Owww, Pete, gently, please! The tape needs to be cut off, not ripped off mercilessly!" Isaac hints.

"No quarter, warrior! We give no quarter here at City..." Pete laughs and continues, "...Ha...Golden Glove recipient, is it? More like Golden Spoon! Tough it out, Isaac!"

Isaac and Samuel finish getting changed out. Isaac is in his same office clothes, and Samuel is in his 'night out' clothes, which are less office and more casual.

Holtz calls out, "Hey, boys, hold on a second, will ya? Need another favor from you."

"Anything, Jim, what's up?"

"I want to get my 'shop' camera and take some photos for City Boxing's Wall of Fame. Hold on...Jesse, take a fiver and come over here. Publicity time!"

"Yes, sir, Mr. Holtz, right away!" Jump says, all respect and proud. "I'm so glad I came here today to work with you two. It has been an honor for me. Really, it has been. Thank you, Isaac!" Jump taps Isaac on the ribs.

Isaac, hiding the flinch well and the jab of pain, tells the kid, "No, Jump, the honor is all mine! Hannah and I are planning to be ringside when you take Gold home! No other youngster is more deserving than you, son!"

Pete sets up the tripod and camera and turns on the lights below Mark Twain's famous quote, which honors the Wall of Fame. It reads, "The two most important days in your life... are... the day you were born... and... the day you find out why!"

Isaac, Samuel, Jesse and Jim Holtz all stand proudly below the quote, all friends for life. Not one of them will ever forget this day. All will fully understand Mr. Twain by the end of the week. Destiny and God's paths arc chosen for each of us. To most without faith, the understanding of these paths would be taken negatively as misfortune. Those with faith, thinking in a positive light, believe their paths are directed from above. Our paths are laid out for us to strengthen us as soldiers for God's plan. This thinking is the thought process of these two friends, Isaac and Samuel. Today has been a day of epic proportions, and it surely hasn't written its final chapter, not by a long shot. God needs a warrior to shed the Earth of its most heinous imaginable. This warrior needs training before he gets there.

God is strengthened by adversity. At one time or another, all of the Apostles who followed Jesus were imprisoned for their faith, strengthening their resolve and spreading their version of what is the New Testament today. Isaac and Samuel have been shown this time and time again. Samuel, finally, by patience tested daily by the many hordes of school-girl crushes he commutes with, never succumbing to these temptations, a subtle lesson in adversity, knows that God will reward him with his Gabriella when he is deserving. This strength will preserve their relationship for the rest of their lives and is well worth the sacrifices. Those who can't withhold from these temptations have toxic relationships fueled by lust. The only gains here are issues, vindictive emotions, and trauma. Carry these into the next relationship and the problems multiply like a virus.

Isaac and Samuel made their way to the College Plaza trolley station, ready to catch a ride down C-Street to the Civic Center stop. If they'd been on their way back to work, this would've been where they got off, taking a walk down 5th to Market instead. They go to the next stop, American Plaza, and backtrack to Karl Strauss' Brewery on 3rd Avenue to toast Isaac's anniversary.

# Chapter 22:

Karl Strauss' Brewery is a popular after-work meeting place for the downtown workforce, especially those who prefer to ride the trolley in uncrowded conditions. A small percentage of driving commuters will also patronize Karl's for dinner, going light on alcoholic beverages and waiting out the mass exodus from downtown streets, highways, and freeways.

Co-workers at Levi and Levi enjoy this establishment over the many others in San Diego. They also enjoy the Spaghetti Factory which sponsors family get-togethers only two blocks from the office. They've tried the Kansas City Bar-B-Que, made famous by the Tom Cruise movie, 'Top Gun'. However, in San Diego, there is no shortage of excellent bar-b-que specialty establishments.

Of course, there is Phil's Bar-B-Que, a very commercialized-version franchise, decent but not family-run. The most popular was Huffman's on Imperial and Euclid by the '4 corners of death'; however, Mr. Huffman passed away, and the location was turned into a mini-mall named Huffman Plaza. Most Huffman patrons now frequent Coop's in Lemon Grove. The owner greets all who enter this eatery as they enter, and they always present a huge igloo with free sweet tea. Levi and Levi's co-workers also enjoy Little Piggies at the Coronado Landing, where patrons can catch the ferry next to the U.S.S. Midway Museum and debark right at Little Piggies. Also, Coronado is one of the most affluent communities in San Diego. A view of downtown city lights is spectacular from here.

Isaac and Samuel prefer the bar over table seating during lunch, usually because lunch has time limitations for them. Elyse, who originally came from a town in Nevada called Winnemucca, in a small area known for gold mining, was greeting them from the opposite end of the bar. The two looked around them and wondered why the bar was so busy that day.

Elyse says, "Hey, boys. Jesus, Isaac, what train hit you? Hannah is gonna want to go after the poor individual!"

Samuel informs her, "Nah. Isaac stepped into this one as a volunteer. The train's name is Jump. Isaac was a crash dummy for that wreck!"

"Yeah, yeah, yeah...I don't remember Sammy pushing me out of the way to get me out of it. I have to go to a four-day stay on Avalon Beach with Hannah, and the worst damage is on my ribs! Thanks, brother!" Isaac blames Samuel as he raises his shirt for Elyse.

"Nice bruising, Isaac. Oh, that's right, four days off work! I remember... happy anniversary, Isaac! I want you to know that I said the same thing to Hannah. Appetizers are on me, fellas; the usual to wash 'em down?"

Isaac produces his American Express Card for Elyse to run up the drinks. She says, "All right, we'll hold onto this until you're ready to total up in case others show up later to celebrate?"

"Sure" Isaac says. It's a usual practice at bars to avoid paying for each order separately. "Elyse, why are there so many people here today?"

"You don't know? This should be easy for you to remember. Your anniversary coincides with Karl's birthday. All beers, appetizers, and entrees are half-price today only! You think this is busy? The after-work crowd will be standing room only with out-the-door lines to get in. We'll need Joey at the door to monitor occupancy to comply with Fire-Marshal's occupancy policy and prevent overcrowding, not just this location either! We'll have four tenders, sixteen waiters, double bus-and-kitchen, too. Foodprep has been storing preps in the fridge for the last two days. The mess has already started." She waves her arms, indicating the already standing-room-only crowd.

Other locals are coming over to Isaac and Samuel to congratulate Isaac on his anniversary. For his better friends, he offers to buy a beer. "What the heck, half-price; it's on me, a round for the bar and a toast!"

Elyse says, "Great, Isaac. Thanks a lot, buddy! One-round premiums for the toast... coming up!"!

Samuel waits for everyone to be served and stands up as Elyse rings the bell: "A toast...to Isaac's first year of bliss with our friend, Hannah! Please drink." They do so.

Isaac adds, "...and a new love found by Samuel this morning..." All the females sound off their disapproval and disappointment. "...please...ladies, now you can all move forward in other pursuits and squash the rumors of his sexuality." The entire bar erupts in laughter. "Now, my non-single best friend, and I must bid you all adieu. We have further commitments to address...and undress!" More laughter.

Elyse brings Isaac's charge card. He adds a $25 tip to it, signs it, and they both leave, with "For they are jolly good fellows, for they are jolly good..." echoing down the sidewalk for half a block. Elyse, being understaffed on this very busy afternoon, unwittingly has made a very bad mistake. One that won't be noticed for several more hours. Inadvertently, she has mixed up the American Express charge cards between two customers. Isaac is on his way to Victoria's Secret in Horton Plaza to buy his beautiful wife, Hannah, lingerie for Avalon and an expensive lace-and-satin robe by Versace, the designer.

# Chapter 23:

Isaac and Samuel walk down 3rd Avenue to Broadway Avenue, then cross at 5th Avenue with Horton Plaza on the right. Isaac walks with Samuel for one block south and says, "See you Monday morning, Sammy. Congratulations on meeting Gabriella. I know she'll be impressed, as we all are. God has favored her with you, as I'm sure you feel He has favored you as well. Hannah and I are off birth control, and this weekend, we will try conception to start our family. That may change once she hears that you have found Gabriella. She may want to hold off a year, hoping you and Gabriella should conceive your firstborn then. Think of it, Sam, just like we grew up, our boys can grow up together! God's favor as destiny!"

"Wow, wouldn't that be a better life than we already have! God is great, isn't He! When you feel life is perfect and beautiful, the gifts keep coming." Samuel agrees. "See you Monday with news of how tonight pans out!" Then they shake hands and embrace as they part, an embrace Samuel won't be able to share again for quite a long time.

Isaac crosses the street and rides the long escalator up to Horton Plaza's street level. He heads straight into the Sav-on Drug Store, craving a double-dip ice cream cone. With a peach-and-cherry-sherbet cone in hand, he steps back outside, crosses in front of Macy's, and makes his way into the Amphitheater Quad to enjoy his treat. The Quad is active with music and roller skaters skating in an invisible rink, all rotating in a 360-degree arena. Isaac takes his time, as he still has three hours to kill before meeting Hannah at Spring Street Station.

Isaac sat there enjoying his sherbet and sugar cone, watching the comings and goings of all types from many locations. There are tourists from docking cruise ships, 'zonie' tourists getting away from 120-degree weather in Phoenix areas, professionals working downtown, homeless who live downtown, those who have court appearances a few blocks away, and many who utilize the parking structure of Horton Plaza to avoid the $20 fees of lot-parking, which is scattered throughout downtown. Parking validation can be had by making a single purchase at one of the mercantile stores or vendors within the plaza.

Isaac and his friends, who have lived in San Diego their entire lives, have witnessed the many changes in the Gas Lamp District, named appropriately after the original gas streetlamps. These were later retrofitted with more modern sodium-vapor lamps, but the flame still burned with a fiery glow, almost like gas was still in use, casting the streets in a warm yellow hue.

San Diego was and still is a military town with its naval harbor, Navy Seal training in Coronado, North Island Air Force, Camp Pendleton, and Mira Mar's Marine bases. When Isaac and Samuel were youngsters they would ride their bicycles through Balboa Park and down Broadway. Along the way, they'd see the wares provided for the military: tattoo shops aplenty, topless bars lining the streets. Massage parlors with scantily-clothed prostitutes advertising their special massage techniques at the curbside. There were also twenty-five-cent porn shops offering short clips in a booth, a curtain on a shower rod for privacy. The streets were crowded with sailors, marines, hustlers, hookers, and anyone else looking for a little entertainment.

San Diego Commerce wanted an improved image to attract up-scale hotels, cruise line contracts, and conventions. First, they had to improve San Diego's image while retaining its colorful history. Called the Gaslamp Revitalization Project, a downtown facelift began. Porn theaters became concert venues; tattoo shops became new specialty shops; old hotels got retrofits; adult stores on corners became fast-food-establishment franchises, trendy coffee shops, and tobacco/cigar shops; liquor stores changed into sidewalk cafes. Horton Plaza was built in a modern mall, four stories tall, complete with high-end merchandise, eateries, and even movie cinemas. Later added were kiosks to give it a street flair, selling crafts, sunglasses, key chains, perfumes and colognes, jewelry and cellphones. Horton Plaza had it all when first conceived, a first of its type, and it worked. San Diego became a trendy city of entertainment for families, tourists, cruise lines, military, and night partners. Isaac smiles at the memories, finishes his cone, and makes his way back across the street to Horton Plaza.

# Chapter 24:

Isaac heads up the escalator to the main courtyard, goes towards the parking structure, and heads up the three-tiered stairs to the Cinnabon Bakery and several other specialty eateries. Past the Foot Locker shoe store and the Hot Licks hot sauce shop, across the plaza bridge to the opposite side of the mall, next to Bath and Beyond, sits the Victoria's Secret boutique.

The perfect robe he came to purchase for Hannah is on the window mannequin model. Designed by Versace from Florida, it is all lace and satin with limited sequins to be tasteful but elegant and most definitely sexy! It is not for the ordinary; the price is $450 plus tax.

The shear print is a light leopard. The back is a snarling face. The arms are the claws, which seem to rake sideways as the wearer moves. The belt resembles the leopard's tail wrapped around its torso. Hannah will simply love it, and he imagines her as a feline crawling across the bedroom floor.

This shop is not conducive to Isaac's well-endowed anatomy, and his erection begins to travel down his thigh. He removes his suit jacket, draping it over his right arm to hide the effect. He must stand still until it subsides, allowing him to walk and shop.

A saleswoman reacts to this as someone waiting for service and rushes to his side. "Good afternoon, sir. Something special for someone special today?" she asks hopefully.

"Yes, Miss, it's my wife. Our first anniversary is today. She is the same size as yourself. A four, I believe, is your size as well?" Isaac knows.

"Very good, sir. You are obviously a man with taste and an eye for women's sizes. Would you like me to model it for you?" she beams.

"You offer that service here? I do have an hour to kill, and that would be wonderful! I may need an ice pack for my pounding head," Isaac laughs to himself at his pun on words. "The ice pack helps control this. Any chance of that?" He blushes due to his needs. She laughs, thinking he is joking.

She says, "Ah, a gentleman with a sense of humor, I see. We are discreet here; there is no need for an ice pack, I assure you!" She gives a hearty laugh as she sashays into the back.

Momentarily, a size-four woman emerges with the robe on and another $200 in accessories. Hannah is, perhaps, a leggier than the model, who wears the robe at mid-calf. "Your wife will love the robe. It feels as good as it looks, especially with the correct apparel underneath it...Monique, please demonstrate for the gentleman."

Monique turns and moves to music only she can hear.

"Very nice. She'll absolutely love it!" Isaac is proud of his choice. "Great accessories, as well. Please add a couple more lingerie outfits to go with the robe...are they Versace as well, by the way?" Isaac asks.

"But of course. Versace has an entire line in this style. If you purchase three additional sets, we discount to $750, and for an additional $100, we add his sunglasses...Monique, please?" Monique displays the pair of sunglasses from her head, places them on the bridge of her very delicate nose, and says, "Stunning, aren't they?"

Isaac thinks to himself, "Who would walk outside with this sexy number where you would need sunglasses?" Then he remembers Hannah's drive to the Spring Street trolley station each morning. He says to the clerk, "I'll take all of it. Please gift-wrap it all for me?"

"Certainly, sir. Thank you, Monique, and well done." Monique could not help but notice the tent in Isaac's lap. She winks at Isaac and sashays to the back with a little extra wag in her step. Before long, there are four other models up front pretending to shop the rack near Isaac. The clerk giggles at him.

He says, "I told you about the ice pack, but you took it as a joke. I'll sit here as you ring it up, OK? Here's my American Express card, and thank you all for your help. Please add a $20 tip for Monique."

"Very good," the clerk says as she returns to her cash register and begins the transaction.

By this time, a customer at Karl Strauss Brewery has been informed that they cannot locate his American Express card. The cardholder contacts American Express to inform them that his card is missing or stolen while at this place of business. This prevents the perpetrator from making any unauthorized purchases. The representative also informs the cardholder that no attempts have been made, as of yet, to complete any transactions.

The cardholder is relieved, thanks the representative, and terminates the call. The representative, with the minimal effort of a few strokes on his keyboard, places a "Code 10" reference at any attempt to use the card. "Code 10, from authorization, comes up at the clerk's end as "Notify Authorities; Card Stolen."

At Victoria's Secret, the clerk receives this "Code 10" and immediately contacts Mall Security. The San Diego Police Department has a constant presence at the mall to expedite arrests for petty theft crimes. Shoplifters are brought to the Security Office by Theft Prevention within the mall and their vendors.

Mall Security, like all private security, needs no warrant to search persons and vehicles on its premises. The San Diego Police Department does need a warrant to search, which is why Mall Security patrols the property's parking lot, public areas, and all its vendors.

While Isaac sits and waits for his gift wrapping, he notices that the models have returned to the back, leaving him alone. Three large men enter the shop, and they immediately approach Isaac. "Excuse me, sir...can you please put on your jacket and come with us? We really apologize for the inconvenience, but this is for your own safety and the safety of the other shoppers as well."

Isaac complies, "Sure, what's up?"

"There is no time to explain here. As soon as we have you secured, we will explain everything to you." Security says, "Please stand and calmly follow us into the Security Office next door."

Isaac, thinking something is going on at the mall and Security is only trying to keep shoppers safe from harm, follows orders. "Yes, sir. What is going on? Is there a shooter in the mall or some other safety concern?"

"Sir, I've already explained to you that we will be able to discuss this once you are at the *Security Office* and we have you secure and safe."

Isaac is escorted. He stays calm, and the security needs no restraints. Isaac offers no physical resistance whatsoever. He looks at the clerk and says, "I'll be right back for my purchases. Remember to please gift-wrap them with paper celebrating an anniversary?"

"Sir, please hurry along with us so as not to attract attention to us, please?" repeats the security leadman.

The four of them exit Victoria's Secret, turn right towards Bath and Beyond, walk over the oversized chessboard, and into the doorway marked Restrooms/Security over the threshold. At the end of the hallway is a window with the word "Security" over it. On the wall is an arrow pointing left that says Restrooms. Two San Diego Police Department officers are waiting, out of sight on the right, for the suspect to reach the end of the hallway.

Isaac approaches the end of the hallway and then notices the quick movement coming up behind him. He says, "Oh, you startled me. Good afternoon, officers." He is then shoved into the wall, face first.

"Not so good! Up against the wall, sir, and spread your legs! Do you have any weapons on you, anything in your pockets that would poke or injure me?" The officer's well-practiced commands are repeated many times a day. Shoplifters and criminals who commit identity theft crimes are usually connected with drug use. Not being able to work due to their addiction, they resort to theft to satisfy their habit, eat, and survive on the harsh streets of addiction.

A used syringe can be dangerous to a police officer reaching into the pocket of an intravenous drug user. Hep-C, HIV, MRSA, and many other forms of the virus can be held suspended within the vacuum seal of a syringe. A single 'poke' can infect the unknowing victim while a search is in progress.

The officer reads Isaac his Miranda rights: "Sir, you are under arrest. You have the right to remain silent." At this point, Isaac turns numb, baffled and has no clue as to what is happening. "Do you understand these rights I have just told you?" the officer continues, "I said, do you understand these rights I have just told you?!?"

"Yes, yes...I work at a law firm, for Christ's sake...I know my rights!" Isaac agrees.

"Great. Let's go then!" He is whisked down the hall and into a Security elevator, which opens up on the 6th Avenue sidewalk. A cruiser is waiting, and off they go.

San Diego Central Jail is only four blocks away. In only a minute, the patrol car pulls up to the 30-foot-tall steel gates with the San Diego County Sheriff seal welded onto them. Isaac can only sit there waiting for these gates to open. Once through these gates, he is in an entirely new world: a world of incomprehensible experiences, a world that frightens even those who frequent this world and, with a recidivism rate of 70%, revisit this world often, the world of San Diego County incarceration.

# PART 2:
# "THE MONSTER WITHIN"

# Chapter 25:

Mark Sutter hears the helicopter fly overhead. He looks out through the cage they put him in during transport from George Bailey County Jail. He spent the last two years in that hellhole, aptly nicknamed "gladiator school" by the inmates who were housed there. He has now arrived at the gates of R.J. Donovan Prison, aptly nicknamed "Rock Mountain" by convicts housed there, and for some permanently.

The helicopter passes, and he can hear alarms and sirens; he is in a high state of alert, Red Alert. The helicopter has become a security risk, and the flight path is low and risky.

Deterrent, flight-control steel cables crisscross the yards. There are no bright orange balls on these cables. The pilot sees these and immediately slows and brings the craft into a vertical trajectory, clearing the cables. The machine tilts forward and, with cameras rolling, shoots the heck out of there, heading north.

Mark has no idea that this news-helicopter pilot has just risked losing his pilot's license due to his flight through restricted air space. Mark has no clue that the pilot risked his career over 30 seconds of video footage of his transport into these gates before him. He glances at the two shotgunners in the back and the one next to the driver, all of them with barrels pointed his way. "Relax," he tells himself, *"Relax. We need Mark to stay with us right now. Don't lose it. Stay calm, it's all cool."* He forces his eyes forward, locking onto the chain links and razor wire ahead. His mind drifts back to the events that led him here...

# Chapter 26:

For the last year before now, Mark Sutter had been making a pretty good living selling entryways for high-end custom homes. "Architectural Entryways," his employer, pays Mark a 20% fee as a commission for each entryway he sells.

These entryways are custom-made from the finest materials. Tiffany-style stained glass and lead-crystal panes greatly enhance the light that pours through them around the maple, oak, cherrywood, and various mahogany woods that create these masterpieces.

This reputable contractor's firm has a lengthy reference base, and its works are very well received in places like Fairbanks Ranch, Del Mar, Rancho Santa Fe, Olivenhain, La CO'sta, all the coastal cities, and the north. However, since Mark began canvassing here in East County areas, he has had nothing but problems with harassment from the San Diego County Sheriff's Department.

Mark's job and income required him to canvas many residential communities, going door to door, talking to homeowners one-on-one, and presenting them with portfolios and references to make the sales. As soon as he started canvassing among the now affluent homeowners around Lake Jennings, the sheriffs started their harassment.

The sheriff deputy's common greeting was, "Hey there, can you step over here, please? You match the description of someone prowling the area. Do you have any I.D. on you, please?"

Then the constant pullovers began with, "Yes, sir, the reason I pulled you over is because your license plate-holder light is covered up," "You have a taillight out," "Your right-turn-indicator light failed to signal," "Your brake lights were flickering instead of staying bright," or the favorite, "You are driving through a known drug area. Your vehicle matches a previous complaint description of a parked vehicle doing drugs inside. Do you mind if we take a look inside?"

At first, he allowed the illegal searches until he was told that they were violating his rights—actually, it was described as trampling on his rights. Then Mark tried to maintain his rights by saying, "Yes, I mind if you search my car! Yes, I mind if you want to violate my rights by a search! Yes, I mind if you trample on my Fourth Amendment rights!"

That's when the real harassment began. "Well then, we will sit here and wait. I'll have to pat you down for weapons. Is there anything in your pockets that will stick me?" they continued to say. Then, once again, they would violate his 4th Amendment rights by going into his pockets. So, Mark read up on the law. He started standing up for his rights to the sheriff's deputies, which should not be a problem, but that only made things worse. Far worse.

Mark would spend hours each night sitting on curbs behind his car. The community would soon associate his face with mischief. After all, he was always being questioned. He must be doing something illegal. Profiling, although illegal in accordance with our Constitutional rights, is done regularly by law enforcement. "Guilty by association" is a form of profiling and exactly that, profiling. Communities all accept the shakedowns in fear of the police; yes, FEAR!

Just last month Mark was eating at a taco shop on Broadway Avenue in El Cajon, across from a Pollo Loco, when the police killed a man, Alfred Chango, holding a cellphone, which the police claimed was a gun. Mark could plainly see from the taco shop that it was a cell phone.

Mark could not believe what he had just witnessed. To him, it seemed that the black man was confused and became erratic because he had cops all around him with their guns drawn, pointed right at him. Mark Sutter tried to come forth as a witness to these facts and has been harassed ever since. Although they were careful not to use the same units and deputies each time, it was still harassment because he spoke to Kristy Lyons of KSDN News.

The community of El Cajon saw the broadcast of her report with Mark Sutter, reliving what he saw and giving his interpretation of the incident. The community almost immediately cried "police-brutality profiling," the killing of a mentally unstable Alfred Chango.

Demonstrations were met with yet more police and sheriff presence. Words were exchanged, decibel levels rose, as did anger. Usually, riots are started by the black population due to the constant killings each year, mostly of black men. This was different. All races and colors stood together in demonstration down Broadway Avenue, escalating into a riot against law-enforcement presence. It got worse when the public was told that no charges would be filed against the deputies who shot the young, mentally unstable, cellphone-threatening black man.

Riots erupted all week long in different areas of El Cajon. In retaliation, law enforcement began mass I.D. checks and searches at the El Cajon Main Street trolley station.

# Chapter 27:

Mark had been having a difficult time getting any sales due to his involvement with KSDN News. His registration on his Nissan pick-up truck couldn't be paid. His rent came first, so his tags had lapsed. Mark had just parked and was going over his leads for the week and his trip to Old Town on the San Diego Trolly Green Line to prepare for a meeting at the office. The salesmen on the phones could nail down leads by offering a discount on Mark's estimates, and Mark would still get his commissions. He never missed these meetings.

Mark was about to step out of his truck to go up the stairs to the trolley platform when he saw a parade of police and sheriff cruisers, There must have been thirty of them from three different directions: Marshall Avenue, East Main Street, and the I-8 Freeway offramp. All converged on the El Cajon trolley station in riot gear and engaged the commuters on the platform as well as in the parking area. MTS Compass passes and I.D.s were requested from all. If warrants resulted from the I.D.'s for whatever reason, arrests were made. Those with no I.D.s were also detained for fingerprint identification.

Mark decided to wait in his truck and even contemplated starting it up to leave, but he was approached from the rear of his vehicle.

"Excuse me, sir. You seem a little agitated. What, exactly, is your business here? Why are you just sitting in your car? Do you have a Compass pass to use the trolley? We'll need to see your I.D., registration, and proof of insurance, please, along with a Compass pass or valid trolley ticket." the officer at Mark's side questions.

Mark, having researched his rights, knowing that the only things he needs to provide are his I.D. and a Compass pass to board a trolley to Old Town, decides to answer the officer's inquiries, "Let's see if I can remember all your questions in order. However, they came at me pretty quickly. I looked through my windshield to see what appeared to resemble an 'armed platoon' descend upon the trolley station that I was about to ascend into. Agitated. I believe if you've noticed here, that all the commuters are agitated by this overwhelming show of force, especially after this last week's event of gunning down one of this city's citizens..."

The officer attempts to cut in, "Sir, please..."

"May I finish? I did not interrupt you, officer! As I was saying...Your presence and show of force for no real or apparent reason, as I see no violence or acts of aggression other than your own...prove to me that agitation and intimidation were your intended goals here!" Mark wants to continue but is cut short.

Mark would have sworn that the officer wanted to rip him out of his truck, as he said in his best Gestapo threat, "That is quite enough! Get out of your vehicle, now!"

"First, please activate your body cams. Both of you, as citizens, request to record your aggression. That is, if you have opposing thumbs to do so..." Mark ridicules.

This initially confuses the Neanderthal officer: "What the... Sir, we gave you an order!"

"And so have I given you. Please activate your body cams prior to any more interaction among us. That is my request, as well as my right, sirs!" Mark's agitated state has now become an activist attitude. The officers sense trouble.

"Yes, sir. We have no choice..." the officer steps back and signals his partner to do the same. The leader reaches up as if to activate his camera, for which taxpayers have paid billions to law enforcement to enable citizens to see events from the cop's perspective. The real problem is that these cameras only get activated by the officers when the footage can prove exoneration of their brutality in the field. Citizens have purchased their own body cams today to prove these interactions. Cellphones are very expensive to replace after confiscation as so-called evidence, either destroyed or lost and never to be seen again or returned to their owners.

Today's cellphones are as expensive as laptops and can exceed $1,000, so citizens prefer inexpensive body cams rather than cellphones to record police pullovers. The real tragedy, of course, is that this is necessary at all.

Rather than activating his body cam, the officer keys in his Rover two-way on his shoulder, saying, "Unit 18 at Main Street location, Operation: Cops Matter, needing back-up near stairwell parking. We have an irate and erratic citizen in an automobile, a Nissan pick-up. Please assist."

"10-4, Unit 18. Back-up on the way!" the radio dispatcher replies.

"Oh, you are good..." Mark says after hearing the call request. "A citizen requests his rights and, typically, he is referred to as 'irate and erratic'. The real problem is your whole approach! We, as your employers, should be 'served,' not 'severed.' I know what's going on now. This whole exercise, what you call Cops Matter, is all about retaliation because we citizens 'demand' our rights! I am being targeted now by law enforcement for demanding my rights, given to me upon my birth here. They are considered inalienable, and, once again, you choose to trample upon them rather than uphold them!"

Back-up arrives in the form of six more cruisers, over-kill it seems; however, a citizen demanding his rights needs to be squashed before becoming a contagion in society. Law enforcement cannot allow these communities to sway judicial outcomes, such as what happened in the O.J. Simpson trial right after the Rodney King riots tore Los Angeles to pieces. All because a video surfaced proving police brutality. It became obvious to everyone that O.J. was found not guilty of murder just because a glove didn't fit (or did it?). The reason O.J. was found not guilty was that the courts didn't want to deal with another city-wide riot. That was the real reason that O.J. got away with murder.

Mark still refuses to cooperate, wanting treatment of civility and respect. The 'force' of the law wants his lack of cooperation to be treated as being 'resistive,' but they have no reason to arrest him yet. Mark says to the officers, "I want to inform you, gentlemen, that I have been recording our interaction since I was first approached."

"What? We'll need to confiscate that phone as evidence then!" the leading officer states.

"Evidence of what? Am I being arrested? What have I done to be arrested? This show of force is retaliation for the demonstrations. That's why it's called Operation Cops Matter. I got it all right here. Not only that, Kristy Lyons of KSDN News has interviewed me and would love to hear about this!" Mark threatens.

The sergeant shows up, and all chaos becomes quiet. Mark is still seated in his truck with his paperwork on the passenger seat. The sergeant asks to be brought up to speed on the problem here. While the sergeant chats with his officers, Mark quickly saves the recording and shoots the file off to Kristy Lyons with a text. After that, he powers down the phone, pops out the battery, and sets both on top of his paperwork.

The sergeant, having calmed down the situation, approaches Mark's driver-side window and says, "Mr. Mark Sutter, correct? We ran your plates, and that is you. Is that correct?"

"Yes...that is correct...that's me." Mark answers.

"Thank you, sir, for your patience. We want to resolve this without escalation." Sergeant of eloquence now, "I would appreciate your exiting your vehicle. We have a tow truck on the way to remove it."

"Remove it! What do you mean, remove it?!" Mark is angry again.

"Relax, sir. Your tags are expired, for one. For two, we are assuming that is the case due to the unresolved fix-it tickets you've received these last couple of months. We don't need an unsafe vehicle on our streets. Please step out of your vehicle now."

Mark is helpless. He stands there with his meager personal belongings in his arms as he watches his truck go by way of tow.

# Chapter 28:

Mark was able to make it to Architectural Entryways before the meeting concluded. Being fifteen minutes late, when he was never late before, was worrisome to his employer, not due to the tardiness but due to Mark's mental condition. Mark's boss has constant access to his therapist and knows just how fragile his state can be. Mark relies on his medications to stay balanced. He's been officially diagnosed with Multiple Personality Disorder (M.P.D.), and it's something he has to manage carefully. Although his medications have been working well, his doctor thinks that the trauma of being witness to a questionable 'death by law enforcement' may impair his improvement. The doctor has only met Mark's other self, who wants to be called Rettus Kram, in a couple of visits enhanced by hypnosis.

Rettus Kram, which is Mark Sutter spelled reversely, is paranoid and a nervous wreck. Sketchy is, to put it very mildly. He only emerges as a defense mechanism once Mark's psyche cannot handle his surroundings, and he feels threatened. Rettus, his eyes darting back and forth, feels as if his life is a T.V. show drama watched by the world around him. He never looks up to the sky for fear of cameras taking photos as they roll.

A large, oversized bill baseball cap, he feels, protects him from this. Embroidered on the back of the cap are the words Rettus Kram.

The doctor is unaware of a third entity. He stays hidden and prefers to be hidden. Neither Rettus nor Mark are even aware he exists. This entity hates Mark; the pansy, the pussy, the conformer, and a sissy! Rettus can't be trusted because he lacks control and is difficult to rely on. The "Monster Within" is Mark's last chance of survival.

The "Monster Within" claims he is the only one of the three who can accomplish what the other two weaklings cannot. His thought process is heinous, evil proportions of violence and vindictiveness. He trusts no one and does all his violence on his own.

Mark would wake some mornings and notice bruising and even punctures in the mirror and on his hands that had been sutured up with dental floss! He has never had to suture up injuries in all his years in construction. He was baffled by his lack of memory of these injuries, which brought him to Dr. Sullivan to begin with.

Doctor Sullivan asked permission to hypnotize Mark. That is when he first met Rettus and assumed that it was Rettus' sketchy movements that caused the injuries. Had he asked Rettus, Rettus would have answered the same reply, "I have no memory of injuring myself."

Mark informs his employer of the day's events and the loss of his truck. He collects his commissions from the previous two weeks but has a look of worry about him. His boss asks Mark. "What is wrong, Mark? Did we forget something? I know East County has been rough to canvas. We think that soon we'll start in Alpine and Descanso. Would that help out for you?"

"Alpine sheriffs, I hear, are the worst of all, Alex. Harassment has been relentless, and even though I have done no wrong, they make it appear to the community that I am a 'person of interest'. The murder of that mentally ill black man was gruesome. I saw the entire thing and am having nightmares because of it!" Mark complains.

"Oh, shit..." Alex says, "...you were there? You actually saw that poor man gunned down?" Alex gapes, shaking his head in disbelief. "Does Dr. Sullivan know what happened to you?"

"Don't worry, Alex. I am taking my medications. I am fine for now but I need to ask a favor of you if you could please help me out. I know you have been very understanding and I really do appreciate your efforts. The sheriffs and El Cajon police raided the Main Street trolley station while I was sitting there, just minding my business and working on my paperwork. Over the past few weeks, I've gotten four bogus fix-it tickets, but I just haven't had the time to deal with them yet.

My registration has expired, and my truck was towed to Impound because of that. No 30-day grace period was extended to me, either. I had to pay rent as a priority and still owe half of that. I need an advance of a few hundred to get my registration, fix-it tickets, and rent up to date. If you could, please?"

Mark has brought in almost half a million in business since he began but he need not remind Alex of that.

Alex answers, "Sure, Mark. It is the least I can do, but please, consider this a gift from me." Alex pulls out his wallet and peels off five C-notes, and gives them to Mark. "Please, Mark, we are partially to blame for having you canvas East County. We had no idea a terrible Gestapo force patrolled it! We will start working leads in Pine Valley and Descanso right away! Go get your truck. Do you need a ride to...?"

"Western Towing on Mission Gorge Avenue and Princess View." Mark finishes.

"Here, Mark..." Alex peels off an extra hundred, "Call a taxi, Uber or Lyft, and I'll take care of that, too! And really, Mark, we are really sorry to have subjected you to all of this."

"Thank you, Alex. I won't forget the help you've extended to me these last several years." Mark doesn't let Alex know of his involvement in protecting his rights and pissing off the cops.

# Chapter 29:

Before leaving the shop, Mark called Western Towing to ask exactly what he needed to get his truck back. He was informed that he needed valid registration, insurance, driver's license, and $340 if he picked it up before the close of business the following day. Mark could not believe the cost, saying, "Three hundred fifty dollars! It was only towed away this afternoon. Why so much? Oh, never mind. I'll go to the DMV first thing tomorrow. I'll be there by closing time at..."

"Five o'clock, sir. Try to be here half an hour before that time in case we need to move cars to get to your vehicle. My name is Stacey. I'll be here waiting. Have a better day, O.K.?" Stacey says and hangs up.

Mark is fuming. "Those damn sheriffs really did stick it to me."

Rettus chimes in, "I told you so, Mark. We should have started the truck and got the hell out of there! I knew something bad was about to happen! I sensed it from the beginning."

Mark says to Rettus, "Oh, shut the hell up and leave me alone, Rettus! It would have been worse if you had taken off. You know you can't drive! You are like a bundle of nerves, an unsprung spring, boing! They would have gotten us for reckless driving, undoubtedly. I told you before, let me handle the cops!"

The Monster Within listens to their conversation taking place within him, and he thinks to himself, "These pansies wouldn't do shit...but do it in their pants! I was there. They were stuck in place like a possum in the headlights, pretending to be dead! I'll just lie here, and maybe they'll roll right over me, and bump-bump get run over with both axles! Pussies..." Monster thinks to himself, "...straight pussies!"

Mark takes the trolley back to his place, an apartment on the east side of Wells Park, next to the YMCA on Madison Avenue. He chooses to walk up Madison from the trolley station to cool off, pissed at the sheriffs who put him on the sidewalk. He phones Lyft as he walks to set up an 8:00 am pick-up to Graves Street DMV next to Highway 67 in El Cajon. Every cruiser he sees makes him angrier. Maybe a walk wasn't the best way to calm down after all.

Mark is sitting on the three-foot cinderblock wall at the entrance to his apartment complex the next morning. A block away, a parade of high school students is on their way to El Cajon Valley High School.

Wells Park, another homeless hangout, is already littered with blankets under trees, the homeless looking for some sleep in peace. Most of the homeless prefer to inhabit the subterranean tunnels, a close-knit community that will exile other homeless for not following the policies and rules in place. Mark walks to the DMV.

Whether above ground or below ground, the homeless have to have order to survive and cohabitate. Without order, chaos would result. This would attract law enforcement, and that would jeopardize all who live to survive on the streets. There is a fine line of tolerance between law enforcement and the homeless. That line was crossed, ironically, when the El Cajon Police Department built new offices by the courthouse on Magnolia Avenue and Park Avenue. Their old office location, across from Home Depot on Broadway Avenue and Magnolia Avenue, stood empty and boarded up for months.

The homeless devised methods to access the building and kept a low profile for months afterward. Word spread, and more homeless took up residency there. The numbers rose. The homeless were even peddling bullet-proof glass in the Home Depot parking lot.

In the dilapidated building, there was a pecking order, just as in a community: someone who called the shots, the mayor; someone who handed out justice, the sheriff; someone who managed the areas, the manager; and so on. Without that, chaos would have shortened the use of the old police facility. The homeless inhabited that property for almost an entire year before it got raided.

On that day, Mark had just finished with the DMV on Graves Street, which took until almost two o'clock. Mark had lunch at the Jack-in-the-Box on Graves Street and called for a Lyft driver to take him to Western Towing.

Once again, as Mark waits at the parking lot under the overpass at Highway 67 and I-8, just like a deja-vu, he sees over twenty sheriff and El Cajon police cruisers coming toward him from all around. Rettus gets paranoid and really nervous. He begins to look for an escape route out of there. He hears honking. Who is honking while he needs to get away? He turns to run and sees that there is a car facing him, the driver motioning for him to get into the car. What the... Mark then takes over, remembers the ride he asked for, and gets into the car.

"Hey, are you Mark?" she asks.

"Yeah, yeah, that's me! What is going on with all these cop cars?" Mark asks.

"I'm not sure. I pulled in and was leaving the drive-thru when I saw them converge. Maybe something happened at Home Depot."

"I'm glad you showed up! After this last week...all these trigger-happy cops scare me. Have you been watching the news? A black man was shot not five blocks from here; he was killed for a cell phone in his hand. I was at the taco shop and saw the whole thing!" Mark explains.

"Oh, my God. You saw it? You were there? Uhm, where do you want to go, Mark?" she says as she goes out the driveway, turns right, and stops at the red light on the other side of the overpass. That's when they see the police presence surrounding the old police department building on the right. "There they all are, got the old offices surrounded. What is going on?"

Mark gives directions, "Can we work our way left so we can turn left on Johnson Street at the end of Westfield Mall? We can catch I-8 from there to Waring Road, up to Princess View, then down to Mission Gorge. I need to go to Western Towing near the Jack-in-the-Box at the bottom of the hill."

"Yeah, sure. I just gave a ride there to someone yesterday. Western Towing is closer to Zion Street; probably be quicker to stay on I-8 to Fairmont Avenue then right on Mission Gorge past Zion Avenue. Western is about two miles down on the left from there." she says.

"Yeah, sure. You are a professional! Let's just get clear of here as quickly as you can. This community is being targeted by law enforcement for demonstrating and standing up to police brutality. The cops are getting really ugly around here. My truck was taken from me in one of their retaliatory shows-of-force yesterday at the trolley station on Main Street." Mark informs her.

"Hey, same with the ride I gave yesterday! He said the same thing!" the driver verified.

Mark has had just about enough. Something has to give! Rettus thinks to himself, "Oh God, oh God, not more trouble, Mark, please, no more!"

The Monster Within thinks to himself, "Pussies! I hate associating with these two pansies. I can't take any more of this crap. I will take an offensive stance and won't get targeted again, never again!"

# Chapter 30:

"This is Kristy Lyons, KSDN News live, reporting from the air. We are high above the west end of Gillespie Field Airport here in El Cajon. El Cajon has been in the news a whole lot these last two weeks, starting with the police shooting of one of its citizens who was armed with a cellphone. The entire community is in an uproar. The police and sheriff's departments have been struggling to reign in the demonstrations. Many callers have reported retaliation by law enforcement that resembles profiling and shake-downs of citizens in public transit stations and targeting homeless encampments, demonstrating power in the form of force! 'Absolute power corrupts absolutely' has been demonstrated by law enforcement, which has not helped the situation. In fact, it has escalated the problem!" Kristy reports as the camera pans below at the Wells Avenue trolley station, then follows the tracks towards Prospect Avenue. Here, there is a large, black cloud of smoke coming from a pickup truck filled with used tires, fully engulfed in flames.

Kristy continues, "It appears that someone set this up early this morning with huge messages on each side of the vehicle; huge signs as seen throughout the El Cajon areas demonstrating against 'police brutality.' One sign simply says 'Enough Is Enough!'; the other says 'Fight Fire with Fire!'. This community is fed up with the Gestapo-style force that has been thrust upon these citizens. If you commute through this area, you may want to make other arrangements this morning. This fire is messy. Burning rubber is extremely difficult to put out, and the fire department is just now showing up. Once again, this is Kristy Lyons, high above El Cajon, probably the safest place to be in this city lately, reporting for KSDN News. Out! Let's get out of here, Don before the cops try to shoot us out of the sky!"

Rettus applauded the scene on the news. The community had had enough, and so had Mark and Rettus. Neither of them knew what The Monster Within was planning.

It hit him while he was at the tow yard, remembering something from the day before. He had passed a Public Auto Auction lot on Fairmont Avenue and I-8 and spotted a retired sheriff detective's cruiser for just $2,200—he plans to buy it soon. On each of his fix-it tickets he began researching the deputies involved with harassing Mark, twelve of them in all.

By phoning the sheriff's department with badge numbers and names of officers, he was able to get this information, all public information, about their work schedules, vacation days, and what sub-stations they report to. He even fell onto a website that, for a nominal fee, could look up phone, address, and criminal information on anyone. With birthdates, the court clerk's office pulled files showing criminal, civil, family, and probate filings on all his harassing deputies. These files he kept hidden under the carpet against the wall below the headboard of Mark's bed.

# Chapter 31:

The Monster Within needed cash to purchase the cruiser, so he began targeting drug dealers in El Cajon, which he first learned were easy targets. Illegally begotten money, when made by selling drugs, was never reported stolen. What was the dealer going to do? Call the cops? Not likely! The Monster Within began his campaign. The perfect place to rob drug dealers would be the Main Street trolley station, as Mark has seen transactions with the many 'blacks' who are blatant about it.

It didn't take long before he was approached, "Hey, my man, what you lookin' for? Some company?"

"Maybe. First, I need something to keep me going, if you know what I mean." The Monster Within replies.

"Yeah, right. Some shit?" the dealer persists.

"Yeah, speed, man, to motivate me for work. Later, we can talk about a lady for company." says Monster.

"Look, my man, what you lookin' for? 'Teener,' 'ball,' a 'quarter,' maybe?" the middleman asks.

"Let's start with a 'teener,' then next time we'll go for the larger if I like it." Says Monster.

"Sure, man. Uh, you ain't the law, right? A cop? Can you show me some cash? I can handle the 'teener'. Anything larger, I'll need to take some cash in advance." hopeful for an advance so he can disappear with it.

"Nah, I'm not a cop. I hate the police. Saw them shoot a guy two weeks ago! I hate all cops!" Monster is emphatic about that. "Are you a cop? Why you asking me?" he shows cash.

"Gotta be careful, is all, no disrespect. Sixty should do it. Price will go down as we see each other more often. They call me Spaz around here."

"Monster is what I call myself." Monster hands over the cash to Spaz.

Spaz doesn't go very far to a bright-green Buick Regal with a white top parked right in the first row in front of the California Recyclers building. Monster wonders if the person knows how obvious the transaction is and how Spaz has identified him so easily.   Spaz returns and says, "Here you go sixty bucks. Next time, I can do fifty, and then we can go from there." Spaz puts the cash in his pocket and disappears.

Monster crosses the street at the Chevron gas station and walks to his truck, parked on Milar Street. Monster dissolves the drug in a bottle of water that he had in the truck. He then locks the truck and starts walking. He pours the water into the gutter as he walks to Palm Avenue where he turns right and continues to the traffic light.

The trolley-station platform is now right in front of him. He has now walked around to the opposite end of the parking lot. The traffic light on Marshall Street turns green, and he walks across the crosswalk and up to the tracks. He then crosses the tracks and accesses the platform from the west-end parking lot. He fakes a swipe on the Compass-pass pedestal, then crosses the tracks and positions himself under the waiting-platform shade structure. He can now watch the activity around the green Buick Regal, his target.

Monster watches Spaz return about a half-dozen times, along with four other middleman runners. He also notices that there is only one occupant in the vehicle.

Monster waits until Spaz leaves the area, then makes his move. Monster walks down the steps, past the MTS Store, and then begins walking north on Marshall Street. As he's walking, he sees that the Buick has both windows down, relief from the rising El Cajon heat. As he nears the car, he pulls out a leather case from a chain around his neck. The case has a fake badge and I.D. inside it. He reaches the car, makes a quick change of direction, and leans into the window, badge and I.D. clearly visible.

"Keep your hands on the wheel, please, sir. Do not make any sudden moves. Detective Monahan, Drug Task Force.

You've been under surveillance for the last couple of hours. Quite a few runner middlemen have been working for you. Look, we can go ahead and arrest you, get you to roll on your source, and so on and so forth. Or we can put you out of business for the day and let you go. The choice is yours, but if we see this vehicle or you using MTS property to conduct business, we'll pull you in. Capisce?" Monster loved the 'Robert De Niro' touch.

"A warning? Really?" Suspicious, the dealer asks, "What's the catch?"

"Confiscation of your proceeds and you keep your product, which should be nearly depleted by now. That should put you out of business for a few days. Saves you the cost of bail and an attorney. Consider it a warning!" Monster says.

"Deal!" the dealer agrees and hands over a roll of cash to Monster.

"Is this all of it? What about your wallet? Hand that over, too!"

"Aww, man, how am I..." argues the dealer.

"Now!" Monster warns.

"Here, and I really appreciate..." says the now humble dealer.

"Just get the fuck out of here before I change my mind!" Monster says. "Go on and Get!"

The dealer starts up his Buick and can't wait to get out of there, thinking how lucky he is. He's never gotten a break from the law before. This must be his lucky day!

Monster walks back to Mark's truck; can't believe how easy that was! The asshole actually thanked Monster for robbing him! Asshole has no idea how lucky he really was. Monster's original plan was to snap his neck, slide into the car, and pull in behind his truck. The side of Milar that he parked on has commercial businesses, but across the street, there are residences and potential witnesses. So Monster opted for the impersonator role, which worked beautifully, and Monster counted out $3,900!

Monster now thinks Mark was in the wrong business. Monster heads back towards Wells Park and home. He uncovers his stash spot and then takes a nap; Mark has to go to work in the morning. This weekend, Monster has an auction to go to at Brown Field to complete the next step in his plan.

# Chapter 32:

Mark wakes up and feels really good today. For some reason he has a feeling that he isn't hurting financially any longer. His employer really helped him out with the $600 he gave Mark. Mark was able to get his truck, change out all the signal lamps to satisfy the sheriff's tickets, had them signed off at the San Diego Municipal Court in Kearny Mesa without seeing a judge, and his registration is now up to date. Back to work!

Architectural Entryways has several leads for Mark. Shadow Mountain Church, on Greenfield Avenue in El Cajon at the base of Crest, is the first. Up into Crest, on top of the hill above the church, there are two residences to estimate. While in Crest, he plans to canvas the many custom homes in the area. Mark feels good about the prospects.

Crest was a great area to canvas. He completed three estimate leads as well as Shadow Mountain Church. Mark spent the entire week there presenting four bids to other homeowners who all wanted bids on their homes as well. After the week's end, as he sat in the parking lot at the El Cajon trolley station getting together his presentations, he was once again approached, but this time not by the cops.

"Hey, Monster, how's it hanging?" Spaz says into the window.

"Excuse me? Do I know you?" Mark returns.

"Oh, uhm, you look like some white boy I met here last week over by the trailer there. Do you have a twin, my man? But now I think about it, he wasn't in a truck, and he wore a Monster Energy Drink cap and shades. My bad, stay cool, brother." and Spaz is gone.

Mark looks around, hoping he isn't being targeted by some sort of law enforcement sting operation again. He quickly gets out of the truck and hurries up the steps to catch the incoming

Green Line to Old Town. He reaches the platform and swipes his Compass card, then waits for the trolley.

Mark does not have to wait long. He sees the tell-tale headlight coming into the station as it crosses over West Main Street. He hurries aboard, happy to see that there are no trolley cops onboard, then finds a window seat facing away from El Cajon.

The meeting went well. He presented his seven solid estimates for the sales closer to sign and he wasn't yet done in Crest. His boss was happy to see that Mark was back on track once again. The help of $600 was well worth it. Seven estimates that he brought in totaled fifty times what he gave him and Mark's confidence level is back to standards. Mark ends up taking home a $3,000 check for the week, plus his expenditures. Not a bad week.

"You forgot to deduct the $600 advance from my check" Mark offers. "Crest is a great area so far. I want to stay in there for a couple more days, if that's O.K. with you?"

"Yeah, sure, Mark. How are you? I mean, have you finally gotten over that bad scene in El Cajon? Is it still affecting you? Any more nightmares?" his boss' empathy was sincere.

"I slept fine, like a baby, last weekend. It felt like I was only asleep a couple of hours, but when I woke..." Mark is still baffled, "...I had slept until almost three in the afternoon on Saturday. I really must have needed the sleep!"

Knowing that this tidbit of news isn't always a good sign, his boss gives him a closer look; no marks or bruises, always a good sign. He asks Mark, "Have you spoken to your therapist lately? How is that going?"

Mark nods, "No problem. I'm taking my medications, and I'm feeling good, especially since I started outside of El Cajon. Where to next week?"

Great, his boss thinks, he's all about work. "We have some solid leads in Harbison Canyon. Ever hear of the Swallows Resort, Mark?"

"Nah. Swallows like the small bird?"

"I certainly hope that's the reference!" They both laugh at that. "How about a bite to eat, Mark? Have you had lunch yet? I'll pay...we can go to China Land Buffet on Rosecrans Boulevard and Midway Drive. You know that place with that entire wall of sushi you like, the $ 9.99 lunch place? We'll see who else is here to join us, too." This is a great way to see how Mark is around others.

"Sounds really good! I am starved but I need to hop in someone's car. I left my truck at the El Cajon trolley station. Got room in your car?" Mark answers.

"No problem, Mark. Let's go. I am starvin' Marvin right now!" They exit the office and the boss offers, "Yummy Buffet lunch is on me, people! Meet you there in fifteen minutes!" and they leave.

Mark really enjoys lunch with the Architectural Entryways staff. Only six were in the office, and the smiling, non-English-speaking waitress was always happy to see them.

The Rosecrans/Midway district also has a bad homeless problem. Because of its proximity to the San Diego River bottom, as well as the many traffic lights, it is crowded with panhandlers. Businesses have started a campaign of 'do not hand out to the homeless' and signs to that effect are posted in all establishments in the area. It is not uncommon for court judges to hand out 'whole-area' restraining orders to the homeless as they exit incarceration.

Mark feels that the city has really overstepped enforcement on its communities when its judges hand out these orders. Mark has a problem understanding how a court judge can order a person to stay out of entire districts. Restraining orders, he thought, are intended for domestic violence, couples who need separating because their relationships have become toxic and violent.

After lunch, Mark is offered a ride to the Old Town trolley station but turns it down. It is only a few blocks from the restaurant. The short walk is crowded with the homeless pushing carts with life's possessions, makeshift tarp tents, and places where the homeless relieve themselves. Mark has to keep his eyes down once past Burger King, not because of dog feces but due to piles of human feces. The old El Rio Hotel, which has a liquor store attached to it, has a rolling, locked fence that encloses the driveway.

Mark glances past the fence and notices four undercover vehicles inside who appear to be eight SWAT cops exiting the vehicles. Their vests all claim them to be probation officers. Mark picks up his pace.

# Chapter 33:

As Mark's trolley rolls past the Amaya Drive stop, he begins to feel paranoid again entering El Cajon City. Rettus exits the trolley and decides to scan the parking lot and areas around the MTS Store for police presence. None are visible, but he does notice the homeless person who called Mark (and him) Monster as Mark left for the office.

Rettus, being ever vigilant and paranoid, lies back and observes this person's behavior. The black man is all over the parking lot, it seems. The man will notice a car entering the lot, someone he knows, and he'll hurry to greet the driver. A nice guy? Probably not!

The man's routine centers around a person sitting in a vehicle in the front row across from the recycling yard. This person is very nervous, sitting in a discolored Ford Taurus, the 'clear coat' on the paint job separating, typical in the hot El Cajon sun. It seems that the occupant of the Taurus is looking for someone, also typical here at this busy trolley station. He's probably here to pick up a commuter. From the south side of the MTS Store building Rettus spots two officers, MTS cops, walking north.

The officers split up. One walks along the last row of parked cars. The second officer walks between the second and third rows. The man in the Taurus spots them as well and starts his vehicle, backs out, and leaves without the pick-up of a commuter. The black man sees his partner drive by. Words are exchanged. The black man crosses at the corner and goes past Chevron Gas. They both disappear as the walking patrol scans the remaining vehicles.

Any of the homeless that the patrol finds loitering are stopped and spoken to. It seems to Rettus that they are asked to produce an I.D., a Compass pass, or a ticket for the waiting platform. Some, it seems, have their I.D.s scrutinized on Rover radio, a warrant check. Rettus can hear the homeless signal other homeless by a series of loud whistles. 'The cops are coming' is the translation. Witnessing from the platform above, Rettus is amazed at the organization of these close-knit homeless here around the trolley station. From this height, he can visibly observe the scattering of humanity as the officer approaches. It's like watching a school of fish scatter and regroup when a predator appears and then leaves the area.

Rettus continues to wait until he sees the two patrol officers turn under the overpass to patrol the west end of the parking lot. Rettus is positive that he has just saved Mark from another harassment tow due to his vigilance. Mark is lucky to have Rettus around. Screw the doctor who tries to limit Rettus through stabilizer medications. Mark needs Rettus now more than ever. Rettus has a premonition about the weeks ahead.

Rettus leaves the shade of the platform and heads for the north stairs and his waiting, parked truck, still vigilant of those around him. Still aware of the traffic on the surrounding streets, he is on the watch for patrol and sheriff vehicles. Now, as he approaches his truck, he begins to relax.

Mark unlocks the driver's-side door, tosses his briefcase onto the passenger seat, slides in, and wastes no time starting his truck. Lately, something inside of him, Rettus perhaps, is influencing his decisions a little. He has changed his routines. He drives north on Marshall Street, past West Main Street, past the Arnelle Avenue trolley station, then turns right at the next street, before Broadway Avenue. Mark drives to the corner where the street 'T's, turns left, then right, into the second driveway, which is the entrance to PetSmart's parking lot. He drives over the two speedbumps at the store entrance, straight through to Chase Bank, where he parks and goes into the bank to deposit his check from the last two weeks.

Mark fills out his deposit slip, goes up to the teller, prepares to receive his receipt, and leave. The teller says, "Sir, one moment, please..." Mark returns to the window and the teller continues, "...your cash back of $800 you requested." She counts out four one-hundred-dollar bills, four fifty-dollar bills, and ten twenty-dollar bills and continues, "...thank you, sir. Have a great weekend, Mr. Sutter."

"Uh, yeah, thank you." Mark accepts the cash. "You have a great weekend as well." Mark walks away, a little confused. Mark has never asked for so much cash back on his checks before. Maybe his subconscious was thinking about paying back his boss' gift, a gift that his boss was adamant about not returning. He has no recollection of filling out that deduction on the bank's deposit slip; very strange.

# Chapter 34:

The Monster Within wakes up early Saturday morning. The Brown Field Auto Auction begins at 7:30 am, so he must leave El Cajon by 6:00 am. Phoning ahead, he is told that there are several unmarked detective vehicles in the lot up for auction. Older, outdated Ford Crown Victoria sedans are the more common patrol vehicles. Markings are not applied to the doors. There are usually numbers on the trunk to identify the vehicle. Spotlights near the side-view mirrors are giveaways as to the vehicle's intent. The headlights have flasher capability to alternate from left to right and there are red/blue strobes behind the grill; all controls disconnected prior to auction.

An easy reconnection can be accomplished since the lights and wiring remain, only needing the controls for a simple relay and flasher to be connected. Hiram's Auto Electric on West Main Street gave Monster a quote of $250 to do the work in an afternoon; cash, no receipt. Monster took out $800 yesterday, just to be sure.

Monster walks amongst the vehicles to be auctioned off today. They have a 'buy it now' price, or you can risk a lower or higher price with the auctioneer. The county Ford Crown Vics, although driven hard and for many more miles than an average vehicle, have been meticulously maintained. There is never a shortage of these cars either, so the 'buy it now' price is always attractive. It is well known, as well, that the power trains in these vehicles are already modified before they come to the county. That's the secondary reason Monster wants one.

He has accumulated five grand for the purchase, two grand more than the cheapest Crown Victoria they have here today. He is sitting really pretty for the one he has his eyes on. He is tempted to just go for the asking price of $3,800 but he came all this way for an auction. He decides to ride it out and see how it goes. It takes several hours before they get to the automobiles; having to sit through the recreation vehicles, boats, watercraft, and ATVs.

The SUVs, favorites of the automobile market, were the first to be put on the block. Nobody is buying sedans much. Large sedans are last on the auction block, and the crowd has been steadily decreasing throughout the day. What started out as over one hundred bidders when the auction began is now down to a half dozen.

Monster is hopeful that the remaining bidders are here for the large luxury and executive sedans. He knows for certain that the one he spotted last week for $2,800 is one of the vehicles still here. It must have been left over after the bidders had all gone home.

The county vehicles are up next. Last week's sedan went for $2,400. Only four bidders are left now, which is a good sign. The one that Monster wants is up next, but there are still three others to follow. His competitor quits at three thousand, and Monster is able to purchase the cruiser for only $3,100, eight hundred less, by waiting the four hours. Two hundred an hour was well worth the patience, and Monster is quite happy with the outcome.

He makes a deal with a flatbed-tow-truck driver for $150 to tow the cruiser to Madison Avenue. Again, it's well worth the cost. The driver parks the cruiser across the street from the apartment complex. On to phase three of 'fight fire with fire' against the sheriff's department.

# Chapter 35:

Mark wakes up at 8:00 pm Saturday night and can't believe that he slept so long. Mark hasn't eaten since lunch yesterday, so he showers and decides to walk to Carl's Jr. on Second Avenue. Mark walks out of his park-view apartment, down the stairs and out the courtyard into the asphalt parking lot. He freezes mid-stride as he looks at an undercover cruiser parked across the street. "Oh, my God. Are they posting up there now, watching me, or waiting for an opportunity to harass me some more?" he wonders to himself.

Mark pretends to search his pockets to play off the reason he stopped and froze, then hurries past the cinderblock wall and turns right up Madison Avenue. At the first corner, he crosses the busy street, taking in the scene, looking for a tail.

Rettus steps up on the curb and continues up the street. Instead of going to Carl's Jr., he goes straight through to Second Avenue and waits for the light to cross Madison Avenue, as if he were going to Jack-in-the-Box. Rettus, ever vigilant, is very good at spotting a tail. Rettus says to himself, "Four right turns or four left turns to spot a tail. If we see the same face twice or the same car twice, we are being tailed by that person!" Rettus agrees with himself. Rettus steps up on the curb, then waits for the green light to re-cross at Second Avenue.

Looking straight down Madison Avenue now, Rettus can see everyone walking or driving towards him from the direction he just came. Nothing suspicious here, he assures himself, so he crosses once again towards the Thrifty gas station on the next corner. As he walks he can see that the car is still parked there, no lights on, no noticeable movement from inside. Rettus turns right again, crosses the street and walks into Carl's Jr., and orders.

"Hi, Mark. How are you this evening?" the cute cashier says to Rettus. She has had her eye on Mark for months now. "How is your weekend going so far?"

Mark says, "Hey there, Denise. I seem to have slept away most of the day. Last week was very busy. I put a lot of miles on my dawgs in Crest. The work has paid off, however. I cleared three thousand on my last paycheck!"

"Really?" Denise asks. "That is really good, Mark, super, super good. To me, that puts you at number one for available dates!" she laughs. "Just joking, Mark, but you know what they say..." she winks at him, "...there is a lot of truth in jest." Denise is wondering what it will take for Mark to get the hint: a slap across the face with her G-string panties.

"I'm still saving up for that date, Denise." They both laugh. "I'll take the usual, please, and one of your special receipts, too!"

Denise has been handwriting a smiley face on Mark's receipts. The last one had a hanging tongue with a piercing in it. "Men can be so clueless," she thinks to herself. "I'll do the same with my cellphone number this time. He should get the hint now!" She has always wondered why she never sees him on a date. He is good-looking, sort of, not really nerdish, more of a yuppy, square type. But he holds a job, it seems, and a really lucrative job at that.

Mark is tall at 6' 3" has a sort of Tom Cruise haircut, and is always clean-shaven. She never noticed any cologne, but she will educate him on that later, she knows. He is shaped well, with not an ounce of fat on him, probably due to his job, which entails lots of footwork. He always smells just showered and never has body odor, compared to the immature 'boys' she's used to. He is dreamy!

"Here you go, handsome." Denise winks again, "All in order with a special receipt, too. Have a nice evening, Mark. Don't do anything really fun without me, good-looking!"

"Thank you, Denise. It's due to you that this is my favorite place to eat out...Yummy!" She melts at that emphasis on 'eat out.' She blushes, which she never does, and can barely get a wave up as he walks out.

"What a hunk!" she manages as he walks out the door. "Next in line, please!"

Rettus leaves Carl's Jr. and is vigilant still. He crosses once again, going south on Second Avenue at the Thrifty gas station, then heads westbound on Madison Avenue. Scanning faces and vehicles in all directions, he sees nothing unusual, mostly homeless heading to or from Wells Park. At the next corner, he crosses north at the crosswalk, then west again.

He comes up behind the undercover Crown Victoria vehicle and notices the vehicle number on the left side of the trunk hatch. In the rear window on the driver's side, he notices a temporary registration paper taped to the inside. Thinking this is strange, he continues his walk-by and sees the police scanner and radio mounted under the console. Rettus continues his walk for another fifty feet, then crosses the driveway to the YMCA.

Rettus enters Wells Park; most of the lawn area still has to snooze the homeless on blankets. The park will close in an hour. An NA/AA meeting is just emptying out at the hall building on the opposite side of the parking lot.

Rettus walks along the grass strip on the park side of the hedges which were placed to hinder soccer balls from straying into Madison Avenue traffic. Trying not to rouse the napping homeless here and there, he finds a spot that is currently vacant and sits down to eat his dinner. Rettus has a view of the Crown Victoria and enjoys his meal. He finds the receipt that Denise had put in the bag with her signature smiley-face, but below that, she had written her phone number. Very brazen of her, Rettus is thinking; he wonders if she does this often. For Mark's benefit, he places the receipt in his shirt pocket. Without seeing any activity around the Crown Victoria, Rettus heads back to the apartment. Maybe the owner is a new tenant in one of the many apartment complexes on this block.

# Chapter 36:

Mark is up early this Monday, hoping to start in Crest early this morning. He has two new construction proposals which he hopes to pitch to the project's general contractor. On his prior visits to these projects, he spoke with the plumbers and electricians, beginning their underground prepping. Mark was told that the general contractor usually starts the week off by being present; sometimes, the architect is as well.

Mark makes coffee, grabs a couple of Danish breakfast snacks and some granola bars, and is soon out the door. He goes down the stairs, through the courtyard, into the parking lot, and slides into his pickup truck. The early morning is just slipping out of darkness, a halo over the eastern foothills of East County. The beginning of a 'Santa Ana' day is promised by Kristy Lyons of KSDN News this morning. The clarity of the mountains and foothills in front of him can already see hints of that forecast.

Mark backs out of his truck and aims it at the driveway. Too early for foot traffic on the sidewalks, little traffic except for an MTS bus heading west on Madison Avenue. As the bus clears by, Mark sees the Crown Victoria parked across the street, ignores it, and heads east. Rather than joining the congested traffic on Second Avenue, he continues straight on Madison Avenue. At East Main Street, he turns left and takes the I-8 eastbound ramp one exit to Greenfield Avenue. Heading east up to Crest, he is anxious to land some leads.

Alberto Rocha – The General Contractor's truck is at the first site, and Mark is greatly impressed by Beto, as he asked to be called. Beto offers Mark coffee and invites him into the work trailer. Beto informs Mark that he has three ongoing projects in Crest and one in the Harbison Canyon area. The one in Harbison Canyon is on a mountaintop accessible from the drive behind the small park and market in the town center.

Mark is able to access the blueprints for all three of Beto's projects and works on estimates on-site. Mark also promises Beto that he will forward these estimates to the owner of Architectural Entryways, a personal friend of Mark's, for an even greater discount for the three projects. The estate project on the mountaintop has three huge entrances. These three alone will total over sixty thousand in custom lead glass and hardwood. Both men are happy about the meeting's results, and Mark leaves the trailer, confident of signing these contracts by the end of the week. He plans on making an extra trip into the office Wednesday morning.

Mark begins canvassing the area, targeting all the homeowners, going door to door, leaving 'door-knobers' and literature on the dwellings with no answer. Mark sits in his truck, eating a tuna sandwich and his granola bars, reflecting on how already great this week is starting out. He isn't parked more than fifteen minutes when a sheriff's deputy cruiser pulls into his rearview and lights him up with the light bar.

Mark continues eating his lunch. After all, he is doing nothing wrong here. The deputies approach his truck from both sides. One stays back on the passenger side while the other comes up to Mark on the driver's side.

"Good afternoon, sir. We've had complaints about an individual matching your description approaching properties in the area," the officer states.

Although Mark's appearance is clean-cut, recent burglaries in the area have put the Neighborhood Watch on alert. "Can I see some form of I.D., registration, and proof of insurance, please?" the officer continues.

"Sure, uh, Officer...?" begins Mark.

"Barnes, Officer Barnes," the deputy answers.

"Here you go, officer. Do you mind if I finish my lunch? I still have half a sandwich here." Mark asks.

"Sure. I'll be right back while you finish." The deputy returns to his cruiser while his partner stays at the back of Mark's truck, scanning the contents in the back. He reaches towards the tool box, checking to see if it is locked.

"Excuse me, deputy. You have no right to open my toolbox, sir." Mark explains his rights.

"Is that right?" The deputy returns to the tailgate of Mark's truck.

Deputy Barnes returns back to Mark and says, "It seems that you and your vehicle have been frequenting the East-County-area residences this last month..."

"And?" Mark asks.

"...and complaints have been made by residents of this area about your presence." Replies Barnes.

"What sort of complaints?" Mark asks. As they sit here conversing, Mark sees two men walking. They are wearing black pants, white button-up shirts with black ties, and carrying books and briefcases; obviously, Jehovah's Witnesses are also going door to door, peddling their cult as religion. Mark continues, "Now those are the real criminals, peddling a cult to unsuspecting atheists when they are actually attempting to remove their names from the Book of Life. Or perhaps they are actually casing the homes of the unsuspecting for later burglaries after they gain their trust. I only sell doors and entryways. I don't break down doors and make illegal entries! Have you received any complaints from neighbors about Jehovah's Witnesses in this area?" Mark has to chuckle at his own wit.

"And your nighttime job is at the Comedy Club, I have to suppose? Better keep your daytime job...of...what, exactly?" Barnes accuses.

"I would show you, but I don't suppose you have a search warrant with my name on it...or one for my toolbox that your partner attempted to open." Mark also accuses.

"All right, smart ass. I see that your lunch is finished here. I will assume that you are, as well. We can all call it a day. Am I right?" Barnes hints at exiling Mark from the Crest neighborhood. "Have a nice day. We'll follow you down the hill!"

# Chapter 37:

Rettus curses during the entire trip down from Crest and Mark is livid once again over the harassment. Mark's resolve not to forfeit any of his rights gave him reason enough not to show Deputy Barnes the estimates from the Crest neighborhood. Only fair, since the deputies weren't about to show Mark the complaints they claimed to have received. Rettus does not doubt that the deputies were dishonest with that crap about receiving complaints from neighbors. He also doubts that he matches 'the description of" as well. Another thing that Rettus doesn't like is the way the Jehovahs were not even scrutinized. The Monster Within is also wondering why these Jehovah's weren't even suspect. It seems to Monster to be the perfect disguise to go along with his revenge for the future.

Rettus is half-expecting to be surrounded by other Sheriff's deputies when he reaches the bottom of the road at Greenfield Avenue. At I-8 Rettus pulls into the Mobil gas station, just to see if the deputies will follow him to the pumps. They do not, so Rettus drives up to a kiosk and purchases some local honey that he knows is sold there.

Monster slides back into Mark's truck and goes east on I-8, one exit to Los Coches, then right up the hill into the Walmart parking lot. Monster goes into Walmart to purchase black slacks, black ties, white-plain-button-up shirts, a black belt, and plain black shoes. He then goes into the stationery department and purchases a black zippered book cover and a plain, black backpack. All items are identical to those of the Jehovah's Witnesses he saw in Crest, the first of his disguises. Monster then pays cash and heads home to stash his purchases in the trunk of the Crown Victoria.

Monster slides back into the truck and continues on Madison Avenue, turns left on First Street, then straight through Main Street and into the Food Land parking lot. He goes in and purchases the Family Carnitas Combo Meal, his favorite, and heads to the cashier. Monster, once again, pays cash. He then goes back out to the truck and heads back to Mark's apartment. He parks and walks through the courtyard and up the stairs to the apartment.

Mark searches his pockets for the keys, opens the apartment door and then reaches down for his briefcase. Mark is surprised to see the Food Land Carnitas at his feet as well. Mark loves their carnitas: beans, rice, and tortillas. He also likes their real and authentic chicharrónes, lathered in Food Land's own homemade salsa.

Mark settles into a chair at his kitchen table and prepares his paperwork. He calls the office and talks to his boss about his four estimates on six entryways. Mark wants to walk them through the office and have the closer work on a better-discounted proposal for Mr. Rocha. A meeting is set up, and Mark makes an early day of it and enjoys his carnitas.

Completely satisfied now, Mark finds the receipt Denise gave to him and decides to give her a call.

"Hello..." a sleepy, sexy Denise answers. "...may I help you? This is Denise."

"That's my favorite cashier..." Mark chuckles, "...always anxious to please and serve!"

"Uh, O.K... may I ask who is calling?" answers Denise, a little confused.

"I apologize, Denise. I should have said so from the start. This is Mark Sutter. Uh, you know... 'smiley face on receipt' Mark." Says Mark, hoping to spark recognition.

"Oh, hi, Mark. How are you? I'm sorry I didn't know who it was. I am just getting up for work. I have the evening shift tonight." Denise's sleepy voice says, a lot sexier now.

"I hope I didn't wake you, Denise. I just didn't want to wait too long to call. I didn't want you to think that I wasn't interested when I most certainly am!" Mark promises.

"I am definitely glad that you called, Mark. I've been wanting you to ask me for my number. I had to take the matter more aggressively to get through your shyness, like most boys!" she laughs.

"Got me there, Denise. I am shy but hardly a boy any longer." Corrects Mark.

"Prove it, Sweetie." Dares Denise.

"Love to! When and where, if you dare!" Accepts Mark.

"Ha ha ha, funny poet and a handsome one to boot! I will get my new schedule tonight. Can I call you back tomorrow with my days off? I am really looking forward to having some fun." Denise pouts over the phone.

"Fun she wants, fun she shall have! I also have been looking forward to spending time without a counter between us. Talk to you tomorrow then?" Agrees Mark

"Great, Mark. Talk to you then," Denise hangs up the phone. Her shower takes a little longer than usual but is much more satisfying.

Mark hops into the shower after a long day of canvassing in Crest. He comes out refreshed and thinks about heading to Westfield Plaza Mall and, perhaps, catching a movie. He is in a great mood after the phone call with Denise. In the past, he's not sure why; he's never had a problem attracting women. He only has had problems keeping them around long.

Three or four women have even gone to court to obtain temporary restraining orders against him, and Mark isn't really clear on why they felt they really needed them. Sure, Mark has lapses of not remembering parts of his day. His doctor has helped clear that up with hypnosis therapy. This knowledge has helped him truly understand why women tend to distance themselves from him after a few dates, but Mark feels great about trying again with Denise.

Mark grabs his wallet, sunglasses, and keys from his dresser and heads out the door. He is feeling confident with his work and strutting like a peacock after his call to Denise. All that changed when he hit the asphalt of the parking lot and, once again, spotted the Crown Victoria, still parked at the curb directly across the street! "Bloody Hell!" Mark thinks to himself. The car hasn't been moved. It's still there. The car brings back memories of Deputy Barnes in Crest, and he begins to get angry and paranoid.

Rettus slides behind the wheel of the pickup. He wants to be vigilant and drive evasively to spot a tail. After Mark's conversation with Denise, Rettus has his mind on a different type of tail.

# Chapter 38:

Rettus and his paranoia make relationships toxic. His jealousies are too frequent and of epic proportions. If Mark's handsome appearance attracts a female, Rettus' paranoia and jealousy quickly repel her. The Monster Within, simply put, has no tolerance for social interaction at all, let alone anything emotional. Rettus knows his failures in relationships and finds his needs better satiated with massage parlors, call girls, and escorts. If his work takes him out of town, he will have escorts from the area come to his hotel room at a cost of two to five hundred dollars; he feels that Mark would spend way more than that for exactly the same results.

While in San Diego, however, call girls would be turned away by Mark once they showed up at his door. Mark would not know about making the appointment with the obviously sexy hooker, after which Mark's apartment manager would have ear-beaten him, stating that the transaction would be illegal, thus violating the terms of his lease. So Rettus turned to Asian massage parlors, of which there is no shortage throughout San Diego.

Rettus has favorite parlors that he patronizes and favorite 'therapists' as well. Rettus prefers a parlor in Mission Village because the 'therapists' are adorably cute, and they know him and welcome him for the extra forty-dollar tip over the sixty-dollar-per-hour fee. Sometimes, he'll pay an extra fifty dollars for the 'four-hand massage.' Rettus also found one on El Cajon Boulevard right off the I-805, which surprised him. The 'therapist' here was an elder Asian woman with gaps in her smile and absolutely no knowledge of the English language whatsoever. The fee was eighty dollars for an hour, twenty dollars more than the others he frequents for an hour. Curiosity got the better of him, however, and he thought maybe this was the mother of the actual 'therapist.'

The elder Asian woman took Rettus to the back area of the converted home, showed him into a private room, and said, "Take off clothing, please."

Rettus said, "Yes, O.K., uh, there is no sheet to cover up with her."

"No need coverup! Take off clothing, please!" then she left and closed the door.

Rettus disrobed, took the eighty dollars out of his wallet, and placed it in one shoe, then placed fifty dollars in the other shoe. He hid his wallet and sunglasses folded deeply in his shirt so they wouldn't be easily accessible while he was being massaged.

Rettus is always cautious around, well, everyone. He heard a light knock on the door, expecting the woman's daughter but it was the elder woman once again.

"You veddy now?" as she eyed Rettus' naked, prone body. "Oh, you veddy tall man!" then she flashed her very best toothless smile at Rettus. "You come veddy special massage? Tip veddy good? Veddy special for you, tip veddy good!"

"How much would be a good tip for a 'happy massage'?" Rettus asked.

"Sitty!" She tried to say sixty and held up six fingers using both hands, her head nodding up and down with her tongue pushing out her cheek. Rettus had only gotten a blow job from his favorite 'therapist' in National City after about six months and a dozen visits. Usually, the only relief found here were one-hand jobs and nipple caressing to bring him off. Still, he believed that the 'therapist' would be someone other than this elder Asian woman.

"I have fifty to tip. Is that O.K.?" Rettus asked.

"Veddy good, for you only, veddy special!" she answered and then removed her house dress to show Rettus her silky, short, kimono lingerie. She then oiled his back and climbed onto his buttocks as she began to work his back. She said, "Ah, you like?"

"Yes, Rettus likes it a lot, thank you. I needed a good rub-down!" Rettus admitted.

"Ah, oh, yes!" she said as sexily as an elder Asian could. Under the kimono, she was naked and shaven clean. Rettus could feel her flesh on his oiled skin. She kneaded his shoulders and began grinding on his buttocks. "Ah, you like?" she asked again.

"Oh, yes, Rettus likes it!" said Rettus satisfactorily.

She slid further up his back, reached back, and began massaging his buttocks while at the same time grinding her labia lips into Rettus' back. Rettus began bucking back in rhythm with her movements.

Once again, she had to ask, "Ah, you like?"

"Oh, yes, Rettus likes much!" as Rettus continued to let her ride his back. She reached back farther and then expertly cupped his testicles while teasing his anus. Old lady or not, she was driving him crazy for relief. He reached back to touch her, but his hands were slapped away.

"No touch, extra to touch!" She reversed her position on his back to face his feet and reached under his belly as he raised his buttocks and lay on his back, her chin resting on his buttocks, and she started to kiss them.

"Ah, you like?" Still grinding on his back, she worked Mark up to an erection. Satisfied, she said, "Roll over now!" as she lifted her body onto her knees, and Mark rolled over under her. She took his full length down her throat. "Ah, you like Ming, veddy special?"

"Oh, yes. Rettus likes. Please do more!" and this is how Rettus met Ming.

Rettus is now a regular of Ming's and although she is an elder Asian, Rettus to this day claims she gives the best head he's ever had.

# Chapter 39:

After Rettus' drive home from visiting Ming, his paranoia returns as he passes by Highway 125 and Severin Drive, as he is now back in El Cajon City and San Diego Sheriff's stomping grounds. He is able to beat the grueling after-work traffic east and makes it back home by four o'clock.

Rettus pulls into the driveway after scoping out the Crown Victoria parked across the street, which still has not been moved. He literally slides out of the truck on the driver's side due to all the oil still coating his body. Rettus checks up and down the street before crossing the parking lot into the courtyard. Rettus feels really good now and lets Mark head up the stairs and open the door to their apartment.

Mark goes to the fridge, gets a Heineken beer, then goes back outside and sits in a patio chair to watch the after-school soccer games below his apartment in Wells Park.

Mark used to go into the park to watch the softball games as well until the many homeless seemed to take control of the trees. Sometimes, he had enjoyed a trip to the dog park there to play with other people's pets since he had none of his own. Today, however, he is content just to sit and watch the comings and goings of the park enthusiasts from his porch. He's perfectly happy just relaxing after a very productive day, although he could have done better had the sheriff's deputies not harassed him and chased him out of Crest! Mark reflects on the day, kicks up his legs, and watches the very talented youth of El Cajon play swarm ball.

When Mark finishes his beer, he goes into the kitchen and eats some more carnitas, beans, rice, and corn tortillas left over from lunch. He clears the table, places his paperwork on the table, and gets his estimates in order for the closer in the morning. Mark wants to limit his time sitting in his truck at the Main Street trolley station. The entire area is beginning to creep him out.

Mark watches a little news on TV with Kristy Lyons doing Traffic at Five, showing traffic starting to bottleneck in the usual places around San Diego. After an hour of that, the six o'clock news begins with the same reports he has already seen, so he turns off the TV and heads for the shower. I'm not sure why his body has a slick oil over it, like suntan oil; he wants to shower it away.

Finding his novel by Ken Follett, the first of a trilogy called Fall of Giants, he retires to his bed for a couple of hours of reading. Mark only gets in about half an hour before his eyelids get heavy. The book falls from his grasp, hitting the carpet beside the bed, and Mark is in la-la land until morning.

# Chapter 40:

Deputy Barnes has passed his detective exam and no longer has to drive a Sheriff's Department patrol cruiser. The only problem is that he has to begin a swing shift for the first probation period of ninety days. Barnes is a widower; his wife of eight years died after her battle with breast cancer. Their only child, Timothy Barnes, is in second grade, and today is his seventh birthday.

Grandma Barnes has planned a party at "The Boardwalk Indoor Amusement Center" next to the "Parkway Bowl" bowling alley. Detective Barnes will drive Timothy there in his new undercover car while Grandma Barnes puts the finishing touches on the party. Planned for after school, she wants the other children to be there at four-thirty so when Timothy comes in with his father, they can all yell, "Surprise!" After which, Detective Barnes has to report in at the Sheriff's Department office in Santee, which is about three miles down Cuyamacca Boulevard, past Prospect and before Mission Gorge Boulevard. Timothy wanted to spend the day with his father, but his father's new title and advancement must take priority. Timothy understands and loves being with his grandma anyway.

The Monster Within wakes and dresses in his best clothes as a detective. Monster's credentials are very realistic, and the I.D. and chain are authentically forged. The sheriff star was purchased at the Del Mar Fairgrounds Gun Show out of a vehicle's trunk, along with a gun and holster clip. He got a Whisper 2000 from the same seller but at an earlier date.

With the Whisper 2000, he was able to eavesdrop on Detectives, including Detective Barnes' parking-lot conversations from across the trolley tracks and across the street from the Cuyamacca station. From these conversations, he has found information not found on public information sources or paid sources. Also, from these parking lot meetings or 'tailgate meets' between deputies, Monster has been compiling a list of addresses, time schedules, vacations, hobbies, birthdays, and any of these officers' children's names. The list only includes the officers who were involved in harassing him while he attempted to work.

In Ramona, Deputy Brown sat in his cruiser on Highway 67 waiting, it seemed, for Mark to come into town to follow his given leads. Monster sat in his vehicle in Von's parking lot along Montecito Avenue, directly across from the Sheriff Deputy Station parking lot. Monster knows that Deputy Brown lives in the Country Estates off Wild Cat Canyon Road. Monster has also learned that his wife works at the Barona Casino farther down the road toward Lakeside.

In Vista, Deputy Duff is also one of the deputies who has harassed Mark in the past. Deputy Vasquez, out of the Mira Mesa office, harassed Mark while he was canvassing the Scripps Ranch areas, along with his partner, Deputy Axleson. Deputy Garcia and his partner, Deputy Gonzalez, out of Lakeside Station on East Main Street, were Mark's harassing officers while he canvassed the Lake Jennings communities. Their office was in the parking lot next to the 99-Cent Store on East Main Street.

This afternoon, he will have his first victim, not counting the drug dealer he robbed at the El Cajon trolley station. Monster has decided that this will happen close to his home, using his props to their fullest. The Crown Victoria has had all its bells and whistles made active. Even the new police scanner has been installed. The main reason that Monster had wanted this one auction vehicle is that it still has the protective expanded-steel barrier between the driver and the rear passenger areas. The clock on his dresser says six o'clock, two hours since Timothy's birthday party has wound down. Time for The Monster Within's debut performance in the fight against law enforcement.

To The Monster Within this is...WAR!

Monster heads out to the apartment parking lot, crosses the street, and slides into his Crown Victoria. Driving straight to First Street, he turns right and follows First Street to Broadway Boulevard and turns into the last driveway on the right. He goes past the Subway Sandwich shop and pulls into an empty carwash bay. The car has been collecting dust, being on the street since he left the auction yard. Monster gives it a quick wash, then vacuums the car meticulously, front and rear, in an attempt to vacuum up any loose fibers that might be present.

Just like checking a plane before take-off, he runs the Crown Victoria through a series of checks:

strobing headlights...check!

flashing strobes in the grill...check!

strobes on the rear...check!

removal of temporary tags...check!

The rear door locks...check!

All systems go; ready to proceed!

The Crown Vic then leaves the carwash. While stopped at the driveway, waiting to exit into the left-turn lane, Monster hears several sirens approaching from the west. Two El Cajon police cruisers and one Sheriff's Department cruiser speed through the intersection, lights flashing and sirens blaring. Monster resists the urge to hit his switches and join in, just to add chaos to the scene. To his amazement, three of the vehicles at the intersection, all different models, hit their hidden lights and joined the pursuit.

Monster flips on the radio to search for the frequency they are all using and finds it. An armed robbery is taking place at the Van's shoe and apparel shop on Second Avenue and Broadway Boulevard. Monster has to wonder if one of the unmarked cars at this intersection was Detective Barnes'. What irony, if so. Monster pulls out and turns left on Broadway Boulevard, follows that all the way through the mall and past Marshall, then right on Cuyamacca Avenue, right again into the Parkway Bowl's parking lot. Monster doesn't need a parking spot. What he requires is to be visible so that Timothy thinks that Monster works with his father. Monster activates his strobes as he parks in front of the big glass windows of the Boardwalk Fun Center. He slips out of the Crown Victoria, makes a show of checking his sidearm, covering it up, and then buttoning his jacket. He pulls out his I.D. to hang from his neck on the chain while he opens the trunk to remove a wrapped birthday gift. He places the gift on the back seat of the cruiser and closes the door.

Monster enters the fun center.

# Chapter 41:

The 'greeter' at the entrance welcomes Monster by saying, "Welcome to the Broadway Fun Center. My name is Alicia. I see you are here for a birthday celebration. Which party are you looking for?"

Monster is looking around to see if he can spot Timothy and, more importantly, to spot Detective Barnes if he attempted to show up after the roll call at the department. He then spots Timothy and points in that direction. "Timothy Barnes party. I am his father's partner, Detective O'Malley. How are you, Alicia? I see Timothy right over there. I understand he is with his grandmother; where might I find her?"

Alicia is blushing a little at this handsome and tall detective who actually remembered her name. Alicia is still in high school and works here after school for work experience credits. "Right this way, Detective. They are in the 'cowpoke' area. I'll show you." Alicia leads the way. "Mrs. Barnes, there is a detective here to see you. Have a nice day, Detective." She then excuses herself and is off to assist other customers in need.

"Nice girl." Monster says to Mrs. Barnes. "I hope she is always so sweet. I see all kinds of meanness every day. Hello. You are Andrew's mother, I presume? I am Chris O'Malley, his new partner on the 'late show,' as we call this shift. Barnes is still in roll call; then he has orientation afterward. He'll be done around eight, then I'll show him around and get him used to the Detective Division."

"How nice, Detective O'Malley. Please, let's not be so formal. Call me Celia, please." Says Grandma Barnes.

"And I'd prefer Chris, as well. Andrew and I thought we'd surprise Timothy for his birthday by having him join us as a ride-along. Really, we have no calls to respond to, as we will still be orientating him. I have been here now for six years and prefer not to have to respond to 'domestic' calls anymore." Lies Monster.

"I, for one, am glad that he is no longer on patrol. Today, I read in the papers about officers involved in shoot-outs with animals. I may still worry... mothers must, I guess. Then we have that mentally unstable man last month, followed by all those riots in El Cajon. The world has gone chaotic, and we really need order. I am proud of Andrew but still worried about his safety on the job." Admits Celia.

"Yes. I do understand. My mother was relieved, as well, when I got this promotion. So, how's the party going? Looks like it's beginning to wind down. Can I help you with all these gifts, take them to your car for you?" Monster offers.

"How sweet of you to offer, Chris. That would be very helpful. Come on, and I'll introduce you to Andrew's son, Timothy, the birthday boy." Celia points her chin in Timothy's direction.

"Santee Sheriff's Detective Division at your service, Mrs. Barnes." Monster is happy with himself, as Barnes' mother has bitten his hook hard, running out his reel. Soon, he will set the hook.

"Timothy, I'd like to introduce you to your father's new partner, Chris O'Malley. This young man is Timothy Barnes." Celia proudly states.

"I recognized you, Detective when you pulled up at the door in your Crown Vic. Then Alicia pointed you out, uh, when you were talking to Grandma."

Monster thinks "that the respectful young man has great manners."

Monster asks, "Are you planning to follow in your father's footsteps when you choose a career? I ask because the reason that I am here while your father is in orientation is to ask the both of you, on behalf of your father, of course, if you'd like to ride along with us as a special birthday gift course." Monster already knows that asking in front of Timothy would excite him, and he would plead to be allowed to go along.

Grandma Barnes says, "Stay here, and I'll talk this over with Chris while I show him where my car is. He is going to carry your gifts to the car."

"I also have a gift in the cruiser to add to the pile. Happy Birthday, Timothy. I hope you like it. It is an educational sort of gift, like a science project in a way." Monster adds.

"I'll be right back, Timmy." says Grandma Barnes.

"I am parked at the door here. Shall I take a load with us as we go to your car, Celia?" asks Monster.

"Good idea. Alicia, can you hold down our table as we carry out our items?" answers Celia.

"Sure thing, Mrs. Barnes. It has been a pleasure to meet you and Timothy. He is such a respectful and kind kid...er...I mean, young man. A pleasure to meet you, too, Detective O'Malley. Be careful out there, all right?" Alicia adds as she blushes.

"Sure thing, Alicia. You stay as sweet as you are! Stay in school and go to college. Oh, and, of course, say no to drugs!" says Monster.

"O.K." says Celia. "I've decided to let Timothy go on the ride-along with you two. It is his birthday, and he's really been wanting to go with his father for a long time now. You are positive that there won't be any calls to respond to?"

"Definitely not! Strictly orientation. We plan to show Timothy the homeless problem and the bad choices made which put them into that way of life, a sort of scared straight ride-along that Andrew says is due for a young man of his age." Monster guarantees.

"So true. The problem may not continue to be so overwhelming if all the young people get the same pointers. Oh, you weren't joking about parking at the front door." Agrees Celia.

"No, and I need to get going before Andrew gets done at the station. Let me get Timothy's gift from the back here." As Monster excuses himself.

"I'm in the Chevrolet Malibu right over there. It's the silver one with the Hawaiian hula dancer in the back window..." Celia adds, "...the only way to tell the difference at my age."

"Oh, stop, Celia. You are still spry!" Monster compliments Celia.

"I have to be with Timothy. You know about his mother? Did Andrew fill you in on that history yet?" Celia asks Monster.

"I'm afraid that the entire department is aware of that period in Andrew's life. We were all praying and pulling for Veronica to recover." Monster's research was very thorough. "How about I run in, grab the packages and we'll get this wrapped up while Alicia is with Timothy?"

"O.K., Chris, and thanks again for showing up to help. When can I expect my son and Timothy to be home? I want to get some grocery shopping done while they are busy."

"Way before Timothy's bedtime of nine o'clock tonight. Orientation is a short day, followed by mostly long days, I'm afraid. This will be a great experience for this young man." Promises Monster.

"I agree," Celia admits. "So, why are we waiting around for this young man? Please, be careful with the two most important persons in my life. Promise me?"

"I promise, Celia." Monster is very believable. "Starting today, they are the most important persons to me, as well!"

Celia and Andrew Barnes never saw Timothy again after this day. No one has, and this has just begun.

# Chapter 42:

Mark is awakened early by his alarm and gets into the shower, preparing to take the trolley to the office. He flicks on the TV remote to hear the familiar voice of traffic reporter Kristy Lyons. Mark decides to make coffee and French toast for breakfast and takes some Jimmy Dean sausage out of the freezer for frying. He places the sausage in the microwave to thaw out as he sits with his cup of coffee.

A breaking news story in East County catches his attention because he hears the name Barnes and the Sheriff's Department mentioned. Mark believes that Deputy Barnes is one of the harassing deputies he encountered in Crest.

The anchorwoman says, "Breaking news this morning in Santee is of the worst scenario." her demeanor is no longer smiling and friendly. "A Detective Barnes, of the Santee Sheriff's Department Detective Division and new to the position as of yesterday, is missing his son, Timothy Barnes. Displayed on your TV screen is a recent photo from his first-grade class. Timothy is seven years old and just turned. He went missing from the El Cajon Bowl and Boardwalk Fun Center yesterday evening. There is an Amber Alert in effect. Any information about this child's whereabouts should be directed to the number listed on the lower section of your screen or by dialing 911. Thank you for joining us. We will be right back after a moment from our sponsor."

Mark finishes his coffee and goes to the microwave to retrieve his sausage, which he starts to fry while, at the same time, dipping his bread in the scrambled eggs and cinnamon. He's completely confused by the news of young Timothy. In the back of his mind, though, way back there somewhere, he has an emotion of vindication towards the deputy and a feeling of apathy.

Mark poured another cup of coffee to have while eating his breakfast and used the remainder in the coffee carafe to take with him his 'to-go' mug. He washes the dishes and pans and wipes the counter and table.

Mark then brushes his teeth and uses the bathroom to relieve his bladder of this morning's coffee. He dresses casually for his commute, wearing '501' jeans, a T-shirt, and a hoody sweatshirt that he can remove and tie around his waist on his return to the heat of El Cajon later this afternoon.

Grabbing his wallet, keys, and sunglasses from his dresser, Mark is on his way out the front door and to the office. Briefcase in hand, he locks his apartment and heads down the stairs, across the courtyard, and into the asphalt parking lot. Before reaching his truck he notices that the undercover vehicle is no longer parked across the street. Happy about that, he climbs into his truck and heads for the El Cajon Street trolley station. It feels unnatural for him to be going into his employer's office on a Tuesday. He can't remember ever going in to submit appraisals this early in the week.

As Mark pulls into the parking lot, he finds a spot close to the stairs leading up to the platform and wastes no time grabbing his briefcase and coffee. As he climbs the stairs, a black man passes him and says, "Hey, Monster, what's happenin'?" Mark ignores the greeting.

Spaz repeats the greeting, "Hey, Monster, how's it hangin', bro? Haven't seen you lately. Need anything today?"

Mark turns and asks, "Excuse me? Need anything? You must have me confused with someone else, guy. I don't know you or what you are talking about. Have a nice day, buddy." He then sits down on the bench by the railing with a view over the parking lot and the Municipal Transit Service Store.

Spaz says, "O.K., have it your way, Monster...er...I mean sir." and continues down the stairs, mumbling to himself, "Crazy cracker mother fucker!" just loud enough to be heard by Mark.

"Yeah, O.K..." Mark mumbles back, "You've been dipping too much into your crack cocaine, my friend!" and chuckles to himself for his wit. "I got wit it, yo!" wondering what is with these crackheads anyway.

While Mark sits there waiting for the Green-Line trolley, he keeps an eye on the crackhead making the rounds again in the parking lot. At the same time, he thought, "Why the hell aren't these cops harassing him? These guys at the trolley stop peddling their drugs all day long. Why don't they lean on them like they do me? All he is doing is working for a living on a job that is a part of the construction process, with a legitimate business that is licensed and tax-paying!"

The black man sees one of his customers coming into the driveway. He hurries over to a shot-out Honda Civic. The driver hands the black man what appears to be money. Mark sees him count it and put it in his pocket.

The black man then heads across the parking lot, straight for his drug connection, parked near the same place as the last time Mark witnessed a transaction; first row, Nissan pickup truck, green and rusty, same male driver without a passenger. The black man and Mark make eye contact as the black man crosses the parking lot. This makes the black man a little sketchy, and he changes course. No longer walking, he pulls out his cell phone and makes a call. Immediately, the green Nissan backs out of his spot and exits the lot.

The driver of the Honda Civic looks at the black man, who makes a chopping motion through his neck and throws up a 5, then a 0. Then he disappears across Marshall Avenue. The Honda Civic pulls out next and drives out of the lot, then picks up the black man.

Mark is flabbergasted by the obviousness of what he just saw happen. If that transaction in drug dealing was visibly apparent to him, then why didn't law enforcement do something about it? Are the police crooked? Are they intentionally blind to the situation here? Even if they all departed so quickly, couldn't they follow them and pull them over under 'suspicion,' a term they used on him numerous times when he was doing nothing wrong?

Mark starts looking around again for the police. This time it is not because he wants to avoid them but to see if there are any around who may have witnessed what he had. Maybe the criminals did their Houdini act, not because of Mark; maybe they got spooked by police presence.

As Mark searches below, bells start clanging. Then he hears the whistle of the Green-Line trolley pulling into the station.

# Chapter 43:

Mark is so enthralled by the comings and goings in the parking lot that he fails to swipe his Compass pass at the pedestal prior to boarding. As soon as he hops aboard, he finds out why he saw no cops at the trolley station. This trolley is full of 'trolley law', and they are handing out tickets aplenty. Mark takes a seat and, briefcase in his lap, opens it to do 'busy work' in the hope that they won't bother him.

"Sir, do you have a ticket or Compass pass on you this morning?" the MTS enforcement officer asks.

"Oh, uh, sure I do." Mark produces his pass.

The officer scans the pass and asks, "Did you forget to swipe your pass prior to boarding, sir?"

"Oh, shoot. I may have been preoccupied. I guess I may have overlooked that. Is that a problem?" Mark queries.

"Well, it could be, but it shows that your pass is good for the entire month so that no ticket will be issued. When we get to the Amaya station, you can hop off, swipe, then hop back on if that is O.K. with you." the officer suggests.

"Yes, sir. I apologize for that. I appreciate the reminder to validate. I will certainly do what you ask." Mark wants to explain to him why he was preoccupied but thinks that this would be inappropriate, as the officer's immediate duty is ticket enforcement.

Mark gathers his papers, closes his briefcase, grabs his coffee, and stands by the sliding door. He hopes to hop off and hop back on. As the trolley pulls into the station, Spaz, the black man Mark spotted in the El Cajon station, is waiting at the platform. Not only is he waiting to board, he is about to board at the same sliding door that Mark is waiting to exit. Mark sits back down, and the enforcement officer watches him.

The black man enters the trolley. He spots Mark, and then he sees the eight MTS cops around him. The black man does a quick 180-degree turn and bolts from the trolley. Mark fails to disembark as he promised and sits there, visibly shaken by the near face-to-face with the black drug dealer.

"Sir, is something the matter? You seem shaken." the enforcement officer asks. "I thought we agreed that you were going to swipe your pass at the Amaya station. That man who attempted to board seemed to recognize you, then wanted to get far away from you...and quickly. Actually, he ran as fast as possible," he says suspiciously.

"Oh, that? I don't even know that crackhead. He seems to believe I know him, however. I have no idea why he thinks that. He is the reason that I sat back down. The guy keeps approaching me, and I thought I'd be safer around you guys." Mark explains.

"Right..." The officer has heard it all in his day, but this one tops it all! "...right. O.K., I'm going to check the new borders first, then my partner and I will get off at the Grossmont station with you while you get your pass swiped. Sound good to you?"

"Yeah, sure, no problem, officer." Mark says compliantly but is thinking to himself "Not again, here comes another shakedown! Once again, they target him when there are drug dealers who are running around, obviously doing their dirty work undisturbed and right under their noses?"

The three get off at the Grossmont trolley station, one of the busiest on the Green Line. Mark starts walking towards a Compass pass pedestal when he hears a booming voice call out at him. "Hey! Hey, you!" the enforcement officer yells towards Mark.

Rettus answers him, "Who? Me? I was just going to swipe my pass, as you asked."

"What I asked? I instructed you to get off with my partner and me..." ordered the enforcement officer.

"...and get my pass swiped' is what you said to me." Rettus repeats word for word.

"Exactly right! So where were you headed just now?"

"Uh, the pedestal right over there." Rettus says in his best sarcastic voice.

"That can wait for now. We have some questions for you in the meantime." Replying to the sarcasm

"Questions? I am on my way to my office for a meeting in thirty minutes. If I don't get back on this trolley, I may miss my meeting." Rettus informs the officer. "Do you want to make me late for work?"

"Sir, I'm not the one who is riding the trolley without a validated pass or ticket. We are on time for our work!" His turn for sarcasm.

"Officer, you can see that we have a monthly Compass pass, which is clearly up to date. Oh, hell. It's a moot point. The trolley is leaving anyway!" Rettus is getting angry.

"We? Not sure who the 'we' is." the officer looks between his partner and himself. "We did request that you exit at the Arroya station to validate." back at Rettus now. "You failed to do so. Now, do you wish us to write you a ticket, or do you, instead, wish to answer a couple of questions?"

Rettus throws up his hands in resignation and says, "I guess 'we' have an extra fifteen minutes on 'our' hands now, don't 'we,' officer? Although I could fight your ticket, that entire court day, of course, would be a wasteful day in court for the three of us." Rettus would definitely fight the ticket. He would call the MTS Enforcement office to find out their days off due to the 'freedom of information act', then schedule his court date for one of those off days. The two officers would have to burn a day off to show up. If they did not show up, the ticket would be dismissed. Rettus knows that this works for all tickets in court. "What are your couple of questions, officer?"

"First..." the officer begins, "...the African American gentleman who began to board at the Amaya station, how do you know him?"

"That black man has, in the past, accosted me at the El Cajon Main Street station on several occasions. He is adamant in his belief that he knows me. I have told him on each occasion that he is mistaken. However, he continues to cost me about this." Rettus answers. "Next question."

"All right, we appreciate your answer. Next question... Why did he choose to exit after he saw you and decide, at almost a run, to leave the station? The individual is known to us, and we would like to know what sort of 'business' you have with him?"

"Next answer...part one...I was under the impression that he left hurriedly because he spotted you two and the other officers, and he didn't have a pass or a ticket. Part two...and final answer...I have no knowledge of that person or his business, which you claim is known to you, and yet, he remains to roam the streets accosting those, like myself, commuting on the trolley." Rettus is done answering, then has a question of his own, "My one question to you is... How is this person 'known' to you?"

"We will be the only ones asking questions here. Do you have an I.D. to go along with your Compass card, please?" insists the officer as he removes his leather ticket case.

"Oh, I see. I do as I am asked, and I still get written up with a ticket?" Rettus snaps back.

"I have not decided yet! Please, I asked you for some identification!" the officer persists.

"Oh, yeah, sure. Here you go." Rettus thinks to himself, "It seems that most times we leave our apartment nowadays, sixty percent of the time, end up handing law enforcement some form of identification!" Rettus chuckles at his next thought.

"Thank you." the officer accepts the I.D., "What seems to be so funny, sir?"

"Just a thought to myself, sir." Then Rettus chuckles again.

"Care to share?" asks the officer.

"No." Rettus stares defiantly.

"Do you mind if we take a look in your briefcase?" asks the officer.

"Yes." Rettus is still defiant.

"Yes, we can? Or yes, you mind?" the officer clarifies.

"Yes, I mind." Rettus is even more defiant.

"Why would you mind, may I ask?" the officer persists.

"Why would you ask me to give up one of my Constitutional Rights, given to me as a U.S. Citizen?"

"Because I suspect your 'association' with a known street criminal and drug dealer is more than you claim it to be. You, yourself, admitted that this person is adamant about believing that he knows you from somewhere. How does one interacting with someone else make a mistake like that, unless you have an identical twin you don't know about?' The officer has no idea how close he is to the truth.

"When you first approached me, as I was sitting down with my briefcase open on my lap, I did not attempt to close it, did I? It was open. Anyone near me could clearly see the contents. Why would anyone with something to hide sit there with the briefcase open for all to see?" Rettus' impatience is becoming more evident and he has answered his last question, "That is all I intend to say on this matter. Now, I need to call my office to explain my tardiness, if I may?" Rettus pulls out his cell phone.

"Sir, please, do not reach into your pockets again like that! We are just about finished here. I need to radio my sergeant first; one more minute, please." he steps a few feet away with his partner. "MTS Rover one-niner-five, repeat one-niner-five. Request contact with Rover zero-two-niner. Sergeant, please come in..."

The sergeant responds, "This is Rover zero-two-niner. What is your request, one-niner-five?"

"I have a commuter here denying a look-see, stating his reason as standing up for his Fourth...how should I proceed?"

What is causing your suspicion: his erratic behavior or his attire? Why are you profiling the commuter?"

Rettus overhears the profiling alert. He knows that this alone is illegal, so he says, "Profiling? Profiling? That is illegal! I can't believe that I'm hearing this right now! I need to call my employer to retain my employment and, possibly, our lawyer."

The sergeant replies, "Shit, the commuter overheard our transmission, one-niner-five! Oh, hell, let him go to his job. Stating that he has a job should have informed you that he has nothing but paperwork in his possession. Zero-two-niner, out!"

Just in time for the next trolley pulling in from the Amaya station, the officer informs Rettus, "Thank you, sir, for your cooperation. Please remember to swipe your pass next time. Please swipe before you board. Have a nice day." and he hesitantly hands back Rettus' identification and Compass pass.

Rettus leaves without another exchange of words as he phones the office on his way to the pedestal, "Hello, Sheri, this is Mark Sutter...yeah, I know...I apologize for being late. I was harassed." Mark says this loud enough for the two MTS enforcers to hear, then puts the phone on speaker. He knows what Sheri is going to add. "Those assholes..." she says, "Their harassment is getting to be ridiculous. I leave from Lemon Grove. They are always harassing us on the Orange Line, as well! I'll let them all know that you'll be here in, what, twenty minutes?" Mark can't help but laugh at his very obvious irritation as a fellow commuter while on speakerphone.

"Thanks, Sheri. Twenty minutes should be good, that is, if I can travel the fifteen miles without another incident with those who are supposed to 'serve'!" More sarcasm.

# Chapter 44:

Mark's office was buzzing with talk about the law-enforcement harassment of their canvassers, Mark and two other employees. All three of them have been harassed lately. They all have opinions as to why but Mark brings up a good point, to which they all take notice.

"The deputies, as well as the police, all patrol in pairs. I've noticed that the Jehovah's Witnesses also travel in pairs. I believe that they do not get harassed due to the fact that it is not one person's word against two cops. Being out there solo opens the door for them to harass and violate our rights because it is two officers' word against one person's word." Mark's words ring true to them all. Mark's boss, his friend, nods in agreement.

"So maybe the solution, in these areas where we have good leads but law enforcement harassment, is to travel in pairs? Alternate leads, perhaps, canvas by going in alternately or sharing the day's commission between two salesmen? We could try that if we need to. I am definitely open to solutions. Maybe problem areas need this?" The owner asks his canvassers for a solution and leaves it up to those who are at risk.

Mark adds, "Sure. I guess among the three of us we can make a list of the areas which have been 'suggested' for us to leave. We could then reappear in those areas in teams. I know that Crest, for one area, has lots to canvas. Look at the estimates I brought in today. These are only for one afternoon. If we could do this or more each day...well...splitting commissions would not be a problem, would it?"

"Great idea, Mark! I'll leave it up to you as to the organization and who will join you. We will test the waters in Crest. You were asked to leave just recently. I think the sooner, the better. Then, we will see how the sheriff reacts to this new plan. Great solution, Mark. Now, let's have a look at what you've got there. On Friday, we will meet with all three of you guys and hit those areas again!" Announces the owner.

Mark is proud of his idea and says, "Thanks. You are going to like what I brought from a contractor in Crest. Alberto Rocha is a very respectable General Contractor in the area of Crest and beyond. Beto has given us three jobs to estimate. He likes what I proposed. I told him there may be a better discount if we land all three. I hope to deliver that discount through our closers here at the office as soon as possible, please!"

"I'll get them on it right away, Mark. I, for one, am really glad that you are on our team, Mark. Thank you!" patting Mark on the back.

Mark prepares to leave, "We'll resolve this problem one way or another. I plan to dress more conservatively and less casually, as the Jehovahs do. The heat will make it difficult, but, hey, if that's what it takes... See you on Friday, then?"

"See you, Mark!" Sheri adds as he leaves the office.

"Bye, Sheri. Have a great day. Watch out for those Lemon Grove 'Gestapo cops'!" Then he gives her the Nazi salute as a joke. They both laugh as the door closes.

Mark decides to walk over to the Old Town Central Park. The Old Town Fiesta 200 is what created this historical area on its 200-year anniversary. There are about a dozen Mexican-style restaurants. There's usually live music in the Bazaar Del Mundo gazebo. The plaza is also surrounded by curio shops, similar to those south of the border in the tourist section of Revolution Boulevard.

Cinco De Mayo and Dia Del Muertos celebrations are spectacular in Old Town. Also plentiful are the historical museums. Whaley House is a popular museum due to stories of it being haunted. The Heritage House section is a mock neighborhood of historical houses, complete with a historical church.

Mark enjoys the central park which is quiet and peaceful most days. The 'coaster' and the trolley station are only a block away and train whistles add to the ambience of the park. The entrance to a public restroom attracts the homeless; however, the park attendants keep that under control.

The park benches in the park are very enjoyable for Mark. Sometimes, he'll finish up his proposals here before continuing on to the office. Mark plans on relaxing for the rest of the day, trying to let the morning's events dissolve away before he heads back into El Cajon City. As he's enjoying one of his granola bars, his cell phone rings. Good thing he decided to stop here, in case he needs to head back in.

The call is from Denise. "Hey, handsome! How is your day going so far? I just woke and thought of you, or maybe that was a dream..." she says sexily, "...so I thought I'd call! I have two days off after tomorrow. Thursday and Friday, then back to work until Tuesday and

Wednesday. I have to tell you, Mark, it has been a while since I've dated, so please be gentle with me!" she jokes around.

"Oh, hey, Denise, glad you called. Gentle is my middle name...that is...until it's time not to be gentle!" Mark jokes back. "At present, I have just finished at the office. Had a great sales day yesterday, so I wanted to get the proposals into the office today."

"Proposals? I hope I'm not too late already." Denise jokes again. "I 'propose' we get together as soon as possible. I am excited about going out with you on our first date."

"Me, too, Denise. It's been a while for me, too. So, Thursday night, then? I'll plan something special and get back to you on the itinerary. Sound good?" Mark says.

"Yeah, it sure does. I am up for anything you want to do. I can't wait! Talk to you soon, Sweetie. Bye for now!" and Denise hangs up.

Mark decides to go to the Fandango Restaurant for a beer and something more substantial than a granola bar for lunch. They are just opening their doors at eleven o'clock, and he has the entire patio to himself. The phone call from Denise puts him in a great mood and the waitress notices.

"Good day, sir. We just opened. A beautiful day for patio dining, isn't it?" she says with a big, radiant smile.

"A great day!" Mark's excitement is contagious.

"Men..." she notices, "...can never hide their emotions when it comes to a new woman, totally transparent! I am guessing, a new girl?" she jokes.

"Is this Fandango's restaurant or 'Fandango fortune tellers'? I mean, you pegged me on the spot! You should open up a 'guessing booth' at the Del Mar Fair!" Mark jokes back.

"Again...men...are so transparent! I'd say you are a fish-taco aficionado. Am I wrong?"

"As a man...I do love a great tuna taco" they both laugh at that. Then Mark orders, "But I know that today is your infamous 'mole' day, so I'll have the Pollo en Mole, please. Extra Mole on the side?"

"And something to drink?" another smile.

"Corona and lime and water with lemon, please," Mark answers, smiling back.

"Back in a flash," the waitress promises.

"I'll be right here!" Mark answers.

He has a very delicious lunch and a lovely view of Old Town Park. His ride home goes by without any harassment and without seeing any drug dealing at the El Cajon trolley station. Mark pulls into his apartment parking space around two in the afternoon. In his apartment, he grabs a beer from his fridge and parks his butt on a lounge on the complex's patio.

After enjoying the park activity below, he finishes his beer and goes inside to read and nap.

# Chapter 45:

The Monster Within is wide awake, gets dressed in his Jehovah's Witness attire, grabs his book and leather case props, and hurries out the door. It is three o'clock, and Deputy Brown's wife will be home by six. Their twelve-year-old rebel daughter has had her new boyfriend over. Both parents know nothing about this boy, who has been wanting to break up with their daughter. Monster only knows that the daughter makes him leave the house by four o'clock before her mom gets home.

Instead of going through the parking lot, Monster hops the fence into the YMCA parking area. He walks towards the dog park and out the back side of the park. Monster has parked the Crown Victoria behind apartments on First Avenue, where they don't assign parking spaces. Being hidden from the street is necessary now that his campaign has started.

Monster knows that apartment managers would never tow an undercover car. Managers prefer to have tenants renting who work in law enforcement or probation. Steady renters and exposure to their vehicles keep criminal activity out of their low-income

apartments.

The Monster Within has had a difficult day, allowing Mark and Rettus to have control. The drug dealer at the Main Street trolley station didn't seem to get the message, and it made Monster angry. He'll have to revisit that virus to mankind one more time. Maybe then he will get the message. Monster's cash reserves are dwindling as well. If that drug dealer thinks he can simply change vehicles and not be noticed, well, he has another robbery coming.

Monster needs to get out to the Country Estates as quickly as he can, so he starts driving like the maniac that he is. He's tempted to hit his grill lights and siren while hitting reckless speeds. That is what he craves; however, it is too soon to be noticed yet. He is sure that Grandma Barnes has given her son a description of Monster's car, and he is sure that it is being sought. This might be the last time he uses it for his war against law enforcement. He will need to dump it soon.

The drive through Lakeside on Highway 67 goes pretty smoothly. There's still about an hour before traffic begins to back it up. Monster takes Highway 67 through Lakeside until he crosses over the San Diego River Bridge. At the Circle K convenience store, he turns right on Willow Drive and follows it through the two-speed circles. The California Highway Patrol usually mans the four-way stop ahead in the evening hours due to the traffic in and out of the Barona Casino. Monster plans to come back through Ramona, and he hopes that he passes Deputy Brown as he returns home from the Sheriff's Department Station while his rebellious daughter is in the back of the Crown Victoria. "Wouldn't that be a hoot?" he thinks to himself.

Monster turns left at the stop sign and heads up Wild Cat Canyon Road at a good clip. The Crown Vic's high-output engine makes the grade to the top quickly. In no time, he is going by the Barona Casino, then the Barona Racetrack, and then the Barona Motocross Track. He goes through the water-crossing dip and turns right at the only stoplight since Highway 67 and Willow Road. Soon, he enters the Country Estates. He passes by the Browns' residence and parks in the driveway of a house two doors down that is for sale. The area is very quiet. Its isolation is why people who live way out here buy here.

Monster's time is running short. Deputy Brown's wife should be home in an hour and the daughter's boyfriend left twenty minutes ago, maybe longer. Monster grabs his leather-cased book and heads up to the front door, posing as a Jehovah's Witness.

Monster rings the doorbell, and a young woman answers. She's been crying.

"Oh, the Lord does his work in mysterious ways indeed, young lady. I won't bother to ask if anything is wrong, as it is clear to me that something has distressed you this afternoon.

My name is Christopher. Would you allow me to pray with you?" says the ever-compassionate Monster.

Stephanie looks up into Monster's handsome features, and her tears begin to clear. She replies, "Oh, hi. I'm so sorry to be like this in front of you. I can't invite you in as my parents aren't home, but I guess a prayer can never hurt, can it?"

"Words of praise are only gratitude to our Lord for the gifts bestowed upon us. He gave us his only Son to save us from our sins. What greater gift is there? It is only right to give Him gratitude for this. We can pray right here on your doorstep." Agrees Pastor Monster.

"Yes, please, and thank you." Agrees Stephanie.

Monster places his hand on her shoulder and says to her, "Let us bow our heads to give thanks, and let us pray."

Stephanie bows her head. Monster removes a chloroform-soaked handkerchief from his back pocket and covers her mouth and nose with it until she collapses in his arms. He easily lifts her up and carries her to the Crown Victoria. He places her in the back he then drives away. He does not even bother to close the front door.

The door stands wide open when Stephanie's mother comes home. She calls her husband, who is only a couple of minutes away from home. It is entirely possible that Deputy Brown passed the Crown Victoria with his unconscious daughter lying in the back. Stephanie was never seen again, just like Timothy Barnes.

# Chapter 46:

Monster is feeling good about his heinous activities and their results. He has two more acts to complete before ditching his cruiser. He takes the route through Ramona, heading back towards El Cajon on Highway 67. This time, he avoids the Willow turnoff at Circle K and continues to Mapleview Avenue. He turns left at the Burger King and past the 7/11 on the right. There are about twenty people or more congregated outside the 7/11, waiting for the Barona Casino bus, and the traffic is now beginning to congest.

Monster hits his turn signal and works his way into the left-turn lane. The signal light turns green and he follows a car into the many who are turning towards the same four-way stop that he passed through two and a half hours ago. At this hour, however, the CHPs will be manning the intersection. He drives past El Cajon High School on his left and begins to slow. He turns on his left-turn signal once again and turns to his next destination: Cactus Park BMX Track.

Monster pulls into the dirt driveway at Cactus Park. He has his strobes and headlights alternating for effect. He is on his P.A. system and speaks into his microphone handset, "Dante Garcia. Looking for Dante Garcia. Dante Garcia. Looking for Dante Garcia. Dante, please approach this cruiser as soon as possible."

Monster then flips a 180-degree turn. Facing the entrance, yet in the middle of the dirt complex, he has made the cruiser and himself very visible. The bogus set of government plates that he stole is the second set that he's changed out since the purchase of the vehicle. He is not worried about someone getting the plate number; he stole the plates from a county auto-body yard off Well Avenue.

"Dante Garcia, very important that you come to the San Diego Sheriff's Vehicle right away. Dante Garcia, very important..." Monster is interrupted by a ten-year-old boy at his window, knocking. Monster rolls it down.

"Yes, Officer. I am Dante. Do you need to see me about something? Is my father O.K.? He isn't hurt, is he?" genuinely concerned.

"No. No, Dante. Your father is fine. He wanted me to come pick up you and your brother and take you home. He has to work late, unfortunately, and I have to join him as soon as I get you two home. I am sorry to say you won't be able to race in any heat. We have to go right away!" Monster explains.

Being a good kid, Dante is understanding, "Oh, that's all right. This actually happens a lot. All my friends are used to Sheriff Squad Cars coming to pick us up. Pop the trunk, and I'll load up my bike."

"We'll have to put it in the back seat, Dante. I'm afraid I have too many dangerous weapons in the trunk. I'd rather your bike be in the seat with you than with my pack of weapons if you know what I mean?" Monster says, concerned for Dante's safety.

"Oh, O.K., sure. Here, I can get it. Should I sit in the back as well? We only live on the other side of Lindo Lake, which is really close. It's just that my dad doesn't want us walking or riding after dark. That's probably why he sent you, huh? O.K., I'm in and ready!" Dante, ever the helpful one, says, "Derrick is at high school. He usually walks home from there. We can wait out front for him or I can go get him. He is most likely already on his way here."

Monster kills his lights and P.A. system, starts the engine, and pulls away from the dirt parking area. He turns right and drives right past the high school. Dante points to a boy coming out the front of the high school. "That's Derrick there. Hey, you missed the turn. He's right there, sir." Dante never got to see Derrick again. Monster actually saw the young boy waving goodbye to his brother. Dante, however, is found not far from where they are now, the Lakeside River bottom on the opposite side of the Rodeo Grounds.

Monster, having been abducted twice this day, has made mistakes; however, mistakes that left evidence behind: his Monster Energy Cap with Rettus Cram embroidered on the back. Monster had to leave it behind without a chance to retrieve it or bury young Dante. It seems he was in too much of a hurry to fully investigate the area in which he chose to hide Dante. The Lakeside River bottom, like almost all of the San Diego River bottoms, is inhabited by homeless communities. He was seen by several witnesses and chased from the scene back to his Crown Victoria.

These witnesses chasing Monster from the river bottom and possibly identifying his vehicle have now changed everything. Campaign Cleansing, his final plan, must be stepped up immediately. Dante would have to be his final target, but Monster is satisfied with his progress. He has also been unable to ditch young Dante's Red-Line Proline BMX bicycle. He decides to use it in the next part of his plan.

# Chapter 47:

Monster stays off Highway 67 towards El Cajon, knowing that the congested traffic on I-8 will slow him down measurably. From the Rodeo Grounds he turns left onto Mapleview Avenue. The new 7/11 is on El Monte Drive, another four-way stop here, also known to lots of law enforcement, Sheriff's deputies in particular. That may possibly be due to having a donut shop here and coffee.

El Monte Drive, Monster knows, is a dead-end street. At the end of it is El Capitan Lake and a boat launch for fishermen. Although this may seem to be an attractive spot to ditch the cruiser, getting in will be easy. Getting out will be an entirely different matter. He goes straight through the four-way stop. Now, he is traveling up and over Lake Jennings Road. This will intersect with I-8 east of El Cajon, one exit past the Walmart where he purchased his clothes.

Interstate-8's intersection has two back-to-back signals and he catches greens on both of them. He then goes around the thirty-mile-per-hour shamrock-loop entrance onto I-8-East. Here, I-8 has been reduced to a four-lane interstate, two lanes in each direction, and the speed limit is seventy rather than sixty-five miles per hour.

At Dunbar Lane, Monster exits once again and continues straight through the exit stop sign, which puts him on the frontage road towards Alpine and Harbison Canyon. He is sure that, by now, the Sheriff's deputies have been alerted by the homeless encampment near the Rodeo Grounds.

Meanwhile, Deputy Brown's wife has finished calling all of Stephanie's friends, and Deputy Brown has reported his daughter's disappearance as being suspicious. Although she is not yet a teenager, the Ramona deputies aren't too worried yet. She may have left the home and forgotten to close the front door. Deputy Brown informs them that, even though rebellious, she is responsible and, in the past, has always been home, usually doing homework in the kitchen, when he or his wife came home.

After Timothy and now Dante, it won't take long to put two and two and two together and come up with a pattern that equals six. Wait! His cap! Then he remembers his cap fell off at the river bottom! His cap has "Rettus" embroidered on the back of it. At the time when Monster allowed Rettus to pay the extra fee for the stitch-work they thought it to be funny.

Mark and Rettus got a laugh out of it when Rettus wore it backward in front of the mirror in the bathroom. Rettus Cram became Mark Sutter. Oh, that was really rich at the time, not so much now.

At the next intersection for Harbison Canyon, Monster turns right, winds around to the left, and down the short grade to the next signal, Harbison Canyon Road, and turns right again. He follows the road straight along the white, picket fences and past the school on the right. From here, the road gets very windy and treacherous, and the speed drops down to forty-five, with some sections dropping to twenty-five miles per hour. He passes a small park and market and Swallows Resort mobile-home park, a nudist community, weather being a factor, of course, for the residents there. A six-foot wooden fence surrounds the park to avoid any traffic distractions.

Monster pulls up to the next intersection, a three-way stop, and turns left. Dehesa Valley Road meanders through Dehesa Valley, then up into Alpine through scrub-oak and juniper trees. Monster, however, isn't going that far. The traffic here is very heavily congested due to the Sycuan Casino at the top of this straight grade.

Most of these commuters and even buses will be turning right into the Casino entrance. Monster does not follow the horde of gamblers but, instead, goes straight for a short distance. He then flicks on his emergency flashers and feigns car trouble, slowing gradually. No one is behind him, so he doesn't need any theatrics about car trouble. He simply pulls over and lifts the hood of his Crown Vic.

Monster removes the bicycle from the back seat and, wearing Mechanix gloves, he removes his stolen plates from the trunk and places them on the back seat. The Jehovah's Witness disguise now looks like casino-employee apparel. He removes a two-gallon can of gas from the trunk and removes the cap to reverse it into a funnel. He opens the gas door on the Crown Vic and sets the can next to the gas-filling aperture on the vehicle's rear quarter panel, giving the appearance of having run out of gas.

When no vehicles are in view, he grabs the can and saturates the back and front seats, as well as the dash and steering column. Monster then saturates the engine compartment and also the trunk area, leaving the partially empty can on its side in the trunk. He then removes a pack of cigarettes and three books of matches from the glove box. He opens the cigarettes, removes three of them, puts the pack of cigarettes in his shirt pocket, and steps back from the car. He puts all three cigarettes in his mouth and lights the three with the same match.

Monster 'hot boxes' the cigarettes, puffing hard and watching the traffic until no one is coming towards him. He once again 'hot boxes' the three 'cancer sticks,' making the cherries good and hot. He takes one 'cancer stick' and places the filter to the end of the matchbook and closes the cover over it, then places it in the trunk. He does the same thing in the driver's seat and in the engine compartment. He then hops on the Red-Line bicycle and starts riding towards the Casino driveway.

Rather than park the bike at the entrance, he goes into the parking structure and leaves it leaning against the wall by the elevator. Monster knows that it won't be there long. The upper-level Red-Line Proline bike is worth about a thousand dollars. He'd be surprised if it is still there by the time, he crosses the bridge walkway into the Casino.

To be certain of this, he sees three youngsters leaving, and he says to them, "Did you forget to lock your Red Line up by the elevator?"

One of them says, "Oh, uhm, yeah. I did forget. Thank you. That's where we were going right now, as a matter of fact!" and he peels off from the group, saying to them, "I'll meet you at the truck on the exit ramp!" Within minutes, Dante's bike is gone; within hours, stripped and built into an entirely different bike.

Monster enters the Casino, goes into the coffee-and-drink service station, and purchases a cheeseburger with onion rings and a coleslaw salad. He leaves a good tip, saying that he hit on a Cleopatra Keno machine. He does the same thing at the drink station, leaving a five-dollar tip. He asks the name of the server and orders a Raspberry Iced Tea and coffee with extra cream and sugar, thereby establishing an alibi with Tran, the drink server.

When he finishes his lunch, he goes back for another coffee and tea, leaving Tran yet another five-dollar tip. He then walks towards the down-escalator to the main entrance lobby, walks to the Services Counter, and asks for a transport schedule for the Marshall Avenue shuttle. The next shuttle will be leaving in ten minutes; he plans to be on it.

Monster meanders through the area between the two escalators and up the steps into the non-smoking area of the Casino. He passes between machines and card tables and then through the rear doors to the shuttle area out back. He finds a seat and relaxes on his way into El Cajon.

Monster walks from the shuttle center towards El Cajon Boulevard. At the same time, he calls for a Lyft driver to meet him on Johnson Avenue and El Cajon Boulevard at the Thrifty gas station. By the time he walks the three short blocks, the driver is sitting there waiting. Once again, Monster asks the driver's name, Lizzy, and he tips her a ten-dollar bill on a fifteen-dollar ride to Wells Park. He walks through the parking lot to Madison Avenue, up to his apartment, and locks himself in, exhausted.

# Chapter 48:

These last few days have been hard for Detective Barnes and his mother, Celia. Celia blames herself for allowing a stranger con artist to abduct her reason for living. Timothy was her everything! Detective Barnes tries to explain to her that it isn't her fault that evil exists. Evil and sadistic people are out in the world, co-existing with normal, compassionate people. They have no compassion whatsoever for those whom they victimize, as well as the many others who are caught in the ripple effect.

It is clear that Detective Barnes' son was targeted. It was not an evil of convenience. The heinous crime took a lot of premeditation and planning to carry it out. Barnes' family had to be carefully watched and spied upon, their routines recorded, all carefully monitored through spy tools and listening devices. All similar to what detectives use in their tool bags on the citizens of the city. Barnes tries to explain to Celia that he thinks Timothy was targeted intentionally. She could not have stopped it, even with her own life, had she thrown it in front of this evil person. He is only glad that he did not lose her at the same time.

These last few days, he's been going over his logs, his arrests, his traffic stops, and any interactions he may have had. He brings home photos of the most violent felons whom he put away and of those who have recently been released. His first suspects: the violent felons capable of doing such a monstrous thing to a child? Barnes didn't sleep much. Even when he could, he would wake up screaming for his son. As for Celia, she really concentrated on each photo for the first hundred or so, and then they all started to look the same. She needed to have some space to rest before she could look at any more of these photos.

However, Barnes keeps telling her to stay strong; there is still hope to have faith in the detectives' abilities to deduce the whereabouts of their son. After all, there hasn't been a body found yet. Detective Barnes' heart sinks when he receives the call of a young boy's body being found near the Rodeo Stadium and under the bridge into the river bottom. The Sheriff's deputies have been there now for fifteen minutes, sealing off the area against evidence contamination, as well as holding witnesses for questioning.

Witnesses! Witnesses? Barnes couldn't get there fast enough for his liking. He's thinking, "Please, please, God, don't let it be my boy! If this maniac did this due to how I represented my badge in an immoral manner, I would change. I swear it to You now, God, if my son can be found, still alive, I will change my ways of law enforcement!"

Detective Barnes pulls into the dirt area being used at present to store those huge, concrete pipe pieces that are ten feet long. He can see the Sheriff's Department cruisers, six of them. Several deputies are busy stringing police line tape so as not to contaminate the scene. He is waved over to two deputies who are detaining several witnesses. As he pulls into the park, it seems that all the witnesses are looking at his undercover vehicle and begin pointing at it. Both deputies stop what they're doing and stare hard at who is the focal point of the witnesses and are now approaching the scene.

One deputy actually guides the witnesses behind their cruiser as if to protect them, while the other deputy unclips his weapon and cautiously approaches Barnes' Crown Victoria. Once the deputy sees who is driving, he relaxes and comes up to the window.

"Hello, Detective Barnes. I apologize for the caution, but..." the deputy looks over at his partner and yells, "...It's O.K., it's Detective Barnes! ...as I was saying, Detective, when you pulled up and parked, the three witnesses who chased our perp claimed that he was driving a vehicle like this one."

"No apologies needed, Deputy. Have we identified the victim?" dismisses Detective Barnes.

"Unofficially, yes, sir. No positive I.D. from the family as yet. Deputy Garcia is en route now to identify." Says the Deputy.

"Deputy Garcia? Are you telling me that the young boy found is Deputy Garcia's boy, Dante, or Derrick? Which one is it?" Barnes asks.

"The younger one, sir, Dante. His older brother, Derrick, is still at Cactus Park with the Park's staff. They are keeping him safe in the office until Deputy Garcia can pick him up. He wants to do the identification first before informing his wife and Derrick." the deputy tells him.

Deputy Barnes steps out of the Crown Victoria and walks over to the witnesses. He says, "I really appreciate all of your time and patience. As you know, this is very important. Our community is being targeted by the worst type of killer, one who targets the innocence of our youth: a coward, really. You three are actually heroes of our community. You really are. Your names are not, I repeat, are not going to be released until we catch this monster. After which I, personally, will make sure that your names are remembered as heroes by the community. If not for you three, the tally of young children may have continued for who knows how many more? Now, I am going to ask each of you probably the same questions that you have already been asked by these fine deputies here, but this needs to be done, no matter how redundant it may seem. Please, bear with me." Barnes says.

Then to one of the deputies, he asks, "Please, Carl, take this..." he hands him a fifty-dollar bill, "...and if you don't mind, can we get these three some cheeseburgers, fries and drinks, going large, heavy all..." He looks at the witnesses, "...sound O.K. to you three?"

They all nod, "Yes."

"O.K., Detective, be back in a flash!" says the Deputy as he hurries over to the Burger King across the street.

"Thank you, Deputy. This may take a long while and while I speak to one, the other two may as well have some dinner." Barnes says, "O.K., let's begin with the young lady. Sound good to you, gentlemen?" Then Barnes begins the questions, and the three are separated to make sure that there are no discrepancies in what they remember.

# Chapter 49:

"Please, be patient while you eat your meals. I have to set up the crime scene for a little while." Barnes says. "I'll be back as soon as I can."

The area is starting to get dark. Light towers are brought in to turn an evening into daytime. The Highway-67 bridge over the San Diego River has only one lane heading towards Ramona. Any southbound traffic is being detoured to the right of the bridge, around Winter Gardens Road and the Highway-67 exit.

The commuters return on their route towards El Cajon. Traffic is backed up all the way to I-8 in La Mesa. That bridge is a main artery for tens of thousands of commuters heading into the foothills of Ramona and even Poway. The entire river bottom under the bridge is lit up. The dirt lot where the killer parked is lit up, and so is the area in between. The body can't be removed until it is photographed and documented.

Deputy Garcia is held back, even though he has his Sheriff's-Deputy I.D., those who access the taped area as investigators sign in as being on the scene; however, to keep the scene sterile, those are kept to a minimum. Deputy Garcia understands this. He also knows that Detective Barnes lost his own son only days ago. Although Barnes cannot be involved in that investigation, he is, however, investigating Dante Garcia's abduction and death, that is, until an M.O. is established that links the two, at which point the F.B.I. will take over both cases.

Deputy Garcia shows up to talk to Detective Barnes. As soon as Barnes finds out that Garcia has shown up he wastes no time in seeing him. "Deputy Garcia, this is terrible, and I want to get back to the scene and the witnesses right away. I can take you down there out of respect and courtesy; however, I have identified Dante's body. I am so sorry. I know, sincerely, how you are feeling. I want to get this creep before the Feds take over. Witnesses have identified the vehicle as a Ford Crown Victoria, dark smoke gray, just like the one my mother says took Timothy."

Deputy Garcia's anger is evident. He says to Barnes, "This creep is targeting 'brothers in arms'? Has your son been found here as well, Barnes?"

"No, not yet. I have to get back. I have released Dante to be brought to you here. Again, Garcia, I want this guy badly! However, I am afraid that once I get my report filed, it will no longer be in our hands. I have to get back. I have witnesses to question. It will be a long night here, and you do have my personal cellphone number if you need anything..." he grabs his shoulder to emphasize this, "...and I mean anything! We have to stop this guy before more of us get targeted."

"Yeah, yeah, I get it. Keep me informed when you get the chance, O.K.? Please, Barnes, I want in on this asshole's takedown, all in!" Garcia stresses this. "Go get him, Barnes, before he gets us again!"

Barnes heads back to the river bottom. The coroner is orchestrating Dante's placement on a canoe, knowing that Dante's father is waiting above. Crime-scene investigators have been busy with plaster casts of shoe prints and tire prints. The baseball cap has been tagged and bagged. Barnes' phone rings.

"Barnes here..." It's his new supervisor who came into the office after Barnes left him a message on his voicemail.

"What have we got, Detective? Is it true that the boy is Dante Garcia, Deputy Garcia's son?" the supervisor asks.

"I'm afraid so...and the witnesses here have described the vehicle as the same one that my mother saw at El Cajon Bowl. I believe that we have a sick person targeting the children of San Diego Sheriff's Department deputies. I will write up a report and have it on your desk by morning."

"Good job, Detective. The reason I'm calling you, however, is that a vehicle fire was just reported just past

Sycuan Casino on Dehesa Valley Road. It appears to be a Ford Crown Victoria. It may be the perpetrator's vehicle. I am having the C.S.I. team go there after they are done at the scene. We want to see if tire prints and shoe prints match up as well. How close are you to being done there?" Barnes' boss asks.

"I have three witnesses to question first. They have been waiting for a couple of hours now. I don't want to wait because they are homeless, and I don't know how to reach them, having no addresses. After that, I can head out to Dehesa Valley." Barnes answered.

"Good. I'll inform the officers there that this is no ordinary car fire and to keep the scene clean." Says the supervisor.

"Thanks. I'd better get busy here. It's going to be a long night!" says Barnes, anxious to get back at it.

"Hate to say it, Barnes, but once that report hits my desk, the Feds are going to want jurisdiction. This is an important break. We may need their help." Warns his Boss.

"I get it. Gotta go. Call if you need to, sir." Then Barnes hangs up the cell phone.

Barnes walks over to the C.S.I. team and says, "Have you guys heard from the Captain yet about the vehicle fire over in Dehesa Valley? He thinks it may be the perp's vehicle. We think he's attempting to remove a trace. How much longer here?"

"We are just waiting for the casts to dry, say, about five more minutes will do, ten tops. I haven't checked messages yet. Are you heading over there next?" Asks the technician.

"You got it. I'll be heading there in a half-hour. Can you give me a call when you can verify that it's one guy?" orders Barnes.

"Immediately, sir. We gotta get this guy ASAP!" replies the Tech.

"I concur, and if we can solve this quickly, it can stay with us rather than the Feds. I want this guy badly. Until I tie this to my son's case there is not yet any conflict. If my witnesses' descriptions of this guy match my mother's description, I'm afraid my Captain will remove me from this case and notify the Feds." Warns Barnes.

"Got you. We will call you from the scene. Good luck, Barnes. Go get him!" said the Tech as he hurried away.

Barnes begins interviewing the witnesses. He asks about the cap, but the perp wasn't seen wearing it when they saw him standing over the boy's body. What they did get, two of them anyway, was the license plate number, E-5921, a government plate. All three described the perp as from 6'2" to 6'3" tall, white male, clean cut, light brown hair, about 200 pounds, fast on his feet, fit and wearing what looked like, or similar to, what a Jehovah's Witness would wear. Their physical appearance matches his mother's description to a 'T.'

There is no doubt that this is the same guy. They have a serial child killer on their hands, targeting what seem to be San Diego Sheriff's deputies' children!

# Chapter 50:

Detective Barnes arrives at the Dehesa-Valley scene one half-hour after the C.S.I. team arrives. The evidence was charred but not destroyed, as the vehicle fire was quickly put under control. The Harbison Canyon and Dehesa Valley areas experienced the destruction of wildfire centers in 2003 when the 'circle of fire' swept up these valleys and canyons.

Places like the Swallows Resort were completely engulfed and leveled. Since then, any hint of fire has been quickly assessed and rapidly responded to. The vehicle was parked in front of 'Fantasy Cars,' originally known for the production of the Batmobile used in the original series of Batman. The property owner was quick to call in the fire. The car manufacturer, Mr. Butts, who passed away years ago, is survived by his wife, Miriam Butts, and her blind sister.

Mrs. Butts witnessed the man pull over his vehicle and open the hood. Standing on her front lawn using binoculars, she witnessed the man, wearing Jehovah-style clothing, remove the gas can from the trunk and pour gas into the car and the engine compartment. She was on the phone immediately, not waiting for the man to light the fuse to start the fire. Mrs. Butts was waiting with Sheriff's deputies when Detective Barnes arrived.

The sergeant on the scene introduced Detective Barnes to Mrs. Butts, "Detective Barnes, this is Mrs. Butts. She owns this property. That is her house over there." The sergeant points to her home. "Mrs. Butts, in front of her home using her binoculars, watched the man intentionally set the car on fire."

"Good evening, Mrs. Butts, and thank you for coming to us on this matter. I am sure that your community also thanks you for your efforts. I can't explain to you the importance of this case, but I can assure you that it is of the utmost importance. What can you tell me about what you saw?" Detective Barnes asks.

Mrs. Butts, being very thorough as the older generation has always been, produces a personal memo recorder, "I can do better than that, Detective. As I watched the man, I spoke into my personal memo recorder all that time so I wouldn't have to rely on memory alone. At my age, Detective, sometimes I'll walk into a room at home and then forget why I came in. I have to chuckle at that and then leave. Sometime later, I'll remember the reason and return to the room."

Detective Barnes is in awe, "You mean that you dictated the event into your recorder?"

"Isn't that what I just said, young man? I guess our generation isn't the only one with memory loss!" Mrs. Butts laughs at her own wit. "To your defense, I guess with your job you have many facts to remember. I'm surprised that you don't have one of these."

Detective Barnes notices that the recorder spools are spinning. "Are you also recording our conversation? You do understand that to do so without permission is illegal."

"So sue me!" she scorns, "Do you want to hear this...lecture me...arrest me...what is your intention, Detective? Sure, this is not admissible in court, but you are on my property, you know. I can do whatever I want on my own property. If I chose to stand here with my twelve-gauge Remington, I could surely do so!"

Detective Barnes thinks to himself, "Now no one, I mean no one, is gonna mess with this firecracker," and he says to her, "All right, all right, Mrs. Butts, can we, please, start over? Can you stop the recording? Then you can rewind your tape, and we can listen to your observations together while you narrate the events as you remember them. Do you mind if I record our interview at the same time?

"Oh, now it's not illegal? What happened to the illegality of recording conversations, young man huh? Do you mean that it's illegal for citizens but legal for law enforcement? Doesn't this seem like a double standard to you? I see it on Cops all the time. Police want to video-record, but when a citizen wants to...well...he gets slammed to the ground...his phone trampled on...his rights ignored." Detective Barnes gives a little chuckle until Mrs. Butts gives him a stern look. He feels like a chastised schoolboy and stops smiling. "Good..." Mrs. Butts says, "...now can we get serious, Detective?"

"Yes, ma'am, please," Barnes says humbly.

"O.K., that's better, Detective. Now, where do you want to do this?" Miriam's dominance was acknowledged.

"How about in my car? Would that be acceptable to you, Mrs. Butts? Would it be possible for us to keep the tape from your memo recorder?" Detective Barnes realizes, with just a look from Mrs. Butts, that he has taken it too far.

"How about this, Detective..." she states her condition to him, "...as soon as I get a replacement cassette, I will then relinquish this one to you. Either that, or you can subpoena me to give it to you!"

Detective Barnes holds up his hands defensively, "Whew, you really know how to intimidate a law officer!"

I've learned to intimidate or be intimidated. Got that from one of those C.S.I. shows, and it works. Now, when can we get serious? We have a really bad person trying to burn my neighbors' property, as well as my own, to the ground!" Again, she is serious.

"Great. Let's get this guy!" Barnes agrees.

Listening to the recording, with Mrs. Butts occasionally pausing the recording to add more of her details, it was as if Detective Barnes was visualizing the entire arson happening before him. With his mother, the three witnesses in Lakeside, and Mrs. Butts all giving identical descriptions of the killer, his case is beginning to build. All he lacks is an identity.

The crime-scene investigators have confirmed that the tire prints and the shoe prints here match the prints and treads at Lakeside. The bike treads will have to wait until the bike is located. The perpetrator must have ridden away on it, but to where?

Detective Barnes looks over at the Casino, and at that moment, he knows that the killer rode over there. The C.S.I. guys were also able to verify the darkened, but still legible, license plate on the rear of the Ford E-5921, so Barnes knows that this is the same vehicle that was used to abduct and murder little Dante.

# Chapter 51:

Detective Barnes drives to the Sycuan Casino and parks at the entrance. He approaches the first security cop he sees and says, "My name is Detective Barnes, here on very important Sheriff's business. Please, take me to your supervisor immediately."

"Yes, sir, follow me, please." He then takes him past the Services Desk into Security and knocks on a door with an enamel plate that says, Supervisor.

They hear, "Come in."

The security officer introduces his supervisor to Detective Barnes. The supervisor asks, "Yes, Detective, how can we help you?"

Detective Barnes explains, "Without going into the details of the crimes that this person allegedly committed, I have to inform you that this is of the utmost importance. The longer it takes our department to apprehend this individual, the longer lives could actually be lost. Therefore, I ask for your cooperation without having to get warrants."

"We always want to cooperate with our brothers in law enforcement, especially in a matter as serious as this!" the supervisor agrees.

"Great! We need access to your camera tapes from five nights ago until an hour ago. We are looking for someone in a white dress shirt, black tie, and black pants. This person may have been riding a bicycle onto the property. This person may have ditched the bicycle and hitched a ride onto the property. If we are lucky, it is entirely possible that he hitched a ride out of Dehesa Valley from your casino entrance. How soon can we take a look at what your cameras can tell us about those hours?" Detective Barnes is hopeful.

"Right this way, Detective. We'd better get to it! We don't have many bicycle riders coming into this casino. Any rider should stand out immediately." The supervisor is right. Within an hour, they not only have video of the killer but also closeup stills as he entered the Casino from the pedestrian bridge. Topping that...they got the license number of the truck that Dante's bicycle was loaded into.

"Thank you so much for your help and cooperation, sir. I need to get back to the office and search our databases now. You've been a great help!" says Detective Barnes gratefully.

"That's why we're here, Detective, and that's why we have our facial-recognition software to catch those who have warrants. We feel it's our civic duty, just like cooperating with law-enforcement entities, the supervisor laying it on thick.

As Detective Barnes is heading back to his office he calls his Captain, "I apologize for interrupting you at home, sir, but I thought you should know..."

"Before you begin, Barnes, please call this deputy in Ramona, Sergeant Brown. His daughter of twelve went missing on the same day as Dante. He lives in the Country Estates between Ramona and the Barona Casino." He says his wife came home to their door being open and their daughter, Stephanie, gone. His home number is (760) 755-8662. He's there right now. Now, tell me what we got?" his Captain asks.

"Well, sir, we may have a conflict of interest here, Captain. My mother, the three Lakeside witnesses, and Mrs. Butts, the woman who saw the man torch his car, agree that it's the same man. I am meeting my mother at the office so she can see our photo from the Sycuan Casino. If she says it's the same person she saw, we'll have a serial child killer loose who is targeting children of Sheriff's deputies. I also want to contact one of my witnesses from Lakeside to get the other two together to see if they can all meet me at the Burger King on Mapleview to look at our perp's photo."

"Great work, Detective! Fabulous work! Until I get your report, we are under no obligation to inform the F.B.I. about this killer. We may need their help to find him if we can't do this ourselves." The Captain adds, "Detective, is there anything we can do to expedite your investigation?"

Detective Barnes gives his idea to his Captain for him to get done. Maybe, with his clout, he can make this happen now, tonight! Barnes says, "Captain, there is something that you can help with. While I'm heading back to the station, call all the deputies involved and see if they can meet me at the station. If this perp is targeting all of us, I want all of us to take a look at the photo and the video. Together, we may jog some memories and come up with where all of our paths have crossed. These are definitely not crimes of coincidence. All of us have something in common with this psycho. We can all put our heads together tonight. If not, there may be another target or targets in the works! We need to stop this guy now!"

"You got it, Detective, right away. I'll make the calls, and there'll be no arguments. I'll make it mandatory to show up, and I'll be there as well. Give me fifteen minutes, and I'll get back to you!" says the Captain.

Not ten minutes later, the Captain calls back, "Detective, we are all 10-8 to the station, with our bells on and strapped for a take-down. We want to get this guy tonight, Detective. We are all willing to stay until we do!"

# Chapter 52:

Detective Barnes is the first one to the station, and he wastes no time getting the conference room set up for viewing. He then calls the number for Ted, one of the Lakeside witnesses, and attaches the photo of the killer to a text message. Ted says that he will show the photo to the other two witnesses right away. The homeless who live at the river bottom or anywhere else, for that matter, rarely cooperate in fingering a suspect for the cops.

A child-killer, however, is different, being the worst of the worst. To violate the innocence of children is frowned upon ANYWHERE! on the streets and within the walls of incarceration.

Still, with time to spare, Detective Barnes begins to pull up his logs for each day that he is a deputy. He's only been a detective for a couple of days. Since his son was abducted on his first day as a detective and the killer knew this, he must have been targeted for months prior.

He places a call to his partner, who answers on the second ring. "What's up, Partner? How are you? I've been really worried about you and Mom."

"The only thing holding me together right now is trying to get this fucker! I want him badly before the Feds take this. Hey, what are you doing right now?" Barnes asks his former partner.

"Let's see, uh, right this second...I am pulling into the station parking lot! Be inside in one minute, Partner!" and he clicks off.

The former partners shake hands and share a brotherly hug. Both are fighting back tears for Detective Barnes' son, Timothy. "I hurt, too, brother. For the last six years, Timmy was my son, too. That's why I'm here, Partner. I want to get this guy with you. I won't sleep until we get this asshole in the downtown jail."

Detective Barnes repeats his theory to his former other half in law enforcement patrol. "Jake, I know how you feel, but right now, the hurt and anger have to be placed aside and replaced with professional resolve. All our 'i's and 't's need to be properly dotted and crossed, then rechecked for, meticulously, no doubt. This perp has been targeting our 'brothers in arms.' I don't believe that these are coincidences or killings of convenience. This guy has been researching his targets, our sons and daughters. Stalking, listening, watching, and, possibly, recording our daily lives to accomplish these heinous killings. It has to be someone with whom we all have had some form of interaction. The Captain has asked all of us fathers of these murdered children and our partners to come here tonight. I've pulled our logs, mine and yours, but I won't have access to the others until the Captain arrives. Sometimes, somewhere, we have dealt with this guy. Tonight we will figure this out; tonight, we will get a warrant signed, no matter who we have to wake up, and by tomorrow morning, we will hit this killer's place of residence and 'black-band' his ass!"

"I am ready to get started; no more wasted time on our logs; let's get this guy! Jake is all jazzed and excited.

Detective Barnes has one of the still-capture photos up on the 65" monitor in the conference room. He and Jake begin to go over their logs going back several months. One by one, other deputies begin to file in. The smell of coffee and cologne begins to fill the room. Printers are busy printing up past logs and interactions.

It is Deputy Brown from Ramona who recognizes the perp first. "Yeah, he looks familiar, not from any arrest in the past but I've had contact with him somewhere...either a traffic stop...or a domestic issue...a nuisance call...I think I've got it! A neighborhood complaint that was it! We got a complaint about an individual walking in a neighborhood in Ramona, who might be a burglar casing the residences. This was an upscale neighborhood near Pio Pico Park, I believe." Deputy

Brown begins to look through his and his partner's logs for a particular entry.

Detective Barnes' former partner, Jake, is the next to remember. He says, "That's right...I remember now, Andrew. Remember the Lake Jennings area, the uppity homes around the lake behind Dunbar Lane, up on the top ridge on the east side of the lake? We had the same type of call, a man walking the neighborhood, going into driveways, and approaching doors...about a month or more ago. Remember Andrew? That's the same guy! We had him sit on the curb for over an hour that day. Said he was losing customers every time a car would drive by and see him sitting there. Remember?"

"Yes, I do remember now!" Detective Barnes agreed. "You are right! That was completely off the radar because there was no ticket and no arrest made."

Within ten minutes all of the deputies have their logs in hand, noting the same person. They have a name and an address on Madison Avenue in El Cajon. Within fifteen minutes, Deputies Garcia and Deputy Gonzalez are in their squad car heading to Wells Park. They park in the lot, in view of the apartment, watching in case their killer decides to run before the warrant is signed. It is nine o'clock in the evening, and a softball game is still in full swing. By nine-fifteen Judge Lazaros, in an El Cajon court, has signed the warrant. By nine-thirty, a Sheriff's swat team is gathering near Carl's Jr. for the take-down. Mark Sutter will soon be in the custody of the San Diego Sheriff's Department.

# Chapter 53:

"This is Kristy Lyons for KSDN News, high above El Cajon City, flying above Wells Park where just east of the park, we are televising live a swat take-down of an alleged serial child-killer. We just arrived on the scene, and the swat team has just entered the parking lot and is now approaching the second-floor apartment of the alleged perpetrator. We are watching the swat team also surround the building." Kristy Lyons reports.

Mark is just getting ready for bed. He has a date with Denise tomorrow night and wants to be well-rested for it, and soon, he will be getting that well-deserved rest. He sees a news alert on KSDN News and turns up the volume. It's Kristy Lyons who interviewed him after that black man was killed at the taco shop in El Cajon. She's in a helicopter over what looks like Wells Park. She's speaking about a serial killer of children. Wow! Who would do such a thing? She seems to be focusing on his apartment building. Yes, the swat team is in his building's parking area!

"My God..." Mark thinks, "...the killer is someone at his apartment building?" He looks over at his door to be sure that it has the deadbolt engaged in case that person tries to evade the swat team by gaining access to his apartment. He needs to stay locked in until it is safe!

Mark watches the swat team come up the stairs right in front of his apartment. Could it be his neighbor? No, not Carlos. Carlos doesn't seem to be the type, but you never know with serial killers. The swat team is grouping at the top of the stairs, right outside his door now, probably going to rush the killer's door farther down the landing. As Mark is watching the TV, no! It can't be! Mark hears a knock on his door. No!!! No!! No!! It can't be him! Noooo!!!

Denise is just getting home from the Westfield Plaza Mall. She had decided to buy a new, sexy outfit for tomorrow's date with Mark. What a hunk! She knows that this new outfit is sexy and hot! It had better be because it cost her over a hundred, with an extra sixty for the 'come fuck me' high-heel pumps that she also purchased. What the hell? First impressions are the longest lasting, they say. He'll never be able to forget her! She sets down her bags and flips on the TV just in time to catch a KSDN News alert. Kristy Lyons is her favorite news broadcaster. She always seems to be on the right spot in all the breaking news alerts. Denise can't believe that Kristy is over El Cajon, actually only one or two blocks from her work. Kristy's helicopter is over Wells Park? Swat team? Serial killer of Sheriff's deputies' children? What the hell! What sort of monster would target children? Here in El Cajon? Denise has to wonder...how many times has she interacted with this demented killer? The swat team has gained access to the creep's apartment now. They are...No, it can't be! Is that...is that...that is...that is...Mark!!! Denise just about faints, catches herself, and sits on a chair at her dining room table. She is looking at Mark. He must be a great actor because he really looks innocent, making it seem that the swat team is making a terrible mistake. He actually looks as surprised as she is about all of this. This can't be happening to her...to him...she was twenty-four hours away from dating a true-life serial killer? Then she faints!

"This is Kristy Lyons, once again, for KSDN News, high above El Cajon City, reporting the apprehension of a suspected serial child-killer. The alleged person of interest is one Mark Sutter, who resides at the address below, where you are witnessing the Sheriff's swat team taking the suspect into custody. Not much is known at this point. What we do know is that the killing spree began several days ago. Detective Barnes' son, Timothy Barnes, was abducted from The Boardwalk in El Cajon, only two to three miles from where his father works. Then, earlier today, Dante Garcia was abducted from Cactus Park, a popular youth sports center that caters to BMX racers. The Sheriff's Department believes that there may be additional victims as well. This investigation is a success due to the exceptional detective work on the part of Detective Barnes, who, if you can believe it, has only been a detective for four days now! He was dispatched to the scene where Dante's body was found this afternoon. He wrapped up this case in mere hours from then. Great work, Detective! Again, this is Kristy Lyons. You heard it first on KSDN News, San Diego.

# PART 3:
## "Incarceration"

# Chapter 54:

Isaac is brought through two huge metal doors into a loading area. There is also a bus sitting there. The S.D.P.D. patrol car parks in the parking spaces to the left of the bus. The two police officers leave him to sit there until they come back for him. The garage reeks of gas and diesel fumes. The entire area is concrete and steel. Huge, round pillars support the nine-floor edifice. Isaac's shoulder is beginning to hurt and the officers left the car running with the heat on. He wonders why they are using the heat in the summer. By the time the two officers return for Isaac, he is dripping sweat and about to pass out. His office shirt is soaking wet, his hair is like a mop, and his face is mottled with hot, dripping sweat.

"Let's go!" he is ordered by the larger of the two; he seems cool and dry.

"Sure..." Isaac says, "...why don't you just pour me out? Why the..."

"I said, let's go, no talking! One more outburst, and I'll put you back into the car!"

While Isaac is attempting to slide and scoot his way out, still cuffed, the officer's partner opens the passenger door and switches the car's temperature to Hi A/C, then closes the door.

"Walk around to the left of the front of the bus, then stop at the front."

Isaac follows the officer's orders and comes to a stop. The bus door is open, and there is a parade of inmates in blue jail clothing boarding the bus. All of them look wrung out, tired, and worn down, like what he would imagine a field worker would be who had been working from sun-up to sun-down. They are in chains and are chained to each other. The two officers know that Isaac has never been arrested before. He has no arrest record and no conviction record.

A conviction record is what a judge examines before sentencing someone before him or her. A superior court judge is there for two main reasons: 1) to ensure that the rights of a defendant are properly maintained; 2) to follow the policies set forth by precedents in applying the appropriate punishment by either sentencing or holding over a defendant for a future appearance. In a perfect world, that is. California judges have been given too much authority today, and they pass their own policies. They even pass their own laws at times, without the voter's consent or his vote. The 'People' don't realize that incarceration is big business, a huge business that lines the pockets of the members of the Good Ol' Boys Club.

An arrest record is information that comes up when a police officer checks your I.D.; this information is given when someone is informed of your 'record.' This is a very misleading account of someone's representation. A normal practice of law enforcement is to pile on the charges. Piling on the charges is due to the officer being lazy and not sure what to actually charge a person for. This leaves it up to the district attorney to look at the evidence to determine what charges will fit the defendant. Having up to a half-dozen charges is not uncommon; the outcome of a plea bargain is only one charge. The other charges are used as threats against a defendant, adding up more time for each charge. The same threats are used if a person wants to exercise his or her rights and take it to trial. They threaten the person with 'maximum time' on each charge to help convince the person to take a plea bargain. Once the deal is made, they will also ask the person to waive a right, which is, in itself, illegal according to our Constitution. California violates everyone's rights all the time by ignoring those inalienable rights.

If we want our Constitutional rights, which are given to us all as citizens of the good, old U.S.A., we have to go to the Supreme Court on a federal level. That level does not feel that California laws are being applied correctly and will overturn violations of one's rights...at a huge cost in legal fees. These costs are far out of reach for the average citizen. Isaac is about to find out all of this firsthand.

Isaac now sees that the rear of the bus is loaded. A gate is closed to seal off the rear area from the rest of the bus. He sees men in green jail clothing coming out next. They are placed in individually caged seating. Isaac wonders what this means, but he hasn't time to wonder any longer as he is ushered into the building and placed in front of a camera.

Sweat is still dripping from his face. His hair is soaked and greasy now from the diesel fumes, and his once-white dress shirt has a dark film on it. Photos are taken from the front and from the side. Still cuffed, he is seated on a bench with rings. After about ten long minutes, he is asked to stand and face the wall, as the cuffs are removed from behind his back. The S.D.P.D. has now relinquished custody to the San Diego Sheriff's County Jail. Isaac is asked to step on a scale, and his weight is recorded. He is then x-rayed to look for hidden weapons and/or hidden contraband. Most people think that this x-ray device can spot drugs that are hidden in a person's anus; simply not true. The x-ray sees bones and metal. No organs are seen here. Incarceration cells and tanks are riddled with illegal drugs of many types.

From the x-ray, Isaac is cuffed back to the bench using Sheriff's cuffs. The S.D.P.D. has now left the building. Isaac is seen by a medical 'professional,' which is putting it very lightly. He has questions about medications, allergies, and whether Isaac is suicidal. He is then put back on the bench for another hour. Isaac asks the nurse if he can use a telephone. She says that he must wait until he is booked and placed in custody. Isaac thinks that Hannah will start to look for him as soon as he doesn't show up at the trolley station in La Mesa. His purchases weren't even bagged up at Victoria's Secret, and this angers him. He is still not sure what happened. He was never informed.

Isaac is finally uncuffed and ushered, once again, out to the smelly garage, where there is yet another bus being loaded with persons in blue outfits. The bus driver tells the deputies with Isaac that they need to return to the room until they bring out the 'yellow banders,' as they call them. So, Isaac is put back on the bench for another hour. More people have been processed since he came in here. The bus is now long gone and there is only one Sheriff's deputy on duty now. All of the support staff seem to have disappeared. Their shift has ended and Isaac must wait for the new shift to finish his processing.

Isaac watches the four other people across from him. All of them have their arms covered with tattoos, and one has tattoos all over his face. He wonders how this person would possibly get a job with these tattoos all over his face. One of the others is yelling at the only deputy there about the charge on which he was brought in here. The officer can only shrug because he has no idea about his charges or his circumstances. This does not quell the man's rants; he actually gets more animated. Another one of the men smells like feces and urine. His pants are clearly stained up the front and down the rear. His hair is matted into what looks like dreadlocks and Isaac has to wonder what sort of parasites are living in them. He can hardly believe there isn't some kind of parasite dip or shower like the ones he's seen on TV and in movies. Maybe that comes later in the process? He certainly hopes so!

The new shift arrives, finally, and gets settled into their mundane jobs. It seems to Isaac that they really hate their work. All of them are wearing latex gloves to help protect them from disease and transferable skin fungi. Isaac wonders about where his protection is in here. Is it legal to expose him to the very same things for which they have protection?

Isaac asks again, "Excuse me, I've been handcuffed to this bench now for several hours. When can I use a telephone to call my wife? I still don't know why I am here. Excuse me! Please!"

"Are you the troublemaker I keep hearing about that won't keep his trap shut? You'll get your chance to use a telephone as soon as you are booked. Now, be quiet while we get our jobs done!" the officer says.

"Troublemaker? What? No, I've been really patient here, really very patient here! The only reason that you have 'work' is due to the taxes that I pay each quarter of each year! Now, I have to demand to use a telephone!" Isaac says more firmly.

"Listen to me one more time, sir. I am not the one who broke the law; you are. I am only here to hold you until a judge is able to hear your case. Same with these others who are sitting around you. We have 72 hours to get this done. That is your right. You will have access to a telephone after, and I will say again after you have been booked! Now, leave us alone so we can get this done for you! Capisce!?"

Fifteen minutes after the deputy's speech, four hours since Isaac was handcuffed to this bench, he is asked to stand after his handcuffs are removed. He is brought back out to the smelly garage and ushered through a door at the west end of the garage. Isaac is asked to face the wall as his handcuffs are removed. His wrists are now purple-ringed and starting to swell. He gives the deputy a scornful look as he rubs life back into them.

"Please, approach the window," he is ordered, "and follow the woman's instructions."

"Good evening, sir. Do you have any other property besides those items noted on this paper that you'd like to declare before going into custody?" she asks.

"Before going into custody? Where have I been these last four hours if not in custody?" Isaac asks.

"Sir, is that a yes or a no, please, sir?"

"That's a no. I have no other property besides my clothes, which I plan to burn because your conditions here have just ruined them!" His anger is apparent.

The clerk gives the deputy 'one of those looks' and says, "O.K., please insert your left arm through the window. Do you have any enemies that you are concerned about here? Any medical issues that we need to know about? Are you suicidal, sir?"

"No, none of those," Isaac says.

"No problem being housed in Mainline, then?"

"Housed? I thought I was going to see a judge from here," he reiterates.

"Yes, sir, within 72 hours of your booking. Now, please, sir, your left arm." she demands.

Isaac places his left arm through the slot in the window, and a blue band with a white strip is placed around his wrist. The white strip has his name, date of birth, and a very long eight-digit number. Below that information is a bar code, which he has always thought one day would be the Mark of the Beast in Revelations. Then to the right of all of that is a photo, a photo of him but not him. He's never before seen a photo of himself looking so badly. He seems to have black-mascara marks on his face, dripping down his cheeks. His hair is wet, and his face is filled with anger as if he's been worked over with an 'ugly stick.' Just then, he remembers seeing similar photos every day, photos in the San Diego Union newspaper that he reads each day, photos of wanted fugitives being sought by the police for parole and probation violations, car theft, burglary, robbery, and, God forbid, crimes against children! All of these photos have the same stare-back at the camera.

Isaac now understands how these photos are created for their worst effect. Just as a photographer, as a professional, would adjust the lighting, props, and background for a desired effect, law-enforcement entities have professionally orchestrated techniques to alter one's appearance prior to taking these photos. Isaac, looking at his own image staring back at him, can now understand the mechanics of subtle tools to achieve the worst visual effect. This is no yearbook photo that one is allowed to dress for, groom for, and prepare for.

Newly-tagged Isaac has officially been booked into the San Diego County Central Jail. As the motorized metal door begins to roll open, a loud clang announces its finality.

"Please, step inside now. The rest will be explained to you through processing beyond this door." the deputy points as the clerk explains.

Isaac steps into a small, ten-by-ten cell that reeks of vomit, urine, and feces. People are actually lying on the concrete in this disgusting environment. He sees three phones on the wall, but only two are operable. He is told this by; it seems the person who controls who gets to use one next. There seems to be no time limit once you get a turn and once you do, he notices, several call attempts can be made while it's your turn. The signal for completing the turn seems to be a slamming of the receiver on its cradle, followed by an expletive curse. Isaac is told that he is eighth, last, in the queue. He begins to think about calling Hannah, and he panics. He doesn't have his home number nor Hannah's cellphone number committed to memory. Actually, he can't remember anyone's phone number! He always uses his cellphone contact list or his speed dial from his home phone. None of his important numbers are committed to memory! So, as Isaac watches others continue to punch in their numbers, then hang up, punch in more, then hang up, then finally get frustrated, then slam down the phone, he now knows why. It seems that the people here can't remember any of their phone numbers.

There is no clock to be seen from here. Someone gets through to a loved one and another in the cell asks the person to ask what time it is. The answer comes back as 11:30 pm! What? Isaac worries about Hannah and what she must be going through.

# Chapter 55:

Hannah, after waiting at the Spring Street trolley station for over an hour past their planned time, is soon approached by the MTS enforcement officers.

"Excuse me, Miss. My partner and I have noticed that you've been sitting here for an hour and a half." Hannah mistakes this for concern. "Do you have in your possession a ticket or a Compass pass, please?"

"A what? Oh, no, you see..." she starts to explain.

"If not, you are loitering on MTS property, which we are employed to enforce against. Are you having car trouble?" the officer cuts her off.

"Car...what? No, no, you see, I am..."

"Then, Miss, we will have to ask you to move along. It is obvious to us that you are not under the influence of drugs or alcohol, so you may leave."

"Leave? Under what? No, you don't understand..." Hannah begins to explain again, but the officer cuts her off once more.

"Miss, please start your vehicle and exit the parking area before we have to issue you a trespass ticket."

"Oh, O.K.. Yes, sir." Hannah gives up, starts her Audi, and reluctantly leaves the station.

Once home, she calls her husband's cellphone, but it goes straight to voicemail. He has it turned off. She then tries Samuel's cell and that number, too, goes straight to voicemail. She tries the office phone, but the office is now closed, and she hangs up when the answering service answers the phone. She doesn't want to worry her grandfather or anyone in her family at that point. She does begin canceling their reservations for their flight to Los Angeles, as well as their accommodations at the Avalon Hotel in Catalina, where their boat transportation from San Pedro was arranged. Isaac has never failed on an itinerary before. However, she is not overly concerned yet. He must be with Samuel for some important reason. She monitors both phones throughout the night, a very long night.

After a very restless night of sleeping alone, Hannah tries Isaac's cell again, then Samuel's. Both go straight to voicemail. She knows that if she calls the office, the entire family will be worried, not just her. She decides to wait a little longer before calling. Without something substantial, she doesn't want to put her family through unnecessary stress or strain.

Hannah begins calling local hospitals: Grossmont Hospital, Alvarado Hospital, Sharps Hospital, Kaiser Hospital, Genesee Hospital, and all the other hospitals in San Diego County. No one named Isaac Stompski has been brought in through admittances or through the emergency trauma centers. Those replying that they had 'John Does' were sent photos of Isaac to compare his description with descriptions of those without identities. After Hannah exhausts all of these inquiries, she calls the La Mesa Police Department. After being asked to hold, she hangs up and decides to go there in person.

Hannah grabs her cell phone, her purse, current photos of Isaac, and her keys, then goes out to their garage. She is near tears as she backs out and drives over Mt. Helix and into La Mesa.

La Mesa is a posh, uppity community with a trendy downtown strip and beautiful parks. There are youth-recreation areas and an active commerce which hosts many great community events. However, as with all the areas through which the trolley travels, crime is increasing, and property values are decreasing. The La Mesa police officers are very thorough and very tough. Criminals spread the word that La Mesa is not the place to commit crimes. Using a La Mesa zip code for car insurance, home insurance and business insurance results in lower premiums here because the crime rate is lower here.

Hannah parks her Audi at a metered parking spot, feeds the meter, and grabs all of her material to report that her husband is missing. She enters the front door and waits to be seen at the counter. The female officer here is very nice and accommodating. She notifies the Missing Persons desk and asks Hannah to have a seat. Half an hour later, she hears, "Mrs. Stompski?"

"Yes, I am she. I hope that you can help me." Hannah says hopefully.

"Please, Mrs. Stompski, come on back to my cubicle, right back here. Can I get you some water? Some coffee?" the officer asks Hannah.

"No. No, thank you."

"Please, have a seat right there and tell me about your missing husband. Then we can go from there." he states.

Hannah begins to hand the officer her photos, but he makes no motion to accept them, so she withdraws them back to her lap. She begins, "Isaac, my husband of one year, as of yesterday..."

"It was your anniversary yesterday?" he interrupts.

"Yes. Yes, yesterday. We have been married for one year."

"O.K., go on, please."

"As I was saying...my husband, Isaac, went to work yesterday. He commutes to downtown on the trolley from Spring Street. We were going to celebrate with a trip to Catalina for a few days, staying at the..." she is interrupted again.

"Excuse me, Mrs. Stompski...did you say he's been missing since he left work yesterday evening? We're talking about twelve hours ago?"

"Yes. Yes, sir, about that long, yes."

"So... actually... he could have gotten home while you have been waiting here to talk to me?"

"Well, I suppose so, but he would have called my cellphone if he got home." she says.

"O.K., here's what I suggest, for now anyway. I will log that we have this report as of ten o'clock this morning. You should go home and see if he tries to contact you. Here is my direct desk number. Call me if he contacts you. If he doesn't contact you by ten o'clock tomorrow morning, call me and say so. Then, we will begin from there. Our policy here is to wait 72 hours before we expend any resources on any missing person reports. Nine times out of ten, the person returns home by then. I believe that this is one of those instances. Is that all right with you? I'm sure that he will be home soon, Mrs. Stompski." the officer reassures her.

"72 hours? Three days? Do you think that I would come here if he did this regularly? He has never, I mean never, missed coming home!" Hannah's anger is evident.

"Please, Mrs. Stompski, I understand that you think he would never do this, but some men do. Please, return home and wait for him." he tries to reassure her again.

"Sorry. I know that you have your rules. I'll have to abide by them. Thank you for your help. I'll let you know if he comes home." she says as tears begin to flow. "Thank you."

The officer escorts her back to the door and leaves her on her own to find her way back to her car. "So much for chivalry in the La Mesa Police Department," she thinks to herself, totally deflated and distraught. Hannah makes her way home, alone again.

# Chapter 56:

Isaac has been on the blue phone now for fifteen minutes. He's tried about twelve different versions of his home number and Hannah's cell number. Sometimes, the recording would say, "Call has been denied," and other times, the recording would say, "Your call was not answered at this time." He knows that Hannah would answer. He knows that she is sitting by the phone, worried sick, but he is helpless. He is pressured to relinquish the phone so that others may use it, and he does.

The holding tank has filled up quickly. One guy with dreadlocks was brought in and given a wide berth; he smelled so bad that even those sleeping got a whiff and moved farther away before falling asleep again. There are drunks with vomit down their clothes; drug addicts worrying about getting sick from withdrawal; meth-heads who can't sit still bouncing all over the cell, pissing off the other occupants. One guy got pounced on when he started talking about his charge of child endangerment. That one had to be removed from the cell but Isaac isn't sure as to where. Someone gets off the phone to inform everyone that it is now four in the morning. At the same time, the door opens, and bags with bologna sandwiches are handed out.

These bags of food wake everyone, and soon, all are gnawing on their bologna sandwich, apple, and two oatmeal cookies. Isaac has no trouble trading his bologna sandwich for an apple. Actually, Isaac thinks that he got the better trade. Before most have even started on their sandwiches, the door opens again, and names are called out.

"Listen for your name. You cannot take food or trash into Processing. If you prefer to finish your breakfast, you may remain; otherwise, come forward." the deputy states. "Cook, Sanchez, Rocha, Miller, Stompski and Gomez. If I did not call your name, please remain seated. We will be calling more names shortly."

Isaac, standing and producing the band on his wrist as identification, is asked what his last four was at the door. "Stompski, last four, please?"

"Uh, 2764, sir." Isaac thinks that the officer means the last four numbers of his social security.

"No, sir, the last four of your booking number, the one on your wristband, please."

"Oh, yes, sir. 0054, sir." Isaac corrects himself.

"O.K., go ahead. Get behind the last person and wait for orders."

"Yes. Thank you, sir."

After the final person comes out, Isaac hears a loud 'clang' behind him. Still not used to this; it makes him jump a little. The deputy says, "Follow the red line straight and then to the left. Please have a seat on the benches to the right and wait to hear your name called.

No one is handcuffed at this point. Why would they need to be in these very secure areas of custody? The only person visible is the one deputy who now goes back to his computer screen, seats himself, and returns to his coffee and Egg McMuffin.

Isaac thinks that this is an appropriate time to ask this deputy, "Uh, sir, excuse me..."

The board deputy seems annoyed by this disturbance and pauses whatever video he is watching and says, "I didn't warn you all yet, so I'll let this one be asked, but no more questions here. Go ahead."

Isaac thinks, "What happened to the 'serve' in their motto, Protect and Serve?"

Isaac asks his question, "I haven't been able to call my wife because I can't remember her cellphone number or our home number..."

"And you think that I might have your wife's cellphone number? Let's see, does my name tag say "Sancho'?"

Everyone on the benches laughs at Isaac's expense. He has no idea who Sancho is. He says, "Is he the person to ask for help to look up the number for me?" More laughter but louder this time.

'Look, I don't have a phone directory. Your problem is not my problem." the helpful deputy makes clear.

"You have the internet there. Can you please look up my office phone number, Levi and Levi..." Isaac is cut off.

"I... said... your problem...is...not...my problem. Now, no more questions!" and he returns to his video. Isaac thinks he saw porn on that screen and thinks, "Our tax dollars, hard at work!"

Straight in front of the benches are windows with open slots beneath them, similar to a box-office cashier. Behind these windows are offices with filing cabinets and computer screens. The lights are all off. No one seems to be at work yet. Obviously, arrests are made around the clock; however, processing is a nine-to-five job here in one of the busiest jails in San Diego County. Isaac can see a clock on the wall inside. It reads six o'clock. This would be the time that Hannah would drop him off at the Spring Street trolley station, that is if he weren't on a vacation day. What a vacation and anniversary this has turned out to be. Thinking of Hannah, he finds himself hoping yet again that someone beyond those windows might help him get Hannah's phone number or the one for his office. The clock reads seven o'clock when the office lighting comes on, but Isaac's hopes are squashed when he sees two men in tan, boat-canvas material with S.D. JAIL silkscreened on the backs of the shirts, as well as down the left pant legs. The two men are being directed by a Hispanic man in street clothing and a collared shirt with a Sheriff on the left breast. The two men empty the trash cans, vacuum the carpet, maintain the restrooms, and perform various other maintenance routines. They leave the lights on when they're done, and ten minutes later, Isaac sees the first signs of life appear. Being County employees, they call no one forward to the one manned window until precisely eight o'clock. Isaac is fifth in line.

One by one, each man is called forward. Isaac is very thankful that Dreadlock is not in his group. Each man is once again handcuffed, this time to a horizontal bar running along the stainless-steel counter below the service windows. There are six windows, only one of which is in use at this hour. Isaac wonders if, at times, all six are manned to expedite this very slow process. He has a comical thought about the last time he went to the Department of Motor Vehicles in El Cajon, which took several hours. Compared to this, the people at the D.M.V. were speed demons!

One by one, the woman, bored and slow, just starting her eight-hour, mundane day, announces to the equally bored deputy, "This one is done. Next, please!"

Acting as though this announcement is ruining his routine, the deputy releases a frustrated breath, pauses his porn video, and is forced to get up and uncuff this person. He says the next name as he orders the served person to return to the benches. The deputy handcuffs the next man, returns to his video, releases another exasperated and overly dramatic breath, and presses Play.

The woman behind the counter looks over at the screen that the deputy is watching and, shaking her head, frowns at the disgusting display. She thinks that all men are like him, and she treats each man as a porn-watching creep!

"Done here, Deputy. Next, please!" she announces.

"Stompski, you're next." the deputy says but is in no hurry to rise from his chair. The woman, tapping her very long, manicured fingernails, each individually decorated, can only shake her head at his demeanor. No one seems to be doing an efficient job here; tax dollars are wasted to the extreme. The deputy lets out another exasperated sigh, pauses his video, and walks over to the window to un-cuff the man who is finished.

"Have a seat on the bench. Stompski, come on up to the window." the woman glares at the deputy with disdain.

Isaac is cuffed to the counter, and the deputy returns to his computer screen. Isaac tries again, "Excuse me, Miss. I can't seem to remember my home, office, or my wife's cellphone..." The woman holds up one of her manicured fingers as if to say, "One moment, please." so Isaac stops.

"Quiet down!" the deputy reiterates to those on the benches who are beginning to wake and stir.

The woman asks, "Stompski, Isaac?"

"Yes, Miss, as I was..."

"You reside in La Mesa?"

"Yes, that's right. Do you possibly..."

"What is your profession, sir?"

"I work for a tax-and-probate law office as a tax accountant and preparer for the firm Levi and Levi..."

"So, an accountant. Does this firm currently employ you?" she asks.

"Yes. Yes. That's what I..."

"Your charges are identity theft, commercial burglary, unauthorized use of a credit card, grand theft over $400.00, and resisting arrest. You have bail of $75,000.00. Your first court appearance is in two days. Excuse me, on Monday due to the weekend, so in four days' time. Do you understand the charges that I have told you and the time of your arraignment on Monday?" she robotically states.

"Yes, I understand, but I don't..."

"This one is done. Next, please!" once again, she cuts him off and goes back to filing her fingernails, making it clear that there are no more services available to Isaac. The deputy, still in no hurry, gives Isaac the time to try again. "Excuse me,

Miss..."

"I am done here. Next, please!"

Isaac is uncuffed and told to have a seat on the bench. Once the last man is seen, the deputy says, "All of you stand. Follow the red line into holding cell number three." As Isaac passes cells one and two, he sees human bodies sleeping on concrete, close enough together to be misinterpreted as 'spooning' with one another. There must be twenty people in each fifteen-by-fifteen-foot cell.

# Chapter 57:

The charges against him mystify Isaac. Although he works for a law firm, he knows nothing about criminal law, absolutely nothing! The whole 'innocent until proven guilty' provision and the American judicial system, formed to protect the citizens of these United States, mean absolutely nothing anymore? He knows that when Levi and Levi have a client charged with a tax or probate crime, white-collar crime, the client is never arrested. There may be an indictment for court, a subpoena for court, even a summons to be seen by a judge; an arrest, however? He has never seen it happen. He has never had to come and represent a client in jail. He has only had to come into court, maybe twice, to testify for his clients. He is finding out that the Superior-Court system works, for the privileged few.

The privileged few with money to buy the best counsel, the best connections, a team of attorneys, and an affordable bail amount can, at times, get away with murder. The people of the State of California have witnessed this before. O.J. Simpson got away with murder. Ted Kennedy got away with murder. He wasn't even charged with a crime. He left a woman to drown in a canal. He let her drown by leaving the scene because he was drunk! Never spent a day in jail; was never even charged with a crime? What about the woman's loved ones? Didn't they deserve justice, closure, or retribution? The privileged few!

Court-appointed attorneys or public defenders (nicknamed public pretenders or dump trucks) are not the best defense. As plea-bargain specialists, they work for the court system hand-in-hand with the district attorney. Their job is to offer plea bargains to avoid a trial scenario. If everyone had a good attorney, it would cripple the courts, clogging the calendars with jury trials. The privileged few, with money to afford a good attorney, have a better opportunity than the underprivileged majority. The first thing a good attorney wants to do to represent you properly is to bail you out and represent you from the streets instead of from jail. Again, only the privileged few can afford this. Is this fair? Absolutely not, but life isn't always fair. This is especially true with incarceration and sentencing. We can control our outcome from 'the outside.' From 'the inside,' however, we are no longer in control. Anything can happen to anyone inside those walls of incarceration, and there isn't anything good that can come from the San Diego County Jail.

Isaac's cell is beginning to fill up with six at a time after being processed. To Isaac's horror, one of the next six to be processed at the window is Dreadlock. As soon as Dreadlock enters the hallway, the deputy in charge picks up a can of Ozium air neutralizer and begins spraying. He even puts on a face mask filter with some Vick's VapoRub dabbed on the outside of it. Isaac can hear the woman with artistic, manicured nails say, "Oh, hell no!" and she leaves her counter. It must be lunchtime because she doesn't return for more than an hour with her own can of Ozium.

Three more deputies finally show up to help; one is a relief for the porn viewer, one is to man a fingerprint station, and one goes onto a computer across from the cells. The computer deputy opens cell number one and begins calling names. The machine of incarceration begins to spin again.

The fingerprint deputy opens cell number two and begins calling names. Isaac's cell number three has to wait for these forty jail detainees to be processed and moved along. The bench deputy walks up to the computer deputy, who has stripes denoting that he is a corporal. The corporal makes a decision, and the bench deputy calls Dreadlock and places him in a cell by himself. This cell is called a suicide watch cell: no sink, no toilet, and nothing from which to make a noose. A button on the wall outside the door flushes a hole in the concrete floor, this cell's toilet. This is Dreadlock's own, personal suite for several hours, maybe days. Those isolated due to being troublemakers or, in Dreadlock's case, being a health risk to others have been forgotten for days until they are due in court. Once the bench area airs out, it is business as usual for the booking counter.

The computer corporal has finished the classifications of the twenty intakes from cell number one. At the same time, Isaac's cell has filled with up to twenty persons. More sack lunches arrive with the same contents as before: bologna, bread, apple, and milk. This time, Isaac tries his bologna sandwich. Others here jokingly call these sandwiches Duffy Burgers. San Diego Sheriff Duffy first started the bologna diet for inmates of the County Jail instead of a hot lunch; probably the only thing for which he will be remembered is bologna! The occupants of holding cell number one are handed their Duffy-Burger lunches as they are told to follow the red line to the right, once again. Isaac cannot see where they went. The operation is now at a stand-still since all the deputy staff are gone, except for the porn-viewing deputy who brings out another six to the unmanned window counter. Half of these seem to be homeless. Their clothes and appearance imply this assumption, as well as the odor emanating into the hallway. Isaac notes their expressions, watching their noses crinkle as they pass Dreadlock's cell; the odor that they have been following is now discovered. The porn viewer takes his can of Ozium and sprays around the cell door, opens the flap door, and sprays into the cell before leaving a trail of spray in his wake as he walks back to his station to resume watching his video.

Those in cell number three with Isaac tell him that since they have received another sack lunch, it must be after four o'clock. They tell him that meals are served at four and ten o'clock in the morning and again at four o'clock in the afternoon. This last sack served signifies to Isaac that he has been detained for twenty-four hours now as a new group of deputies and a new woman at the window counter take charge.

Isaac's door is opened with a loud clang, waking those curled up on the concrete, which utterly disgusts the senses that Isaac has known. He has seen cleaning crews for the office, but after using the stained, stainless-steel toilet, he knows that it hasn't been cleaned for, possibly, years. He wonders, "Isn't stainless steel supposed to be stain-free?"

The fingerprint deputy begins his boring job, which requires actual contact with these walking viruses and joining them in the petri dish. One by one, persons are called from cell number three and fingerprinted as they continue the process. Isaac is called mid-way through their group.

"Stompski, you're next, please!" Isaac steps up to the station. "Place your feet on those patterns stenciled on the concrete. Give me your left hand. Keep your other hand in your pocket."

"Yes, sir. Can I ask..." Isaac begins.

"No, you cannot ask. This is fingerprinting only. Now, relax your hands and fingers as I roll them over the glass reader. I said relax!" the deputy reiterates.

"Yes, sir. Sorry, sir." Isaac apologizes.

While Isaac's group is being fingerprinted, those in cell number two are getting classified by the corporal deputy at the computer. Those from the benches are filling cell number one. These processes are endless, the same, day in and day out. Isaac sees a group of new recruits being escorted through, and he is sure that their brief walk-through seems exciting to them.

A career in a county job as a housing deputy is a first step into law enforcement. It is possible, while working in the jails, to further their education in other specialized areas. Deputies working in the courtrooms are desirable, as are the trustees in the reentry facilities, where the inmates have privilege.

The higher-classification criminals being processed for violent crimes are housed in more secure jails with dorms and cells. Crowded conditions are boiling, conditions of uprisings among races and rival neighborhoods. These areas are less desirable, that is unless you enjoy the conflict hazards or even agitate to instigate conflicts.

Isaac's group in cell number three is finished with fingerprinting. Those in cell number two have been taken down the hallway following the red line to areas unknown. Cell number one has now reached its maximum of twenty occupants, and the benches are, once again, filled. The rotation of incarceration, called recidivism, reported to be at a 70% rate in California, continues. The swing-shift skeleton crew is back once again, the porn-viewer has returned, and those in the cells begin to seek available footage to park and nap. The movement has, again, slowed into the early morning hours of Friday. Even Isaac sits on the stainless bench, leans against the half-wall at the toilet and sink, wedges himself into the corner, and falls asleep.

# Chapter 58:

Clang! The door slams open. "Everyone, up! If you want to eat, get up!" the deputy orders. "One at a time, come to the door, get your wristband scanned, get your meal!" Isaac was so tired that he had to be awakened.

It's six in the morning, Friday, his second day through this process, and Hannah's second morning waking up alone. Isaac's heart is about to explode inside his chest with anxiety, frustration and, now, heartache.

Names start being called for the corporal at the computer and cell number two has started to accept those processed at the counter window. Fingerprinting has begun in cell number one. Isaac's name is called around eight o'clock; he notices as he walks up to the desk.

"Mr. Stompski?" the corporal asks.

"Yes, sir," Isaac answers.

"I see that your charges are serious but non-violent, however. I see that this is your first arrest?"

"I haven't been able to remember my office, home or cellphone number. Can you help me with this problem?" Isaac is very thrilled that he was able to get out of this request before being interrupted or told to be quiet. Maybe, Isaac thought, this one can help.

"I completely understand your dilemma, Mr. Stompski, and I've heard it asked before. Unfortunately, all I can suggest to you is this...once you are housed...after this process...you write an inmate request to a counselor asking for the phone number of your office. The chances of finding that number are better than finding a home or cellphone number. Have your office contact your wife. I would tell you to contact a bail bondsman... if you had a credit card in your property. However, it says on your charges that the credit card found on you does not belong to you and was taken as evidence. If you had your valid credit card, a bail bondsman could pick up your property and help with your bail to have you released. Says here that bail is set at $75,000.00, so 10% of that is $7,500.00, which you also do not have." The corporal was helpful but also dismal, with the very vital information.

"I do appreciate your answering my question. No one has even attempted an answer thus far. An inmate request, you say? Thank you."

"You are welcome. Since this is your first arrest, your custody points would place you in a dorm setting once your arraignment date is over... Done here! Next is Gonzalez?"

Isaac goes back to cell number three and his last chance to use a 'free phone' for local calls only. After two more hours, cell number three has seen the last classification.

Isaac sees that the porn-viewer at a bench has begun yelling at Dreadlock, still in the suicide cell, isolated from the rest. There is not enough Ozium in the entire facility to rid this floor of the sick, overwhelming fecal odor assaulting everyone's sense of smell. The porn-viewer can, in hand, investigate the cell and completely lose it! Apparently, Dreadlock has taken a dump, but not in the hole, not in his pants, but at the threshold of the clanging door! As soon as the porn-viewer begins his rant, Dreadlock reaches down, fills his hand with feces, and smears it all over the portal window on the door. The porn viewer actually flinches at this as if Dreadlock had thrown it at him. Hysterical laughter can be heard. Then Dreadlock strips naked, bends over at his hips, and, with both hands on his buttocks, laughs again!

All of the cells are closed and secured at this point. The only deputy present is the porn-viewer with his Vicks-treated dust mask firmly in place. Magnetic blinds are placed over the window portal, and someone in Isaac's cell mentions something about cell extraction.

Loud orders can be heard, "Get on the ground, now!"

"Kiss my shit-covered ass!" followed by laughter.

"Stop resisting! Get on the ground now! This is your last warning!" the extraction-team sergeant commands, followed by more hysterical laughter.

"Hose him!" the order comes.

The door clangs open, and a high-pressure hose can be heard spraying, followed by screaming. They hear another order, "Get on the ground, now!"

"Kiss my..."

"Hose him again!" followed by more screaming and "Get on the ground, now! Don't resist, or you'll get the hose again! We are coming in to cuff you! Let's get the restraint seat in here, NOW!" the extraction-team sergeant orders. Then, all goes quiet as they wheel Dreadlock out of the cell and into another isolation cell. Isaac never sees Dreadlock again after that.

A team of inmates in tan jail attire instead of blue is brought in next. These inmates seem to have free movement through the hallways; Isaac believes these to be "Trustees." After the magnetic blinds are removed, water and feces can be seen throughout the corridor. The stench is everywhere and people are gag reflexing and retching out their many bologna meals consumed.

One of the trustees throws down his mop and quits on the spot! He says, "Hell no. Put me back in blues. I didn't sign up for this shit!"

He gets what he wants.

# Chapter 59:

After the corridor is cleaned and back to operational status, Isaac's cell number three opens with the now-familiar clang. The group of twenty men is told to exit the cell, get their blue band scanned, grab another sack meal, and follow the red line to the elevator. The elevator rises one floor. The group exits to a waiting female deputy. Her name tag says Bean. Those who have returned from previous incarcerations have nicknamed her Butter Bean, probably due to her complexion and obesity, not her disposition by any means.

"Everyone, out! Face the wall! When I call your name, follow the red line to my partner and enter the cell that he indicates for you to enter! No talking!" Bean orders.

Names are called. The twenty men are placed into an empty cell where they consume their fourth bologna sandwich meal since the first tank, Wednesday night. Just like the bench deputy, porn-viewer, Bean calls out six men at a time into the next area, off to the side of this cell.

Isaac's group of six men is the third group to enter. There are numbers on the wall, 1 to 6, with a shower-type curtain separating each and a privacy screen. Deputy Bean and her partner stand in front of a bin with T-shirt rolls containing a T-shirt, underwear, and socks. Another bin has S.D. JAIL-logo-ed canvas pants and pullover shirts. A third bin has plastic sandals.

Isaac's group has two white men, including Isaac, two Mexican men, and two African-American men.

Bean orders all six, "Everyone, disrobe down to your birthday suit. Do not, I repeat, do not shake your clothes before placing them into the black zipper bag with the hanger. Shoes and socks go into the bag first, then your clothing. As soon as the bag is placed in front of you, you may begin."

Isaac wonders, "Why is a female officer put into this part of the process? Did she request it? Maybe she is one of those man-hating lesbians and enjoys the dehumanization of stripping a man of his clothing. What drives this person, and what sort of response will a person such as Dreadlock get from her?" A bag with a tag, similar to the wristband with information on the face of it, is placed in front of each man.

"Check your name tag on your bag first to ensure that you receive your proper clothing upon your release. Begin, please!" Bean orders and watches.

Isaac drops his pants, removes his shirt and T-shirt, and lastly, his underwear. Bean's reaction to his manhood is immediate, which causes the entire group to look over at curtain number four. Some even take a step forward to peer around Isaac's curtain, shocked at the anaconda-like penis hanging between his legs.

Bean says, "You! Number four! Stompski, is it?"

"Yes, Deputy Butter...er... I mean, Bean."

"What are you trying to pull there? Do you really believe that you can pass off that prosthetic device as real to us professionals?"

"This is not a pros..." Isaac begins.

"Do not speak, Stompski!" Bean demands as she steps forward, reaches down, and gives Isaac's member a hard tug. "I see that these days they really do have these new devices, looking and feeling natural, Partner..." then she stops, "...I think that you are using this prosthetic to smuggle drugs or contraband into my facility, Stompski!" Then Bean grabs his penis with both hands and gives it a much harder tug.

"Hey, ouch, Deputy! I swear..."

"Shut it, Stompski!" Bean turns it in her hands in an attempt to search for a seam where it is attached and finds none. "Has this person already been x-rayed, Partner?"

"Says here, yes, he has..." hardly able to contain his humor at this scene. "...maybe, try pulling harder with some hand lube, and you'll find out what he's smuggling."

"Shut it, Partner!" Bean flushes red, and the whole room erupts in laughter. "I said, shut...it...now!" as she backed away from Isaac. "That can't be real. I can't believe that THAT is real!"

By now, everyone is dressed except for Isaac. The door to the next-side cell opens with a clang. Everyone shuffles by Isaac as if chased by a bear. The door clangs closed, and Bean approaches Isaac, saying, "I've got my eyes on you, Big Boy. If I see that your dorm has a problem with dope, I'm coming straight for you! Now get out of here!" Then she removes her latex gloves and squirts hand sanitizer on her hands.

Isaac says, "Hey, what about some sanitizer for my Big Boy, Deputy Bean?"

Clang...the door opens, and Deputy Bean orders, "Stompski, you and Big Boy, get your asses out of my sight, NOW!"

As Isaac walks through the door, the fifteen or so already in there are on their knees, giving Isaac a bow-down, respect salute, as a tribe would do to show respect for their chief. They all laugh and joke about his 'contraband.' Some are still carrying their bag lunches, not having had a chance yet to eat them.

One of the Mexicans says, "Hey, Homie, I wish that I had eaten my sliced bologna before I was in there with you. I swear on my skin, Ese, I have been traumatized after seeing your 'verga,' Homie!" Again, everyone starts to laugh.

Butter Bean turns into a Kidney Bean, due to her blood rushing to her head.

# Chapter 60:

Names continue to be called, and men continue to return to the cell. Some haven't returned yet, and some wonder where they have gone. Isaac's name is called. As he leaves the cell, he is not told to follow a red line or enter another cell. He is informed that he is going to arraignment court this afternoon, and he wonders, "Has it been 3 days in this process of hell?" Isaac is ushered into the elevator up another floor. When the elevator door opens, he steps out to another waiting floor deputy.

He orders, "Name and last four?"

"Stompski, five-nine-two-one." Isaac answers.

"Right. Follow this corridor down to my partner and follow his instructions. Next! Name and last four?" as the next person steps out of the elevator.

Isaac walks along the corridor, and the next deputy says, "Follow this corridor up to the metal detector. Go into the cell to the left of it. The court is in about an hour from now."

"Yes, sir." and Isaac goes into the cell as ordered. Along this corridor, cells on the left are packed full. Cells on the right have only one individual inside. One or two are in green suits with S.D. JAIL stenciled on the pants and shirts. Others are in the same blues as Isaac, except that these have different-colored wristbands. Isaac learned after he asked another inmate that yellow bands are for those in protective custody, or P.C.'s. They cannot be held with blue banders for the yellow bander's protection. Isaac also learns that if you are in the same cell with a yellow banner, it is mandatory that you attack this person.

'Full-flighting' is what was explained to Isaac. If you fail to 'full-flight' a P.C. who is put in the same cell with you...then you will be 'full-flighted' by two of your own race. It's called two-on-ones.

Protective-custody convicts in the California prison system have become so numerous that entire prisons are populated with P.C.s. Support yards for these P.C. prisons house Mainline convicts who are used for work crews in kitchens and for yard maintenance outside the gates. P.C. proudly wears tattoos of 'Deuce Five' or '25' or 'P.C. Pride' or many other symbols to signify solidarity.

P.C.s or 'snitches' are targeted because they have, in court or out of court, singled out others to get them arrested, even by just giving up their names as part of a group.

Prison gang groups, just like in neighborhoods, have formed as a protection in numbers. Their affiliations are proudly tattooed on their skin, making them identifiable as members. Smart ones hide these tattoos by tattooing their scalps, hiding by the hair when on the streets, and shaving clean when locked up. These members are identified and listed, so when they hit a prison yard they are then isolated into confinement called 'solitary housing units' or S.H.U.s. These limit movement to very little yard time and lots of lock-down time. Some can't handle this and choose to 'drop out.'

"Drop-outs' are asked to 'debrief' information. In exchange for this information, they are pulled out of the S.H.U. and placed in a P.C. yard. All that this has accomplished is the duplication of gangs inside the walls and out. Gangs are formed on the streets in neighborhoods for personal protection. When not in the protection of one's home, members will venture out with other members to have each other's back. Despite the influence of the brainiacs at the California Department of Correction to break up these gangs...all they've done is create duplicates of these gangs with a 'deuce five' sect.

Bus transports from jails to courtrooms and back are now 50%, 75%, and even 100% filled with P.C.s being transported instead of 5%, creating an entirely new problem of housing those needing protection. Incarceration is a 'beast' created by lawmakers and

voters: a 'beast' that has grown too large to control. Voters have been trying to reverse this trend. The courts have come up with their own methods to circumvent what the voters want while, at the same time, violating the rights of those whom they incarcerate.

Isaac has entered this world of incarceration because of a scenario in which he was innocent. He had no knowledge that the card he produced was not his. A simple mistake had, apparently, been made by the bartender. In a Mayberry-R.F.D. world, Sheriff Taylor, played by Andy Griffith, would have straightened out the entire problem, and Isaac would now be in Catalina, celebrating his anniversary with his wife, Hannah.

In today's world, California's world, the 'beast' must be fed. A 'beast' whose insatiable hunger is devouring California's sons, brothers, uncles, fathers, grandfathers and women, too. The 'beast' will regurgitate these meals, then feast on them again and again, caught in a revolving door called "recidivism." A money-making machine with a return rate of 70%.

Clang! Isaac's cell door opens yet again. No longer does this sound startle him from his sleep. At first, he was disgusted watching others lie around on these blackened, dirty concrete floors. After three full days of this, his clothing, his skin, and his person have been absorbing the malodorous stench of all around him. He hasn't been offered a shower before court either, hasn't brushed his teeth or his hair, hasn't had a deodorant, and hasn't even washed his face.

Now, he is being ushered into a courtroom filled with his community peers for his arraignment proceeding. Although he has the means of the 'privileged few,' he has no access to his funds; therefore, his treatment is the same as, well, someone like Dreadlock.

"Stompski, what are your last four?" asks yet another Deputy.

"Stompski, five-nine-two-one!" Isaac answers automatically now, the question, sadly, getting familiar to him.

"Go through the metal detector, then follow the red line to my partner and the others in front of you. No talking!" orders the Deputy.

Isaac follows the order.

"Single-file line, follow the red line across this bridge, then down the stairwell to our waiting partner on the next floor. No talking!" the redundant order again.

The bridge over Front Street allows those incarcerated to go to the San Diego Superior Court on West Broadway Street without having to leave custody by transporting. The bridge is completely enclosed without windows to the streets below. The old jail used to be part of the courthouse until the incarceration 'beast' outgrew its host, and it continues to outgrow it. The incarceration 'beast' is 'big business' in California.

The long line of inmates is split into the appropriate cells, according to the courtrooms that are requesting the inmates' mandatory appearances. Isaac's appearance is for arraignment court. The courts must arraign a person within 72 hours, one of our Constitutional Rights. As with all rights, the courts have come up with ways for them to have them waived, which, in all legal and moral aspects, is illegal. They will call an inmate to the gate whose 72 hours were exceeded and tell him that he needs to sign a paper to be released. Once the waiver is signed, there is no release. The inmate was duped. He was misrepresented, intimidated, and pressured into signing away a right. This is a commonplace practice, and they get away with it. They tell the person that he can't be released until it is signed, a dirty practice, and they get away with it.

Clang! Isaac's door opens and he hears his name called, "Stompski, last four, please?"

"Stompski, five-nine-two-one." Says Isaac once again.

"Stand against the wall, place your feet on the stenciled feet on the concrete. When asked, raise a leg, your left leg." They put a cuff on his ankle. "Right leg." They put a cuff on his other ankle with a heavy chain connecting both ankles. "When the chain goes around your midsection, drop your left arm." Isaac's left hand gets cuffed. "Now, your right arm." His right hand gets cuffed.

The 'shuffle of shame' is the clanging gait one is forced to walk while chained up in this manner; yet another form of dehumanization and humiliation, another reason that an attorney would want his client to walk in off the street for his appearances.

A line of restrained court-bodies leaves the cell corridor where they had been lined up. They exit into a hallway at the top of the escalators on the second floor of the courthouse. A public hallway filled with citizens waiting for their court appearances. The court hallway is packed with those readying themselves for a 1:00 pm court appearance. Those with children protectively wrap them up in their arms as these chain gangs shuffle down the hallway. Isaac is reminded of the old Tom Hanks movie, The Green Mile, and the quote, "Dead Man Walking," by the sadistic co-star.

Almost all those in the hallway back up to the walls. They would back up farther if the walls weren't present. These chain-gang inmates are doing the 'shuffle of shame' and want to crawl into a hole to hide.

Humiliated, deflated of confidence, shamed, appalling appearance, unshaven and ungroomed, and smelling of the disgusting dungeons in which they have been sleeping, they are made to appear in court. Damaged psyches, humbled and hobbled, they are led down the corridor as if brought off the island of Papillon. Only three days ago Isaac was dressed as a professional man of business, a successful citizen. Today, he has been reduced to dungeon filth, and he reeks of vomit, urine, feces, and, of course, bologna.

The chain gang is led partway down the corridor and, to the visible relief of many, led into a side door that leads into a back hallway. This back hallway leads around the side of the courtrooms. The chain gang stops at each courtroom and drops off its court body, then continues on to the next courtroom. Isaac's courtroom is second to last. An enamel sign says, 'Court 28: Arraignment, Judge Polanski Presiding'.

"Stompski, name and last four!" the deputy states.

"Stompski, five-nine-two-one." Once again, Isaac answers.

"Enter here. Court is in session, so no talking and no noise or trying to communicate with anyone in the seating area or you will catch the last bus back, got it? Enter and follow my partner's next orders."

Isaac shuffles through the door with two others. The enclosed bench area is surrounded by plexiglass with holes drilled through it to allow someone to speak. Isaac wonders why they have all the chains when they go from locked room to locked room. The 'privileged few' are called up first from the courtroom seating, properly dressed and presentable, although some of their charges, Isaac hears, are as bad as manslaughter and even armed robbery.

Judge Polanski, known as Blind Justice by those who have been arraigned many times here, sits with his wife next to him. His wife acts as his eyes and relays the visuals through her eyes to his ears. Arraignment court only needs a public defender (pretender) to represent. It is only a statement of "How do you plead guilty or not guilty?" However, no one says "Guilty" here. If they do, they are told to only answer "Not guilty" instead.

Isaac, only finding out a day ago what his felony charges are, meets his 'public pretender' for the first time at the proceeding.

"Stompski, Isaac?" asks the pretty little woman in a short miniskirt.

"Yes, I am Isaac." Answers the filthy Isaac.

"Mr. Stompski, my name is Jewel Jamison. I work for the Public Defenders Office. I am only your temporary defender in this arraignment process." His appearance and stench assault her senses, but she has seen it many times before. "This will be done quickly. The court clerk is going to state your charges. The judge will ask you to state your name and how you plead. You will say 'Not guilty,' and a new court date will be given to you. Before that date, you will be contacted by someone else in our office who will defend you unless you provide your own counsel. Do you understand what I have explained to you?" in her robotic, monotone voice.

"Uh, yes, sure." Seems to Isaac the only response possible.

"When your name is called, I will step up to that podium on the other side of the glass. You will, please, step up to the glass. Don't worry, the judge can't smell you from the other side." she assures him.

"Great, but you can smell me? Just wonderful!" Isaac says.

"I am sorry. I understand the holding tanks you were forced to come through. I do understand." she reassures Isaac. Then she speaks to two others in the 'plexi-cage.'

When done, she enters the courtroom. Those in the 'plexi-cage' could care less about what their charges are, "Did you see her legs? Did you notice how she looked at me? I think she wrote a smiley-face on my file." All they cared about was 'hot legs'!

"Stompski, Isaac," the clerk calls.

Isaac steps up to the drilled holes and hears what he thinks is English, but spoken so rapidly that he isn't 100% sure that it is.

"How do you plead, Mr. Stompski?" The clerk has to repeat the question, "Mr. Stompski? How do you plead, sir?" He sees the wife of Blind Justice talking into his ear. Isaac knows that she is filling his senses with Isaac's disheveled appearance. He wants to shrink below the partition.

"Uhm..." the pretty miniskirt mouths, "Not guilty" for Isaac as a prompt,

"...Not guilty, your honor," Isaac says in his defense.

More foreign language as the clerk rattles off dates and times. Then Isaac's moment has passed, as another name is called to the plexiglass. Name after name, hour after hour, day after day, every week of every year, these courts take away the freedoms of many.

# Chapter 61:

Hannah has lost her confidence in the La Mesa Police Department. She has left two messages a day for the detective in Missing Persons, as she was instructed, and still has never received a return call. Now, she is told that the detective will be out of the office until Monday. What, people don't go missing over the weekends?

She continues to call Samuel's cellphone, as well as her husband's. Still, going straight to voicemail, both of them? What, did they go to Las Vegas on a gambling binge together? Of course not! Isaac would never do such a thing and Samuel would never allow his best friend to worry her in such a way.

She refuses to call the office just yet. After the detective exhausts his resources, she may go to the firm, but not until the detective is back on Monday. Hannah is beginning to get angry at the 72-hour policy of the La Mesa Police Department.

Hannah begins her search through the twenty-three San Diego hospitals on the list that she has compiled. She has the photo of Isaac to send to any hospitals that have any John Does. This time, in her search, she has included Samuel's name as well, in case they were together. Hannah refuses to check with the county coroner. That is not an option and, anyway, Isaac had plenty of valid identification on his person. If something that serious had happened, she would have been notified. Hannah has heard horror stories about travelers in foreign countries being abducted and held for ransom. But here in San Diego? That thought hit her: their proximity to the Mexico border. She has seen stories of women abducted by cartel members. Then, instead of being held for ransom, they are held and trained by injecting them with heroin until hooked. After months or maybe a year as addicts, they are trained to be sex slaves.

Could that have happened to Isaac and Samuel? Do they even do that to men? If not, what about organ harvesting that she has seen in MSN News stories? For Isaac not to contact her, he has to be held captive someplace, held captive against his will, a prisoner in a dungeon somewhere. Hannah has no idea how close she is to figuring out her dilemma.

# Chapter 62:

Clang! Isaac is put back into the exact same cell after court as he was before court. He was given another sack lunch as he headed into the elevator back to this floor, his ninth bologna meal since he arrived.

"Stompski, name and last four!" the deputy calls.

"Stompski, five-nine-two-one." Now becoming mundane.

"Step on the scales, remember your weight, and have a seat in front of the nurse." The deputy cuffs Isaac to the nurse's counter.

"Are you suicidal, or do you have any medical emergency or special medications to declare?" the male nurse asks.

"No, nothing like that. I do need the eyeglasses that they took from me. Metal frames, I believe, was the reason." says Isaac.

"Do you have your prescription on you?" asks the nurse.

"Uh, no, I don't." Isaac chuckles, "Who on earth carries their eyeglass prescription around with them?"

"No? Then you can purchase reading glasses on commissary when you order." the nurse says. "Did you come in with any money on your books?"

"Uh, no, I don't think so. My credit card was taken from me, too." Isaac still doesn't understand that the card that they took as evidence was not his.

"I'll make a note for you to get glasses. Anything else?" the male nurse asks.

"No. Not medically," Says Isaac.

"Done here, officer. Next, please." Orders the robotic nurse.

Isaac is uncuffed and told to, once again, follow the red line to his partner. This time, he passes by cells with some of the people with whom he had been in previous cells. He is then put into a cage by the elevator. He is soon joined by the three others who were called when he was. The elevator door opens, and a voice-over speaker calls out their four names and tells them to get on the elevator. One of the men had been through the change-out area with Isaac.

The man laughs and says, "Hey, Stompski, that was the funniest damn shit I ever seen in there with that Butter-Bean Bitch!"

Isaac says, "Yeah, to you, maybe, but you didn't have 300 pounds of man-hater hanging off your penis either!"

The entire area erupts in laughter.

"Man, you are the sheee-it, my man! My name is Spaz, from El Cajon. Mind if I call you Stomp, my man?" asks Spaz.

"No. That is fine, I guess." And Isaac got his handle.

"Cool," Spaz says, "Looks like we got us some love here. We got us a straight shot to the Thunder Dome, no shitty-ass, fourth-flo' shots!"

"The Thunder, what?" says Isaac, not understanding Spaz.

"The Thunder Dome, my man, George, Mutha-Fuckin', Bailey. Stomp, is this yo' first rodeo, man?" Spaz asks.

"Yeah, I guess it is. I still haven't been able to..." Isaac begins, but the elevator door opens.

"Step out and face the wall. No talking!" the deputy says. "When you hear your name called, give me your last four and step out, then follow my partner's directions."

They all file out, one by one, until all are against the wall. They are sent into a large cell littered with hundreds of used sack lunches from a previous crowd.

Spaz is in before Isaac, going through all the sacks. "Looking for apples, my man. You should look, too. We gonna be awhile in here!"

Isaac comes up with three apples and finds a seat on the opposite side of Spaz.

Spaz calls over to an acquaintance with whom he's been locked up before, a white guy. "Yo', Tyler, my man, how are ya?" Spaz asks.

"What's up, Spaz? Did they get you again? At the trolley station, El Cajon?" Asked Tyler.

"That's right, some weird shit goin' down in 'the zone', man. Some crazy white guy killin' cop-kids and some snitchin' muthas at the station. Hey, Wood, this here is Stomp, hung like a damn horse, he is! New fish needs some political advice from a fellow 'wood'! Can you help him out for me?" Spaz asks.

"Oh, fuck yeah, Spaz. Gotta run it down to him before he gets lumped up for getting stupid! I got him, Spaz, and thanks for looking out for him!" Tyler says.

Tyler takes Isaac under his wing, and he's got his work cut out here. Stomp, he realizes, is as green as they come. "Look..." Tyler begins, "...I got a lot to cover, so try not to interrupt until I finish, then ask questions, O.K.?"

Isaac only nods 'yes', and the education begins.

# Chapter 63:

Incarceration in county jail and Prison places a person in a hyper-polite society. Racially segregated into five main groups: Whites, or Woods, have segregations such as Peckerwoods, Skin Heads, Aryans, Nazi Low Riders, and so on; Blacks have their segregations as well, such as Bloods, Crips, and so on. Even though these gangs have been broken up in the cities from which they came. Others who are Native American, Asian, Middle Eastern, Russian, European, and Pacific-Islander natives are only a few. Mexicans have designations such as South Sider, Norteno, Buster, and Paisa, which have also been broken up into the neighborhoods and cities from which they came.

Respect and manners, socially, are very important within the walls, especially between races or sects. One doesn't cut in front of, interrupt a conversation, approach for any reason, or eavesdrop without a resounding, "Excuse me?" Hyper-polite.

Respect is always given, but it is also earned for a higher degree of respect. Your word is the first example of respect. You say what you do, and you do what you say, being righteous. Cleanliness is self-respect, as well as respect for those around you. The entire system is 'nuts and bolts.' They crowd you together into areas that must be kept clean and orderly to maintain health and respect for all.

Rules and discipline are not only handled by the facility and housing deputies. The sects also have their own rules, which, when broken, carry disciplines. The deputies carry their status visibly on their shirt sleeves with bars, chevrons, and stars. Those incarcerated carry theirs in respect and word. These are not visible. Actually, their names are handles or nicknames so that their identities are protected. This is much the same way a battalion would protect its officers. One would not use a handle in front of deputies. One would not approach a deputy without being accompanied by another to guarantee that the conversation was not a snitch move. It's the same with inmate correspondence.

Having another to 'shadow' a request or written page of paper is required to guarantee against an accusation of dropping a 'snitch kite'. An example would be if housing were raided because of drugs or porno and somebody saw someone drop a 'kite' without being 'shadowed', that someone would be suspect. Rules are too plentiful for Tyler to go through each and everyone for Isaac, so he tries to keep it basic.

Tyler tells Isaac where they are. San Diego Central Jail has ten floors. The bottom two are for booking and processing. The top two are for administration and support staff. Floors three through eight are for housing; each of these floors has four modular living areas. Some are dorms, but most are cells. Each 'mod' has a representative or 'rep' for each race. Any racial issues are discussed and resolved by these 'reps,', and any disciplines required are handed out by each 'rep.' A discipline would start out as a physical exercise such as pushups, squats and many variations of these. Sets of 1-2-3 would increase to 2-4-6 and up, depending on the severity or repetition of the infraction. South Siders would use denominations of 1-1-3, then 2-2-6, and so on.

Harsher disciplines are also handed out once these are exhausted or for disrespecting another race. The 'rep' decides the discipline. His 'right hand' will hand it down to the responsible individual or take over should the 'rep' not be available for any reason. The hierarchy among the 'mods' is controlled by someone who has the keys to each facility.

San Diego's seven jails house, on average, 5,000 inmates. Each of the seven jails has a key holder who answers to another with the keys to all seven jails. The same goes for the prison system hierarchy; the same breakdown with a big difference. The 'shot caller' with the keys to his race, usually housed in a maximum-security prison such as Pelican Bay, not only runs his race within the walls but also outside the walls. Respect through intimidation and fear of retribution is the sole tool needed to carry out orders from within.

Isaac has a lot to absorb from Tyler and he has only given Isaac the basics of this society. Tyler has his own, personal advice for Stomp. "Stomp is your handle now. Introduce yourself as Stomp, claiming San Diego, or for others from San Diego, you can claim East County, as La Mesa is in East County." Tyler continues, "On the streets, I have two basic rules: 1) Always maintain. If you cannot do this, do not leave the protection of your home; 2) Never, and I mean never, tell on yourself. Myself, I never even offer my name to law enforcement. All of my paperwork states, 'Mr. Arlington handed me his I.D. and said, 'You figure out who I am, and I plead the Fifth!' Remember, Stomp, that no matter what runs out of your mouth, the cops will twist it around to use against you! Got that so far?" And the final rule 3) Never ever stick your dick in crazy!"

"O.K., Tyler, what is your handle?"

"You catch on quick, Stomp. I like that! My folks, being pot-heads, started calling me T-Stick for Tai-stick. That was made even shorter by dropping the 'Stick' and calling me 'T.' Around the '50,' they call me Tyler or Arlington." Proudly states Tyler.

"Good looking out, 'T.' You are right. This is a whole lot to consume. I appreciate this." Isaac's sincerity is recognized.

Tyler's schooling continues. He informs Isaac as to where they are headed: George Bailey Detention Facility, commonly known as "The Thunder Dome". As Tyler goes into describing the Thunder Dome, the sally-port tank that they are in gets fuller by the minute as court bodies are done in the courts and await transport back to George Bailey. They are on the late bus back, the one that hits traffic the whole way. They most likely won't be chained together and Tyler definitely won't be housed with Isaac. Tyler is being housed in the high-power tanks; his charges will lead him to prison.

"Back to school, Stomp, before the bus comes. We won't be going to the same housing. I am going to high-power tanks and cell living. You are going to low-power dorm living, but I don't envy you. I prefer cell living over dorm living. There is more respect where I'm going. More respect, less problems; less respect, more problems. Capisce, my friend?" Tyler explains to Isaac how the dorms work. "When we pull up, we will be searched and separated into the housing cells in groups, so we have to get this done before we get chained up."

Tyler continues, "When you get to your dorm..." Tyler explains to Stomp what will happen when he goes through the gate at his 'mod,' most likely House One, either 'A,' 'B,' 'C', or 'D.' Each 'mod' has four dorms: House 1-A will have dorms 101, 102, 103, and 104; House 1-B will have 105, 106, 107, and 108, and so on until House Two. House Two's numbers coincide with House One's.

Stomp will be instructed to put his bedroll on a table. Standards are that the back tables, back by the stairs, are for the 'woods'. All Stomp needs to know is which dorm is his, never mind the rack number given to him. He will be assigned a rack by the 'rep's righthand man. The 'right hand' will explain the rules to Stomp: which tables are the 'woods' tables, which phones are the 'woods' phones, and not walking between other races' tables during chow. If Stomp has any questions, if there is anything that Tyler hasn't covered and Stomp isn't sure about, the 'right hand' is the one he should ask in order to make the right choice.

Isaac and Tyler hear chains in the corridor, and Tyler says, "All right, Stomp, you'll do fine. Just remember what I've told you and stay away from gambling and debts, and don't let a queer suck you off. We have a saying here, 'You can't un-tell, and you can't un-suck a dick!' Good luck to you!"

"Thanks again, 'T'. I'll need it!"

# Chapter 64:

Clang! The drab-green metal door slams open. There are sixty or more grown men in this 1200-foot holding tank. These are the last to be put on buses to leave here until the next day.

"Listen for your name. Give me your last four, then walk down to my partner at the end of the hallway." The sally-port deputy calls out. Stomp sees 'T' being called and gives him a fist bump. 'T' says his thanks, then he is gone. Another ten get called, then...

"Stompski, Isaac!" Came the order.

"Stompski, five-nine-two-one!" Stomp declares.

"Go ahead to my partner!" final order.

"Turn here and hands up on the wall. When the chains go on, drop each hand when directed to!" sally-port-deputy's partner orders, as chains are thrown around Stomp's midsection. Then Stomp is chained to another man. He can see 'T' farther up the queue.

"All right, line up in the next room, starting on the left side!" says the transport Deputy.

Ten groups of two line up against the wall while a cart with property, mail, and belly chains is wheeled out to the waiting bus. The garage is filled with diesel exhaust. This is now Stomp's third full day without a shower. Stomp and nineteen others, chained together, fill half of the back of the first bus. The other half is filled with P.C.s, some in individual cages, all separated by a gate running down the main side of the bus. The blue-banders closest to this gate begin calling the P.C.s names, such as 'rats,' 'snitches,' 'creeps', and many other expletives. Some try to spit at them. Although there is plexiglass, the sentiment is still sent forward with the colorful, spewed saliva.

At this hour, the southbound I-5 is at a standstill through South Bay cities, so the transport takes the Pacific Highway past Logan Heights and the many shipyards of San Diego

Harbor. This continues until the highway comes into the Naval Housing and Officers Golf Course on Main Street in National City. The transport heads east on Main Street to Broadway Avenue, then heads south to H-Street in Chula Vista, then east again past the South Bay Courthouse and Jail, then south on I-805, effectively skirting the standstill traffic of hurried after-work commuters. At this point, the transport heads east on the I-905 to the Otay-Mesa border crossing.

'T' is seated two rows in front of Stomp. He points out the border crossing to Stomp. "Stomp, across that border, is the Tijuana Airport, and not far from that is the infamous Mexican Mesa Prison. Hey, Stomp, have you ever seen the Mel Gibson movie, 'Get the Gringo'? I swear, Stomp, it is just like that in a Mexican prison, much like a little ghetto in the city. There are vendors of food, alcohol, cigarettes, and drugs, all run by prison gangs, all at a cost. You can rent a private area, much like an apartment. Men are incarcerated with their families as well, un-fucking-believable!"

"What? Is that the same here?" Stomp asks. Those around him laugh at his naivete.

"Hell, no." 'T' exclaims. "Up here on the left is R.J. Donovan Prison, Stomp. You'll see as we drive down the dip in the canyon. Look out at it as we rise up the hill. It is immense!"

"All of that is only one jail?" Stomp says unbelievingly.

"Not one jail, one prison, state penitentiary, La Pinta, as we call it, Rock Mountain Pen! To get there you ride on 'the chain' from George Bailey to there. It's a five-minute ride to reception yard four. All levels are put there together for about sixteen weeks until classified. Murderers are put in the same yard as drunk drivers or shoplifters.

"Not like the movies, is it?" Stomp gets another laugh.

"No, Stomp, you are not in Kansas anymore...," 'T' says. Then he quotes a line from the movie starring Tina Turner and

Mel Gibson, 'The Thunder Dome.' "Rickety Man, welcome to the Thunder Dome!" More laughter.

The P.C.s come off the bus first and are quickly ushered into the metal, sally-port gate on the right and out of sight of the Mainline blue banners. Then, the rest of the bus is unloaded. Stomp can't comprehend that this facility is actually older and in far worse condition than where he came from downtown. The metal gate noisily struggles to open and stops after eight inches of travel. A deputy has to come over and manually pull it free for the motor to engage and finish its business. After it opens, Stomp's jaw drops to the concrete. There, standing in the corridor before him, is his nemesis, Deputy Bean. She is smiling at Stomp and nodding her head as if to say, "I told you. I got my eyes on you!"

'T' looks over at Stomp and says, "Stomp, uh, Butter Bean is acting like she knows you. If this is your first time, how does she know you?"

"That, my mentor friend, is a LONG story. I'm afraid that more will be revealed to you soon. Uh, is it possible to get a T.R.O. against a stalker-deputy in here?" Stomp is serious, but the laughter says otherwise.

"Stop talking! Everyone, listen up! Walk down to the end of the hallway to my waiting partners. Face the wall to your right. When your hands are un-cuffed, place them high on the wall in front of you. After the chains are removed from your waist, step up to the wall and place your hands in your waistband. No talking, or you'll be spending most of the evening in these holding cells! Now, walk!" the sally-port deputy, Garcia, orders.

This is the first bus to arrive back, so all of the cells on the left are empty. By the end of the day, they will all be packed, and the talking will rise to a roar that will be deafening.

"Well, well, Mr. Stompski, how was your day in court today? Now you are on my playground. Welcome to my Thunder-Dome, Rickety Man!" Deputy Bean warns.

The laughter is met with Garcia's demand, "Shut the hell up! This is your very last warning! Deputy Bean, we got this from here. Thank you for your assistance."

Deputy Bean winks at Stomp, then leaves the post to resume her duties. Her message was sent loud and clear. 'T' gives Stomp a look like 'What the Fuck?' and Stomp mouths to 'T,' 'She wants my dick.' Then it comes back to 'T' what Spaz told him, 'He's hung like a horse!'. 'T' looks over at Spaz, who mouths, 'I told you so!'.

"All right, Ladies, step out of your shoes and place them behind you with your paperwork!" The deputies go through it all, looking for contraband. "Turn around and lift your shirts and T-shirts up over your heads so that we can see your underarms!" They are all checked down the line. "Pull your shirts down and drop your pants and briefs down to your knees until you're told to pull them up!" Everyone does so, and 'T' looks over at Stomp for verification of what Spaz said. He isn't the only one, either. All of the deputies are pointing at Stomp's shaft down his leg. His head is still in the briefs, even though the pants are around his knees.

"You, Stompski, is it? I guess you'd better drop your pants to your ankles. Uh, is that thing real, young man? All right, the show's over. Pull up your pants and listen for your name. Enter the cell that you are directed to enter!"

Stomp, Spaz, and 'T' are separated, going to different areas according to their classification needs. Spaz and 'T' are still on parole, so they will be housed in House Six, while Stomp will go to the dorms in House One. The holding cells fill, and yet another sack lunch is handed out for dinner. Stomp's tenth or eleventh bologna meal, he has lost count since Wednesday night and his arrest. Headaches are the result of these echo chambers, and everyone's hopes of going home with time served or being released from custody on their own recognizance are dashed.

Other hopes for a reduced sentence or a drop in charges are also dashed. Moods are glum, anger is rising, conflicts are mounting, and Stomp, as the new fish, is an easy target. He asks another 'wood' about trying to call his wife and is explaining his situation when a hothead looks at Stomp with hate in his eyes and gets in his face.

"Hey, why don't you just stop your fucking whining, already! I am sick of hearing your voice already! Especially about your whoring wife! One more word..." The hothead says disrespectfully.

To hear someone disrespect Hannah was more than he could tolerate. Stomp stands up and says, "WORD!"

"What? Mother Fucker!" The hot head wants clarification. "What?" louder this time.

Those who saw the argument would not even call it a fight. Actually, had you blinked, you would have missed the entire event. Who did miss the event, it was said, was the skinhead who took a swing at the new fish, Stomp. Without padded protection, the skinhead's ribs did not take much coaxing to collapse. A final, downward cross to his jaw finished off the hot-head.

Stomp very calmly sat back down, and everyone was quiet. The tension was felt in the other cells, although no one saw what happened but the stunned crowd in Stomp's cell. Word got to 'T' and Spaz that their new friend, the guy hung like a horse, obviously had a kick like one, too!

The hardest kick was yet to come.

# Chapter 65:

"When you hear your name, give me your last four and step out here. Line up against the wall!" Here at Bailey Jail there is no loud Clang! These gates are barred with old-type locks. After several names are called, Stomp hears his name.

"Stompski!" The Deputy calls out.

"Stompski, five-nine-two-one!" Almost automatic now for Isaac.

After twelve men are called, they are Marked out through two double doors and through a metal detector.

"Everyone, grab one roll and turn to your right, to my partner!" instructs the Deputy.

Stomp follows suit and removes what looks like a blanket rolled out of a big, blue bin. The skinhead with whom he had the problem is holding his side and quietly absorbing his pain. Stomp can see workers in tan canvas suits on the other side of fencing in an outdoor courtyard, cleaning kitchen tubs. The twelve men are led around an outdoor quad courtyard with two gates; one reads Houses 1-3, and the other reads Houses 4-6.

"If you know which house you are from, stay where you are. If you are just getting here, step back one step!" Continues the Deputy.

Stomp and one other step back.

"Name and last four?" Asks the Deputy.

"Aguilar, four-six-one-three." The Southsider answers.

"Aguilar, you are in House 1-B! Next?" The Deputy is giving house assignments.

"Stompski, five-nine-two-one." Isaacs turn.

"Stompski, you are in House 1-A! Anyone else in House 1, step back one step!" Orders the Deputy.

Four others step back.

"Go through the gate to my partner!" Final Deputy orders.

The six follow each other to another Deputy who is waiting by an open gate in front of a shed.

"The two new House-1 inmates, grab a sleeping mat, then line up in the corridor!"

The other four go around and line up against the wall in the corridor. Stomp and Aguilar line in the rear.

"Who is in House 1-A? Please come forward and walk through the gate." Says the Deputy, gatekeeper, to "Thunder Dome."

A door is ajar, and a motorized gate is opening, without a Clang! It stops before being fully open. Stomp is the only one to enter here. Remembering what 'T' had explained to him, he knows that the nearest tables, all empty now because everyone is locked into their dorms, are for the Blacks. Stomp walks back to the metal staircase on the right and sets his bedroll and mat on the table at the bottom of the stairs. It is exactly how 'T' had described it, but it is still overwhelming compared to all the cells that Stomp has been in so far. Stomp counts twenty stainless-steel tables in the huge room, each of which will seat eight persons. There must be 160 inmates in the four housing units, which, he quickly calculates, would be 40 in each unit. However, he can look into the lower dorms, where he only sees two inmates lying on their mats on the floor.

Stomp looks to the upper dorms. All are very active with movement. The one above him, labeled '203', is a lot more active. '203' has just received their newspaper after lunch; the "Crime Stopper" section shows a 'parole violator at large' photo. The description information states child molesters and sex offenders.

Although everyone's paperwork is checked when they arrive, those whose recording simply states parole violation slip through the cracks of the Rep through scrutiny.

Mohammed Aziz, whom those in the dorm call Mo for short, is the 'parolee at large' shown in the Crime Stoppers and got here the day before. When checked over the San Diego

Sheriff Information System on the inmate's phones, his charges stated parole violation. As an 'other,' his 'rep' would be an 'other' or a 'black.' At that point a request for paperwork should have been made to get more detail. Sometimes, the follow-up on this is lacking, and the person gambles on that to enable him to be housed with more freedom to be less restricted of movement.

The newspaper photo pulled back the sheets on Mo, so to speak, and the 'black/other' race was approached to take action against Mo. The keyholder for that race was housed in '201' next to '203' and a kite, or message, was sent to the 'Rep' to handle him, 'put the boot' to him, and eject the "Chomo," or child molester, from this House. Mo, knowing that it was coming, had grabbed his important property in his arms and was at the door, expecting his ejection.

"Stompski, you are housed in dorm '203'. Head up the stairs with your roll and mat!" orders a voice from the P.A. system.

Stomp hears over the P.A. Speaker. So he grabs his things to head up the stairs, sets his things down on the landing, and waits for the locked door to open. Mo sees the group gathering and pulling out their well-hidden weapons, shivs or shanks, or anything that can be sharpened. Bars of soap, wrapped up in socks, become blackjacks, and just about anything can be used to strike a "Chomo." Mo turns and begins to push the button next to the wall speaker at the door, screaming for help.

"They're gonna kill me! Pop the door. Pop the door!" Screams the frightened Mo.

The door pops open as Mo gets rushed, and he squirts through the opening. Stomp sees the angry mob rushing towards him and turns to follow Mo. Stomp has the mob at his back and feels a hard two-handed push, and at the same time, his feet become entangled in his bedroll on the landing. He is launched from the landing, right towards Mo's back. Stomp throws his arms around Mo as a reflex to survive, and they both are thrown forward down the concrete and steel steps.

Unfortunately for Mo, and most would say deservedly, he catches the brunt of the impact with 180 pounds of Stomp on his back. The 'crack' sound was loudly heard in all four dorms as Stomp rode it out on top of Mo. The stunned silence was followed by an eruption of cheers from all four dorms.

Sirens sounded, followed by orders over the P.A. System for all those in the dorms and for Stomp in the dayroom. "Everyone, get down on the floor! Those in the dorms, all of you, on your racks! On your racks, NOW!"

Everyone in all four dorms was crowding the glass, trying to get a view of the "Chomo" Mo, lying at the foot of the stairs with his neck at an unnatural angle and unmoving.

Parole won't have to worry about Mohammed Aziz molesting another child...ever again.

# Chapter 66:

Stomp is cuffed with plastic zip-ties while he is lying on the floor next to the deceased "Chomo," Mo. He is then led away to a side cell just outside the gate. He is then told that he must stay there until a sergeant works on paperwork. He is informed that the sergeant is reviewing recordings of the incident in order to make a documented well informed determination on the attack.

The San Diego Sheriff's detention deputies knew of Mohammed Aziz's prior record before housing him. It is not known or documented by Mohammed's signature that it was his choice to be housed in Mainline rather than to be housed as a P.C. inmate. Housing Mohammed without informing him of the danger present for him, without protection, places the fault with the San Diego Sheriff's Department.

Had Mohammed been informed of the danger and had he denied protection, the fault would have been reduced to a small degree. However, as professionals in their domain, should sexual predators be given a choice of custody by the Processing Deputies?

Although those deputies who work on housing do not work on the streets and actually arrest individuals, they do have 'hit lists' of persons whom they want to be brought into their custody. These 'hot lists' are illegal and immoral and are done as favors to deputies who have problems with certain people. Abuse of authority is far-reaching throughout the judicial system and may not surface until years or decades later. A district attorney, for example, would have background investigators look into the past of his daughter's ex-husband due to child custody issues. Using taxpayer dollars to run a personal investigation is illegal. Will these abuses of authority ever result in criminal charges when exposed? Probably not.

So, who are the real criminals? If these 'civil servants' are prosecuting us, who prosecutes the 'civil servants'? They are left to the investigations of inter-departmental investigators and dealt with from within and then swept under the rug. Absolute power corrupts absolutely. How is an incarcerated person able to defend himself when the facility's detention deputies accumulate all the available evidence? Any and all evidence would be used to build a case against the individual, not in his favor!

The word among inmates spreads very quickly. The death of a known and documented child molester by another inmate is important news that needs to reach the keyholder of Bailey Jail. This happens within hours of the attack, as the entire jail is soon placed on lock-down status. Those housed in cells are kept in cells without movement. Those housed in dorms are told to stay in their racks except for trips to the restroom. This could last for days or weeks, depending on the severity of the incident.

Visits get cancelled for all races and all races get pissed due to not getting privileges. Green-lights to violence are carefully given so as not to disrupt privilege, knowing what the outcome of any violent incident would be. However, child molesters are always green-lighted. It is mandatory to deal with these types without waiting for a decision to come down from the top echelon of the hierarchy.

Inmates, with charges of violence and charges resulting in decades of prison time, would gladly accept the chance to take out a child molester as Stomp has done. Going to prison with that credential would sky-rocket one's respect and reputation instantly and immensely. Legacies within the walls are built up on these credentials; while at the same time, these credentials would be called upon for more violent duties to your sect, or 'car'. These actions cannot be denied when called upon but, instead, accepted with gratitude to put in work for your 'car'.

Stomp is in 'the hole' for three, maybe four, hours before a black-shirt detective comes in with a stack of papers in his hands.

"Mr. Stompski, I am Investigator Jones." Says the Detective.

"Yes, sir." Answers the worried Isaac.

"Upon reviewing the video and questioning you, I need to read you your rights once again. You have the right to remain silent; you have the right to counsel; anything that is said between us, from you, can be used against you in a court of law. Do you understand these rights that I have told you?" asks the Detective.

"Yes, sir, I do." Says Isaac.

"Are you willing to answer any questions that I would like to ask you today?" Asks the now friendly Detective.

"No, sir, I am not. I'd like an attorney present."

"O.K.....well...then I guess we are done here. Are you willing to sign any forms that I have for you to sign?" Hopes the Detective.

"No, sir, not without my attorney present. I think that our conversation is concluded, sir." Stomp has learned that 'T's advice about not telling on yourself is exactly what an attorney would have advised in this situation.

The Detective continues, "All right, Mr. Stompski, we do need to re-book you on one new charge and change your custody level. Did you leave any property in 1-A besides what was issued to you?" the Detective asks.

"That would be a question you're asking, sir. Pleading the Fifth was my request, sir!" Stomp ends it with finality.

Stomp is led back out the way he came in and, brought into Administration and, fingerprinted, then checked by a nurse for scratches to his elbows and hands. These are now documented in the incident report. The classification process is done quickly and his housing status is changed to high-level housing. Stomp is walked back out of Administration. He is told to grab a blanket roll, is walked through the metal detector, and is taken to the gate for Houses 4-6. He is led through the gate, told to grab a mat at the shed, and told that he will be housed in House 6-A, which is still on lockdown.

The gate rolls open halfway, and Stomp takes his roll into the dayroom and, once again, lays it on the table by the stairs on the right. He hears his name being yelled out from someplace upstairs, but he can't tell from where. Then he hears his name being yelled out again in Spaz's voice from downstairs, very close to him.

"Hey, Stomp! What up, my man? Why are you being..." Spaz begins to ask, then "...Oh, shit, Stomp! Was that you, my brother? Say it wasn't, Stomp! Are you the reason we are all in lockdown?"

"Not sure, Spaz..." Stomp answers, "...where I was going to go, they chased someone out of an upper dorm, and I turned to go down and, well..."

"Oh, shit! That was you?" says Spaz.

"Hey, Stomp, up here!" 'T' shouts from his cell.

"Who is yelling for me, Spaz?" Isaac asks.

"That's 'T' up there, in 215, top of the stairs on the other side!" says Spaz.

Stomp looks up at 215 and sees 'T'. He yells up there, "What's up, 'T'? I had a little problem where they tried to put me, big trouble!"

"Oh, man, that was you, Stomp? You are the man, Stomp! We are proud to have you here. Hey, I have an empty rack up here. I'll see about getting you moved up here when they pop us out, O.K.? Stay tough, Stomp. We got you!" 'T' yells out.

"Stompski, you are living in 211, 211, go there, now!" the P.A. Speaker orders.

As Stomp walks by 'T's cell, 'T' can see the bandages on his arms, hands, and chin. "Damn, Stomp, you look like you got run over since I saw you last!"

Stomp agrees, "Yeah, maybe you should see the condition of the other guy."

At least I got up and walked away!

# Chapter 67:

Hannah, come Saturday morning, finally receives a call from Samuel, frantic and astonished after reading Hannah's messages.

"Hannah, I am so sorry that I am just now getting back to you. I will explain my absence later. First, I need to find out why you are not in Catalina and what do you mean by 'Isaac is missing'? Is he still missing?" Asks Samuel, astonished by the news.

"Oh, Sammy! I have had absolutely no help from the police. Their 72-hour, missing-person policy has them all sitting on their hands until then. I haven't even called my family yet. I don't want to upset them and Isaac's family, also. I've been calling every hospital in San Diego every day since Thursday. Oh, Sammy, I am so worried for him. Do you think that he was kidnapped?" Hannah's tears are still flowing.

"Hannah, go back to the La Mesa Police, now! I'll meet you there right away. We won't leave until we get some action from them. I mean it!" Samuel states angrily. "Bring photos and any information, such as medical, describing his physical size and weight, to help. Meet you there!"

A half-hour later, Hannah and Samuel arrive at the front lobby doors of the La Mesa City Police Station. Samuel cannot believe how distraught his best friend's wife is. Obviously, she hasn't slept in days.

"Hannah, have you slept at all?" Samuel's worry is evident.

"Oh, Sammy, not much, no, catnaps mostly. I keep getting awakened by the imaginary ringing of phones, hoping they are Isaac, but they are only my imagination." Hannah cries.

"Better let me speak to them first, Hannah." Samuel wisely states.

As they walk in and wait in line at the counter, the impatience in Samuel's demeanor is obvious. He hands the counter-officer the business card that Hannah was given and says, "My best friend sitting over there..." he points over at Hannah sitting and crying, "has been here several times about her husband. Isaac has been missing since I saw him leave work on Wednesday. I believe the 72-hour wait has come and gone. This detective has not even replied to her phone calls. I would like to speak to his supervisor or your Captain, please?" Although it is Saturday, Samuel is wearing his business suit, and his appearance is that of a highly paid-attorney. He wants to give this impression.

"The detective on this business card is out of the office until..." the counter officer begins, then is interrupted by Samuel.

"This detective has had his chance! I asked to see his supervising officer or the Captain, please."

"One moment, please." He punches three digits into his console and speaks to someone. "Please have a seat. A duty officer will be up as soon as he is done with a meeting. It might take fifteen minutes or so if that is O.K.?"

"Thank you. We'll be right over there." Samuel points at Hannah and the seat next to her.

Fifteen minutes turn into thirty minutes, which turn into forty minutes. Samuel gets up once again to approach the counter when the door opens.

"Yes, sir, I'm Sergeant Rodriguez. I apologize for the wait. Please come on back." as the sergeant steps back and holds the door open for Hannah and Samuel. "Right this way, please." He then leads them into an office then closes the door. "Please have a seat. I can offer you water or coffee if you'd like."

"No, thank you." Samuel replies to both of them.

"Fine, what can I do to be of assistance?" asks the Sergeant.

"Thank you. My best friend, Isaac Stompski, has been missing since I saw him last Wednesday around two in the afternoon. His wife here, Hannah Stompski, is obviously at her wits' end. She has met with your detective in charge of Missing Persons and has left several messages but has not received any replies." Samuel motions to Hannah.

"I have c-c-called every h-h-hospital in San Diego every day since Wednesday. P-p-please, help me find my h-h-husband, S-s-sergeant!" Her tears are flowing freely again. She hands over her list of hospitals and Isaac's photos to the sergeant. The sergeant accepts Hannah's list and photos, takes a look at his description from his last doctor's physical, and says, "Let me check a few things while you're here. Excuse me for a couple of minutes. Are you sure you wouldn't like some water or coffee while you wait?"

"Not for me, thank you," Samuel says as Hannah shakes her head to say, "No." and the sergeant leaves the office.

"I just don't get it, Sammy. Why does it take a man to get men to do what is expected of them? I swear, I was treated like a child when I was here before. They spoke down to me as if I were an overly emotional...wreck! Oh, my God, Sammy, I am that emotional wreck, aren't I?" Hannah begins to cry again. Samuel takes Hannah into a hug to comfort his friend.

"Oh, Hannah, please don't cry. We won't leave here, I promise you that, until we find an answer or see some action towards that answer!" Samuel guarantees her. "I also want to share something with you...but right now may not be the time...but it is important. It's just that right now, we need to concentrate on Isaac."

Hannah stops crying and, looking at Samuel with love in her eyes, smiles and says, "I believe you, Sammy, I really do. As soon as I find an answer here, I swear, your important news will have OUR undivided attention. Can it wait?"

"Of course, Hannah. Isaac's disappearance is our priority now! There is nothing more imp..." Samuel begins, but the sergeant comes in through the door.

Sergeant Rodriguez walks around his desk, pulls his keyboard closer to himself, and says, "I think I may have found your husband, Mrs. Stompski. I'm afraid..."

"Oh, no!! Please, don't let him be dead!" Hannah screams.

"Oh, no, Miss. I'm sorry if I sounded like that was the case. No, Mrs. Stompski, he is, for the most part, not hurt...much."

"Is he in the hospital?" Hannah screams again.

"No. However, he is in serious trouble..." and then he turns the monitor to face Samuel and Hannah and asks, "Is this your husband, Isaac Stompski?"

"He looks like he's been run over by a bus! Why does he look so terrible, and where was this photo taken?" Samuel asks.

"I'm sorry to have to tell you this...Mr. Stompski has been arrested and has been in custody since Wednesday afternoon. His charges, I'm afraid, are very serious. He is being held without bail until his new arraignment date next week. He is being charged with the murder of another inmate while in custody. I'm sorry to have to tell you this." Offers the Sergeant.

Hannah faints in her chair at hearing the news about her husband.

Chapter 66:

High-power House 6, cell 211, is home to Triple-X Greg Forbes, who has been fighting a charge of assault with deadly force while protecting one of his pornographic film stars. Busty Bries, who seems to attract violent masochistic types, is a sweetheart who happens to love the feel of leather. Her clothing is suggestive of S&M, and she does love the feel of leather straps being dragged across her shaved labia and clitoris, but gently done.

Some men in the genre of fetish tend to get way too carried away. They go too far over the threshold of that infamous, thin line between lust and pain. As Busty Bries' manager, Triple-X must be her protector at all times, professionally as well as recreationally. Waiting outside her room for her pleasure to be satiated, he is well-versed in her screams of orgasm. The door to the room came flying off its hinges when those screams went beyond pleasure.

Triple-X's brass knuckles, custom-made with XXX raised in brass, leave imprints on flesh, marking their passage in black and blue, raised welts. However, these welts were never found or produced for court evidence. The video, which was in vivid 4K resolution, another Triple-X trademark, continued recording while the beating was taking place, unknown to Triple-X at the time.

Stomp gets further educated by his new cellmate, Triple-X, and gets the whole rundown on his many court hearings. After all, they had an entire seven days in lockdown due to the investigation of Mo's demise in 1-A.

"Don't let them scare you, Stomp, into a murder charge. The most that they can get out of you is a six-to-eight-year stretch in the pen for manslaughter when, in real terms, you did them a favor. Hell, you did San Diego a favor! That video they have is damning. It will look really bad in front of a jury. They slowed mine down, and you could actually see drops of blood fly across the air, coming off my fists." Greg was impressed by the quality of 4K resolution in slow motion.

"I was pushed from behind, Triple-X, and I got my legs tangled up in my bedding at my feet." insisted Stomp.

"Hell, Stomp, do you really think that any convict in here intended for his opponent to hit his head on the rim of a sink or toilet to cause death? Believe me, when you start swinging, there is no stopping it until your threat stops moving. Fight-or-flight is the name of Survival-101 and, in here, there is nowhere to fly to!" Greg is putting it out there real.

"But, Triple-X, I really didn't mean to..." Stomp begins. Then he is cut off.

"Stomp, this is what I believe, and you may not believe what I say because of my business empire in the pornography trade, but here it is. Our world is a world of good, but with the good, there is also evil. The child molester preys on the innocents of the world, children. Our God, at times, seems cruel, but He loves His children above all else. They are true innocents. Stomp, maybe you have been chosen by God; your purpose, your reason for being born..." Triple-X takes a moment to emphasize this.

"I hear what you're saying, like destiny? At my gym, there is a quote from Mark Twain on our Wall of Fame. It says, 'The two most important days in our lives are the day we are born, and the day we learn the reason why we were born!'" Like a lightning bolt, this strikes him.

"Exactly, Stomp! Now you're getting it! It very well could be the reason that you are here, not by happenstance but by His Will! It may not seem like it presently, but I am pretty sure if this is what it is, your work has only just begun." The conniving Triple X continues his pitch, "I say this because Satan has been very busy here on our earth; his playground and Good Soldiers are few and far between!"

Stomp nods his head, then seems to come out of a fog into a new clarity and says, "I can't believe I did not get this purpose until you slapped me in the face with this!

"Stomp, do not get me messed up now. My love for fast cars, faster women, and the fastest distribution of the best drugs hardly makes me a religious zealot. Especially the way I tend to exploit the female body, in many ways with my addiction to the flesh of women. The adult entertainment industry and its exploitation, I'm just offering you a P.O.V., an expression used in the flesh trade, or a different point of view, to consider." Admits Greg of his weaknesses.

"Just like...for instance...the reason I am in this cell with you, Triple-X, is for us to have this conversation as a message, allowing me to recognize my greater purpose. Now I get the message. It has sunk in deep. I need to get out a message. I need help...how can I call my home when I can't remember my phone number or my wife's?" Stomp pleads.

"That's right! You haven't even had access to a phone yet! Or a shower, my friend; not to be disrespectful, Stomp, but whew! On lockdown, it may still be a couple of days until we get access to a phone or a shower. Fortunately for you, Stomp, I have one of my 'stars' on the outside checking charges and researching addresses and phone numbers. Once we get to a phone, we'll take care of that for you as well." Triple-X says while crinkling his nose.

"I'd appreciate that, Triple-X, and all your advice as well." Says Stomp gratefully.

"No problem, 'wood, love.' We take care of our own in here. How about some 'wood, love' reciprocation, huh? Here's a bar of soap and a washcloth. Do you know what a birdbath is, Stomp?" Triple-X says in a nasal voice while pinching his nose shut.

"Yeah, we have one on our back patio in La Mesa." Stomp says, wondering.

"In here, a birdbath isn't for the birds of flight. In here, it's for jailbirds, Stomp! Now, for your cellmate, please, please strip it down and cleanse it. We live in far too little space, and until they bless us with control showers, be a good bird and take that bath!" Pleads Triple-X.

As Stomp strips down to washcloth his body, removing the caked-on soot and filth from booking and processing, he can't believe the density of black soot that covers his exposed flesh. All were well-orchestrated by the cops and bus diesel fumes. He scrubs until he is sure that a layer of tainted skin has been removed, along with the clingy stench. Stomp dries off, then turns around to hand back Triple-X's washcloth.

"Stomp, uh, go ahead and keep that! It's now yours. Uh, do you have a name for your friend there?" Triple-X starts his sales pitch. "I got it! Stomp, have you ever given a thought to having a career in pornography? Rip-Torn would be a perfect handle in the business! Stomp, I am serious here, 'wood.' I could make you a star!"

Triple-X is forever on the hustle.

# PART 4:
## "RJ Donovan"

# Chapter 68:

Stomp and Sampson have had all of the credit-card-theft charges thrown out immediately after Elyse, the bartender from Karl Strauss Brewery, came to court and cried her heart out to Isaac to please forgive her. She even told the judge that she was to blame for all of Isaac's charges and that she should be switched out instead of Isaac. Not a dry eye was to be found in that courtroom, and the presiding judge dismissed all of those charges from the record.

"Now..." Sampson informs Stomp," ...we get the same honorable Judge Donaldson to hear our case in his courtroom. He is aware of your being arrested due to a simple mistake by a bartender. I, too, never, ever look at my card when it's returned to me by a waiter at a bar or a restaurant. None of us do. Our problem is this, Isaac: the video depicting your grabbing Mr. Aziz, causing the both of you to fall down the concrete steps, ending, as we all know, in the death of Mr. Aziz. Understand that this is not the first accidental death in a prison or jail resulting from a fight or beat-down. Precedents are many. Here are some for example..." Sampson shows Stomp other cases with similar deaths-by-misfortune while incarcerated or imprisoned.

"So, Mr. Sampson, it makes no difference that, had I not been arrested and placed in jail, this would never have happened?" Stomp interjects.

"That would be called conjecture, Isaac. We are not fortune tellers. We cannot foretell destiny. We can only bring to the attention of jurors, if tried, and judges, if plead-out, prior precedents in similar cases; like the examples I have shown you there. Take this one, for example..." Sampson pulls out a case of an auto accident resulting in death, "...this gentleman worked hard and, for all intents and purposes, had never broken the law. He did, however, fail to properly maintain his vehicle properly, resulting in a brake failure. The district attorney was able to prove to the court that this man was driving a vehicle on the public roadways beyond the recommended service-record maintenance schedule. He hit a family in a crosswalk, and the mother died pushing her children to safety. He was not under the influence; he was not talking or texting on a cellphone, but it was proven that he was beyond being due for his vehicle manufacturer's brake service. He had no record, not even a traffic violation. He was given six years in prison for vehicular manslaughter. Just an accident, yes, but the family of the victim thought that he got off easy." Sampson, ever the realist, lays it out for Stomp. "That district attorney didn't have a video, as our does, which is going to be damning if shown to jurors or Aziz's family in the courtroom audience." Sampson finishes.

"Mr. Sampson, I am sure that you have a plan. I can see that you are a deliberate man in your craft. I have no idea or experience in any of these matters. I have 100% faith in your ability to apply whatever eloquence must be presented on my behalf. Work your magic, be tactful, and present your plan to Hannah and Sammy so that they aren't even a little bit surprised or shocked. If I have to do..." Stomp looks at some of the precedents of previous cases ranging from six to twenty-three years in prison," ...even ten years, I will only be forty-something, right? Hannah and I were just trying to conceive a child. We will still have time to do so, right?" Isaac is beginning to tear up for Hannah, not for himself.

"Yes, Mr. Stompski, I do have a plan in mind. Today, we may have Judge Donaldson's compassion for your demise as well. Trust me here, Isaac, we need to present a planned plea to solve this mess as soon as possible, within the week, to take advantage of that empathy. Hearing what you just told me about you and your wife's planned parenting, I might be able to include that as well. I will work through the night, filing a presentation and plea and, hopefully, talk it over with Donaldson before the District Attorney's Office can argue. Hopefully, by tomorrow night or the next day, we can meet again, and if you agree, I will explain it all to Hannah and your good friend, Samuel." Sampson begins shuffling papers back into his briefcase, then adds, "Don't worry, Isaac, this is my playground and my ball. If they want to play, it will be by my rules!" They shake hands and Sampson lets the courtroom deputy know that they are done, then leaves. Stomp waits for the courtroom deputy to chain him up for the reverse walk back across the bridge to await the transport bus going back to George Bailey Detention and House 6-A.

When Stomp gets back to the Thunder Dome high-power, it is well after dinner. They served the court bodies in the sully-port holding cells where the bus drops off its passengers. The upper tier has the dayroom, and the Wood Pile wants Stomp to fill them in on his day in court. All that he discusses with his buddies and Flaco is that all charges, except for the death of Aziz, have been dismissed and that the whole episode was an error on the part of the now-distraught Elyse, the bartender at Karl Strauss downtown. He apologizes to them all, especially Flaco, for not being able to discuss the Aziz charges with any of them, per his attorney. "Charges are still pending, so they can't be discussed. I apologize."

"No, Hermano, you are right to be careful, even in here where most of us are convicts. You are right, Mi Amigo. No apologies are necessary. Flaco grabs onto Stomp's shoulder, "Sampson is the best, Stomp. I have no doubt that he will work out the best possible solution for you and your wife; you will see!"

"I really am appreciative of all your help, Flaco, and of yours, Art, and of all the Wood Pile's. I have learned a lot through this experience, not all of it bad, either. Whatever happens next, I have made some good friends and comrades through all of you. In order to keep your friendship...however...I had better get in that shitter, then the shower. It's been a long day in holding cells! Triple, can I get a few minutes alone to use the shitter? Maybe grab me a razor if they do razor-call while I'm in the shower?" asks Stomp.

"No problem, Stomp. If they call razors, I'll get one up to you. We'll talk later, Cellmate. Go get your shower." agrees Triple.

Clang! The door to 211 pops open. Tinny-voice says, "Stompski, you have a professional visit in ten minutes. Get ready and wait at the gate."

"Wow, Stomp, that Sampson is good, really good. I've never seen an attorney work as hard on a case as yours is!"

"Yeah, this might be it. I think that he is coming to tell me their pitch for a plea bargain. Triple, what kind of deal can I expect?"

"The last in-house death caused by a fight here through mutual combat was accidental, and with a paid attorney, the deal was eight years, which was a great deal. I've seen anywhere from ten to fifteen years; however, eight years have set a precedent. I wouldn't expect Sampson to take any more than eight years; probably a strike they will want to give you." suggests Triple.

"Thanks. Gotta face the music now. At least Donaldson now knows that I am here through an innocent mistake by a bartender. Sampson wanted to strike a deal while the D.A. and Judge were sympathetic to my circumstances, which sounds like he did. We'll find out soon." Then Stomp goes out the door.

# Chapter 69:

In East County Court, attorneys De Santo and Mott are meeting with Judge Lazarus in his office. "Well, gentlemen, what have we come up with?" Lazarus wants his solution. "You first, Counselor Mott."

Terrence, wanting the harshest possible that justice can hand out, states, "Your honor, speaking for the representation of the victims, which, as you know, all law enforcement officers do, we must set an example of the highest and harshest possible. If we don't...then when will this stop? The citizens have got to be assured that our office will protect those who protect them. Whether the perpetrator is sane or otherwise, these crimes are capital crimes against children..." Mott is cut short by the Judge.

"Yes, yes, yes, I understand all of this, and I'm sure that even the defense can see our predicament here. My concern, actually all of our concern, should be to fully close any loopholes by following proper laws and policies. That is my job. What have you two brought to me? Please, let's get through this with as little lecturing, posturing, and legalese speeches as possible into areas with which I am already familiar and understand. Now, continue, please, Counselor Mott."

"We, Mr. De Santo and I have not yet come to an acceptable plea-bargain deal. Any plea bargain would have to include from the defendant the disclosure of the other victims' bodies and their locations, allowing full disclosure for the victims' families, but, as the polygraph shows, Mr. Sutter has no knowledge of any of these crimes, let alone having hidden any bodies. This case, as far as I know, is unprecedented. To get to any sort of solution, the District Attorney's Office and Mr. De Santo will agree on one thing: further psychological and psychiatric testing will need to be accomplished to get past this...uhm...gray matter in Mr. Sutter's head. A typical psyche evaluation is only ninety days to ensure competency. However, after speaking to the administration official at Patton Prison for the mentally unstable, I was told that a ninety-day evaluation would not be sufficient to come up with any answers to prove competency. Mr. Hodanovich suggested that they would need closer to a year to be positive in their findings. My office would accept that as a prelude to any further steps toward trial." Mott thought this to be a safe solution for all concerned.

Judge Lazarus, nodding his head in earnest approval, asks, "Counselor De Santo, you are up next. Please, do you concur with the District Attorney on this as a solution?"

De Santo, ever wary, states his conditions to them both, "I think that this would be fair to my client, as well as the victims...however...to be sure, in all fairness, I would request, please, a monthly report of progress and testing. If my client has any, and I mean any, problems concerning any of the methods used, we have the right to discontinue and come back to your office for another solution. Agreed?"

Judge Lazarus, still nodding, says, "I have no problem with such an order. Counselor Mott?"

"Agreed."

"Very well. Any further proceedings will be suspended for, say...a year and a half? R.J. Donovan Reception Yard takes months to trans-pack a housed convict to their appropriately ordered facility, and we want Patton to have their requested full-year. Agreed, gentlemen?"

"Agreed." says Mott.

"Agreed." says De Santo.

"Agreed." says Judge Lazarus. "Then let us schedule a hearing at my calendar's soonest opportunity, shall we? Please speak to my clerk on the scheduling, and one sure thing, gentlemen, it's been a pleasure coming to this solution with you. Good day, then." The meeting is over.

As the two attorneys walk from Judge Lazarus' chambers, they speak to his clerk to schedule a court date, stressing the

Judge's desire to schedule as soon as possible. Both attorneys consult their daily schedules and assistants at their respective offices. The Judge's court calendar shows an open date two months away and that date is agreed upon. With that done, the Judge grants a forthwith motion placing Mr. Sutter on the first available special transport to R.J. Donovan so as to expedite the process.

"It seems that Judge Lazarus is willing to prioritize this case as if he were cultivating a prized orchid in his greenhouse, a hobby of his." says his clerk, Judith Statham.

"This is a high-profile case, and I am positive that what happens here will be watched very carefully." says Mott.

That is another reason that Attorney De Santo wants his client to be evaluated for up to one year. This moratorium will buffer his client from the pressures of the community, as well as from the families of the victims. The gag order will still be in place, as well, until an outcome is reached. De Santo feels that he did a very good job for his client, being aware that his client has been set up for violence at least once already.

"Well, you two, if there is nothing else that we need to accomplish here together, I need to meet with my client downtown to inform him of his upcoming hearing and our decision to postpone the trial until he is evaluated. Have a great day." De Santo thinks to himself, "I know that we did."

# Chapter 70:

Stomp is taken upstairs to one of the four private (if such a thing exists while incarcerated) holding tanks reserved for professional visits. Herb Sampson is, once again, already seated and submerged in reading the many documents laid out on the stainless-steel counter at which he is sitting. He has a large Starbucks coffee with him, but it is untouched. He actually brought the coffee for his client, along with a cinnamon/raisin bagel with cream cheese and bacon, Isaac's favorite.

"Hello, Mr. Sampson. I wasn't expecting you back so soon. How are you?" says Stomp as the deputy cuffs him to the eye bolt mounted on the counter.

"I am well, Isaac, and so are Hannah and Samuel. I just had one of her delicious breakfasts as we waited for Samuel's arrival. She is still teary-eyed when we discuss your situation. Isaac, she has a deep love for you, and it is evident that all of your friends and family do. I also have grown fond of you and now consider you not just as a client but as a friend. I personally do believe that you did our society a great deed by ending Mr. Aziz's life. I read his file, and by criminal standards, it was a lengthy, habitual commission of child molestation, over a half-dozen instances of sexual assaults on minors, all under the age of twelve. He was being housed and monitored as a sexual predator of children. Within hours of his cutting off his monitor, he was found at a nearby elementary school parking lot in the East Lake area. No doubt he was looking for another victim to sedate his sick appetite, which is now forever quenched. I'm pretty sure that there is a place for his soul to satisfy his evil hunger. I, for one of many, give thanks for your bravery and courage, Isaac. It has been a privilege to represent you. I will be seeing you one more time after your move. I promised Samuel that I would represent you as his best man. He and Gabriella are getting married next

April on the 21st. After which, the four of us, Hannah, Samuel, Gabriella, and I, will visit with a video clip on my iPad to share with you." says Herb.

"You have been a good friend, Herb. I can't tell you how much we all appreciate your hard work and care. So, please, I am nervous and anxious to hear how long I will be apart from my Hannah."

"Judge Donaldson, in his empathy for you, has set new precedents, I am glad to tell you. Although his hands are tied when it comes to the charge of violence, you will be given a strike; however, upon successful parole, once discharged, the strike will be expunged. We agreed on six years, all time to be served here at R.J. Donovan on the 3-Yard, with conjugal visits four times a year, each visit lasting a weekend, extensions being available on holidays. You will still be able to consummate your family intention while there and with all of the Milestone credits in today's California Department of Corrections system, you could knock down the six years to four years by taking classes while there. How does that sound?"

"Really? I was prepared for eight years due to your precedent examples! How did you pull this off, Herb? Does this mean that I don't have court anymore? No more court transports or trials?"

"Well, we have one more appearance, really just a technicality, for you to accept your plea sentence. We've already agreed to a forthwith agreement, which means immediately. You'll probably be on the first available transport from court to R.J. Donovan."

"So, all the secrecy is over? I can talk to my cellmates and buddies where I'm housed? I can speak to Hannah on the phone about anything now. We are all good?" Stomp is astonished; relief is apparent in his excitement.

"Yes, to all of your questions. I gather that I don't have to ask if you are pleased with the deal. I can move forward to accept these conditions?" Sampson asks, back to being a professional.

"Hell, yes! Sign me up, Herb! Thank you, and I couldn't ask for a better, best man to represent me in any facet of life, whether at my friend's wedding or in court.

"Oh, Samuel told me to tell you that...after you are released...Gabriella and he will retake their wedding vows with you as their best man when they do." Herb is beaming with grins as he pushes the button to summon the housing deputy.

"Thank you, Herb, my friend!" a tear-filled Isaac embraces Herb after he is uncuffed, "And thanks for breakfast!" Then Stomp is led back to 6-A.

"A true hero to our city!" Stomp hears Herb say as he is led off, the deputy wholeheartedly agreeing.

The upper tier has a dayroom this morning since they had a dayroom last night. The whole crew is out and playing pinochle, four to a table. Chaz is doing laps with his cellmate, Bob Bitchin (also his best man when Bob got married), and as Stomp enters 6-A, the two are just coming up to the gate.

"Hey, Stomp, what's up, brother? What did your attorney have to say? Did he get jiggy with it?" was Bob's favorite expression.

"Yes, Bob, he did get jiggy with it. All that I have left now is a formal hearing for sentencing next week and no more court buses, only a chain-gang bus after that! I am so happy that it's over. I'll tell all of you about it; the secrecy has been lifted, finally!"

Chaz, always the one to call for a celebration, inside and outside the walls, says to Stomp, "Yeah, brother, what a difference a day makes, huh? Let's celebrate! Our batch is ready to drink now. We were just waiting for you!"

Those at the 'wood' table see the smiles in the group, and they are called over to hear the news, but first, Stomp has to go thank Flaco for the South Sider's part in retaining Sampson. Later, he will call Jesse with the good news. Stomp shares the good news among the four tables, thirty-two of his new friends, a camaraderie that he will never forget.

"So, four years with Milestones? That is fantastic news, Stomp, and you get to stay here with quarterly conjugal, with immediate sentencing? How many of us are waiting for the chain?" Art asks. Six 'woods' sitting among them are waiting for the next bus to Donovan. "Cool. We can keep our crew together a little while longer then. One...two...three...WOODS RULE!" The celebration has begun.

# Chapter 71:

Clang! Tinny-voice says, "Sutter, you have a professional visit in ten minutes. Get ready and go to the gate to get chained up!"

Mark rolls out of his solitary rack. He has the cell all to himself and a shower every three days. Time crawls by in isolation, it seems to him. Of course, Mark has no recollection of any wrongdoing at all, and he would know if Rettus had done those awful things, but Rettus also has no recollection of these awful charges. Mark woke up to find a note from Rettus on their little, steel writing desk; Rettus said, "I swear, Mark, I may have paranoia, but I am no child-killer. I am not crazy!"

Mark heads down to the gate where, once again, he is met by four, huge deputies to chain him up and lead him up the flight of stairs to have his professional visit with De Santo. His leg and belly chains remain on, and another set of cuffs is attached to the chain around his belly and to the eye-bolt mounted on the stainless-steel table. Attorney De Santo waits for the deputies to leave before he begins.

"Mr. Sutter, how have you been? Any more problems with other inmates that I need to know about?" asks De Santo.

"No, Mr. De Santo. I haven't spoken to anyone else since I last saw you. Rettus and I have been leaving notes for each other..." Mark begins.

"Rettus?"

"Oh, yes. Dr. Sullivan told me that while I was under hypnosis, he met Rettus, my split person, who takes over when I am threatened; my defense mechanism, it seems. Don't worry, Mr. De Santo, Rettus also claims that he wouldn't do such terrible things as are being charged."

Mr. De Santo is beginning to think that this year of psyche evaluation is most definitely a great idea now. He wonders if the County should pay him a double fee for representing the two of them. Hmmm, he's going to have to request this; it just might take that much more work in the long run. Gabriella's wedding is coming up in April and he will need the extra cash to give her the best that he can. Their daughter, Gabriella, is the love of his and his wife's life together.

"Well, Mark, the District Attorney the Judge, and I met twice last week and came up with a solution to satisfy all four of us, I believe. Rather than have specialists come into these facilities and conduct their tests under these harsh living conditions here, we decided that it would be best if left to a group of professionals in a setting where you are better accommodated, a setting where there are, as well, no threats to your wellbeing. Normally, a judge will order a ninety-day psyche evaluation to determine if a person is of sound mind to stand trial; however, in your case, your doctor, Dr. Sullivan, believes that this time needs to be extended. So does the lead psychologist at the facility to which the Judge is going to remand your custody. The California Department of Corrections has a hospital/prison named Patton. As your attorney, I think that after a year of testing by these professionals, it will be proven with no doubt that you do not know the crimes charged against you. At the same time, the year of being out of the sight of the media will calm things down for us to better defend you. Do you understand?" De Santo asks.

"Like some sort of crazy hospital, a place for the...uhm...criminally insane? Do you really think that I am insane, Mr. De Santo? Does Dr. Sullivan believe that I'm insane?"

"No one mentioned the word 'insane', Mr. Sutter. The term used was 'evaluated'. I've also requested that a monthly report of progress be recorded and sent to my office to be sure that your rights are being protected at each step. This may or may not include a physical visit by my office to determine your well-being as you are being evaluated. You will not go through this without my office by your side. You will, as well, have access to phone me regarding your progress. I, for one, feel that the environment there will be a more positive environment than here, with all of these chains and locks everywhere, weighing you down." De Santo says convincingly. As he looks around and at the chains on Mark.

"Well, Mr. De Santo, it doesn't sound like I have much of a choice in this matter, do I? So when do we start? How long until I get sent from this shit-hole to that better environment that you have colorfully painted for me?"

"Judge Lazarus will have a hearing in two months to make it formal, another month to catch the transport to R.J. Donovan in Otay Mesa, another two months there at the Reception yard. Once you are medically screened, you will be transported to Patton Hospital. The Judge will want you back in his courtroom in a year-and-a-half's time. It took much deliberating to convince the District Attorney to accept this before a trial could commence. Of course, he wanted it tried while it was still high-profile. What he really wants is a plea bargain from you with information leading to other victims who still have not been found. That is the only option but you proved that you have no knowledge of that. Is that still the case, Mark?" De Santo asks, hoping.

"I already told you that neither Rettus nor I would ever do any harm to a child. We are both dumbfounded by all of this." Mark reminds De Santo. "So with this evaluation, if they determine that I still do not know these acts, then what happens, Mr. De Santo?"

"Then we prove that you do not know the charges brought against you, and we will request that the charges be dismissed due to the mountains of documented truth. You will be a free man in a year and a half or a little longer once we file the motion. Sound good?" De Santo says with a smile. "In any case, Mark, we really have no choice in the matter. You will be evaluated before we can go any farther with proceedings. I am only here to inform you of the Judge's decision before your next court date. As I said, from this I will be able to defend you better. The District Attorney will then have to follow the guidelines handed down by your evaluation professionals in mental health and even the court will have to follow their reports to the letter." De Santo's eyes sparkle with a shine of victory.

"I apologize if I seem ungrateful to you, Mr. De Santo; I really mean it. I know that you have worked very hard to achieve this for me. I really do thank you. You have been my champion, and I want you to know that I recognize that. I will fully do what we have to do to get to the truth concerning these abductions. I know...from my heart...that I had nothing to do with any of it. I, too, do believe that this plan will prove that. At any rate, I know that this shit-hole is not the answer. Thank you."

"You are welcome, Mr. Sutter. If there are no more questions, we will proceed." Mr. De Santo summons the four deputies to escort Mr. Sutter back to his P.C. Housing.

# Chapter 72:

Due to his clout and true to his word, Sampson has a court date for Stomp two days later. The court transport from Otay Mesa to downtown is excruciatingly tiring, worse than for East County; the very worst is going to North County Vista courts. Those inmates who decide to take their charges to trial proceedings from George Bailey turn into zombies halfway into the first week of the process, a process that possibly could last from a few to many weeks of daily transport, leaving their housing unit at four in the morning and not returning until nine in the evening; only to do it all over again the next day and the next and the next, all week long, for weeks at a time. This will wear down a defendant who, 90% of the time, ends up taking a plea bargain to step off the train-wreck process; all of it is orchestrated so that the defendant simply can't stand anymore. "Where do I sign?" is the result.

Time and time again, one will read in the paper of someone being interrogated for many hours into days until that person eventually agrees to a confession just to stop the harassment. Coercion, torture, water-boarding, and court bus-transports for many hours day after day are all the same thing. The courts do this for a specific reason: the results prove that it works. It has been tested and perfected for decades, and it guarantees a plea-bargain result. That is not all. The violation of rights really kicks into effect when you agree to a plea bargain; a waiver of rights is a violation of rights. These rights are waived while a defendant is, for all intents and purposes, under duress. The defendant is exhausted from the process, and he doesn't really understand the process or the legalese language. Attorneys are there to explain the language, sure, but still, he is left with a gaping mouth, shaking his head, not understanding what was just said.

Stomp works in a law office, Levi and Levi: Tax and Probate. Still, he has no clue regarding the process that he has just undergone. Stomp is intelligent. He somewhat understands the language of legalese, and yet, he is left wondering what all that has happened to him means. Eighty percent of those fighting charges are poor, with very little resources and minimum education requirements. Most of the 80% have no clue as to the process. If they do, it is out of repeat offenses and many times through the process. Then, some have language barriers throughout the entire process.

San Diego is a border city with Mexico to the south. The courts are clogged with charges of 'drug mules.' Clint Eastwood's movie, "The Mule," depicts this crime. Smugglers bring vehicles across the U.S./Mexico border packed with kilos of drugs on a daily basis. The Border Patrol, maybe, catches one percent of the vehicles that cross with drugs hidden onboard, one out of every hundred, one thousand out of every hundred thousand that cross daily.

One thousand mules get arrested and charged with being 'blind mules' because, of course, they claim no knowledge of drugs being onboard the vehicles that they are driving. These drivers are mostly Pisa or Border Brothers. Some other races, such as White, Black, or Asian, also get desperate for the easy-money pay-out of several thousand to mule or transport illegal, controlled substances or even people across the U.S./Mexico border, paid for by the drug cartels in Mexico. Sixty percent of the population in San Diego County Detention is Hispanic. The other forty percent is Black, White, and Other. The same goes for the population at R.J. Donovan Prison.

Stomp's last court transport is a relief to Stomp. Sampson did exactly what he had promised he'd do. "Mr. Stompski, are you ready to accept the plea bargain that we spoke about?"

"Yes, Mr. Sampson, Herb. Please, call me Isaac. I consider you a friend, and so do my wife and family. Samuel is very happy that you've accepted his offer for you to stand in for me at his wedding in April. Thank you." Stomp says excitedly.

"It has been a pleasure to meet all of you. Judge Donaldson is more than willing to accommodate our plea deal. The D.A. hemmed-and-hawed a bit, but Donaldson made it clear that he will consider the D.A.'s recommendation but that the sentencing will fall on the Judge's shoulders." Sampson explained.

"Everyone stands. The Honorable Judge Donaldson is now presiding over Courtroom 31, sentencing court." the bailiff states. "Please, be seated and refrain from speaking unless addressed to do so."

"First on the calendar, Isaac Stompski. Herb Sampson is representing Mr. Stompski. Counselor?" says the court clerk.

"Present, and so is my client, sitting here next to me, Your Honor." answers Herb Sampson.

"Mr. Stompski, how are you today?" asks Donaldson.

"Fine, Your Honor. Thank you." says Stomp.

"Has your attorney, Mr. Sampson, explained your plea agreement to you prior to coming to my courtroom today?"

"Yes, Your Honor, he has, but I would appreciate hearing it from you to document it all in the transcript." answers Stomp, looking over at Sampson. Sampson simply nods his head as if to say, "Smart on your part, Isaac."

"Very well, Mr. Stompski, your charge is serious in nature: manslaughter resulting in the death of an inmate by the name of Mohammed Aziz. Although the video depicts the action as accidental, there are still charges filed by the people of this county. For that reason, I will hand down six years and a strike. The latter may be expunged in my courtroom after you have completed the requirements of your parole. At the same time, I state for the record that you will be housed here in San Diego in R.J. Donovan Prison for your entire term. I also state your eligibility for four conjugal visits per year, each lasting for 72 hours, starting forthwith, once permanently housed. I also state that you are eligible to earn Milestone credits to help reduce your sentence. Of course, all of that depends on your staying out of trouble while housed there for your term. Do you agree to these conditions that I have presented to you today?" states Donaldson.

"Yes, Your Honor. Thank you, sir." says Stomp.

"Counselor Sampson, have we covered all that was discussed by the three of us, you and the District Attorney and myself?"

"Yes, Your Honor. The only other request that hasn't yet been covered is for immediate sentencing and for my client to be on the next available transport to R.J. Donovan...uhm...for the record, sir." Sampson wants to make it clear.

"Yes, yes, very well, Counselor. Let the record show that I request immediate sentencing forthwith so that Mr. Stompski can get his term started. Will that be all, gentlemen?" asks Judge Donaldson.

"Yes, sir." says Sampson.

"Yes, sir." says Stomp.

"Good day, then, gentlemen. Good luck to you, Mr. Stompski. You are definitely due for some, in my eyes. Next on the calendar, Bailiff?"

"Mr. Tyler Arlington, Your Honor." the bailiff states.

Stomp nods to 'T' and mouths, "Good luck, Bro." as they switch places in the plexiglass booth. Before Stomp can hear 'T's sentencing, he is led out of the courtroom, shackled, and led back down the Hall of Shame and into one of the holding cells on the opposite side of the bridge.

# Chapter 73:

Tyler and Stomp are both waiting in the court sally-port, deep in the belly of the Beast, Downtown Central Jail. Although inmates say that the Thunder Dome is the most violent housing, this simply is not true. Central Jail is the worst of the detention centers and the first housing location of the Beast's process: five floors of four modular housing units, A-D. The D-units on each floor contain yellow-band inmates and the worst of the worst, black-band inmates who require isolation, called solitary confinement. The facility, although not as old as George Bailey, is far more disgusting and filthier. A poorly maintained environment can become very costly to bring back to a healthy standard. Inmates having to live in a poorly maintained housing unit can only become resentful and negative, breeding anger and hatred. This is known and orchestrated as such by the landlords of the Beast of Incarceration.

Health and safety, for which laws are created for enforcement, fall by the wayside of those paid to enforce these laws. It is no wonder that MRSA and other medicinally resistive virus infections are rampant here. Nurses are trained to label these infections as spider bites, blamed on the brown-recluse spider, which is not indigenous to the San Diego region, unless present as a hitch-hiker on goods transported from its normal region.

Homeless men oozing with Hepatitis-A virus due to unsanitary living spread it through proximity. Media scream bloody murder when refugees are depicted as being housed in inhumane cages in Border-cities in the south, while here in their own backyard, the scenario of citizens in the belly of the Beast is a day-to-day reality. The real crime is the Beast which, although fed millions of dollars each budget, cannot take proper care of those for whom it is paid to be responsible.

Program funding to be used to assist inmates all gets soaked up and misappropriated. Don't sit there, open-mouthed and shocked. This is a real, global problem and not just in incarceration. If you really believe that the relief efforts reach those for whom donations are collected, you are living in a fantasy world. Wake up and research your own facts, not by the internet, where facts can be manipulated for a desired result. Follow the money, the greed, the ruination of lives and families due to the cost of feeding the Beast that is never sated. This is the conversation today in these dingy, dark, and rank-holding cells among Stomp, 'T,' Chaz, and Spaz as they sit for hours in a sea of trash.

There are half-eaten bologna sandwiches, apple cores, all types of condiment packaging leaking into the concrete floor and bags of discarded lunch sacks being used as pillows by those awaiting their transport back to their detention housing. Tyler, Chaz, and Stomp were all sentenced forthwith and will not return to court and this filthy sallyport. Their next transport will occur very early in the morning for a short ride across the canyon below George Bailey Detention to R.J. Donovan Prison.

Chains can be heard in the corridor, along with clanging, key noises. This signals the presence of activity and the arrival of a San Diego County Sheriff bus transport. The last of that afternoon's court bodies gets jammed into the holding cell, now filled to twice its capacity, according to the signage above the door and Health and Safety Codes, making it impossible for the four from 6-A to continue their conversation. Those who continue to make conversation have to raise the decibel level to the point of shouting at one another. It seems that no one is listening, while everyone is shouting to be heard. The presence of the transportation deputies soon has everyone crammed up against the door, like caged animals expecting to be fed. This does little good, however, as no one crosses that narrow threshold without hearing their name called and giving the last four of their booking numbers. Stomp and those from 6-A were all called close to each other, so Stomp gets chained up with Chaz. In cell living, the only interaction with others is during an unlock period. Since 6-A has been in lockdown for half of the time that Stomp has been housed there, he hasn't had any in-depth conversations with Chaz. Stomp finds out on the bus transport that Chaz, who has been in the system on and off for many years, comes from an affluent family just like he does. This is very rare in the belly of the Beast, whose main diet consists of the poor and homeless, regurgitating them back onto the streets. Recidivism can be imagined as one opening up the underside of a man-eating shark and then releasing it. The shark will swim in circles, eating its own entrails.

Chaz explains to Stomp what keeps bringing him back time after time: one of the conditions of his parole is '5B: no alcohol'. "Stomp, I am a grown man; alcohol is legal. I am not here for any DUI, but my parole officer caught me pulling into my driveway after I had two beers at a friend's house, well under the .08 BAC level of intoxication, but the violation is still on my file. Every condition of parole or protection is there as a trap to bring you back." Chaz says. Those chained up around them all agree, "We are all grown men whom the system watches under its microscopic scrutiny!"

"Part of my deal is to get my strike removed once I complete my parole. Is parole that difficult?" asks Stomp.

"Probably not for you, Stomp. You are the one-percent exception here. You were actually innocent when brought here. You were charged with manslaughter that was truly accidental, not an act of premeditation, and yet, here you are, chained up to me and heading to prison on the same bus when we catch 'the chain.' Stomp, one has to imagine that you are either the most unlucky man that I have ever known or some Divine Order has you here for a purpose. Most of us on this bus are either addicts to illegal drugs, addicts to the game that comes along with selling those drugs, or addicts to the fast, large sums of money that illegal drugs can make. Most crimes are committed to support the drugs and lifestyle. Now, replace the word 'drugs' with a word like 'politics.' Politicians get caught up in their game to support their lifestyle. They take or misappropriate their campaign funds; however, you'll never see them chained up next to all of us. They get away with murder; Ted Kennedy, for example, with the same charge as yours, is worse, I think, because he left a woman to die in a car submerged in a canal when he could have saved her. Mr. Kennedy was so worried about his political career that he left her to die. He never even spent a day in jail.

"Yes, I remember that! They call that the Good Ol' Boys Club. Affluence and influence let him get away with murder. It's no surprise to me that members of that family died tragically, that is, except for the matriarch, who died from natural causes. Karma, brothers!" says Tyler.

Chaz shares a story, "My father, may he rest in peace, started with J.C. Penny years ago in merchandising. When he interviewed old man Penny, the two did so during a luncheon. My wise, old man received his meal, tasted it before seasoning it, then seasoned it with salt and pepper. Mr. Penny told him that he was hired on the spot! Mr. Penny told my father that he would never hire anyone who used table seasoning before tasting his meal, especially at an eatery or restaurant where one has never dined previously. He worked at J.C. Penny for his entire life and left my family lots of stock in the business." Chaz continues, "O.K., Stomp, it's your turn to share something with us. Let's have it."

Stomp thinks. He only has one thought, "I've only slept with one woman in my entire life, and I don't want to sleep with any other!"

Laughter comes from the entire bus now. Chaz says, "Come on, Stomp. We all know that you're hung like an elephant! Some of us thought that you worked with Triple-X on some of his projects. Wait a minute...you're serious...nah...you ARE serious?" as Chaz sees Stomp's expression. "You have only been with your wife? What about in high school? College?"

"Hannah and I have been in love since we were twelve years old, Chaz. Our families took vacations together most years. We've always known that one day, we would marry and continue the family lineage through our consummation. We planned to get Hannah pregnant this year well before this happened. Sampson, my attorney, worked into my deal to house me here with conjugal visits four times a year." Stomp says, hopefully.

Tyler turns around and asks, "Attorneys can do that in court?"

"Attorneys can request it. The judge can order it, but it is left to the state to grant it." Chaz answers. In most cases, the state will grant what the judge orders."

The bus takes the Pacific Coast Highway route due to bad traffic on the I-5 Interstate. As the transport passes under the I-5 overpass at Main Street, everyone can see that traffic is at a standstill. The bus goes to Downtown National City and heads south, then east on H-Street, right before Third Avenue. The bus then turns right into a tunnel.

"Where are we?" asks Stomp.

"This is South Bay Detention. We must be dropping off inmates here and picking up others after their court hearings today." says Chaz.

"Another jail?"

"Wait until we get to the Pen that, like most of the fifty-four others in Cali, is a virtual city!" says Chaz. "Each of its five yards is the size of Bailey!"

The transport bus pulls up to one of two huge gates, which has another bus sitting inside. The gate at the front of the other bus begins to open, and the other bus pulls forward, and the gate closes. Then, the gate in front of their bus begins to open. Once open, their bus pulls forward to the closed gate.

"Those of you housed here at South Bay Detention Center, please, stand. The man on the left will exit the bus first. The rest of you, stay seated and stay quiet!"

"Watch what everyone does as they walk by the P.C. cages, Stomp." Chaz whispers. "The transport deputies are both outside intentionally, Stomp."

Just about every blue-band mainliner walks past the P.C. yellow-banders and spits into their enclosed cages, calling out names like rat, snitch, dropout, cho-mo, bitch, or punk. Only about a half-dozen inmates step off the bus, but the ruckus gets everyone laughing and hollering. Four others are brought onto the bus with the same verbal and salivary exchanges. Once the deputies board the bus, everyone settles down except for the deputies, who are chuckling over the exchange. The rest of the trip is uneventful up to the point where the transport bus crosses the intersection of 442 Alta Road and the entrance to R.J. Donovan Prison. From the rear of the bus, looking forward, one can tell who was sentenced to the chain. Those catching it turn their heads to the left and gaze at the mini-city as they pass by.

"There, Stomp..." Chaz says quietly, "...is our new address."

# Chapter 74:

The chain-gang wake-up call comes to High-Power on Tuesday mornings at 2:00 am. Usually, those expecting to hear their names called have been preparing all month, accumulating stamped envelopes. Having a postal money order or two sent in a letter and put on your property list ensures a fish draw for the canteen at the soonest possible time. Envelopes are currency on the 4-yard, which is the reception yard. Cans of Bugler Tobacco were once sold at the canteen for $11.00; a bag of cheaper 4-Aces went for $4.50. Tobacco is no longer sold there; however, it is still available through correction officers who smuggle it in and sell it for $300.00 a can. Those who smoke cigarettes are more than willing to pay six stamped envelopes, or three dollars, for a very slim cigarette, mostly rolled in paper wrapped around toilet paper tissue, called mil-tex, barely any wider than a #2 pencil lead, never the size of a factory-rolled cigarette.

Since tobacco is no longer for sale, neither are cigarette lighters. All the cells in prison have light switches and a receptacle to use for acceptable devices, purchasable in the canteen. Water-stingers, used to heat a cup of water for coffee or Top Ramen soup, are sold in the canteen. A salt-water lighter is fabricated using a plastic cup, two paperclip leads submerged into the salty water, and a pencil lead or a spring from a pen's plunger. When the leads are inserted into an electrical receptacle, the pencil lead or pen spring will glow red, and a wick can be started.

A wick is a length of toilet paper several feet long, twisted tightly as a rope. Once lit, constant airflow keeps it lit, similar to starting a fire by placing paper or kindling on hot coals and blowing on the hot embers to catch the kindling on fire. Wicks are dropped into the return-air vent with a few inches protruding and glowing red. Similar to a fuse, the wick will slowly be consumed. Since the air is drawn over the wick and out of the cell, there is no smoke. Wicks, once started, can be passed around to others. Simply ask the building porter to get one to you at his convenience. It's always wise to take care of a porter when purchasing canteen or cigarettes; offer him something to continue receiving his favors. A jar of coffee can guarantee a slot at fish-draw canteen sales. A jar of coffee is also used as a form of currency.

All of this information is expressed to Stomp as his next level of education begins. Stomp has two $200.00 postal money orders, sent in letters and placed on his list of small, personal property. These will be put directly into his account, while any money in his account at George Bailey will take six weeks to show up. Although Stomp doesn't smoke, he purchased sixty envelopes since he was told that the reception yard has no phones and it takes nearly four months to get classified there. Hannah made Stomp promise to write to her every other day. Triple-X suggested that he purchase a deck of cards and place one card in each of the envelopes. Four months of cell-living, with one hour in the yard every three days, requires cards to help pass the time.

During the last dayroom, Art took a chain roll call to determine who was awaiting the call that morning. Stomp, Triple, Chaz, 'T,' Chris Beckman, Cake, Sickness, Bob Bitchin, Thumper, and Art himself are all expecting to go for the Wood Pile.

"We got ten solid hardwoods going together on the Chain Wood Pile! We all stick together as long as we can, ten deep walking the yard. We know that Stomp will go to the 3-yard permanently, while most of us will go there and the 2-yard temporarily. Chaz has done the 5-yard twice already, and there's a really good chance that he'll go there again. While housed in the Reception Yard, workouts are mandatory and also sound off. No matter what...we have each other's backs. Everyone has his paperwork to bring. Right?" Everyone nods. "I am proud of all of you. Love and respect. Wood Pile, one-two-three...WOOD PILE!"

"WOOD PILE!" everyone yells in unison.

Sleep has been difficult for both Stomp and Triple-X as Stomp's education continues. Both are still awake when a voice, barely perceptible and tinny, says, "Stompski, Forbes, roll up your property and head to the gate!" The call that they were waiting for all week long has finally come. Their cell door opens with a loud "clang," along with a dozen others in 6-A. Twenty-eight out of two hundred housed in 6-A are catching the chain this early morning, almost enough to fill an entire bus. All ten of the 'woods,' hoping to go, got the call. All the men are down at the tables and talking about the next step in their journey.

"Stomp. Hey, Stomp, it's Flaco up here, Amigo!" Stomp sees Flaco at his window. "Venga aca, por favor!" he calls Stomp to come up.

Stomp is happy to see that Flaco is awake and that he gets to thank him for everything that he has done for him. "Flaco, I'll never forget your friendship, not ever, my friend." He continues, "I am glad that you're awake to allow me to thank you."

"Gracias a ti, Stomp! Do not worry, ever, Stomp. We have your back everywhere you go. Never forget that. Capone has you set up already with all you need at Donovan. I have your hook-up and we'll see each other again, I promise you! Vaya con Dios, mi Compadre! Mucho gusto! Are you ready to do God's work, Stomp?" Flaco asks.

"Siempre con Dios!" Stomp's Spanish has improved.

Clang! The gate begins to open. "Thanks again, Stomp. Get going now. You are blessed to be going with ten of your most righteous. We got you, Stomp!" Flaco says again.

Stomp heads to the stairs and down just as the deputy begins calling names. The inmates' bedrolls, mattresses, and brown paper bags are no longer County property; they are now the property of the State of California. Any letters of correspondence from loved ones or friends will be returned with a red stamp reading 'Released from Custody.' This confuses the families, leaving them wondering, "If released, why are they not home?"

Names are called one by one, "Stompski, last four?"

"Stompski, five-nine-two-one."

"Toss your bedroll and mattress there. Grab your property bag and stand behind the last man in the corridor." After the deputy calls the last man, "All right, follow around to the right and stop at the next gate!" The twenty-eight are met by others from House-4 and House-5, a line of about sixty now; all led around to three holding cells. Each man is handed a hot breakfast on a tray, a brown paper bag containing milk, bread, and a spoon. Not too long after that, two buses arrive with the words California Department of Corrections on their sides instead of the words San Diego County Sheriff being there.

The men are chained up, just like for court, except that the CDC uses ankle chains for transport as well. The bus interior has two P.C. cages with an added cage at the rear, where a Corrections officer sits with a shotgun in both hands.

"Sit and stay quiet, and we will have no problems. Any talking and you will be placed upside down into one of the cages until we get there!" a no-nonsense demeanor, obvious and serious. Stomp is shackled to Art for the short trip across the canyon.

They exit the gate at George Bailey, drive around the helipad, and then start down the canyon, leaving the second transport behind to load up the second set of thirty. Sixty men a week are transported; distribution of goods translated into flesh and freedom and torn-apart families. Seventy percent of the releases are returned to custody, again and again. The Beast is insatiable. The greed, the gluttony, and the lack of compassion towards those being harvested into Beast-feed are comparable to the treatment of cattle being herded to market. It is not about rehabilitation or being held responsible for one's actions. This is simply about big business and greed.

The bus is allowed into the mini-city walls of double-fenced, razor-wire topped, electrified fencing after being scrutinized with mirrors along the undercarriage as if someone would try to smuggle themselves 'into' the prison. The bus pulls through and into the center of the city behind a building stating R&R, "Reception and Release."

"Line up on the wall! When the chains come off, step up to the wall and do not turn around! Do not talk. Do not make a sound and no questions!" the Corrections officer commands. He is one out of the fifteen male and female Corrections officers at the facility. A prison worker wheels out a large, blue bin. Another rolls out a rack of orange jumpsuits, T-shirts, boxers, socks, and flip-flops. The workers are all wearing denim pants, blue button-collar shirts, brown boots, and denim jackets. The sun still has not risen, and the morning fog gives the ambiance a creepy, haunted feel.

The chains all come off. Stomp already knows what will happen next. "Everyone, take one step back, remove all of the County clothing, all of it, dropping it behind you, then step back up to the wall! Do it now!" The thirty men do as instructed, then step back up to the wall. The two prison workers roll the large, blue bin behind them and collect all of the County-owned laundry. They bag it all up and store it in the underbelly of the bus to be returned back to George Bailey in two days. Once the clothing is collected and stored, the fifteen Corrections officers spread out behind the naked men, two men to one Corrections officer, with their batons out, slapping their palms in unison. The air is damp and cold. The ground is asphalt and painful to the soles of their feet. Some attempt to clear the small rocks from under their foot pads. The wait is intentional to humiliate and cause discomfort.

"Gentlemen, welcome to R.J. Donovan State Penitentiary. You are currently behind in the Reception and Release processing area. Unfortunately for all of you, you are not being released today." These words are all spoken slowly and loudly to make the men wait nakedly in the cold. "Your property will be searched. Your personal items and clothing will either be shipped to an address that you will provide or will be donated. While in processing, you will remain quiet as we work. Names will be called out once and only once, so you will need to pay close attention. You are fortunate to be the first bus load to be processed, as you will be the first to receive your new housing units. Quiet is the key to getting this done quickly. Only answer questions asked and ask no questions."

"Once processed here, you will be walked to the 4-yard for classification. Until classified and housed appropriately, you will be housed with all levels of convicts, from white-collar crime to murder. We no longer use a chow hall for feeding on the 4-yard since we've had too many fights and riots while walking to the chow hall and within the hall itself. You will receive a shower every third day and be in the yard for one hour every third day. Meals will be brought to you in the morning: a cold breakfast and a sack lunch. A cold dinner will follow later. Hygiene will be given at the building podium if you require soap or toothpowder. Indigent envelopes will be provided until you receive your first draw in the canteen. The canteen is once a month unless you have immediate money in your account, for which we will allow a fish draw one time. Draws for canteen are one through four, designated by the last two digits of the CDC number on the I.D. issued to you." All of this information is available, as well, in the Title 15 book everyone gets or by asking for it from the building porter. It is given now to stall and freeze the men standing naked.

"Now, we will do this in pairs, gentlemen. The CO behind you will walk you into the building. Your photo will be taken to create your I.D., and then you will enter your holding cell and listen for your name to be called. When called, step up to the counter to the officer requesting your presence and proceed to the next holding cell. If you stay quiet, we can accomplish this quickly. If you get loud or ask questions, we will lock the holding cells until it is quiet and then resume. Now, first, two men, take one step back, bend at the waist, cough twice, turn around, open your mouth, bend forward, shake out your head, squat and lift your package to your belly button, turn to your right, accept the boxers and T-shirt, put them on, step up to the camera, wait for the flash, turn right again and walk into the open cell. When I say, 'Next two,' they will follow suit. Now, first two men!”

“Next two!”

“Next two!”

“Next two!”

“Next two!”

Stomp steps back and bends over to spread his legs, and he hears, “Stop right there!” a female voice. He turns around to see who said to stop. “Do not turn to face me! Stay bent over. What the fuck is...” the female CO taps Stomp's penis with her baton, thump, thump, thump and says, “...is that thing real?” thump, thump, “What the hell do you feed that thing?” she asks. “O.K., turn around!”

Stomp turns around and sees the female CO, who resembles the character, Elvira, in a skin-tight uniform, apparent cleft resembling a camel toe, and a button-popping shirt with huge cleavage. Stomp's dry mouth opens as Stomp tries to control the drool spewing from his open mouth, and then, she just gives a sexy wink.

# Chapter 75:

Stomp and Chris Beckman are in 'Elvira's group of two. She had positioned herself at the door to R&R before instructing the two, "All right, you two, turn to your right and walk towards the two workers." her eyes never leaving Stomp's manhood, her head swaying in sync with the pendulum-swing of Stomp's penis, his size having the black men feeling inferior. The two workers can't believe the way the head of his penis protrudes from the hem of the plain, white boxer underwear that the State has provided. 'Elvira' offers, "I can tie a knot in a cherry stem with my tongue. I bet I could do the same with that!"

"All right, gentlemen, fun is over. Let's move along. Next two! But that was a hard act to follow!"

Chris walks into the photo booth. He is CDC #P-41877. Stomp is next with CDC #P-41878. These numbers, just like the ones for Social Security and a driver's license, are numbers that one never, ever forgets. After the photo, they join the men before them, going into a cold, concrete holding cell with one toilet. Art and Bob Bitchin are at the front, and Stomp joins them, as does Chris. No names have been called yet. The counter COs are waiting for the laminated IDs to arrive so that they can start the processing.

This is Art's and Bob's first rodeo here at Donovan. Keeping the conversation at a whisper, Bob says, "Stomp, what do you think of 'camel toe'? Don't be surprised if she stalks you at first. She will put you in situations and tempt you, and she has seduced many. Hell, I got jiggy with it!" The four laugh.

Art adds, "Well, I suppose I didn't...uhm...stand out..." more laughter, "...as you two did! I was never approached, but it does happen, and not just by female COs either. Stomp, about a decade ago, one of the homosexuals on the 3-Yard was forced to blow a CO at his workplace. The man spits the CO's sperm into a cloth, saving the DNA of the CO. A couple of weeks later, a friend of his was paroled and took the sample still on the cloth, straight to the victim's attorney, who picked him up at the gate waiting for it. Well, the shit hit the fan when the CO was forced to give up a DNA sample, which of course matched. It turned out that the man had complained about the sexual abuse and harassment, but no one took him seriously. Well, they do now!"

"Dietrick, counter!" the first name is called. Art goes out the cell door and steps up to the counter. The cell gets quiet as more men enter from the alley where the bus is unloaded. A second bus can now be heard pulling into the alley, with another thirty mento process. Names continue to be called, and Stomp hears his name called.

"Mr. Stompski, counter!" Stomp steps up to the CO at the counter. "Mr. Stompski, here is your A2-B I.D. card. Once you are permanently housed and obtain a job within the facility, you will receive a new A1-A I.D. card. You have two $200.00 postal money orders on your incoming property. Please, sign the back of them both so we may add the funds to your account."

Experienced parolees, after release, purchase $200.00 postal money orders and keep them in their wallets. This is done because discharging the parole number is not done easily. A person can be sent back on violations as petty as not following suggestions from your parole officer or not gaining full-time employment and many other violations. Most are sent back due to dirty tests, most likely dirty as they left, as drugs are accessible within the walls. Some are sent back due to arguing with their significant others over infidelity while they are absent. Then there are those who are institutionalized; they cannot function on the streets, cannot find a job, or cannot support themselves; committing crimes is all that they know. Living within the walls becomes all that they know as well. Being housed and fed and surrounded by all their 'homies' is comfortable for them.

"Mr. Stompski, do you have any tattoos on your body anywhere?"

"No, sir."

"Are you claiming White or Caucasian ethnicity?"

"Yes, sir."

"Do you have any enemies here? Any reason why you can't be housed on Mainline?"

"No, sir."

"All right, your clothing and personal property...do you want to provide us with an address to mail them to...or do you wish to donate them?"

Stomp was warned about providing an address that would be documented on file. Samuel had suggested that he use his address instead. "Yes, sir. Please send them to 6041 Lee Avenue, La Mesa, California 92064." The items are boxed, and the label is affixed.

"The postage will be deducted from your account, once sent. Before we do, let's go through your property items." The CO allows the envelopes, the Bible, two writing tablets, and a dozen pencils. "We can't allow the hygiene products purchased in County, as they aren't in transparent packaging. Donate or place in the box?"

"Donate, please." Stomp wants no items from jail sent home. All allowed items are placed in a brown paper bag and given to Stomp.

"All right, Mr. Stompski, we are done here. Walk over to the R&R worker there and receive your carrot-suit. Good luck to you."

"Thank you." The R&R worker cracks up as Stomp walks up to him with the head of his penis hanging out of his boxers. Stomp slips on his elastic-waistband pants and slip-over shirt, both orange; hence, the nickname, carrot-suit.

"Mr. Uhlman, counter!" Bob steps up to the counter. "Bob, back again, I see. The usual?"

"CO Muldonato, yes, sir. Donate all except the allowable. How's the family?"

"A lot safer now that you are locked up again." They both laugh. "Tattoos? Yeah, got it here, except for the dragon on your back that looks like an alligator-lizard, and your body still has to grow to fit with that big-ass head of yours." More laughter.

"Yeah, oh yeah, ask your Missus about my big head! It's because of her that my body got so shriveled up while I was out there!" More laughter.

"Yeah, Bob, she'd love to get to know your friend, Stompski, there. You see the size of his chorizo, there?"

"Yeah, Muldonato, I can see you salivating for some of that breakfast sausage!"

More laughter.

"All right, Bob, you know the routine. Stay out of the way of trouble and get released on your date, for once!"

"Yeah, right. Like that will happen!" Then Bob goes for his carrot-suit and enters the cell.

The first thirty get processed and are all in the second holding cell when they hear the exact same welcoming speech out back for the second busload. It is just starting to turn to dawn, and the new day has just begun in prison.

# Chapter 76:

Stomp and the other twenty-nine from the first bus are led out of R&R. Bob is walking with Stomp and points to their left, "That far yard is the 3-Yard. That one there is the 2-Yard...," he points to the right, "...straight down there are the Parole Hearing Board offices and Visiting. To the right of that are the caged-in cottages for conjugal visits over the weekends." Bob points to the right of that and says, "That is the 5-yard, low-level, and two-level housing. Killers with a gate pass, less than twenty-four months, and zero points, are bussed to the trolley maintenance yard and put to work cleaning and washing the trolleys. They also have the Rock Mountain Rock Crew, which is outside the grounds. You will probably go to the 3-Yard after the classification process. Where we are going now is Building 16, the most disgusting and shot-out housing at Donovan. The 3-Yard is called the lifer-yard. The cells there are dialed in because those housed there have the grip of time."

The group steps up to the large gate, large enough to drive a bus through. The yard is empty at present, as the sun is just peaking up over Otay Mountain to the east. All thirty are Marked through the gate and down the length of the yard on the track, which runs around the yard. Building 16 is next to the trailers on the east end of the track used for medical screening and classification processes. First-timers have to take an education-level screening to establish if they qualify for HSET (high school equivalency testing) classes. All thirty are instructed to sit at the six rows of benches where a hygiene kit, two stamped envelopes, and a Title-15 book are set out for each.

The Title-15 book has all the rules and regulations, rights, appeals, procedures and the processes to accomplish all of these. The book states how to properly file a grievance (602) and how to appeal a discipline of serious nature (115) or of a minor nature (128). Convicts (prisoners of prison), not to be confused with inmates (prisoners of jail), separate once men step out of George Bailey and into R.J. Donovan. The Title-15 book is all in legalese language, so all have access to a law library with a worker to help along with any process. Again, it is always best to hook-up, tip or show appreciation by sharing a gift with anyone who assists you in any capacity. Take care of those who take care of you, especially if further assistance is needed later down the line. Respect and appreciation should be given; they cannot be taken or demanded. Bob explains all of this to Stomp.

"Plan on being locked up on this yard for sixteen weeks, Stomp; not in this building but in 17-19. Building 20 is for the he-shes and the semi-crazies. The 1-Yard is for the medicated psyche inmates, called Hot Meds. This is orientation here and we'll be here for the first week until we clear medical, classification and S.A.T. testing. The judge ordered for your housing to remain here, as your time may be shorter. Chaz and I have been to the 5-Yard before, so we may go there if there is available housing. If not, they could temp-house us on the 3-yard until they trans-pack us somewhere. No matter where you go to Stomp, you will be taken care of. Just like Flaco did for you in Bailey, someone will do for you here. You have friends in high places, while I have high friends in places." Bob cracks up at this tidbit of wit.

"I can't imagine the problems that I would have had if I didn't have all of you as friends. Really, Bob, I am very grateful to all of you. I look around here, and it is very obvious who the nervous ones are; the ones who are new to this, trying to appear brave, but fear is just beneath the skin." notices Stomp. "I know that I am here among friends. I consider all of you as my friends and I mean that, Bob."

"Good to know that, Stomp. I know that you mean it, too. Thank you, my friend."

Orientation begins, and, almost verbatim, the book is explained just as Bob explained it to Stomp. The entire process is explained just as he explained it. Those who have been here many times don't need their Title-15 books, and Bob asks for them from those who don't want them.

"Why do you want all those, Bob?" Stomp is curious.

"It takes four books to make a deck of playing cards. I brought dice, six of them, but no cards."

"Dice? How did you get dice through the R&R counter?"

"I hooped them before we left Bailey, Stomp, inside some latex gloves. I do it every time I come here. That's a lot better than making them, and I can sell them to the brothers for fifty dollars a pair. I can make $150.00 from them!"

It has been a long day and it's just about breakfast time as the bunk assignments are given out.

"Uhlman, you are in 108, bunked with Stompski. Take your property into it and secure your door!" the CO orders.

"Brauel, you are with Dietrick in 109. Take your property into it and secure your door!"

"Beckman, you are with Forbes in 110. Take your property into it and secure your door!"

Once all thirty are housed in their cells, the next thirty are set up with books and hygiene kits and then brought in from the yard for orientation. Before orientation, the kitchen workers roll in the breakfast carts and lunch sacks. The CO tells the kitchen workers to set up but to wait until all are housed before serving the meals. While the CO begins his speech, the dorm porter goes around to the new cells.

"Welcome, 'woods'. Bob Bitchin, what's up, homeboy? Who came here with you?" Matt Dixon asks.

"Hey, Matt. Hell, you know, same ol', same ol'! Art's here, Chaz's here, Chris is here, Thumper's here, Forbes is here, Sickness, too, and this here is Stomp. Stomp, meet another legend, Matt Dixon!"

"Stomp, already heard about you, homeboy! Been told to hook you up on everything and pass the word to each unit. Your deeds precede you; our respect to you, homeboy. If you need anything, and I mean ANYTHING, just holler at me. All right, Stomp?"

"Thanks, Matt."

"We got you. Gotta go check in with Art and the rest. I will get you hooked up, no worries!" and Matt goes down to 109.

"Stomp, the first thing we do in here is don't touch anything until Matt brings us some bleach and towels. I, for one, need to scrub this disgusting cell before anything is done. Matt knows. He'll hook it up for all of us." says Bob as he inspects the thick cotton mats for stains and odors. "These aren't too bad, seen worse."

As if on cue, the door to 108 rolls open, and Matt is there, hugging Bob and greeting them both. Bob says to Matt, "Bro, this is Stomp, a righteous 'wood' with mad chuck'em skills. I'm pretty sure that his reputation has preceded him?"

"Yes, it did, Stomp. It is an honor to have you with us! I hear that the South Siders look up to you for mentoring the USA's next boxing gold medalist. Jumpin' Jesse, Capone's son from Logan? So you know, Stomp, I got you a spot at the first canteen fish draw. I will walk you over there myself and handle it all for you. This here..." Matt drops off a bag of canteen items and hygiene, "...is from all of us to you and Bob. The South Siders' car also has something for you but the 'rep' 'Papa' wants to meet you and send his respects. Bob, here's the bleach and water spray bottle and two anti-bacterial Fabreze cans for your mattresses. Take those with you after your medical and classification screenings. I got you both spots in Building 18 together. Sound good?" asks Matt.

"Hell, yeah, Matt. You're always taking care of the Pile, I mean always!" Bob hails on Matt.

"Gotta go, Stomp, a pleasure and respect."

"Same to you, and thanks, Matt, for everything." says the ever-grateful Stomp.

"No worries, I got you both. Off to take care of our other homies!" says Matt.

"Time to disinfect our new pad! Otherwise... my skin crawls just thinking of all those micro-critters getting jiggy with it on my flesh!" says Bob. "First, we spray with the bleach and water. Bleach kills everything, a sanitizer. Let it sit for a minute, then wipe it down. We'll let the toilet sit for a lot longer. I can't get over how stainless steel stains in here! Science experiment shit! The last things we do are; spray our mattresses, let them dry, then tie our sheets, spray again, let dry, place blankets, spray again, let dry...you get the routine, Stomp? Before we start, the CO will be coming by to give us our trays for breakfast. Stash these chemicals under our shit before he sees them." As Bob says this, the door rolls open again.

"108, come out and get your trays and lunch, then lock down. When the door opens again, slide out your trays, but keep your cups and sporks. They are yours until you leave!"

Bob and Stomp step out to receive the meals and cups, then return to their cell. Bob says, "I don't eat until this place is disinfected. The food is cold, anyway. What do you say, Stomp? Shall we get jiggy with it? I'd feel better!"

"Let's do this!" says Stomp.

# Chapter 77:

Everyone's been up, well, since the night before last, actually, and after disinfecting the cell, Bob and Stomp take their time eating their cold-ass breakfasts: coffee cake and oatmeal. Stomp has a jar of Folger's in the care package that Matt dropped off. The sack lunches went up on the shelf.

"I don't know about you, Stomp, but today, all I'm doing is 123 burpees for a workout. I am exhausted!" says Bob.

"Sounds good to me. I want to write to Hannah and Sammy. Not being able to call, she made me promise to write daily and mail one out every other day!"

"I don't have that much to say for that much writing!" admits Bob.

"Well, I do. Now that I'm sentenced, I can say whatever I want without worrying about anyone using it against me in court!" says Stomp. "It all happened so fast, from being arrested to now. It all went sideways so quickly!"

"Amen to that, Stomp! We all share that. We all can relate to that part there. The best part in your situation is, and be thankful for it, that your neck isn't the one that snapped, or Hannah would not be able to see you, hold you, or start a family with you. Do not feel sorry for that creep who died, either, Stomp. He would have passed on his sickness or even victimized other children before the same result. Do not ever feel sorry for his demise!" clarifies Bob. "Be sure to say hello to me. Now, get to writing."

Bob gets his 123 burpees done, and Stomp is about to start his when the door rolls open again. Bob places the trays and trash outside for Matt to collect for the kitchen. Matt brings in another bag of canteen from 'Papa' and the South Siders.

"Man, Stomp, did Triple-X and you get the same love in 6-A as we get here?" Bob pulls out a spiral device with a cord attached to it. "You know what this is, Stomp?"

"It can't be what I am guessing it to be, with no women to please here!" They both laugh. Bob gives a sideways glance at Stomp and shakes his head.

"I don't even want to know what that is, Stomp. No, no, stop right there. Do not explain that! Anyway, this is what we call a stinger. Here's the thing with this. We use it to heat up water. Never plug it in unless it is submerged in water. Always unplug it after the water gets hot and let it sit for a minute to allow the element to cool before removing it from the water. The end result, Stomp... is now we get a hot cup of coffee in the morning!"

Stomp pulls a note from the bag from Papa. It reads:

"Respecto, Stomp! Anytime I get notified by my big homie to take someone under my wing, I take that seriously. I do take your protection seriously, Stomp, and if you need ANYTHING, please come to me first so I can honor my word. At first yard, please, allow me an introduction. Papa – 212."

"Stomp, now you should show your respect and appreciation to 'Papa' and the South Siders' car with a sound-off. Like this...'This is Stomp for the Wood Pile in 108, sounding off. Respect and appreciation to Papa in 212 and all the South Siders. GRACIAS!' Then you will hear the South Siders return with an... 'A ti!'." says Bob.

"Yell it through the gap in the door as loud as you can."

Stomp does exactly that and is amazed at the thunderous response. Then he surprises Bob by sounding off a thank-you to the Wood Pile in the same manner and to an even louder "THANK YOU."

"We really do love you, homeboy!" says Bob. Then he sounds off, "This is Bob Bitchin in 108 for the Wood Pile. Finished my mandatory workout. Thank you!"

"THANK YOU!" another thunderous reply.

"Now that's what I'm talking about, Stomp! That is the Wood-Pile unity I love! Now I am gonna take a nap until dinner. Sound off after your burpees, just like I did, every day!" teaches Bob.

Stomp does so; then he lies down to read his Bible, the only book that they allow through R&R. He is enjoying the New Testament and Philippians, the first chapter, about Paul in prison, and he dozes off.

Unlike George Bailey with its opaque windows which allow light to come in but with no visual view, Donovan has clear windows, three feet tall and six inches wide, that you can see through. The day turns from daylight to dusk before the door opens for delivery of dinner. Again, the meals are cold but were prepared hot before the cart pushers delivered them to each building. The kitchen workers live in the gym of the 4-Yard and deliver to Buildings 16, 17, 18, 19 and 20, twice a day. Problems with convicts on the reception yard during walks to the dining hall (chow hall) prompted the change from that to delivery service.

Problems began with efforts to get gang members to drop out and debrief on their fellow members, giving up names and information to charge and arrest, ridding the streets of members. Documented members go directly to the SHU, the hole, Solitary Housing Units. The only way out is to drop out. Once released from their P.C. yard, they return to the streets, then return again to the yard. Being on the 4-Yard for reception exposes them to retribution by their former members. The walk to the chow hall was notorious for being able to walk up behind a target and stab that target from behind. Those attempting to slip through the cracks become noticed by their avoiding the one-hour-yard every third day. Paperwork to verify the P.C. status is always required. They all carry with them their proof of charges and arrest history for any requested verification. Roll calls performed by the Wood Pile, where you must give your name and birthdate to verify your charges and history, are mandatory for the building 'rep'. The door rolls open again. The dinner trays are collected by the kitchen workers, and fifty-nine of the new bodies go back to sleep.

Stomp reads his Bible until his eyelids get heavy, and then he, too, soon slumbers away the long day.

# Chapter 78:

Both Stomp and Bob are awakened by some sort of commotion in the dayroom. Bob explains to Stomp, "Watch this, Stomp. That black CO's name is Marshall, sitting in that chair in the middle of the dayroom. He is cool. See what he's doing with his hands?"

"Yeah. Is he doing sign language?" asks Stomp.

Bob laughs, "Street-wise, yes. The letters in each hand represent an area, a neighborhood, gang signs, and a salute to their cliques. He knows them all. It's his hobby. He usually..." Bob starts.

"What's he doing now? He put something on the floor in the middle of the dayroom."

"I was going to say he usually lays out a pouch of Bugler tobacco for the new bodies to shoot out their lines to try to pull the pouch into their cells. Watch, Stomp..." Bob starts making a line from his sheet.

As Stomp watches, he sees lines being shot out from under the cell doors, trying to gauge the distance to the stationary pouch of tobacco. Bob found the sole of a flip-flop shoe, left on the shelf by a previous convict, and he didn't throw it out. He told Stomp that it would come in handy later. He now attaches his line through a small hole and ties it off. Then, he carefully lays out the string so that it will follow the heel out under the door without tangling itself. When he thinks that there is enough line, he shoots it out under the door. The heel flies out on the freshly waxed floor and whips around to the side of the pouch, but a little short of the target...

"About six feet short, Stomp!" He pulls out ten feet more and lays it out, ties the end to the door, then reels in his line. "The trick is Stomp, to shoot it past the pouch at an angle. When the end jerks to a stop, it will snap to the side, hopefully close enough to go around the pouch so we can pull it in. That pouch can make thirty-to-forty cigarettes, Stomp!" He holds his two fingers close together, demonstrating thin, "Pinners, maybe, but all our homies will appreciate a smoke!" He shoots it out again.

As Stomp watches, he can count a dozen lines out there now, a couple of them even coming from the upper tier. "How are the upper-tier lines going to pull the pouch up to their cells?" he asks.

"If they can, they'll pull it closer to the cells below to pull in. All it takes is a lucky shot, and we are all smoking!" Bob's excitement is growing. "This one is the...ONE!" and he shoots the flip-flop sole just past the pouch, then snaps it back as the line reaches its apex, circling the pouch. "That's what I'm talking about!"

Bob begins to reel in his line slowly. The line curls around the blue pouch and the corner sticks to the edge and begins a slow drag, right to cell 108. Now, other lines begin to shoot out in earnest, not any from the 'woods,' as Bob says, "Wood Pile, this is Bob and Stomp from 108, pulling in the pouch to us!" Some of the lines cease to shoot, as South Siders also let the line be drawn. CO Marshall now stands up and follows the pouch at a distance, right up to the door of 108.

"Is that you in there, Bob Bitchin?" Marshall recognizes Bob, "Got a wick ready?"

"Got one right here, Marshall. Thank you, CO!"

The door rolls open, and Marshall uses his personal lighter to light a short wick for Bob. Bob places the wick in the vent and immediately starts to make one six feet long to last, marking the last foot with a band of pencil writing as a warning to make another wick. Bob teaches Stomp proper wick-twisting and proper cigarette-rolling techniques.

"First, we take care of those who take care of us, Stomp," Bob says. "Matt Dixon, Papa, Art, and two to share with our homies in the next yard. One for us right now."

"No, Bob, not for me, don't touch the stuff, bad for the stamina!"

"One for me, then, right now. It's been four or five months. My lungs are screaming at me right now!"

"You knock yourself out, Bob. I'm gonna read my Bible and hope to fall back to sleep. Catch you at breakfast wake-up tomorrow. O.K.?"

"Yeah, Stomp. I'm right behind you. I want to make a proper wick, have a smoke, then get those dice out of my ass while you sleep. We'll be playing 10,000 by tomorrow night!" promises Bob.

"Uhm...Bob, play with dice that you have up your ass? Uhm... can't promise on that one!" says Stomp while laughing.

"Come on, Stomp. I got them in latex fingers, and I'll wash them and bleach them clean. You gotta learn 10,000. Did you get your cards, though? Or should I make some out of the Title-15s?"

"Yeah, they made it. The CO never opened one of my envelopes. We're good." As Stomp verifies.

"Great. I'll teach you cribbage, too!"

"Sounds good. See you in the morning. I'm really exhausted."

"Yeah, me, too. Hasta manana!"

# Chapter 79:

Two days later, after six games of 10,000, with dice that Stomp insisted be soaked in bleach and water for a couple of hours, and Bob's attempt to teach Stomp how to play a card game called cribbage, with terms like fifteen-two, fifteen-four and a double run for eight equals twelve, terminology that seems to Stomp to be comparable to a foreign language, the building is given the yard.

"Let's go, Stomp. We only get an hour and a half. Come on, let's get jiggy with it!" Bob grabs a short wick, grabs five of the cigarettes, and says, "Let's go, Amigo!"

They both step into the short hallway where a gauntlet of CO's, all with metal detectors, are in full search mode. They don't care about the wick burning between Bob's fingers as they sweep their bodies and legs for metal. Once through the checkpoint, they step out onto the yard, the same size as a football field with an asphalt track around the circumference. Before long, Art, Chaz, Sickness, Thumper, Chris, Tyler, and Matt are all gathered together, exchanging fist bumps and slaps across their backs. Papa comes out and meets Stomp for the first time and instantly likes him.

"Mucho gusto, Stomp. I am an old friend of Capone and have known Jesse since he was still sucking on his mother's tit. I have much respect for Capone and his son, Jesse. My friend, your presence must match your image. We have to work on that. You need some ink, and my homie, Fletcha, can make your image pop!" says Papa.

"You are a fresh skin canvas. This must be done with careful thought, my friend. Fletcher did the dragon on Bob's back. Show him, Bob!"

Bob lifts his shirt and turns to show an amazing dragon whose scales glitter and pop. "I know, I know, she looks more like an alligator lizard right now, but I'll get my size back soon!" The group chuckles, since each time that Bob returns to the 4-Yard, the dragon's head is large, and the body is all sucked up and shriveled. Stomp looks at the amazing detail and has an idea. First, he'll run it by Bob and Art, his confidants. He has learned to value their judgment and something as permanent as a tattoo...well...Papa is right...it will take some consideration.

Bob presents Papa with a cigarette, lights it for him, and watches him get dizzy and wobbly. He then hands one to Art and Matt, lights it, enjoys watching their head-rush and hands out the rest to share as they start to walk. As they walk past the dip bars, Stomp sees someone whom he recognizes from his first day at George Bailey. It's the angry skinhead who insulted Stomp's love, Hannah. Their eyes meet, and the guy comes over.

"Art, Bob, Matt, the gang's all here again, huh? I wanted to come over and express my apology to this man here..." he nods at Stomp. "...I was very angry after I was sentenced, and I apologize for coming at you sideways. My name is Chaos, from Lakeside."

"Stomp, La Mesa. I appreciate your apology. I hope I wasn't too rough on you?"

"Hell, Stomp, your handle is a perfect description, and I really deserved it, bro! I can't remember ever being hit that hard before, except by that big Scat, Marshall Pritchard," says Chaos, as he rubs his jaw.

"Chaos, how are you, brother?' Bob gives him a hug. Then Chaos fist-bumps and hugs the rest of the crew. "I gather that you two..." he nods at Stomp and Chaos, "...have you already met?" Stomp and Chaos chuckle. "Great! Nothing like mutual respect for one another. Some of my best friendships include a mutual combat or two!"

Everyone laughs now. "Where does Matt have you housed, Chaos?"

"Probably same as you, 18 in cell 204. Looks like we got one hell of a crew showing, huh, fellas? Hey, Stomp, man, you got a perfectly shaped dome. Ever thought of shaving your head, maybe a tattoo on the back? A great place because to hide it, all you do is let your hair grow back!" says Chaos.

"Peddle the image, Chaos, but not the sect. Stomp has no interest in being a skinhead, and his last name is Stompski, a Christian with a Jewish lineage. Doesn't the 88 Precepts disallow that recruitment?" says Art, knowing full well that, although asked to recognize the rules and policies of the precepts, all are into drugs and sales of drugs. Art has a protective wing around Stomp.

Chaos knows that recruitment of Stomp would score high credentials for the 'skins.' He recognizes and respects Art's rebuke and joins the group as they walk the track.

"Stomp, today we stroll and see who's who here and make introductions of you to the homies. Next yard, we will spend on the bars, working out all day, then in the cell as well, before we sound off." Bob explains. "All of us may not be going to the same yard from here. Some of us will even be transported to a different CDC pen from here but connected to the yard. Here is how we take care of each other. Matt here..." Bob throws an arm around Matt, "...knows now that your permanent housing will most likely be on the 3-yard because he just found out. He also found out that you are under Art's wing and all of ours. Matt, as a personal favor to you and all of us, will use his influence to hook you up, through his clerk's influence, for a great job with a great pay number. Matt can get this done for us. Anyone else gets a charge, but he has already told you that he expects nothing. We all know that he is willing to assist out of respect, but, Stomp, we will take good care of Matt whether or not a favor is extended."

Stomp fully understands the camaraderie here. After all, he has been the recipient of generous support since his first day in 6-A at George Bailey. At RJ Donovan and any CDC prison, the convicts run everything. The COs may oversee the running of the facility, but the hiring, the bed moves, the clerical, and everything except for the releasing and receiving are done by the convicts; and not just the planning from the inside, they also run the rackets outside, as well. If anyone deserves to be fast-tracked into a premium job spot, Matt knows that Stomp will make him look good, too. Stomp is not the type to do heroin, and when it hits, fuck-off on his job. He is not a sloth who prefers rack-riding and slumbers his days away. No, Stomp would be a fantastic referral and, thus, any referral thereafter would be taken seriously. Matt has just figured out the perfect job for Stomp. Everyone will appreciate this hook-up. Now, Matt is anxious to get back and begin work on Stomp's fast track.

"Hey, Art, Bob, Stomp..." Matt begins, "...we need to hold off on Stomp's transformation. I have the perfect job for Stomp...Inmate Day Labor. It needs someone with skill and who is responsibility-minded. That sounds like our boy, here!"

Art says, "Perfect, Matt. Make it happen! We love you, Matt!"

Their walk is interrupted by, "Yard Recall. Yard Recall! Everyone head back to your housing units immediately! Yard Recall!" coming from the tower over the unusable dining hall. Lines of COs with metal-detecting wands are positioned at each building entrance. Reverse gauntlets!

# Chapter 80:

The first death Stomp helped create. The second death happens fifteen feet from him and Bob as they leave their cell and begin to walk toward the yard. Bob grabs the back of Stomp's carrot suit and holds him stationary as three South Siders come up behind one another. Blind-siding him, the first one comes up and puts an arm around him as if a comrade, while the other two come up from behind and begin stabbing him multiple times. He tries to spin, to run, to hide but the first one holds him in place and upright. The other two are both holding shanks in their hands with socks over them. When the snitch's legs buckle, he is laid down gently and spit at. The two with weapons simply peel off the socks over the weapons and deposit them into a trash can by the door. Bob turns Stomp around, and they head back to their cell and close their door.

Matt Dixon is collecting trash and collects the bag out of the receptacle the weapon was just deposited in. The action was so smooth that the convict or CO never noticed it. Before the alarms even sounded, the trash would be in the compactor and on the way to being incinerated.

"Obviously, we aren't getting yard for a few days, Stomp. I grabbed you because I felt what was about to happen. I could sense the tension sense the urgency that the two had on their faces as the first one distracted the target. All the COs are outside, creating a gauntlet to search. Oh, sure, they'll check out a video and take the two out to the hole. Dollars to doughnuts, they both are getting over twenty years already and this here won't get them more than a couple to five more years. What's the difference to them? And this is only their first torpedo strike. They've already let it be known that they have nothing to lose. They've already lost it all, so make them a legend." Bob explains.

"What the..." Stomp's mouth is agape, "What the fuck, Bob?"

"Stomp, that is none of our business. That is their business. That snitch probably ended a life by putting someone in here for the rest of his life. If he takes the freedom from another for life, why not take his? Believe me, Stomp, that is not done without proof of it and, in documentation, paperwork from the court. The kill order is due to some serious shit. Otherwise, they would have just three-on-one or five-on-one him. Again, none of our business! If asked or interviewed, your answer is, 'It was none of my business!' Believe me, Papa had to take the order and make the call. He is still our friend. It isn't easy to be in his position or Art's. Do not treat him any differently. He is still our friend."

"Yeah, Bob. Thanks. I do understand. I had never experienced a death until I got locked up. Now, after only a couple of months, two deaths within five yards of me hit really close to home. I've still got years to go, too." Stomp shakes his head.

"Never, I mean never, walk the yard alone! We always walk with at least two or three others when we're in the yard. To be caught alone is to have 'target' written across your back. Every group in here has homies in the hole. These two will end up there for months now. While there, they will be taken care of by a steady stream of other homies with their asses packed with drugs and tobacco. Delivery service! How do you think that they will be sent to the hole? Some unsuspecting solo walker will be attacked, not like this, though, but just by starting a fight, just enough to get the yard alarms going and everyone on their bellies. The two or three get hauled off to the hole for a few days. Delivery made! The victim should not take it personally. He should not have made it so easy. We never make it easy. We always have each other's back. Have you noticed, as we walk, that our eyes are always observing what's around us? We are not distracted. We are our own security."

"I am glad that I have all of you as friends, Bob. I still have so much to learn, and all of you have already taught me so much in these last two months, but I am still so naive about all this." realizes Stomp.

"Stomp, do not worry. We have you, and we are working on paving the way for you on the 3-yard once you arrive. We got you a job already. Has Matt or Art told you yet?"

"I heard something about IDL, whatever that is?" Asks Stomp.

"Stomp, IDL, which stands for Inmate Day Labor, is the best-paying job in a CDC yard. Pay is one dollar an hour, one-hundred-sixty a month. We can only spend one hundred and forty a month at the canteen. IDL's work is usually outside the gate, so a gate pass is given when your points are low enough. Not all work is outside the gate, however. Hell, Stomp, most here gets kitchen jobs, dorm-porter jobs, yard recreation, and maintenance jobs, all for about five cents an hour. Matt has hooked you up, Stomp, out of respect and because he likes you, as well. I have an idea about how to pay him back in a real way later after you get your job. I'll explain it all later. For now, when we get you to the canteen, we can each get him a jar of coffee as a gift." recommends Bob.

"Hell, Bob, at least that!" agrees Stomp. "Matt has really..." Stomp is interrupted by yard alarms going off and shouts of, "Get down. Everyone down!"

The COs finally spot the guy lying by the trash can under the bubble, basically hidden from view. Those who made it outside Building 16 have to hit the yard on their bellies until they are searched for weapons and their hands are checked for bruising or cuts. They trickle back in after being scrutinized. Bob and Stomp avoided this by heading back to their cell before the hit went down.

"Also, Stomp, always check your cell when you come back from the yard, from work, or from showering. Those youngsters could have easily slid those shanks under a cell door after the hit. The trash-can drop was not smart, but better than going through the gauntlet search at the yard gate. Had it been in the yard, the weapons would have been handed off

302

several times and hidden, disposed of, or buried in the yard under the gravel. As I said, things get slid under doors all the time, especially drugs, to keep from getting caught in possession. It won't take them long to watch the video and recover the weapons. The three involved have already hooped dope and tobacco for the hole. I can pretty much guarantee that." says Bob. "This yard is probably the most active due to the level 4. The 3-yard is less active because lifers are housed there, and there is more respect there. Still, …"

"Watch my and our backs on a daily basis." Finishes Stomp.

# Chapter 81:

It takes two weeks until they are all screened in the medical trailers next to Building 16 and moved to Building 18. Some go to the gym to work kitchen jobs. Bob and Stomp stay cellmates for the next ten weeks and Stomp gets really good at cribbage and 10,000 by then. He also scores a 12.1 on the educational scale test, which is the highest possible level; 12.1 signifies that Stomp is at the college level of education. Lower than that would necessitate HSET classes. Some attempt an intentionally low score, enabling them to take classes and achieve a Milestone credit of a six-month reduction of their sentences.

While Stomp meets with his counselor, she verifies all of the judge's orders and hands him all of the necessary packets for visits and conjugal visits, to be filled out by those needing to be approved. Bob helps Stomp with his fish-draw order, and Matt, always true to his influence, is able to get Stomp's ID to the head of the line at the canteen. Stomp gets a jar of coffee for everyone who has no canteen and gets three jars for Matt in appreciation. Although Matt tries to refuse, Stomp insists that Matt accept his gift of gratitude.

It is around their twelfth week when Matt informs several that they will be trans-packing to other facilities that day, leaving early in the morning. Chaz and Bob are being trans-packed to Eagle Mountain CCF near Indio. They have both been there several times and both are excited to get there, probably the best place to be sent. Eagle Mountain CCF is run by a private contractor for the State of California, and those with level-one and level-two points can be sent there. Also, applications for work furlough can be requested there, which release applicants to six months in programs such as Model X, Bachelor Flats, and Volunteers of America, all of which are located downtown and monitored by parole. Gainful employment is a requirement and they assist with resources to get paroled convicts working. Half of the convict's paycheck is collected as room and board; the other half is held in an account and doled out, upon request, for weekend passes. Receipts must be provided afterward. All monies must be accounted for to prevent any money from being used to purchase drugs. Random drug testing is frequent, and any positive test will send the person back into custody.

Stomp is going to miss his friends, but they tell him that they will stay in touch, and they exchange information to stay in contact. Matt returns to Bob's and Stomp's cell to inform Stomp that he will be moving, as well, that day to the 3-Yard, along with Art, Chris, Sickness, and Chaos. Matt lets them know to start packing their property and brings them each a plastic trash bag. Papa is also going to the 3-Yard to represent the South Siders car. Stomp will be housed in Building 13 with a lifer named Dan Nelson, who is also a co-worker in IDL as an electrician in the yard.

Matt says, "Stomp, Nelson also works at IDL, and he's going to pull you into it to work with him. It's all arranged with the clerk. Within a week, you will be called in for an interview with the free staff electrician for whom Nelson works. He is an electrical contractor on the streets and runs projects here for the CDC where you already are. This is just a formality. Hey, Stomp, it's been a real honor to meet you. We'll see each other when you have projects in the yard. Your boss can bring you cans of Bugler tobacco, so if he asks if you need anything, say tobacco and hook us up over here if you can. Good luck, Homeboy!"

Stomp goes around and says his farewells to those with whom he has become friends. Then, the five are called to the gate to move to the 3-Yard. Stomp, once again, learns what a difference a day makes in the CDC.

Stomp and the others are Marked out to the track and wait until others are brought out from Buildings 19, 20, and the gym. The line of transfers is Marked down the track towards the gym and told to wait for the others to join the March. Once the convicts from the gym join the group, they are marked to the same gate from which they all originally came in. Once through the gate, they turned right, and Markh passed R&R on the left and up to the new yard. About half of those in line are called out of line and told to wait at the 2-yard gate. The rest are told to continue on to the next yard, the 3-yard, and up to its gate.

Like night and day, the 4-yard was all dirt and gravel and depressing, but as Stomp walks onto the 3-yard, he sees grass, a volleyball court, a work-out pit, a baseball field, and, to his surprise, a heavy bag, and a speed bag hanging from chains on one side. Not only that, the yard is full of convicts taking advantage of the yard, not an empty, unused yard area like the moonscape of the previous yard. Here people are wearing gym shorts and tennis shoes, playing Hacky Sack and Horseshoes.

Art says, "What a difference a day makes, huh, Stomp? A functional yard where, although some have no out-date, they at least have some normalcy."

"Much better, Art! Much better." Agrees Stomp.

The line marks to the left, and a couple of convicts get dropped off at Building 11. Sickness and Chaos get dropped off at Building 12. Art, Chris, and Stomp are dropped off at Building 13, and the rest continue on to the last two buildings.

"Building 15 is the program building. The Amity Program has some benefits for addicts wanting change and hoping to start here. If successful here, Amity assists them on the streets as well. SAAP is another program in there as well. We won't get yard with them, bad influence on programmers.", says Art. "Building 13 is a lifer building, also temporary housing for those like us. You'll stay here...ordered by your judge and attorney, Sampson. It's not a bad yard, a lot better than in the desert CDC prisons like Ironwood or Chuckawalla CDC. The heat there is terrible in the summer. The rest of us are hoping to catch the bus to the fire camp, Jamestown S.C.C., up near Modesto. Your points won't allow you to go there. Still, we'll

be here together for a couple of months more, probably.",
continues Art.

"Stompski, you are in 213!" he hears over the P.A. speaker
and sees the door to 213 open.

"Dietrick, you are in 208!"

"Beckman, you are in 217! Gentlemen, please, head up the
stairs and secure your doors!" The three head up to their new
homes on the 3-yard.

Stomp realizes, as he walks up these concrete and steel
steps, that this will be his permanent home for almost half a
decade.

# Chapter 82:

Stomp steps into 213 and feels as if he should remove his shoes. The cell, unlike the previous cells at Donovan, is clean and polished to a waxed, brilliant shine. His new cellmate put in a lot of time making this fifty-square-foot concrete box a home. Dan Nelson was expecting his new cellmate, it seems, since he left a note that was on Stomp's bunk. It reads:

"Stomp, make yourself at home. I know, and I've heard that you are solid and respectful, and I look forward to knowing you. I usually get back from work near 3:30 or 4:00 each day. We will go to dinner together; I'll buy it! Lol. Your new cellmate, Dan."

Stomp reads and re-reads the thoughtful welcome note left for him by Mr. Nelson. He even knew Stomp's name. Then he takes another look at Mr. Nelson's self-made home. The stainless-steel sink, the faucets, the toilet, and the mirror are all shining his reflection back at him. The concrete floor and even the concrete walls are waxed and polished to the point that they appear to be wet. The walls, in addition to the two metal shelving units, have thickened cardboard shelves three or four layers thick to support the weight of books or clothing. There is shelving over the sink and mirror to accommodate hygiene products. All the shelves are in sets of two; one set is already occupied, while the second set is bare. These, too, have been painted and waxed to a shine. Even with all these added items, the cell is uncrowded, and Stomp feels comfortable here.

Mr. Nelson's rack is tightly made, with not a wrinkle in the blanket, corners folded, and a perfectly centered pillow at the wall. Underneath the rack are Xerox boxes and lids, painted and waxed the same as the shelves; storage for his life's belongings, a life spent in here for many past years. The writing table is organized, and the seat has a padded leather cover, just like a motorcycle seat. Appliances? The incredible Mr. Nelson has a large crockpot and a transparent television set hooked up to speakers for stereo effects. Hanging by each rack is a set of earbuds hooked up to a splitter switch to enable one to listen to the TV while the other cellmate is sleeping.

Stomp carefully begins to prepare his mattress, making every effort to duplicate the neatness of his new cellmate, successfully creating a spitting image of the mattress below his. Afterward, he places his property on the steel shelving that was left empty for him. Without assuming that any of the other shelves are meant for him, they are left empty. Once all of his property is placed on the shelves, Stomp sits at the table and writes to Hannah.

The cell door to 213 rolls open, and a salt-and-pepper-haired gentleman with an Aesthetic Electric ball cap strolls into the cell. He's about the same height as Stomp, with a new-cut-style haircut, wide shoulders, and Popeye forearms. He is wearing black workman boots instead of the brown leather CDC boots typical for everyone else in the yard. He sees Stomp, and his smile is ear-to-ear, a genuine smile that is instantly contagious.

"Isaac Stompski? I apologize. You prefer to use the handle, Stomp. Is that right?" Mr. Nelson asks.

"Stomp is the new nickname given to me by my friends in Bailey. I sort of got used to it. My wife calls me Isaac, as did my friends before I was arrested. I liked it very much to hear you use it as now you are my family. Please don't stop calling me Isaac. Do you mind calling me Isaac?"

"I'll tell you what...you call me Dan... I'll call you Isaac except when we are in the yard... There it will be Stomp, and you call me Nelson. A deal?" Dan asks.

"Perfect, Dan.", Stomp responds.

"Great for me, too. I just got home from work, so I'm gonna hop in the shower. The COs here are cool with us A-1-A workers taking showers after work. I just have to grab my towel and hygiene items. We'll talk after and at chow. Be right back." says Dan.

"I'll be right here.", says Stomp, then adds, "I noticed that your cap says Aesthetic Electric. I know the owner, Paul. Did you work for him before coming here?"

"Actually, yes, and I still do, and so will you, starting next week! Paul is my free-man boss here.", answers Dan. "How do you know Paul?"

"He's been doing electrical work for our family business and all of our homes since 1984. We love the guy; they always took good care of us, best in the business here in San Diego."

"Yeah, I'll say! He really knows his trade! I've learned a lot working for him, and he takes care of us." The door pops open. "I'll be right back, Isaac.", and Dan heads to the shower. Stomp continues writing his letter to Hannah.

Before Stomp finishes his letter, the door rolls open once again, and Dan walks back in. "Please, Isaac, go ahead and finish what you're doing. We have plenty of time to get to know one another. I still have to get ready for chow, which is in..." Dan looks at the clock mounted next to the upper set of shelves, "...about twenty-five minutes. Here, we all walk to the dining hall for dinner and breakfast. Until you start working with us next week, you will go to breakfast on your own. I'll leave you a couple of cigarettes to share with your friends in the yard. I'll leave you a lighter, too, but we aren't supposed to have either, so don't be obvious about it. The free staff for each trade takes care of us at IDL; the only thing is, we don't say where we get it. Don't worry, the CO's never ask. They know that we won't say anyway." Dan is saying all this as he gets ready for chow. "By the way, Isaac, the shelves that have nothing on them are for you to use, and I have some Xerox boxes under my rack for you to use as well. I try to keep food items on the shelves and clothing in the boxes to deter any rodents from having a meal. The empty shelf above the sink is also for you to use."

"Thank you, Dan, for your hospitality. Do you mind my asking how long you've lived here?" asks Stomp.

"No problem. This next February will be ten years here at Donovan. Before here I was at Old Folsom for five years.", answers Dan. "In ten more years, I'll be up for parole."

"Whew!" Stomp's shock is obvious "You seem to be taking it pretty good."

"Well, Isaac, the good part is...I have a date for eligibility. You also have a date. Some here do not, and while in the yard, it is best not to discuss any out-dates and how much time is left. As I said, some are here for life." Dan buttons his blue shirt. "We have to stay in good spirits here, and the COs pretty much leave us alone as long as we behave ourselves."

"The yard looks a lot better than where we were on the 4-Yard; a lot of activities here to do. At least there is grass here." Says Stomp.

Dan laughs at that; then the door rolls open again. "Come on, Isaac, let's go eat. Chicken and potatoes tonight!"

# Chapter 83:

The five buildings on the 3-Yard each hold two hundred convicts; one hundred on the lower tier and one hundred on the upper tier. Chow releases one building at a time. Upon release onto the track, everyone walks around to their right. In front of the chow hall and under the tower, the line forms to enter the dining room. Those walking the track form up in groups to share tables with whom they choose. Stomp introduces Art and Chris to Dan and Dan introduces them all to his co-workers at IDL. They now number eight and stay together in an attempt to sit together.

Art says, "Like day and night coming here from the 4-yard, huh, Stomp? This is one of my all-time favorite yards, Stomp."

"You should see Nelson's cell, Art. I mean, he has it dialed in with a television, shelves, and storage boxes under his rack!" Stomp is still amazed. "Nelson says that I will be working with him, too. Get this, too; Art, the electrical contractor who is our boss, is a friend of my family."

"What? Nelson's boss, and now yours, is a friend of your family on the streets? Wow, how small this world really is, huh, Stomp?" answers Art. "What are the chances of that? Does he know yet that you are in here and going to work for him?"

"Not sure. I wrote to Hannah but the letter is still on the writing table. I'll call as soon as I can... that's right... I can call now! Nelson, when can I make a call?" asks Stomp.

"When we get back from chow, I'll check with the CO, Adams. He's cool. He'll let you, I'm pretty sure, but we'll ask him first.", says Dan.

"Right on. I'll have her call Paul to let him know so he won't be shocked the first time he sees me here. I mean, he knows me and my family from doing work for us but I doubt that Hannah called everyone we know about what happened to me. Thanks, Nelson. I appreciate it. I haven't heard my wife's voice in months, nor she mine."

"No problem, uhm, Stomp. I got you.", says Dan as the group walks up to the long line going into the hall. "It's also been months since you've all had a hot meal, huh? Tonight, it's chicken, an entire half of a chicken, too! Yard bird!" laughs Dan. "Stomp, you'll find that everything is better in this yard. Matt Mimms is here, too, when you want some art done on you."

"Matt is here?" asks Art. "That's my boy, Stomp. Now we can get an 'SD' done on you, recognizing you for the work. We can do an 'SD Padres' tattoo on the back of your head after we shave it. That way, once you are out, you can grow your hair out, and it won't be visible. Where is Matt housed, Nelson?"

"He's A-1-A, too, Building 11. We'll get yard at night together once Stomp starts his job next week. I'll set it up. I can set up the barber, too, but there is no hurry. Best if Stomp waits until he gets hired so that the IDL office has the best impression of him. We'll keep any tattoos above the sleeve and not visible unless his shirt is removed." Says Nelson. "Prison tattoos are scrutinized by the cops when visible on the streets. You're a blank canvas, Stomp. Matt is going to love that."

When Stomp and Nelson get back to Building 13, CO Adams is at the podium in the center of the dayroom. Nelson goes up to him and says, "CO, how are you?"

"Just happy to be here! How are you, Mr. Nelson? Mr. Stompski, how are you? Do you two need anything?"

Nelson nods at Stomp, who asks Adams, "Pleased to meet you, sir. If I may, I haven't spoken to my wife in several months. Is it possible for me to make a call to her?"

"Of course, Mr. Stompski. Would you like to make it now or later?"

"The sooner, the better, sir. Could I make it now? I don't believe that I get evening yard until I begin my job." Asks Stomp.

"That reminds me, Mr. Stompski, here is a ducat for tomorrow at the IDL office at 9:00 am. Nelson will be at work then. Do you think that you can be ready for that time?" Adams speaks into his radio, "Tower, please, turn on phone #1 for Mr. Stompski here."

"Thank you, CO sir. Yes, I'll be up and ready to go for tomorrow," says Stomp. "Really, I do appreciate this."

"No problem. Mr. Nelson, head back up for now, please."

"Thanks, Adams.", Nelson says. "Have a good call, Isaac. Let Hannah know that we got you in here, and tell her not to worry about you."

"Will do, Dan. See you upstairs." Returns Stomp.

Stomp knows, however, that Hannah will always worry until she has her Isaac back home again.

# Chapter 84:

Judge Lazarus is glad that this is the last court appearance for Mark Sutter. The media circus on this high-profile case has become intolerable. Mark Sutter's portrayal as a monster just doesn't sit well with the judge. True, almost all serial killers caught had charm and a chameleon-like personality. Almost all of them shocked everyone once they were caught due to their apparent normalcy. This one, Mark Sutter, is very different, indeed.

Mr. Sutter's sincere lack of knowledge of these heinous crimes that were committed was confirmed by the polygraph testing as well. The public, catered to by the media, has already tried and convicted Mr. Sutter. The overwhelming evidence makes it difficult to accept Mark's innocence. Something is just not right here and if Mr. Sutter has some sort of mental disconnect, then that is up to the professionals with expertise to prove. For right now his job, for the people, is to rule on the order before him and to see that the order is carried out.

"All rise, please. The honorable Judge Lazarus is presiding in East County Court. The people versus Mark Sutter is first on the docket. Representing Mr. Sutter is Nicolas De Santo. Please, be seated.", the bailiff states.

"Mr. De Santo, Mr. District Attorney, as we have previously determined, Mr. Sutter's condition, as stated by Dr. Sullivan, proves to this court that he cannot stand trial at this moment. We are all in agreement that Mr. Sutter needs to be evaluated by professionals to determine if or when we can continue. I am ordering a one-year psyche evaluation while still in custody at Patton State Prison. They have a year to complete a full report for me. At that time we will all meet back in this courtroom to continue this case. Are you aware of my order, Mr. Sutter?" asks Judge Lazarus.

"Yes, your honor, I am." Answers Mark.

"I am also ordering that this man be isolated from all other men in incarceration, as well as in treatment, due to the severity of these charges. I am also ordering that any tools necessary to reach the truth in this case be left to the professionals at Patton. I am, however, eliminating the use of chemical truth serums, which leave the brain damaged. Any of these are out of the question. Is that clear?"

"Yes, your honor."

"Yes, your honor."

"Thank you, your honor.", says Mark.

"Let it be so ordered. Mr. Sutter, we will see you again back here no later than one and a half years from this date. Court adjourned." Orders the Judge.

"Please, stand.", says the bailiff. The judge rises and walks out of the courtroom. The bailiff opens the door to the holding cell, the same cell where Mark was attacked on his first court date. Mark sees that there is already a man in the cell awaiting court. Rather than enter the cell, Mark turns and sits on the floor. His attorney sees this refusal to enter. De Santo walks over to Mark, stands next to him protectively, and gives the bailiff a hard stare. The bailiff stares back, and De Santo says, "Please, will someone ask Judge Lazarus to come out here right now?"

The clerk does so. "What is the meaning of this? Why am I being asked to return to an adjourned courtroom? Mr. De Santo?" asks Lazarus.

"Your honor, see my client seated on the floor here? He was following my instructions after the last incident here at your courtroom when Mr. Sutter was attacked by an inmate by the name of Matt Simms. Here, we have the possibility of another assault in your courtroom. I am making you aware of this possible assault by the sworn officers of your court.", says De Santo.

"What?" Lazarus walks over to the bailiff standing by the door and looks for himself. "Bailiff, what is the meaning of this?"

"Your honor, I was in here with you when this man was placed in here..." the bailiff begins.

"...and why did the defendant have to sit on my courtroom floor instead of you intervening as your job-description action requires? Can you tell me what action you are required to take?" instructs Judge Lazarus.

"Uhm...action? The policy is to protect the defendant from others on the premises. Uhm...if a threat exists, the defendant is to remain in your courtroom until the threat is removed?" the bailiff queries.

"Is that all, bailiff? Continue, please. What then? After the threat is removed, what then?", the instruction of Lazarus continues.

"Uhm...you are to be notified of the threat? We have just done so, your honor."

"No, bailiff! No, we have not! Mr. De Santo has not been my staff nor my on-duty Sheriff deputies! Why is that? What happens next, bailiff, as my security staff member in my courtroom? What needs to happen next?" continues the Judge.

"Uhm...next? I am to keep the defendant restrained at the defense table, under protection with his, uhm, attorney present, as well as the court staff, Uhm. At the same time, I personally investigate how this inmate was brought into the cell prior to Mr. Sutter?"

"Finish, please."

"Once investigated, I am to report to you how this happened as well as the identity of the individuals who escorted that inmate to the cell and all of those involved in this, Uhm, mistake?" asks the bailiff.

"Then why, sir, is this man still sitting on the floor, being protected by his attorney rather than by my staff? And why are you not taking what action is required of you? Why?" demands the Judge.

"Yes, your honor. Right away, sir!" as the court bailiff helps Mark to his feet and leads him back to the defense table. Nicolas De Santo re-takes his seat while all the staff stays seated. Two additional bailiffs, both sergeants, enter from the spectator hall and stand as protection for those at the table.

"I want answers, gentlemen! I want to know where this threat originated and who is involved, and I want it now! If any heads are to roll, it won't be this man's again! We will all wait while you do your duty, sir!" and Lazarus sits back in his position of authority. After the bailiff leaves through the holding cell, taking the waiting inmate with him, Judge Lazarus calls to a sergeant, "Sergeant, please, approach my bench!"

"Yes, your honor." He then approaches the bench in front of the judge, "Yes, your honor?"

"Sergeant, the reason that my courtroom is having to be held here, frozen, is due to your deputies. Mr. Sutter, sitting there with his attorney, Mr. De Santo, has claimed that he was attacked after his arraignment hearing. Mr. De Santo identified the inmate who attacked Mr. Sutter as Matthew Simms, a registered Red Belt in martial arts. Your deputies knew of Mr. Simms' skills prior to their placing Mr. Sutter in the holding cell, still cuffed. As a sergeant for the San Diego Sheriff's Department, do you believe in coincidences?"

"Your honor, I do not, sir, as I do not believe that Mr. Sutter could possibly..." the Sergeant begins.

"Enough! Sergeant, your belief is not the issue here in my courtroom, nor did I ask you for it! Here is what I believe, sir, and my belief is important here! Your attitude towards disrespecting these proceedings is contagious for those whom you command. It is not your responsibility to purvey your belief to your men that this man is guilty before he has had his day in court. Proving that this man is or is not guilty beyond a reasonable doubt, sir, is my responsibility, not yours!", interrupts Lazarus.

"Your honor..." the Sergeant begins again, "...those children..."

"I am not finished, Sergeant, and for you to say what I just heard shows to me a conflict of my orders. My courtroom and those who staff it are to remain neutral and unbiased at all times, as your duty requires. If you believe or feel that you are not able to follow your job duties, what should you do then? Answer me, please.", the extremely angry Judge Lazarus questions.

"Sir, your honor, if a conflict of interest becomes apparent in any capacity of your staff, that staff member is to be excused from his duties, sir?" the Sergeant answers questioningly.

"Is that an answer, sir, or a question?" Before you answer that...if that is an answer and said staff member continues to perform his duties, although there is an apparent conflict, then what happens if this conflict becomes documented?" the very wise Judge continues.

"Your honor, that was an answer. The answer to your next question would be that the staff member who does not excuse himself would be in contempt of your courtroom, sir.", the Sergeant answers.

"Correct, Sergeant. Now, I want you, as commanding officer, to personally go after your deputy who just left and bring me those involved in this travesty of justice. Is that clear, sir?"

"Yes, your honor." The Sergeant leaves through the same door and holding cell, but not before he shoots Mark a look of hatred and vigilance.

"Thank you, your honor. May I approach the bench, sir?" Mr. De Santo asks.

"No, you may not! I am not happy at this moment. I need to reflect in silence, please." The Judge thinks to himself, "I cannot wait to send this man, guilty or innocent, away from the already affected morale of my staff. The hatred and lack of professionalism that I have seen so far are unprecedented. I understand, but I can't condone the vigilante attitudes that I have witnessed from my own city officials. Heads are going to roll so that this never happens again."

And heads do roll in East County Court!

# Chapter 85:

The Sergeant and the three deputy officers under his command are brought forth in front of Judge Lazarus.

"I want this on the record, Clerk.", begins the Judge. "This court will not tolerate any vigilante vengeance in Mr. Sutter's case or any other case in the future. Mr. Sutter has not yet been found guilty of any crime, especially not the crimes for which he has been accused. The admitted voluntary polygraph test verifies his innocence and the only reason that he is still being held is due to the overwhelming physical evidence that has been documented. Mr. Sutter, while in my court, will not be victimized any longer by those employed by this County. These deputies may claim that a mistake has been made, which I'm sure that they will do, so I won't even bother to ask the question. My concern is this: it takes more than one mistake to make this happen. This was no coincidence. Therefore, I want to charge these four in front of me with contempt of court. In consideration of their service up to this point, I will not levy this charge but, instead, will recommend suspension for a period of one week without pay. This should give them adequate time to think about the extent of damage that could have been caused to my courtroom, especially with all the media outside in the courtyard. Sergeant. Although you were not directly involved in the alleged mistakes that occurred in our holding cell, I find it bothersome to hear of your judgment of Mr. Sutter before I have made my judgment. Your attitude of pre-judgment is contagious to those whom you manage and direct. These three deputies here may have made these grievous mistakes while thinking that their actions would coincide with your thinking. Therefore, the buck is being passed along to you, as well." The Judge's stare towards these deputies is one of anger and disbelief. "To explain why I am dealing with this situation so harshly, let us play this through, hypothetically: Mr. Sutter, while cuffed, walks into the cell already occupied by another inmate. I have no idea why the other inmate was un-cuffed, as he should have been cuffed waiting for court; another mistake. The assault by an un-cuffed inmate on a cuffed inmate could have been extensive, if not lethal. Worst-case scenario...Mr. Sutter is beaten to death while in protective custody in my courthouse. Gentlemen, have you noticed the media circus in the courtyard at the front doors of my courthouse? Mr. Sutter, by his quick thinking and, I'm sure, Mr. De Santo's instructions after his last visit here, saved all of your jobs. Not only were your careers saved, thereby avoiding embarrassment to your profession and the entire County that employs you, but possibly my career as a judge as well. All of us owe Mr. Sutter and Mr. De Santo a sincere thank-you for avoiding this public display of gross negligence. Thank you, Mr. Sutter, and you, as well, Mr. De Santo." The Judge is just about finished, "Off the record, Clerk, please. Sergeant and Deputies, a week's suspension is light for your actions, believe me. My courtroom and judgment are never light but are always fair. You, gentlemen, play your own scenarios forward and weigh your own outcomes. Trust this...none of your outcomes will end as lightly as what I have ordered. That will be all. You four are dismissed from your duties forthwith for a period of one week." The Judge looks at the Clerk and nods, "Back on record, this court is adjourned." Judge Lazarus stands, all those in attendance stand, and the honorable Judge leaves the courtroom.

A new deputy enters from the hallway and guides Mark into the now-empty holding cell. Attorney De Santo insists that he be allowed to accompany Mark back to the cells below. Once Mark is placed in a cell downstairs with no other inmates, Mr. DeSanto nods at Mark and then says to the deputy, "That was very close to creating a major incident. If I were you, I would spread the word that my client is to be handled with respect and caution until he is no longer under your protection." De Santo then leaves,

shaking his head in disbelief.

Mr. De Santo has been told by Mark and by many other clients about the instances of retribution to which those in protective custody are subjected. There are claims of negligence due to the lack of information about those incarcerated, leading to improper housing or classification. Yet, those housing new bodies have all of the inmates' files in front of them, including their gang-member affiliations, their documented enemies, and their custody status. All information regarding custody is red-flagged during the booking process. Mistakes are frequent and always preventable. Absolute power is frequently abused but blame is always avoided with claims of 'not enough available information'. These games have lethal consequences more often than not. The person in harm's way is not the only victim. The inmates used as tools for retribution are also victims. They are given additional time in most cases, sometimes large amounts of time, depending on the severity of the injuries. Thus, the families of the inmates involved are also victimized due to the ripple effect of any act of retribution, seen as entertainment for the deputies in charge, whose duty it is to provide safety for those same inmates.

Newspapers around our nation document instances in all levels of incarceration of inmates hanging themselves out of hopelessness, improper handling of medications that leads to death, and improper medical attention when something appears to be non-lethal, as with a hernia, normally treated by doctors with immediate surgery due to the complications an untreated hernia can cause. While in custody, these conditions are always ignored. Complaints of pain are treated with aspirin and suggestions to drink more water; by nurses, not doctors. These abuses are common in a system where care should be a concern but is ignored instead. Ignorance is always the defense of those who are responsible. Ignorance is intolerable for those charged but tolerable for those in charge. That is the nature of the Beast created by incarceration, tolerated by all.

# Chapter 86:

Hannah hasn't heard her husband's voice in several months now. Although she has received a couple of letters a week, she needs to hear his voice. Being parted from Isaac this way, Hannah feels that for their relationship to endure is a test from above. God needs her husband to do this and the only acceptable way for her to deal with this is to cope with it. She knows that she is suffering, but this selfish thought must be pushed aside as she thinks about how he must be enduring the separation. Her suffering is nothing compared with what Isaac must be suffering, being separated from all of them. Her thoughts are interrupted by the ringing phone.

"Hello?" Hannah answers.

"You have a collect call...from an inmate at a California correctional facility. If you choose to accept this call, press one now." Hannah presses one.

"Hannah, Hannah, Honey, is that you?" Isaac stammers.

"Yes, Isaac. Yes, yes, yes, it is me; I miss you so much, Sweetie! Are you finally someplace with phone access? Are you all right?" says Hannah as a teardrop trails down her cheek.

"Yes, Baby. I am as good as can be expected. The other place that I was in was terrible, and so was that incident that I wrote to you about, right in front of us. I just got to this new place today. It's like night and day! My new cellmate is a guy named Dan Nelson, an electrician. We're going to be working together. Are you crying, my lovely?" Says Stomp as his voice begins to crack.

"I am Isaac, but tears of happiness. What did Dan, your new roommate, do, Isaac? I don't know, honey... an electrician? Oh, Isaac, isn't that dangerous work? You know how accident-prone you can be... I mean... you are all... oh, Isaac, isn't there something else? Can't they use you at something like you do here for Grandpa?" asks Hannah worriedly.

"Hannah, I am not accident-prone... oh, OK, maybe just a little bit. I mean, look where I am." Isaac laughs, "Oh, Hannah, I miss you so much! Oh, yeah, I have to finish letting you know. My boss here is Paul, the electrician and owner of Aesthetic Electric. How cool is that? Hannah, honey, call Paul. I'm sure that he will be able to bring me little gifts from home, from you. Maybe not at first, but ask him and find out. Once I get my A-1-A status, you can come to visit Sammy, Jesse, and you too. Please schedule our quarterly weekend visits, too. I love you, Hannah, honey."

"Mr. Stompski, 213, please finish your call for now. We need to get the count done after chow. Please inform your loved one that you will have access to a phone tomorrow after you get hired. Thank you.", the tower speaker states.

"Did you hear that, Hannah, honey? I have to go...I love you, Hannah, and always will!" Says Isaac hurriedly.

"Oh, Isaac, get hired quickly, please! I'll call Paul right away to inform him. To be safe, he probably will only want you to know about his relationship with you, you know...conflict issues. I love you, Isaac!" says the now hopeful Hannah.

"I know, Baby. Oh, do you mind if I get a tattoo in here? You know, one or two that are only visible to you and no one else?" Promises Isaac.

"Where only I can see them? That doesn't mean..." Hannah visions his penis with a tattoo. "As long as only I can see them, Isaac! Nothing evil like skulls, only good-natured ones, and I'll have to OK them. How do you mean that only I can see them?" queries Hannah.

"The CO is here, Babe. Gotta go now. Love you!"

# Chapter 87:

Stomp is sitting in a seat in the Administration Office, waiting to be interviewed by the CO in charge of Inmate Day Labor, Carmen Diaz, thirty-four and a sweetheart. Amazingly, she still remains unmarried but no longer available, while just about every CO here at Donovan Prison has tried to date her. Miss Diaz has strict rules against dating other COs, as her father and both brothers are also correctional officers. Her father has been a CO for thirty years as of last October. He is in Transportation. Both of her brothers reside near El Centro. One works at Ironwood CDC, and the other at Centinela CDC, both are in Imperial County. Being around Correctional Officers for her entire life, she cannot imagine dating another, let alone being married to one.

A string bikini and G-string greatly enhance her striking beauty and figure. She prefers to date watermen, such as Paul Provencio, the owner of Aesthetic Electric and free-staff foreman of the IDL Electrical Department. His insatiable prowess in bed is amazingly thorough and compassionate. He's not Magnum-PI-like handsome, but he has taken her to places that she has never been before; more than one-way trips, they were round-trips and many trips a night. The sight of him instantly affects her. She has had more than one orgasm just by sitting next to him in his truck, just traveling to check out the surf. She'll always remember their first date. There was no dinner, no movie, no stroll under the moonlit night but an afternoon at Scripps Pier, surfing on a longboard made by Skip Frye in the cool water of La Jolla's clean Pacific Ocean. The memory is still an aphrodisiac to her, as are many more.

Carmen has to bring her thoughts back to the present before she gets wet again. She looks at the file in front of her: Isaac Stompski, highly educated, married, and happily loyal to his wife of only one year. He is not only recommended by Mr. Dixon, the porter from Building 16 on the 4-Yard but also by her man, Paul. If Paul wants him to be hired, she will move mountains to make it happen for him. There goes her mind again as she shifts her position in her seat, wanting to run her fingers across her labia but restraining. "Back to work, girl!" she reminds herself. "Mr. Stompski, please, come in and have a seat." Stomp does so. "Mr. Stompski, how are you today?"

"Fine, thank you, CO Diaz." Answers Stomp.

"Under the circumstances anyway, right? Anyway, the position for which you are being considered is probably one of the best that Donovan offers. I am in charge of Inmate Day Labor, IDL, for an acronym. We work in all construction trades. You are being hired to work with your cellmate, Daniel Nelson, in the electrical trade. Mr. Nelson is more than willing to take you, with your lack of previous knowledge, and mentor you into this trade. Are you O.K. with working in and learning the electrical trade, probably the most hazardous of all the trades?" Diaz asks, prideful of her man as a Master in the field.

"Yes, CO Diaz. I have full confidence in my cellmate and your free staff not to place me in harm's way. As long as I follow directions from these two, I am confident of my safety and theirs.", replies Stomp.

Diaz is impressed by his answer, very impressed, indeed! "Very good answer, Mr. Stompski. Your eloquence, I have no doubt, precedes your actions. I will do the paperwork today. After dinner, your new I.D. for A-1-A status will be in effect. You will begin work on Monday morning. Paul, your free-staff boss, will be here then and..." she wiggles and shifts in her seat, blushing, "...he is very thorough and likes to welcome his new employees. Your A-1-A status will begin immediately, which means that your visits and conjugal requests will be granted as of today."

"Thank you so very much, CO Diaz. I will not let you down! Ever!" Stomp thinks to himself, "Why is she blushing like a high-school girl? What am I missing here?"

Stomp then asks the CO, "Will that be all then?"

"Oh, yes, yes. Sorry, Mr. Stompski, I was daydreaming just now. Thank you, that will be all. You are excused."

Stomp rises from his seat at her desk. "Thank you, CO Diaz."

"Please, Mr. Stompski, close the door on your way out?"

Stomp does so. Carmen picks up her phone and calls Paul's office, hoping to catch him before he heads out for the day.

"Aesthetic Electric, your complete service contractor, how may I direct your call?" Marcie, the receptionist, answers.

"Hi, Marcie, this is Carmen. Has Paul left for the day yet?" asks Carmen. "Oh, no, Miss Diaz. He has been expecting your call before heading out...just a second." Marcie patches her through.

"Hi, Baby, I was hoping it was you!" says Paul, grinning ear to ear.

"Honey, I gotta see you tonight, sooner if possible." Says Carmen after hearing his voice and getting even more aroused.

"Of course, Babe. Is something wrong?" Paul's worry is evident.

"Wrong? Wrong? No, Honey, everything is soooo right! I just need you! I mean, really, really need you! I can't think about anything but...but..." she is getting wet again. The baritone of his voice is at bone depth, and she is melting.

"O.K., Carmen. What have I created? I feel the same way, Sweetie. I have to taste you and your sweet nectar before I can enjoy another breath!", Paul's ever-thirsty appetite never quenched.

"Oh, Honey, you just made my day seem longer than any I've ever had. I'll get out of here as soon as I can. I'll call you." breathes Carmen. "And I'll wait for it, breath held! Have a great day, Baby. See you tonight!" Then Paul hangs up.

Now, the door closed, Carmen puts her hand over her throbbing labia between her legs; a long, long day ahead of her.

Stomp gets led back to the 3-yard, shows his I.D., and is let back in through the gate. It's yard time for those not at work, and Art and Chris see him and walk up to the gate. They greet one another, and Art asks, "So how did it go in there, Stomp? Did you get the IDL job?"

"Yes, I did. My A-1-A status and I.D. are effective immediately. I can get visits now and conjugal weekends four times a year now, too. Matt really came through for me, Art... first chance I got...I gotta shoot him an entire can of Bugler. How do I do that?" asks the very appreciative Stomp.

"First, you gotta get in good with your free-staff boss at IDL, establish a sense of trust so he knows that you won't let anyone know that anything came from him; same as anything here, Stomp, 'hold your mud'. It's really not a problem if it's only tobacco, Stomp. Never use the source for illicit drugs, no matter who asks you. You are not a mule, Stomp. Make that clear if approached. No matter how hard they lean on you, lean right back. Set your boundary right from the gate, no gray areas. Got it?" Art makes the point clearly.

"Yeah. Never mule drugs or paraphernalia. Got it!" clarifies Stomp.

"Do not try to bullshit your boss. Let him know exactly what your intention is for the tobacco if asked; 'I need to return a favor' or 'I want to share it with Dan and my friends.' See my hands, Stomp? What do you see on my fingertips? Show him your hands, Chris." Art demonstrates.

"I see tobacco stains on your fingers, Art. You, too, Chris. Same stains." answers Stomp.

"Now, look at your own." Says Art.

"No stains." Returns Stomp.

"This is what is always looked at. The COs all chew their tobacco, and so do some housed convicts. The COs carry a cup or container to spit in; have you noticed? Same with those on night-yard who have access to chew, you'll see. Rather than being obvious in the yard by smoking, they chew, smoking only in the cells. I know that you don't smoke, but..." Art still schooling Stomp.

"That reminds me, guys, here..." Stomp digs out the two smokes that Dan gave him this morning for his friends, "...these are from Nelson to share with you guys. He even gave me a lighter to use out here."

"Right on, Stomp!" Art takes one and breaks it in half, half for Chris and his cellmate, half for Art and his cellmate. They then walk clear of the gate before Art and Chris light up and share the other one. Stomp can see their eyes get hazy as the nicotine hits their systems. Still, he has no desire to smoke. Stomp, for these last months, has seen the effects of heroin, crystal, Suboxone, and even Remeron on other inmates. Art has explained to Stomp that he may use a drug when it hits, but he takes his responsibility for the Wood Pile car seriously. He never does an excessive amount that would incapacitate him. He also makes it clear to any 'wood' not to take it to that point.

When drugs hit the yard or building, it's not apparent at first. It does become obvious to those who pay attention, however, not just to the other inmates who are familiar with the symptoms either. The Sheriff's deputies and the COs are trained to recognize the effects of using. Odd behavior from drug abuse will eventually become evident. Those who cannot handle or maintain it get blamed for the heat when the building gets hit or is scrutinized and searched.

This will cause problems, eventually, either for those who get fronts and can't pay on their next one or for those whose lack of control becomes obvious. Phone calls to home and loved ones asking for money to be put on someone else's account become frequent and are monitored. That may get tiring for a loved one trying to make ends meet to survive without a breadwinner out there to help. Soon, the money can't be sent, and a problem arises. Maybe a rep as good as Art can take care of the issue and maybe get some more time to pay if he is made aware of the debt before it becomes a problem. A good rep, like Art, will have rules in place stating that no drug debts are allowed, avoiding issues. At times, a solid 'wood's debt can be resolved within the 'wood' car, but that, too, gets old.

Stomp's wisdom has experienced all of these problems, and he has learned from Art the proper way to handle these issues. Those who make the same mistakes over and over have to be dealt with; it is always preferable to deal with it within your own car and before another car asks you to deal with it.

"We deal with our own, Stomp. I would rather have my homies discipline my actions than have them let another race discipline me." teaches Art. He also taught Stomp that if a debt can't be settled, 'hands laid...debt paid'. If the person owed the debt can't wait for reconciliation of payment, we will discipline but that will resolve the debt. No more issues.

Incarceration is a complicated society with respect, rules, and discipline. The best way to get through incarceration is to be without vices.

# Chapter 88:

Stomp, Art, and Chris continue to walk the track, Stomp's first walk on the 3-yard. Stomp is full of questions for Art, the first being when he can use the heavy bag and the speed bag to exercise.

"Stomp, do you see many convicts with gloves on? Once a year they have a Track Meet/Olympic Event competition. Boxing is one of the events, and a month or two before the competition, you will see people train. That's why you won't see anyone now and why I recommend that you set up your own equipment at the IDL yard, so you don't expose your skills in the yard." instructs Art.

"I don't get it, Art. I mean, of course, I trust your reasoning and will definitely follow your advice, but why not?" To Stomp, the equipment is like a beehive to a bee. The attraction is strong.

"Stomp, there is a lot of testosterone cooped up in these yards. Youngsters are searching for ways to get their stripes, taking a chance for legend status. They are street-scrappers. Don't get me wrong, they have heart and will not give in easily. You've read plenty of Louis Lamour novels while here. They're young gunfighters wanting to make a name for themselves. What is the one thing they search out?" asks Art.

"I guess they always target a legendary name to be the one who wins against him in a gun battle?" Stomp answers.

"Bingo! Stomp, consider this place the Wild West. All of these young cannons are threats to your legendary status. The Woods and the South Siders are protecting you from the highest levels. However, there are some legend-seekers who would ignore that, taking the discipline in a trade-off for a name. Never let your guard down, Stomp. Never show off your weapons and skills to allow someone to spot a weakness in your armor." Art continued.

"So, to exercise my skills in the yard will expose my skills, allowing an adversary to plan an attack against me? Is that the reason, Art?" clarifies Stomp.

"Part of it, Stomp. Of course, one never really knows what lurks in the minds of men who want what others have. This is especially true if they see how well you are being treated while they aren't. Greed and jealousy are prevalent in all walks of life. It is simply not enough that you knowingly gave up years of freedom to rid the Earth of a threat to our children. Some youngsters, jealous of your status, may overlook that respect. Even in my position as a rep, my decisions are not made lightly. If a wrong decision is made, I could be scrutinized by a youngster who claims a wrong decision and that my status as a rep should be taken or stripped from me and given to him. It only takes one 'Oh, Shit!' to take away a lifetime of 'Atta Boy's'. I never make a decision lightly, and neither should you in here where it could come down to life or death." Says Art, with all seriousness.

"With each tidbit of wisdom out of your mouth I understand why you are in the position that you are in. I am also in agreement that we have the right man to represent us all. I am also proud to call you a friend and comrade, Art." Stomp says to his mentor.

"Thank you, Stomp. I have the same respect for you. To finish your question on the heavy bag, keep your pugilistic skills to yourself until called upon. I can admit that you are the top gunslinger in the yard if not the whole prison. There will be those who want to challenge you. It is not a question of... if... but when? The proper arena for this, for everyone's protection, is under proper guidelines and supervision. It's the difference between a bout and a brawl, sport or otherwise. Nelson will show you how you can get the bag work done where you work. Once your IDL boss sees your skills, he can, and probably will, help set you up in an area.", suggests Art.

Stomp thinks that Paul will definitely help him set up bags. Paul might even bring his own equipment for sparring.

"Thanks, Art. I'll take things slow until I get to know my IDL boss." Stomp has to keep this to himself but doesn't like keeping it from Art.

"Yard recall! Yard recall! Everyone, return to your buildings immediately! Yard recall!" The loud tower-speaker reverberates around the entire yard, sparking a mass exodus.

# Chapter 89:

As Stomp, Art, and Chris walks into Building 13, the CO is at the podium and calls Stomp over, "Stompski, head upstairs and bring me your A-2-B I.D. card to exchange it for your new A-1-A I.D. and congratulations on your new IDL job."

"Cool! Thank you, CO Adams. I'll head right up. Give me a couple of seconds." as Stomp heads up the stairs.

"That's right, Stomp!" Both Art and Chris congratulate him on his job. Stomp goes into 213, grabs his I.D., heads back down to the podium, and gives Adams the old ID.

CO Adams explains to Stomp, "Mr. Stompski, this entitles you to many new privileges. Ask Mr. Nelson what they are. What I can inform you from here is that you can now attend night-yard, you now have phone usage at unlock, and you now have nightly shower access. If you have any questions that Mr. Nelson cannot answer, please do not hesitate to approach me or any other COs working the podium." Adams then holds out Stomp's new I.D. and, with it, the key to visit with his family and friends.

"Thank you, CO Adams. You failed to address the priority advantage of this thin, laminated photo I.D., which doubles as the key to being able to see my friends and family and for my wife and partner to start a family. This thin passport of a future is most dear to me. Thank you, sir." as Stomp begins to tear up.

"Mr. Stompski, I can read those whom I house in here pretty darn well. I see and read them all. You, sir, are a breath of fresh air, and please, do not allow this place to change you. I can honestly say that I am here for you in any way that I can be, as long as you are straight with me, and I will be the same for you. Congratulations on your new job. You will find that the weeks will fly by now. I will leave your cell door open if you'd like to get a shower before the workers get back from work. Otherwise, you can secure your door.", adds CO Adams, respectfully.

"Thank you, sir. I will take that shower." Says Stomp as he hurries up the stairs.

"Tower, start showers for the lower tier. When you are ready, leave cell 213 open as well. Go ahead, Mr. Stompski.", Adams announces. "When you are done, I will allow a phone call as well, if you'd like. Just leave the cell door open until you are done."

"Once again, thank you." Stomp continues up the stairs to get his hygiene items, then heads to the shower.

The tower speaker sounds, "Beginning showers for lower tier first. First three cells, go!" Three cells roll open to occupy two lower-tier and one upper-tier shower.

Stomp is in the shower near his cell. Showers have a fifteen-minute limit, then the next set of four cells will go. The shower cube has three shower heads. Each cell has two convicts. The cube is five feet by five feet. On the 4-Yard they utilize every shower head, so three convicts per cube. Those coming from work, however, get shower cubes for themselves. Stomp gets to enjoy his first solo shower in months but, still, for only fifteen minutes. He then heads back to 213 to await Nelson.

Nelson's arrival is telegraphed by the cell door rolling open. "Well, Isaac, tell me, brother. Don't keep me in suspense here." Then he looks down on the shelf and sees Stomp's new I.D., "All right, Isaac! I guess it all went well with Diaz? Isn't she just the sweetest CO you'll ever meet? What a sweetheart she is!"

Stomp, who never lusts after other women, has to agree with Dan. "Yeah, Dan, she was very nice to me. It seemed as if her mind was elsewhere, however. I think that she was glowing from thoughts of sex, you know, flustered like?"

"You need to keep this to yourself and me, Isaac. Paul and Diaz have been seeing each other for over a year now, I think.

She has eyes for no other and it's obvious to see when she comes by at lunch every day. I mean, there is nothing inappropriate at work or anything, but it's very obvious by her movements and the way her smile lights up when they are together." Dan's smile gets bigger, "I, for one, am happy for her. She deserves happiness, and so does Paul."

"It's funny, Dan, that Hannah and I haven't met sweet Miss Diaz yet, but they've only been going out for a year. By the looks of her fluster and blushing, they are still exploring each other and very well, indeed!" says Stomp. "By the way, Dan, my wife thinks that it's best to keep my relationship with Paul on the low-down unless he brings it up, anyway. Is that cool with you?"

"Certainly...but if I know Paul, his excitement on seeing you will be difficult to hide. Isaac is the one doing the CDC. a favor, not the other way around. I guess you're being hired tomorrow is the reason that he'll be here first thing in the morning. He never said why; he just said that he'd see you first thing. Congratulations, Isaac. I look forward to teaching you the trade." Guarantees Dan.

"I really appreciate you, Dan. I am a fast learner. Oh, Art wants me to ask you...Art thinks that it's a poor idea to use the heavy bag or the speed bag in the yard. Do we have an area out there to set up the bags?" asks Stomp.

"Really, Isaac? I thought you said that you knew our boss. Doesn't he train with you and Danny, is it?" asks Dan.

"Sammy. My best friend is Samuel, Dan.", corrects Stomp.

"And Jumping Jesse, too? That is Paul's main topic most days at work. Isaac, Paul has both sets of bags, focus pads, gloves, and headgear out there as well. He just doesn't have a suitable sparring partner anymore, and I am too old to get punched on. Art is right, Isaac. If your pugilistic skills are well-honed, you'd best not show them off and telegraph a challenge to the yard. The youngsters will be relentless to go with you. Art has good advice. Keep your skills to yourself in the yard.

At work, there are only a few of us, and we are all yard-wise and mind our own business.", Nelson says.

"You are right. Paul's shop even has a makeshift ring in the warehouse. Of course, he'd have a set-up here." Says Stomp excitedly.

"I'm pretty sure that we are gonna get more new boxing equipment now, too. We also have a weight pit out there. Nowhere else can we use weights here, but we have our own bars and cinder blocks, ropes, and pulleys; pretty ingenious, I gotta admit. You'll see, Isaac. I gotta get ready for chow. Hamburgers tonight and corn on the cob. I'll fill you in on the rest as we all walk to chow." Then Nelson is out the door to get his shower.

On the track to the chow hall, Nelson, Art and Chris are listening to Nelson inform Stomp, "We will get woke up together at the same time as I do every day. The difference is that you and I will leave Building 13 together at 5:30 in the morning. We will have breakfast in the chow hall at 6:00 in the morning, only a handful of us, though. I believe that our crew is the earliest to use the hall. Paul likes to get started at 7:00 in the morning. He runs a business out there and several crews, so he'll usually leave after he gets lunches for us from the 'Officers Dining Room.' The lunch sacks we get, we take in case he has to leave early but, usually, one of the other contractors will pick up our lunches for us. Paul's get-down is this...if we work through dinner, he buys us ODR; if we start early for some reason, he buys ODR any meal when he is here, and he takes very good care of us. Rare, but sometimes he brings us Starbucks. Since it's only you and I, Stomp, he may even bring bagels with cream cheese and bacon. Always, no matter what, CO Diaz joins us at each meal...well, not really us but Paul." Nelson runs it all down, "You will get new, black construction boots and a real camp jacket instead of a denim one. We just can't wear the boots except to and from work. The jackets are cool, though."

"It can't get any better than IDL, Stomp. You get all sorts of privileges because you are skilled labor, and the COs treat you better. You get all that.", says Art.

"You deserve this, Stomp. Hell, you shouldn't even be here at this..." Chris begins.

"No, Chris. I believe that I am here because it is God's will. That is my perspective and my faith. I am here with all of you for some reason that hasn't been made apparent to me, but to God, I am His tool. I believe that!" Stomp interrupts.

"Well, destiny or not, your attitude alone brings me faith in humanity and, now, divinity as well! Thank you, Stomp. It is an honor to be here with you and to know you as well.", Chris says sincerely.

Art and Nelson concur with Chris' sentiments. "Now, let's get some hamburgers, Wood Pile!"

# Chapter 90:

Nelson and Stomp are awakened by a tinny voice over the speaker at the door, "Nelson, Stompski, time to rise and shine. You guys up?"

"Yeah, CO, we are up, thank you. We'll be ready to go in fifteen minutes.", says Nelson.

"All right, fellas. Stompski, good luck today.", says the tower CO.

"Thank you, sir.", replies Stomp. Then, they hear the click of the intercom turning off.

Nelson says, "We don't need coffee or anything here. We'll get all that at work. Did you notice how friendly the tower CO treated us? We'll get the same respect and friendliness from all of them throughout the day. See what I mean? About the only ones who are assholes to us are the Goon Squads. They are the black-uniformed CDC officer squads that come through our work areas and search for drugs, porno, and contraband, like cell phones. Yes, you heard me right, cell phones. You won't see them here, but a lot of us have them. Most hide them here outside the gate at work because the areas aren't searched like they are in our buildings. I have one hidden, too. I'm sure that Paul will hook you up, too. Let's get going. This is the closest thing to freedom that I have, Isaac, and I can't wait to leave!"

"Ready? Let's hit it, Dan!", the excited Stomp says.

"Just bring yourself. We'll hook you up with all the new stuff at work. We also get new clothing at the end of each day. We also get long-sleeved T-shirts issued to us. Others get laundry bags and have to send their clothes through the laundry, but not us." brags Nelson.

They leave 213, secure their door, and start down the stairs to the CO, who is waiting at the building gate. "Have a great day, gentlemen," says Adams.

"You, too, Adams.", says Nelson.

"Have a good one, CO", says Stomp.

They walk out of the building into an early fog that makes it difficult to see the tower. Because of this, they come across a CO at each entrance path to Buildings 13, 12, and 11. Nelson, familiar with all of them, says hello to them by name. All of them know of Stomp and greet him, as well as Nelson.

The two walk into the chow hall, cinnamon-roll day, one of Nelson's favorite breakfasts. The cinnamon rolls are as big as dinner plates. The oatmeal is steaming, and a large scoop of peanut butter awaits both of them. There are only fifteen or twenty others seated in the huge dining room, and Nelson introduces Stomp to all of them.

"Good morning, fan club! Hey, fellas, this is my cellmate, Stomp. He will be with us for a few years. Stomp, these are all of your co-workers for IDL...you can be introduced to each other later. For now...let me at them rolls!" says Nelson.

"Hey, Stomp!" they all say, "See you out there."

Nelson and Stomp sit and eat. CO Diaz walks in and says, "Good morning, crew!"

"Morning, Miss Diaz!", they all say together.

"What a drive in this morning...the fog on the freeways is epic.", a word she picked up from Paul, "Assholes slamming on their brakes all at once...I felt like hitting them just to teach them a lesson!"

"Teach me a lesson, Diaz." someone decides to hint to her bravely.

"Oh, really?" as she removes her baton and slaps her hand with it, "Now, or at change-out after work?"

"Uh, uhm..." the now not-so-brave man stammers.

"I thought so. Now, Mr. Stompski, how are you today? It is nice to have a respectful sort among us...a real gentleman." She looks around the chow hall with disdain. Nelson is still digging into his cinnamon roll. "Would you like me to get you another tray, Nelson?"

"Yes, Miss Diaz!" Nelson says, with a huge mouthful.

"Anyone else?" Diaz asks.

Everyone says at once, "Yes."

"Go ahead and walk back through the line. Hey, kitchen server, get my men another tray, please?" asks Diaz.

"Yes, Miss Diaz, anything to keep you in here longer!" the server returns.

"Save the energy, fellas. I'm all worn out today!" says Diaz to a cacophony of catcalls and hollers.

# Chapter 91:

Miss Diaz takes all of the IDL workers through the 3-yard gate, stops off at the Laundry, and picks up Stomp's new boots, camp jacket, a ten-pack of new socks, and a six-pack of new boxer shorts. She has the Laundry put all of it into a new mesh laundry bag for Stomp to carry his items to the shop and back to the 3-yard at the end of the work day. All done, she leads the group to their current project, converting an empty warehouse into an injection-mold-manufacturing building.

Donovan is working with a supplier of landscape, sprinkler heads, and other accessories. P.I.A. is an employer of prisoners who assemble these parts and they pay prisoners a fair wage to compensate them. Prison Industry Authority accepts contracts from manufacturers and creates jobs within the walls of incarceration, not just at Donovan but throughout the State of California. Men who are employed there receive wages; a third goes to pay off their restitution decreed by the judge and state; a third goes into the men's accounts; a third is saved into another account for their release dates.

The men are led into the construction area, past the con-ex box. "Mr. Stompski here is where you will check out any of the specialized tools, including your tool bag, that you will need to accomplish your duties. Each of you has ten washers with a number stamped on them. Here are your ten. Your number is 33. Mr. Nelson will instruct you in the process.", says CO Diaz, who seems to be impatient and in a hurry as they walk into the project warehouse.

The warehouse is about one hundred yards long by forty yards wide, constructed of steel. The center core has newly constructed bathrooms with a room for electrical controls built on the side. A mezzanine on top has transformers humming away. The control room has unfinished walls, and the Allan-Bradley control gear is lined up against the walls. A rack of conduits, neatly bent and spaced, is hung on uni-strut supports out of these conduits and stubbed out through the unfinished walls and into the manufacturing area. A job box has already been unlocked, and the plans are on a makeshift table being studied by his friend, Paul.

Paul's six-foot-one-inch frame is what would be expected of a San Diego local who has surfed since he was eight years of age. He has wide shoulders with wavy, black hair, slightly graying at the temples. He is wearing Dickie shorts, an Aesthetic Electric collared shirt, and a required hard hat with the same logo on it. A sticker on the back of the hard hat says, "If you want to come in 2nd place, follow me!" His smile is very infectious, and he beams one of his best at the sight of Carmen Diaz as she walks straight at him.

CO Diaz has to stand on tip-toes to give her man a kiss. His touch makes her arm hair tingle. Her sex flutters from the nearness of her lovely partner. Between the two, their smiles can light up the sky, like a show of the Northern Lights. This affection that they share makes all of them, especially Stomp, miss their individual 'Hannahs.'

Nelson and Stomp approach the open job box. Paul sees Stomp and says, "Isaac, I heard about what happened to you, and I couldn't believe it until now. I received a call from Hannah last night. Carmen and I swung by your house to visit her. She and Carmen both had a good cry, Stomp. Carmen here is a tough CO and can put men twice her size on their butts and cuff them, but she was teary-eyed from Hannah's take on this situation."

Discretion now out the window, Stomp says, "Paul, it sure is good to see a familiar face while here. My poor Hannah. I get to see her on weekends four times a year. I filed the paperwork." He looks at Diaz for verification.

"Isaac..." Diaz verifies, "...I think we can do a lot better than that for you two. Basically, I am going to get that for you on any weekend that a cottage is not in use. You will have your allotted four visits and as many more as I can swing for you. Actually, not this weekend, but next weekend is open for you two, and I'll swing by your home and let your lovely wife know. Sound good?"

"Really, CO Diaz? That would be terrific!" says Stomp, practically jumping up and down.

"On one condition. You call me Carmen, except around staff, and I'll call you Isaac, except around staff. Deal?" says Carmen. "Paul, I'll see you for break and lunch today, right?"

"What about dinner? The surf's really good at the Cliffs on the way in, and after that… tuna pitas for dinner at the Sea Trader?" asks Paul.

"Me for dessert?" asks Carmen.

"Yummy!" says Paul, licking his lips.

"You got that right!" as Carmen heads out the door.

"Man, Isaac, what a woman!" Paul whistles as she picks up the sashay in her hips, and everyone cat-calls and hollers as she leaves. The other free-staff members laugh and shake their heads.

"I always enjoy telling people that I am dating Carmen Diaz. I can't help it if they believe that I'm talking about the actress. Isaac, Carmen will take care of everything for you to make your time go better. I've brought you both a can of Bugler here. A cellphone for you, Isaac, on a pre-paid card. Nelson will instruct you on how to stash it and it didn't come from me."

"Really, Paul, that is so great! I can call Hannah from work here. She will love that.", says Stomp.

"Yeah, I just told her not to text or call you. We don't want to hear it ring. Even if the ringer is off, it will vibrate, and the Goon Squad will find it. I also brought you two bagels and coffee. Today will be light. Nelson will show you around our project here, and explain the do's and don'ts. I will bring you another can of tobacco tomorrow for your friend, Dixon, on the 4-yard. Carmen will get it to him for me. Matt will appreciate that.", says Paul.

"Thanks, Paul, for everything. I just don't want you to get in trouble or fired from here in any way. I have learned how to be off the radar, but I am new at this and will never get used to it.", says Stomp.

"Let's hope not. Some have out-dates here like yours, some don't, like Nelson...Lots keep coming back for whatever reasons. What I have learned, Isaac, is that most are good men, stuck in the revolving door so many times that it is evident that this system is broken. I see it, and so do other voters. We vote, but the courts come up with ways to work around the new laws. I don't understand why these judges allow it to happen. They are the ones who are supposed to protect our laws and our rights but they are the ones violating them. You had a good attorney, I hear and got a great deal, but too many others here can't pull that off and get twice as long or break off and strike out. My heart goes out to them all, all good guys and a couple not so good. Anyway, I'll check in with you before I go. We got you, Isaac.", reminds Paul.

"All right, please, tell Hannah not to worry and that I can't wait to see her in two weeks.", says Stomp.

"You got it!" says Paul as he walks off.

# Chapter 92:

Nelson and Stomp sit at the makeshift plan table and enjoy their second breakfast: bagels from Einstein's and coffee from Starbucks. "Amazing how Paul still knows that I like my coffee like candy, with all the mocha and whipped cream, but he got you a black, no-frills coffee.", Stomp notices.

"That's the thing with him, Isaac. He always remembers what he promises, always does what he says he'll do, and is always there for you when you need him the most. Those are CO Diaz's words. I'll never forget them because they ring true. I know. I try to live the same way and I know, as you are his friend, that you do, as well. The first thing we'll do is set up your phone and charge it; then, we'll take a tour of the P.I.A. buildings. It is also our job to maintain the manufacturing buildings, as well as the lighting towers, work orders requesting work, and new construction. We, basically, have keys to every gate in every yard. I have no problem dropping off care packages of legitimate items to others on other yards; coffee and even tobacco and chew. I just let the CO at the gate know that I have these items and that it is OK to take them to a buddy. The COs are all OK with that as long as you declare the items, like at the border, 'Do you have anything that I need to know about?'. Don't say no when you do. If they search and find it, they'll never trust you again. If they take what you declare, it's no big deal. Try again the next day. We never drop off hot kites or drug kites because we would lose our jobs. If asked to do so, my response is always, 'Why are you asking me to risk my job, my only part of this hell-hole that gets me out of here? I would never ask that of you!' No one asks me anymore, but you may be approached. They may even make it look innocent, but hidden in an item, a drug can be saturated into a card or paper. If they want a message sent, do not accept the kite unless it is written in front of you on paper that you provide." Nelson must get this across until it is understood.

"We've got it good out here, all of us, not just you and I, and we'd like to keep it good!"

"Got it, Dan, and thank you. For now, I only do what you suggest. I will always check with you before doing anything.", agrees Stomp.

"O.K., probably best at first. Let's get your phone charging." Nelson unwraps the cell phone, grabs the multi-outlet strip, and heads up the stairs above the rooms to the mezzanine power room. He removes a side panel on one of the service gears and sees two other phones being charged from an outlet installed inside the gear. Nelson checks his phone for messages, knowing that he won't have any, but he still checks from habit. He unplugs one phone charger, plugs in the outlet strip, and then plugs Stomp's phone in to charge. He grabs one of the phones and then replaces the side panel. "We're going to bring this to Matt Mimms. He works with the welders' crew."

They walk down the stairs, and Nelson leads Stomp over to the welder's lockbox area. "Matt, this is my cellmate, Stomp. I think that Art may have spoken to you about him."

Matt Mimms stands up and shakes Stomp's hand, "Pleased to meet you, Stomp. Heard good things about you from Art. He told me about your work and that you are a blank canvas. Are you interested in some tattoos?" Matt asks.

"Hey, Matt, Art has told me that you are righteous, as well. He told me not to let anyone art me up but you. I've never had one. My wife says that she approves if the tattoo is visible only to her and is not below the sleeves. You are the man, so just let me know what I need to pay or do to get it done.", says Stomp.

"First, Stomp, you've earned yours already, and we out here have all been taken care of already. We can do the work a little at a time. Let me think about it, and I'll get back to you. Sound good?" says Matt.

"Let me know, Matt. I appreciate you.", says Stomp.

"It is we who appreciate you, Stomp.", returns Matt. "We'll spend some time later. We can talk, and you can tell me your story. Then I'll come up with something that is all you. What's your wife's name?" asks Matt.

"Hannah. The love of my life since we were kids." Answers Stomp.

"Got it. We'll talk, Homie.", ends Matt.

Nelson then leads Stomp around to the other job boxes and the Con-E's toolbox. He is issued ten chits with the number 33 on them. Nelson hands over one chit to receive his hand-tool pouch. "We won't use your tool pouch today. We'll put your chits in our box, then do the maintenance rounds."

Nelson explains to Stomp what happens when a tool goes unaccounted for. "When we were laying the foundation for this building, doing the underground piping and sewer, a plumber lost a large screwdriver in one of the trenches. The Goon Squad, the only CDC COs who fuck with us out here, the investigative squad, had us out here until three in the morning. We dug up every trench as they worked the metal detectors until we dug up the screwdriver. They were pissed. We all were pissed, although it was an accident. The screwdriver just fell out of the plumber's back pocket. He lost his job here, and they moved him into the gym with a five-cent-an-hour kitchen job. All of our tools are accounted for by the end of the day. Before we go back, we all meet at two in the afternoon. It takes the Goon Squad an hour to check all the tools in the shed. We pretty much knock off at one-thirty, tools in by two, to the Laundry by three, changed out, and on the 3-Yard by three-thirty, every day, no overtime. Sometimes, Diaz and Paul need us on a Saturday as volunteers, and we are happy to comply to return the many favors that they do for us. Now, let's go check out the manufacturing buildings for P.I.A.". Nelson grabs his tool belt, leaves a chit for a voltage/amperage meter, and off they go.

# Chapter 93:

Nelson and Stomp walk up to a John Deere farm cart, throw the tools into a milk crate in the back, and the tour of P.I.A. is underway.

"I was asked yesterday to fire up all the light towers on all of the yards and assess the hours to do the yearly maintenance on them. The towers stand a hundred and twenty feet high. Due to Federal requirements, we do this once a year. P.I.A. is next to 1-Yard, so we'll dip into the electric room there first. It takes fifteen to twenty minutes for the HID lighting to fire up. Paul is working on a bid to retrofit to LED to save power. An HID lamp burns at 1,000 watts, while an LED burns at 35 watts. San Diego Gas and Electric has a program to pay some of the cost but they do so in monthly credits. The initial cost can be very substantial, and budgets need to be approved. Until then, we will maintain all existing fixtures."

They walk into an electrical control room, head up a ladder to a roof hatch, and then step out onto a roof. "The photocell control is up here, away from any lighting." Nelson tapes up the photo-eye. "If lighting gets to the photo-eye, what will happen is that the lights will stop working, the photo-eye will turn them off, then back on, once dark, so the lights will go on and stay on all night long. At daybreak, the lights turn off and stay off all day long." They climb back down the hatch, go to the cart and take off to the P.I.A. bread plant. "Not sure if you noticed, Isaac, but you'll never see me eat the P.I.A. bread, nor will you see anyone who works there eat it. It's not only P.I.A. bread, either. I'm pretty sure that Wonder and any other bread manufacturers have the same problems that P.I.A. has with critters getting into their equipment. It was enough to get me to stop eating it! I still eat my Hostess products, though!"

Nelson leads Stomp into the P.I.A. bread plant and into the free-staff office. "Mr. Richards, how are you today? I have a new recruit here, Isaac Stompski. Isaac, this here is Paul Richards. Any problems or concerns today on any of the equipment, Paul?"

"No, Dan. All seems to be running like a well-oiled machine at present. Should we do a walk-through while you're here?" asks Mr. Richards.

"May as well, Paul. Can I grab the clipboard to make it official?" returns Nelson.

"Please do." Instructs Paul.

"Isaac, we do maintenance checks throughout the facility, checking off and initialling on each item. I last did this two weeks ago, so we'll go through it all for you. Ready, Paul? I'll lock up my tool bag in the office while we're walking. Always keep your tools in sight or under lock and key.", instructs Nelson.

The three walk the plant, staying within the well-defined walkway. Each piece of equipment has a control panel with a solid, painted red line three feet in front, as accorded by N.E.C. (National Electrical Code) requirements. As they walk, Nelson points out to Stomp the scurrying rodents and insects. Richards is unphased by the commonplace scurrying. Rodent problems here at R.J. Donovan are visibly uncontrollable. Those housed in the gyms see more than their share of the problem. Second tiers are preferred housing over floor tiers due to rodent issues, but the rodents are still present. Insects get ground up in the manufacturing process and are baked every day, and there are no health inspections. If there were, there is no doubt that the plant would be shut down. All the processed bread supplies not only the prison but also the County jail facilities in the State. The walk-through takes half an hour. The three return to the office. Nelson returns the completed clipboard, and he and Stomp continue on their tour.

Nelson and Stomp return to the 1-yard and are allowed through the gate, driving the utility cart. Each tower holds eight fixtures. Nelson counts two lights out on one tower and three lights out on a second tower, a total of five. He then drives the cart to the base of the first one, which is thirty-six inches wide, mounted on a concrete pad which is ten feet by ten feet. Nelson grabs his tool bag and removes the inspection plate at the base.

"O.K., Isaac, here is where we attach a telescoping bar onto this one-inch drive adapter. We will use a one-inch-drive Milwaukee crank drill, the same one we use to pull wire on large conduits; this will lower the light tower down to us so we can work on the lights. The cable runs through a pulley system similar to an elevator car. As the tower lowers, so does the cable. A reel of stainless-steel cable will unroll the cable so as not to kink or tangle. At times, the reel will jam on us, and we need a crane to hoist us up to the top to repair it. The 4-yard has one such problem. We haven't repaired it yet, but a report has been filled out to start a work order. Of course, that takes time." Nelson replaces the inspection plate and notes his observations on yet another clipboard. Then it's back to the electrical room to remove the tape on the photocell, then on to the 2-yard to repeat the process of documenting on the clipboard the lights needing repair, then reversing the process. "O.K., Isaac, lunchtime! Let's see what Paul brought us for lunch." Nelson and Stomp return to the construction site, carrying all of the tools in the milk crates. Paul and Diaz are there waiting, with Filippi's Pizza for everyone. Ten pizzas to feed all twenty-two people, split by five free-staff members, is only about forty dollars each. Usually, it is up to each free-staff member to buy for his guys, and they do this once a month.

"All right!" says Nelson, "Filippi's Pizza!"

"Dig in, fellas, these are the last two that we've been waiting for.", says Diaz, and they swoop on the pizzas like it could be their last meal on Earth. "We'll call it an early day today, guys. I've got plans for the rest of the day...", more catcalls and whistles, "...gentlemen, and I use the term loosely... please, tomorrow we'll get a full day out of you, so no worries! So, get a good night's rest and

stay off the shower packs, people!" raucous laughter from all.

The rest of the week is spent doing a light-tower audit and an estimate of the hours required to do the repairs. Each day Stomp gets to call Hannah from his new cellphone from Paul. Hannah lets Stomp know that Carmen has become a good friend. Hannah also tells Stomp that he and she have a weekend together coming up in seven days.

Which can't come soon enough for both of them.

# Chapter 94:

CO Adams and CO Diaz are waiting for Stomp when that weekend comes. Stomp is as nervous as a high-school-boy-virgin going out with the class slut at Prom.

"Are you O.K., Mr. Stompski?" giggles Carmen.

"How do I look, CO Diaz?" asks Stomp. He has now shaved his head and lost his sunburned scalp. Matt has put an 'S.D. Padre's logo on the back of Stomp's head, complete with a bat-swinging Friar.

"Well, let's have a look. She probably is not used to P.I.A. denim and blue-collar shirts, but I doubt that she will even notice this. Myself, I actually think that the shaved head is an improvement but I would never want it for my man. If it wasn't for me being in love with my man, I would fuck you..." begins Carmen.

"All right, I'm sorry I asked already..." says the blushing Stomp.

"... and if Hannah wasn't becoming my new, best friend to share all our intimate secrets... is it true, Isaac... what she says?"

"I'm sure that if Hannah says it, it's definitely true...uhm...what has she said?" asks Stomp.

"Oh, nothing. Just girt talk. I have no complaints about my guy, anyway, my Mr. Plum!"

"Your what?" asks Stomp.

"My..."

"Oh, never mind answering that one... I get it." Says Stomp.

They are at the gate to the cottages now. Hannah is outside, sitting at a picnic bench, when she sees them coming. CO Diaz unlocks the gate to allow Isaac entry as he and his wife run into each other's arms and, together, they cry; cry tears of long-awaited happiness, cry tears of agony and torment, their tears intermingle with a flurry of emotions. She is his wife of one and a half years, his love since childhood and his partner for life.

Carmen, too, cries, standing there, witnessing this endearing love shared between these two. She cries, as even here, surrounded by hopelessness and desperation, all that is completely smothered and forgotten by their love for each other. In all her years here, she has never seen this pure and untainted love within these walls. The reunifications that she is used to seeing here are purely carnal in nature. Those getting married while incarcerated in George Bailey seem to be doing so for only one purpose: these conjugal visits. That is what Diaz has been used to, so she cries for all those that she has witnessed before now. She cries because until she met Paul and these two friends of Paul's, now her friends, she had almost given up on, well, people in general.

People can be cruel and greedy towards one another, caring only for their own gain in life, completely apathetic, and lacking all empathy and compassion for their fellow man or woman. Chivalry, it seems to Diaz, is a lost culture; thinking, well, women, you wished for it, to be treated equally. Be careful what you wish for! Yes, she wants to be treated as an equal, as a human being, but she wants her man to treat her as a lady, as well. Now she cries, too, for women everywhere.

Carmen gives them a long moment. Usually, she would quietly close and lock the gate, retreating without any sign of emotion, not with her new friends, however. She slowly comes to them and wraps her loving arms around both of them. For a moment the tears really burst out, sobbing tears, now, bawling tears. The three look at each other, and then all three start to laugh hysterically while continuing to embrace one another.

Miss Diaz says to them both, "Isaac, you and Hannah have this place until nine in the morning on Monday. I'll come and get you both and escort you back. Don't worry about work on Monday. Nelson and Paul will be working on the tower estimates, going to the warehouse to inventory parts and then putting in an order. You won't be needed there, just here. I've really grown to love you both, Hannah, so don't worry about your husband. He will be taken care of by all of us. Now, go enjoy each other, and if you need any groceries, Hannah, just call me, and I'll bring them with Paul. See you Monday, if not."

Hannah gives Carmen a huge hug and kisses on her cheek, "We love you, too, Carmen. Thank you and Paul so much for all you two have done for us." Hannah releases Carmen and reaches out her hand to Isaac. "Come on, Honey, let's celebrate our first-year anniversary now. Whether it's here or on Catalina, my view will be the same!" They all laugh and Hannah leads her man into the cottage, while Carmen cries her way back to her office, then goes straight to a phone.

"Hello, Baby, how did it go? Are they OK?" asks Paul.

"Oh, Honey, are you at home? I need you so badly right now. Hannah is a doll, and Isaac is the same. We all cried together in a group hug. I've never done that with any other couple who've worked for me before. Promise me, Darling, that one day, our love for each other will be exactly like what Hannah has for her husband and Isaac has for his wife. They are so damn cute together, both of them staring into the other's eyes in that damn cage, but that was unimportant to them, being totally oblivious of being locked into a cage in a prison. What was important to them both was that they were finally together." Carmen is deeply impressed by the love that Isaac and Hannah displayed. "I really need that, Paul. Can you fulfil my need?" then she begins to cry.

Paul has to chuckle, "Now, now, Baby, please, don't cry, my rough, tough correctional officer! I can promise you this...get over here, and I will most definitely fill your need."

"Paul, I'm serious here."

"So am I, Baby...let me finish and get your mind out of the gutter! I will fulfil your need to be loved and cherished. I believe that we demonstrate this to each other without words...I love you with all my being, Carmen." Paul answers sincerely.

"Thank you, honey," Carmen says chokingly.

"Not done, Babe." Paul continues.

"Better not be. Keep going, you!" Orders Carmen.

"Carmen, we don't need to be separated for four months to get there...no hiatus from each other, please! I can't stand to be away from you each day while we are at work already. If we didn't work together as we do...think how difficult that would be! Again, I love you and I always will, Carmen." Paul reinforces his love for her but can still hear her crying in the background. "Carmen, please, stop crying, Baby."

"No, honey. These are tears of joy now. I love you with all my heart, Paul. I am so happy with you, my Prince Charming, my devil-tongued charmer!" begins Carmen.

"Get over here, Carmen. I'll show you a devil tongue...uhm...hurry, please!" says Paul with a swollen tongue.

"Me first, Paul. On my way, Lover!" finishes Carmen.

They hang up their phones. She grabs her bag and keys and begins jogging through all the gates. Anyone attempting to slow her down with conversation is met with the same reply, "Sorry, in a rush and can't talk now...sorry...in a hurry...see you Monday morning!" All those whom she encounters just stare after her, dust rising from her heels.

Neither Carmen and Paul nor Hannah and Isaac come up for air or nutrients for two whole days!

# Chapter 95:

On Monday morning, Carmen meets her IDL crew in the dining hall for breakfast, consisting of silver-dollar pancakes and sausage with milk and coffee. She comes over to Nelson's table to say good morning. "Mr. Nelson, how was your weekend in that great, big cell all alone?" she giggles, "Maybe Isaac was not the only one with a conjugal visit, huh?"

Nelson is still not used to a beautiful woman such as Diaz speaking to him as one of the guys. He almost chokes on a bit of sausage, "Nascar is great to entertain, CO Diaz, but, unfortunately, not on the level." he laughs with her, "Are you going to check out my cellmate this morning? You may need to bring a medical team with you for his wife, Hannah. I, for one, cannot believe that a woman can handle my cellmate without some ripping or tearing involved!" more laughter.

"You men think that you're all that, don't you? You're always trying to measure up to one another. I met his wife, Hannah, Nelson. Actually, we have become friends and I share dinners with her and Paul. His best friend, Samuel, and his girlfriend, Gabriella, also have dinners with us. They are all top-shelf people, Nelson. Hannah is a gorgeous, petite girl. They are in the most loving and committed relationship that I've ever seen. I want what they have, and I believe that I have a relationship that's close to it once Paul finally slips a ring on my finger. Until then, we enjoy sitting on longboards and watching the sunset." heart-struck Carmen sighs.

"Oh, yeah, sitting on a longboard, is it? So that's what you're calling it nowadays?" Nelson laughs and shares it across the dining hall. "Hear that, fellas? CO Diaz, here, sits on a longboard until the sun sets!" Catcalls and whistles reverberate and echo throughout the near-empty room.

"O.K., all you short boarders, finish up and stop stalling. I've got a job to do here!" returns Carmen, with humor of her own, to a chorus of boos. "Nelson, Paul has brought us breakfast, so don't fill up on State food; machaca burritos from Hilberto's down the street, quesadillas, and horchata to drink. Please, don't broadcast that, though!" She then walks to the exit door, signaling that it's time to go.

The IDL workforce is led through the gate and around the fabrication and manufacturing buildings, then into the new plastic injection mold building. As usual, the men split up to go to their respective areas while CO Diaz hurries over to Paul, who is already at work at his planning table. She comes up behind him, and her arms encircle him around his chest as she presses her ample bosom into his warm, wide shoulders and back.

"Yum!" Paul says. "I've missed you, Carmen."

"Missed me? I left at 4:00 am this morning. It's only been two hours! as she nuzzles and kisses his neck. "It's cold in here! How come you are always warm, and I am always cold?"

"The reason is that we complement each other, Doll, and it's been seven hours since we fell asleep last night, you first again, as I admired the steady rise and fall of my chocolate kisses!" He refers to her delicious nipples as chocolate kisses. "Do you really think that we would enjoy each other if we were both heaters in bed?" Paul usually kicks off the comforter as Carmen wraps herself around him and the comforter. "Good morning, Nelson."

"Morning, Paul. I was starting to think that I was invisible, standing over here!" jokes Nelson.

Paul looks over at him with Carmen still latched onto his back. "I'm sure that Carmen thinks of your jealousy as flattering; at least the jealousy had better be towards her!" and he laughs.

"Mr. Nelson had his Nascar fix this weekend, Lover. He only has jealousy for horsepower in over the one-thousand range.", replies Carmen.

"I brought you a breakfast burrito and Mexican fast food, Nelson. Carmen and I are going to go eat with Isaac and

Hannah. Care to join us, as long as it's O.K. with Carmen, that is?" asks Paul, looking between the two.

Carmen thinks and answers, "Sure if Nelson wants to meet Hannah. I know that she'd like that, too. She has told me so. I'll tell you what, Nelson,...check out your tools...if questioned, I can say that you are checking out the maintenance there."

"You got it, CO!" Nelson goes to the box, grabs a chit, and retrieves his tools.

Paul and Carmen meet Nelson at the work cart with the breakfast, and all three drive to the visit cottages for an eight-o'clock wake-up call.

# Chapter 96:

Carmen, Nelson, and Paul pull up to the visit cottages to find Isaac sitting at the picnic bench in front. Hannah is in his lap and nestled in his arms, the two totally immersed in their love and comfort. Isaac sees his new friends as Carmen unlocks the gate, and they enter. He greets them all with a smile and a wink. Hannah senses their presence and slowly lifts her head from the crook of Isaac's neck, waves at them, kisses Isaac, and walks over to Carmen for a hug. Hannah helps Carmen set out the Mexican food for their men, as Isaac introduces his wife to his co-worker and cellmate.

"Nelson, I'm glad that Diaz let you join us. I want you to meet my reason for living, my wife, Hannah. Hannah, this is my cellmate and my mentor in the IDL electrical trade, Mr. Daniel Nelson. I told you about him." Hannah gives Nelson one of her best hugs.

"Nelson, I doubt that Isaac said anything to you...so I will now...my husband is a gift from God...however, to God, there is no such thing as perfection. My Isaac's imperfection and God's sense of humor is his clumsiness. No arguments, Isaac! Honey, your two left feet are the whole reason that you are here! God did not push you onto that terrible person, as you claim, my lover. You tripped onto him. Nelson, you need to be aware of this...for the safety of both of you at work. Isaac has been accident-prone since he was ten years old, so please be careful! Oh, and it's so very nice to meet you."

"Now, Hannah..." begins Isaac.

"No, Isaac, I had to say it, and I did. I've lost you temporarily, and I refuse to allow this to become permanent!" she turns serious. "Thank you, all three of you, for being our friends through all of this...now...can we, please, eat? I am starved right now!" All three laugh, and then the two women talk together as they all feed on the needed substance.

"Paul, stay with your workers as I drive Hannah back to the Visiting Office. Then I'll come back and take Isaac back to his housing. I'll be back!" They pull away with kisses being blown by the two teary-eyed beauties.

"Hannah brought me some tennis shoes here and gym shorts, tank tops, socks, and underwear. Here, Nelson, one set for me and one set for you.", says Stomp.

"What..." begins Nelson.

"I told her your shoe size and clothes, the same size as mine, so she just duplicated it all. We can send a thank-you in a letter later, O.K.?" asks Stomp.

"Thank you both.", Nelson says.

"I'm sure that Carmen will escort you back with both bags of items. Here, put this in there, too..." Stomp then pulls a can of Bugler tobacco and a six-pack of microbic lighters out of his bag and buries them under the clothes, "... she knows about these already, but we bury them so as not to expose her in any way."

"Thanks, Paul.", says both Nelson and Stomp.

"I know that Nelson knows how to be discreet with it all. He shares it with others, too," says Paul.

CO Diaz is coming down the roadway now, and Paul is admiring her beauty. He says, "Isaac, Nelson, isn't she something? With her, beauty isn't only skin deep, either. She is a beautiful person, too. She has really become a good friend to Hannah, Isaac."

"I know. Hannah has expressed her gratitude to her. She says that she and Carmen are like twins of the soul, where one cries and the other feels it; the same as I feel when Hannah is upset or sad, I feel it, too." Admits Stomp.

"I think that I want to spend the rest of my life with her, Isaac. I mean, I know that I do! I could spend two lifetimes with her. I really believe that we have what you and Hannah have. I have been looking at wedding rings lately. She has no idea, though, but soon I am going to ask her. I have to speak to her father first." Paul's lack of confidence is apparent.

"If you are asking my advice, Paul, I would do it, ask her father first, I mean. It's traditional. Her father will respect you for it, as well. It's pretty obvious to all of us what her answer will be, and her father would give his daughter his approval to make her happy. So, if you want to keep this confidential, we had better end this before she parks!", finishes Stomp.

Carmen stops the cart, looks at the three men standing there like schoolyard boys getting caught in the act by the principle, and says, "All right, you boys, what gives? I pull up to the three of you smiling from ear to ear, staring at me, without catcalls and whistles like I usually hear from you. Something is up!"

"Yeah, Carmen, we are all awed by your beauty, awed as in speechless, tongue-tied awe! Yes, there are three things up, standing at attention here. I think that I can speak for all three of us here...we love you!" says Paul.

Carmen laughs, "The answer is yes, yes and yes. To whatever you three want, the answer is yes!" Then they all laugh. "Let's go, Isaac. Grab your property and climb in, all of you." Then they drive to the 3-yard. "Let me escort Isaac into Building 13 to his cell to get his property through, and I'll be right back."

As she walks away, Paul says to Nelson, "Nelson, I have to admit that I love it when she walks towards me with her quick gait, but...I think that I like the view even better when she hurries away!" They both laugh as she turns around and flips them off with her middle finger!

"That's my Baby!" Paul says.

Carmen escorts Stomp through the gate to Building 13, says her greeting to CO Adams, and explains to him that Mr. Stompski will have the rest of the day off but will go back to work in the morning. Yes, she has already searched his property in both bags. Stomp thanks them both, then walks up the stairs to 213 in no great hurry. He enters his cell, then secures the door after waving to them both, as Carmen, once again, begins to fight back the tears, an emotional wreck, thinking, "Am I for real here? Is this what happens when a woman falls in love?" She feels a higher sense of compassion for all others in love.

Whatever it is, she smiles. She really likes it a lot! She feels like a... Woman.

# Chapter 97:

Stomp lays out his and Nelson's new clothes and shoes, all identical. They will appear funny-looking in the yard, though. He wonders if Hannah did that intentionally to mark her property with her way of shopping. Her sense of humor brings a smile to his face. He starts to feel empathy for the hundreds of others locked up here who aren't as blessed as he is to be afforded this assistance all the way around. Is this God's mysterious way of taking care of His tool on Earth, His angel of redemption? All of this simply cannot be coincidental, can it; one right after the other? Stomp's knees get weak, as he seems to be pushed down onto the floor, as if two hands are on his shoulders, pressing him into a praying position. He begins to give thanks.

"Dear Father, I am here. I am ready to serve You in any capacity necessary. I want to express my humble gratitude for Your continuing blessings bestowed upon me and my family. I believe in Your works, Your blessings, Your love, and Your redemption. Please do the same for my wife, Hannah. She may not understand Your ways as I do. I know that I felt Your hands on my back, pushing me down those stairs and onto that terrible man; I felt Your presence. I do believe, although my Hannah does not know, that she will one day. Please bless her as You bless me. Without her, there is no me to do Your work. Thank you, Father. Amen." Stomp feels the pressure on his shoulders release, and he stands back up on his feet.

Stomp walks to the bathroom sink mirror to brush his teeth and wash his face. He then notices his shirt at the shoulders. There appear to be two imprints of palms and fingers in the fabric, plain to see, two very distinct impressions. He smoothens them out, but as soon as he does, they appear once again. How can he not believe it when His message is so obvious? He was here with Stomp, and they prayed together.

Stomp decides to change into his new gym clothes and new tennis shoes for the yard to see who's out there and to work out.

The first thing that he does is package up some tobacco for Art and Chris, including a lighter for each of them. He still hasn't mastered the art of rolling a cigarette. He always has a large lump in the middle, like a pregnant earthworm. Instead, he puts a few papers in each baggie.

The doors open for the morning yard. Stomp walks out and turns left to Chris' cell 217 just as Chris is stepping out. "Hold on a second, Chris. I have a care package for you.", says Stomp as he hands Chris a pack of tobacco. "Roll one up. I have one for Art, too. I need to catch him before he secures his door."

"Thanks, Stomp. Don't mind if I do. Meet you both downstairs.", says Chris, as Stomp begins walking towards cell 208. Art is still getting his boots on when Stomp walks to the door.

"Morning, Art. Got a care package for you here. Meet you downstairs when you're ready. I have the day off today. Are you going to the yard?" asks Stomp.

"Yeah, of course. Thank you for the smoke. I'll roll one and meet you downstairs.", says Art.

"I just came in from the yard, no searches that I could see. Your lighter should be fine to walk out with this morning. See you downstairs!" Then Stomp walks back to his cell 213, rolls the door closed and walks down the stairs to greet CO Adams. "Morning, again, Adams. Have a good day."

"You, as well, Mr. Stompski. Did your visit go well over the weekend? Is your wife taking it as good as could be expected?", cordially asks Adams.

"Yeah, my boss is very cool. Both bosses are good to me. As for Hannah and I, we were together, and that was what mattered the most to us. Thank you for asking. I'm going to work out for a while. See you later.", says Stomp, and he walks outside to the track and looks at his surroundings as the morning fog begins to lift.

Art and Chris walk out, and the three begin their walk in silence. Art and Chris know that Stomp has just had his first-weekend visit. They don't need to know how it went. That and Stomp's silence let them know that he is trying to hold onto that as far through the day as possible. The three get to the workout pit, where high bars, dip bars, push-up bars, and crunch bars are grouped in a pit of gravel.

Stomp peels off. "I'm gonna get my workout in while you both enjoy your morning smokes. Catch up with you all later."

"You got it, Stomp. We'll be right here on the track if you need us.", reminds Art. "You aren't alone out here."

"Thanks, Stomp, for the tobacco and all.", says Chris.

"You guys are very welcome. I really appreciate all you've done for me; I'm glad I can do something for you guys, too." Says the very appreciative Stomp.

"You missed breakfast with us...no sack lunch. If you need something, just holler at us. We got you.", Art reiterates.

"I know, fellas. I appreciate you both. Just need to work out and think a bit. We'll talk later, cool?" Says Stomp as stretching begins.

"Cool!" Art and Chris walk off and light up their smokes.

Stomp is still thinking about the hand impressions on his shirt shoulders that he saw in the mirror. What does it all mean? He is not an insane person. He is a man with faith in God. He has never been one to attend church every Sunday; however, he and Hannah had been regulars at the Rock Church in Point Loma, less rigid than the Catholic religion, praising God through song and music. Miles McPherson and his assistant pastors always brought a good message to the congregation. They really enjoyed the Ministry Recruitment Month when the entire roadway in front of the doors of the church was an encampment of kiosks representing every ministry imaginable. The message and hope of this encampment was to get those in the congregation into God's work by getting involved. Hannah has been wanting Isaac to become more involved in God's work. Well, Hannah, be careful what you wish for! Isaac chuckles at this cliché as he thinks it to himself.

Five sets of twenty-five dips done...on to the pull-up bars for five sets of fifteen in all three types of pull-ups; five sets of twenty-five in all three types of push-ups; five sets of twenty on the crunch bars on all three types; finally, to the high bar for his hanging crunches.

During the entire time, his thoughts are of his wife and how she is troubled, believing that his clumsiness caused him to trip into that very bad man. He thinks about feeling two hands on his back and being pushed. Even Stomp had doubts about his memory after watching the video presented to the court. The video clearly shows that no one was pushing his back. He almost completely doubted it, that is, until this afternoon when he felt those same two hands on him in his cell, forcing him to his knees.

His thoughts are interrupted by loud, blaring alarms and another sound, "Whump, whump, whump, whump...", and the tower speaker saying, "Yard down. Everybody, down on the ground! Yard down. Everybody, down on the ground, now!"

Stomp feels the air wash over him as a helicopter flies very low over the yard, a KSDN News helicopter. He can see a female sitting on board, looking at him, hanging from the bar by his knees.

Then Stomp hears, "You, too, Stomp. Get down on the ground! Now!", from the tower.

Oh, shit, Stomp thinks; I was so into my thoughts that I continued to crunch while the rest of the yard was down on their bellies. Stomp does a backflip from the high bar and executes a perfect 10-score gymnastic move, landing in a crouch. He thinks of his brand-new gym clothes that Hannah bought for him...he contemplates whether to lie down in the dirt with his new clothes when he hears, "I guess that's good enough, Stomp. Thank you!" from the tower voice as the helicopter lifts and pulls away to a safer altitude, turns and rapidly leaves the restricted airspace. "Yard recall! Yard recall! Everyone, up and return to your buildings at once! Yard recall!"

Stomp, still in a crouch, has another one of those premonitions that the news helicopter has some sort of significance. He catches up with Art and Chris and says so.

Art says to Stomp, "That was strange, all right. There are very strict regulations on airspace over State and Federal prisons. See that sign on the tower that reads, 'No Warning Shot'? That sign is there for a reason. I'm sure that, had that helicopter's skids touched the track, shots would have been fired. I also believe that the pilot of that news helicopter will be losing his license to fly. I, for one, have never seen that happen." says Art.

"I swear, Art... Chris, that gave me an eerie feeling of some significance. I didn't say anything before to you guys but before unlock, in my cell...Oh, never mind! It sounds crazy!" says Stomp.

"No, Stomp..." says Chris, "...we want to hear. We know that you are not crazy. Tell us, please."

"The reason that I wasn't talkative when we first came out here is that, while I was changing into my new shorts, I felt the same two hands on my shoulders that I felt on my back when I was pushed onto Aziz, except that this time I was being pushed down onto my knees to pray! The prayer came from my mouth and was in my voice, but it was as if the words were being spoken through me, not from me!"

"You're right, Stomp, that is crazy!" says Chris.

"Crazy, yes, but, Stomp, you are righteous, as we all know. Your faith and my confidence in our belief in you give me the belief and acceptance to believe that what you are telling us is 100% true! Your word is golden to us all, brother." Confirms Art.

They are just about to reach the sidewalk of Building 13 when Stomp really lets them have it. "My very best of comrades, there is more...more crazy than that...leaving me speechless! I got up from my knees and went to splash my face with water...and...and I clearly saw two hand prints on my shoulders where I had felt the pressure pushing me onto my knees!" finishes Stomp.

"Maybe your cell is haunted?" Offers Chris.

"I'll ask Nelson but I know Whom I felt! Now, I got the same feeling from the helicopter flying over us. There is some significance...has to be, don't you guys think?"

Art, Chris, and Stomp walk into the building, and they ask CO Adams about the news helicopter.

"It's all new news to me! I was here with you guys. I do know that someone will catch hell over it! Go up to your cells and check the news!" Adams directing all to lock up.

"Great idea!" they all say as they take the stairs two at a time to their cells.

Stomp goes straight to Nelson's TV and tunes in to KSDN News.

# Chapter 98:

Marc Sutter's special transport is allowed through the gate at R.J. Donovan Prison. The correctional officer at the gate steps aboard and sees the sole passenger and does not understand the wasted use of manpower and transportation. He checks his manifest. What he reads thoroughly disgusts him, and his glare at Marc shows his obvious distaste for this new addition to Donovan. He steps off the bus, spits a huge, dark-colored wad of chew juice onto the ground, and mutters a volley of ugly expletives at Marc Sutter.

The second gate opens for the transport driver, Diaz, and he continues into the center of the State facility, then turns into the dead end behind Reception and Release. Diaz puts the bus into a kneel position, then deploys the step and door to step out. The shotgunner in the rear is silent with a stare that dares the passenger to attempt a move, any move, so that he can end it right here and now. Marc doesn't take the bait and sits as perfectly still as the air around him.

Although he is the sole passenger onboard, an army of correctional officers exits the building and creates two lines of muscle, batons-in-hand and ready. CO Diaz confirms the transfer of property into R&R, confers with the sergeant in charge, gets permission to transfer the high-profile transportee into State Prison custody, and then reboards the bus. He passes through the locked gates of the bus to the area where Marc is sitting and orders him to stand up and exit the bus. Diaz's professionalism of many years is seriously stretched to the limit with this one and everyone sees it in his demeanor. Diaz steps off the bus and turns his back to the passenger, spitting a huge wad of chew onto the asphalt, refusing to acknowledge the passenger. Marc steps off the bus and is told to turn around, facing the bus. His transport chains are removed and stored in the storage bin in the belly of the bus. He is then told to turn around and strip off the County clothes that he came with and is asked to bend over and cough.

After being searched thoroughly and invasively, he is led to a waiting CO with a set of boxers, a T-shirt, and a white jumpsuit that is nearly transparent. The lack of a worker convict and the white jumpsuit is indicative of an administrative, segregated housing convict.

Marc is led to the photo equipment, told to hold up his CDC number plate, and a photo is taken, recorded, and received. Although he is only being processed for a psyche evaluation, he must still be given a CDC number.

Rather than being put into a holding cell, he is put into a locked cage that faces the counter. He will be processed while he's in the cage instead of at the counter. His personal property remains in County Booking, as does his small property, so this process goes quickly. However, the COs make him wait in that cage for four hours while the counter and all of R&R are empty and the sergeant is in his office. He has contact with the sergeant once when he is given a sack lunch and a pouch of drink mix but no water to mix with it.

It's four hours later, and Marc is dozing off in the cage when he is awakened by three batons hitting the screen of the cage.

"O.K., Asshole, time to go to your new housing until we can get rid of you. Let's go!" the sergeant yells.

Six COs, all huge at three hundred pounds or more, chain him up with leg and belly chains and begin the walk onto the 4-yard. Here, they do not close the yard for the transfer of administrative-segregation inmates. They march him right through the ongoing yard, right into Building 17.

Once inside, he is chained to a bench and then left there to wait for another two hours. The sergeant comes in, takes the CO aside, and speaks to him, casting his gaze toward Marc, and then the sergeant leaves.

"Mr. Sutter, you are here temporarily until we can trans-pack you to Patton Psychological Hospital. You will be spending almost all of your time locked up in Isolation due to your protective custody order. Next to you are your hygiene items, toilet paper, and a Title-15 book. Please pick up these items and proceed to cell 109. Dinner will be here real soon. When it arrives, it will be placed at your door. Once the kitchen workers have left the building, your door will open for you to pull in your tray. A reverse order will take place for you to set your tray outside your door. This will happen twice a day until you leave. Any questions, sir?" asks the CO.

"No, sir.", says Marc.

The CO unlocks Marc's leg and belly chains and the cuffs securing him to the bench. "Go ahead and walk to your cell and secure your door." This is the last time that Marc will see this CO for the next three weeks. The only other contact he has during his time is with a pastor who places a Bible at his door.

# Chapter 99:

Stomp, Nelson, and Paul are huddled at the planning table, with Carmen getting their coffees and bagels from Einstein's Bagels laid out for them. Nelson has noticed a huge difference in the relationship that they all share since his new friend started working with them. CO Diaz has always been professional, even with her intimacy with his boss, but now, she seems, well, domesticated. A doting hostess for the three of them only. Nelson doesn't see the same change among the other IDL workers; of course, none of them are in this area, either, so none of them see the change as he does. Diaz is even more attractive to him like this. He wonders if this is the 'new' Diaz or not. He has to admit to himself that the intimacy between Isaac and Hannah is a contagious emotion; even he felt it around other couples after their exposure to their loving relationship.

Another thought enters Nelson's mind. When he got home from work yesterday, Isaac asked him if it was possible that their cell was haunted. "Haunted?" Nelson had to laugh, "Haunted? Now, Isaac, what makes you ask that? What a bizarre thing to ask me. Why? Did you see items being flung across the room? Maybe a cloudy figure floats across your view?"

"I am being serious here, Nelson! Something did happen but I want to be taken seriously before I try to explain it to you. Can you do this?" The look on Stomp's face was not just serious but a little bit worried, as well.

"O.K., Isaac, I am sorry. Yes, I can take you seriously, when you put it that way. I'll tell you what...I am going to get cleaned up for dinner and shower, then as we wait for unlock for chow, we will sit and discuss it. Sound good to you?" asks Nelson as he grabs his towel and hygiene.

"Thank you, Nelson. I need an ear right now." again, that worried look from Stomp.

"Be right back, Isaac." reasons Nelson.

The two have a very serious discussion about what Isaac felt on his shoulders, how he was forced to his knees to pray, and about the handprints seen in the mirror. Stomp explains to Nelson how he felt the push on his back, throwing him onto Aziz's back at George Bailey; then how shocked he was when he saw the video showing that no one was behind him at the time. Nelson sits through it all, amazed and openmouthed, not being a huge believer in Divine Intervention, until now, that is.

"Your wife doesn't believe that you were pushed. She even told me so. You do believe it, however. Are you going to tell her about what happened after you came back here?" asks Nelson.

"Of course I am. I never lie to my wife or keep anything from her. I just needed to ask you if you had ever felt anything in this cell before. I mean, before I tell her, I need to know." Stomp asks again.

"Never, Isaac. It is all very strange. Handprints in our mirror? Visible like some sort of stigmata?" Now, Nelson and Stomp leave for dinner.

The next morning at work, Nelson is having trouble concentrating on the plans in front of him as Paul discusses the maintenance project for the next week. "So we have parts to change out ballasts and igniters on six of the 1000-watt H.I.D. fixtures, and we have the remaining twelve on order, plus an extra three to have on hand. Now, as to the 4-yard tower that we cannot lower due to the jammed pulley system, what do you think about renting a boom truck with a telescoping bucket that can reach the height of the fixtures? We can open up the mid-inspection and top-inspection plates to diagnose the repair of the pulley. After taking a look, we can do any of the repairs on the..." Paul takes a look at his report, "... six of the eight H.I.D. lamps that are not functioning."

Nelson confirms the count while looking at Stomp. "Yes, that tower only has two functioning fixtures on it. That part of the yard is very dim. They have no night yard, however, which is why no one has really complained to the officers in that yard. Only when they transport from here to another facility do they supervise prisoners in the dark?"

"That is one of their concerns. So, we troubleshoot and do what repairs are possible with the rented, boom truck. I want to be clear here: in no way is that bucket to be used as a crane in making these repairs. It cannot handle the weight of two men and the light tower at the same time. If we need to relieve the weight of the light tower from the post, we can make a separate work-order report for the next time that we either retrofit to L.E.D. or make repairs in the future, incorporating cranes to do so. Are we clear, gentlemen?" warns Paul.

"Yes. Understood. Bucket for repairs only, not for lifting weight or supporting weight, too dangerous with one or two men aboard." says Nelson, as Paul nods yes.

"Especially with my clumsy luck!" says Stomp.

"Especially!" emphasizes Paul.

"Boys and their toys." chuckles Carmen.

"Girls and their boys," winks Paul, then adds, "Thank you two for your thorough report. I hope that this maintenance report will be the last before the L.E.D. retrofit. The L.E.D. fixtures bolt right into the existing housings so we can remove the H.I.D. guts and install the new L.E.D. guts in their place. They may opt to retrofit the bad pulley tower while we have the bucket truck rented, but first, we have to troubleshoot the pulleys. A decision is yet to be made by Facilities. They want a full budget cost and time for payback from energy savings. I want to include you two in that process as instructors on how it works. Sound good?"

"Thanks, Paul!" say both Nelson and Stomp.

"Now, let's eat these wonderful bagels prepared for us by my lovely fiancé newly proposed," says Paul, as Carmen shows off her engagement ring.

"What?" says Nelson.

"Congratulations, Carmen and Paul. You must have gotten her in a weakened emotional state. Where did you propose to her?" asks Stomp.

Carmen's smile lights up. "We were surfing out at 'Out-of-Sights' in Sunset Cliffs for the evening glass off, with one of the most beautiful sunsets we've seen in a long time, saw a green flash and Paul leaned over for a kiss, then leaned back, took my hand and asked me to be his partner for life!"

"What did you do then, Carmen?" asks Stomp.

"She fell off of her board, Isaac after she let out an ear-piercing scream!" Paul and Carmen laugh together. "I then told her that I got her father's permission after he got his wife's permission, of course. Behind every scary father is an even scarier mother!" They all laugh.

"Paul, my mother is an angel, my father is a total softy. Don't make it sound like a lot of dangerous territory was crossed here. They both love you! As I do!" and she jumps into Paul's arms. "But I have a question to ask you, Isaac, please?"

"Just one question?" Marvels Stomp.

"I want your permission to ask Hannah to be my Maid of Honor." Asks Carmen.

"Hannah would love that, Carmen, but you need to ask her, not me. I feel that that would take her mind off of my situation here. Do you want me to talk to her first? No. You should surprise her if you ask me. Show off your engagement ring, then ask her." Says Stomp relieved.

"Thank you, Isaac." Says Carmen.

"All right, everyone. Back to work. I have to go to the office and work on this project, crunch the numbers, and get prices. The pallet over there has our high-bay L.E.D. fixtures, a contactor, pull box, conduit, and all fittings, wire, and lube. We work on this for now to light up this place for all the trades. Chop chop!" says Paul.

"First, I have a question for the three of you, my closest friends here. Nelson already knows the details, but I know that Paul is spiritual. I need advice." Stomp gets serious.

"Paul, Isaac is serious here. Please, give him a straight answer without any wit or humor!" warns Carmen.

"Who? Moi? Of course, Isaac, shoot.", returns Paul.

"I do have faith in God. I mean, I do believe, but how do I know if God has chosen me to do His work?" asks Stomp.

"Hmmm, that is a good one, Isaac. Belief is the start, and praying for guidance, as well. The key is this... you must have a relationship with God to know God. You do not just believe that He has chosen you; you will know that He has done so because you know each other. There will be no mistaking it. The signs will be visible to you and, probably, only to you. Moses, Jesus, John, and Paul were all chosen. However, the many chosen but unrecorded are vast and far-reaching. Be 100% receptive to Him, and you will know. What you do not fully understand now will be made clear to you by Him."

"Nice job, honey.", says Carmen.

"Thank you, Paul." Says Stomp.

"No. Thank you, Isaac." Says Paul. "Now I must crack that whip!"

Carmen and Paul leave Nelson and Stomp to their project. Nelson tells Stomp, "Isaac, why don't we go up and get your phone so you can call your wife? I'll come down here and begin unloading our pallet of material. Sound like a plan?"

"Perfect. Thanks, Nelson." and they head up to the mezzanine to the service gear. Nelson then leaves Stomp for his phone call.

"Hi, Baby..." Stomp says when Hannah answers.

"Hi, Honey..." says his wife.

"Hannah, I am at work with Nelson..." Warns Stomp.

"Make sure to say hello to me..." His wife ignored the warning.

"Of course, Sweetheart. I want to tell you something very important that happened to me and straighten out one other fact when I tripped into that terrible child predator. I need to clear up something..." Begins Stomp.

"Oh, Isaac, the video..." Interrupts Hannah.

"Please, let me finish, Hannah. Have I ever in my life exaggerated or not been truthful about anything? When I was on top of those stairs, I was definitely pushed, not tripped, pushed! I felt two hands on my back, no matter what that surveillance video shows. I know what I felt!" Continued Stomp.

"O.K., Isaac, whatever you say.", says Hannah.

"Something else happened, Hannah... it has me scared and worried. Never has anything like this affected me so..."

"What, Isaac, what..." Hannah is now worried.

"I felt it again! This time in my cell, on both of my shoulders, forcing me to my knees and into prayer. The prayer was as if God prayed with me or through me! When we finished I went to the sink to splash water on my face... and... that's when I saw them...two hand prints, clearly as if the hands were still pressing down...still on my shoulders!" Stomp hears a gasp.

"What does that mean, Isaac?" More worry.

"It means, Hannah, that I am being chosen to do His work on this Earth!" confirms Stomp. "And, Hannah, I need for you to believe me. I need you to pray for us and to open your heart and not just believe in God and me but to know Him as I do. Hannah, I want you to have a better relationship with God starting, well, starting right this minute. Ask for His love and His compassion for us both. I love you and I want God to love you and you Him. Bye, Honey."

"Isaac, wait! Isaac? I do want to know Him, as you say. I will pray as soon as I tell you that I love you. Bye, Honey, and please, be safe!" Then Hannah prays.

# Chapter 100:

The next week goes by quickly for Stomp. Nelson is a great mentor in explaining the mechanics of the installation of the high-bay lighting in the plant and the layout above all of the equipment and areas in between to illuminate the workspace best. Nelson teaches Stomp how to lay out the fixtures, the layout of the conduit, and how to bend the conduit from the contactor pull-box to the fixtures. By the time they complete the task, Stomp is proficient at all of it.

"Nelson, I am really enjoying this work. Thank you for being such a good instructor. I had a desk job for too long and this is a good skill set that I could get used to." Says Stomp, the electrician.

"Isaac, I can't remember the last time that I had someone learn as well as you have. Myself, I love the trade. It has always been something that I enjoy doing each day. It sounds like you are another who enjoys it, too. Paul is the same way. Everywhere that I drive out in San Diego, I can point here, point there, and proudly state that I was a part of building that or this: turning an area into a high-tech production facility or a sewer-treatment plant or conveyor systems with huge cabinets with motor controls that automate and ship products on the same line. I love it all. What we did this week is only the beginning of this project. Once we install the machinery, we will utilize electric, photo, pneumatic, and proximity controls to accomplish one aspect, then a second, a third, and so on, until a product is made and shipped. It is all fascinating, like building with an erector set as a child, piece by piece.", explains Nelson.

"So, these plans that we work from...is this what Paul does at the office...creates plans?" asks Stomp.

"No, Isaac. Engineers in all of the trades engineer plans. The engineering results are then given to an architect who takes the data and transfers that to large prints with all the engineered data and specs on the installation process." Nelson shows Stomp the entire scope of the prints. "We are working from pages of the electrical set here. This page depicts the underground below the concrete slab. It shows all of our stub-ups into service gear and from distribution to control and from control to equipment. This next page depicts the layout for the lighting. Notice the lines between fixtures and the dashes across them with circuit numbers on the dashes. Those are the conduits that we ran. The dashes are the load conductors from the contactor and breakers. At the contactor, the conductor changes from 'line' to 'load.' The switches at each door operate the coil at the contactor, the control." Nelson explains the entire electrical end of the job, as Stomp absorbs all of the instruction.

Nelson continues with his explanation of the plans, "The first pages of the blueprints depict the finished building's appearance, as seen through an architect's vision; the first page is the front view, the next page shows side views. The pages after that contain structural specs, types of materials, and steel beams with sizes and locations down to the nuts and bolts. There are mechanical illustrations that depict the ducting for any H.V.A.C., which stands for heating, ventilation, and air conditioning. We refer to these prints for heat pump and air-conditioning locations in order to run power to them, as well as bathroom ventilation equipment if they require ventilation. Plumbing encompasses any type of hydro needs, as well as pneumatic needs, for equipment. Pneumatic controls are common for anything from thermostats to equipment controls. Each piece of equipment that we install also has an attachment for control wiring shown as dotted or dashed lines with a note: see attachment so and so. At the end of the set of plans, the Panel Distribution and Control Equipment that you see here at the core will be shown. When we have hooked up all of the installed equipment, the conductors will all be landed on circuit breakers as designated on these prints."

"All of that is why Paul is at the planning table well before you and I show up for work?" asks Stomp.

"Yes, and he has a second set at his office and, probably, one in his truck. Specs for the job, since this a Government project, state what brand and type of material, even as small as a conduit strap or connector, is to be. If this project were up for bids from several contractors, a spec sheet for material would be on file at suppliers, and a material cost to estimate the job would be available to all those bidding on the project."

"Dan, how long have you been an electrician? Were you also a contractor, like Paul? I'm not sure if you are comfortable with my asking this...but what brought you here? If you don't want to say, I won't ask again." Asks the ever-curious Stomp.

"Well, Isaac, I have been an electrician for my entire adult life since I was seventeen years old. Yes, I have had my 'C-10' contractor's license since 1984 and my own business, which was successful for decades. Unfortunately, to start a contracting business consumes a lot of time to be successful. My wife wanted children, and so did I, but a couple needs to spend time together to consummate a relationship and bear a child. We grew distant, although I now see that her loneliness was my doing. I had a difficult time trying to understand why she couldn't see that I was working hard to be successful for us both. You know the saying, "Too much work makes Dan a bore," well, too much work made Deanna a whore! I came home for a minute to retrieve a set of plans that I had left behind, and I caught Deanna in bed with our neighbor. I shot them both where they slept, but I was too much of a coward to shoot myself. I thought that if I couldn't shoot myself, I would let the police do it for me, you know, suicide by cop? You always read how trigger-happy the cops are and how the swat team takes out an armed man who refuses to come out of his home. I called 911 and the dispatcher was a woman, a very nice woman. She seemed to understand my situation and kept talking to me. A combination of her empathy and then seeing Deanna dead in bed finally made me break down and cry uncontrollably. I didn't even notice that the police had come through the garage as I was crying. I was in handcuffs without even knowing it. I got twenty-three years for a crime of passion. My attorney did his best, I know. That was fifteen years ago, Isaac. I think that I will be eligible for parole in three or four years, but I'm not in a hurry. I have no one and nothing out there.", concludes Nelson.

"Dan, you have Hannah, Paul, Carmen, and me! I really mean that, too! You have good friends, and I can honestly say that you can depend on and rely on friends like us to be there for you, and I also mean that! Are you listening to me here, Dan? I mean, really comprehending what I am telling you here? You have us!" comforts Nelson's new friend. "We are now family to you!"

Nelson is near to tears. No one in almost two decades has ever told him this.

# **Chapter 101:**

At five o'clock on this foggy morning, Paul drives the rented bucket truck through the gate into Donovan and onto the 4-yard. He parks it at the base of the light tower with the faulty pulley system, then walks back to the gate. Carmen is there waiting for him, along with CO Murtaugh, who is stationed at the 4-yard gate.

"Thank you, Murtaugh. We will round up the troops and get an early start here. Obviously, there will be no yard today, right? I have the keys and the vehicle is secured. We will get this done as soon as we can, but it should take the entire day." Says Paul while looking at Carmen for verification...

"I've spoken to him and R&R. The only movement today will be a trans-pack to Patton Hospital for a psych evaluation. He will be under heavy escort due to his Ad-Seg housing. We will be able to work through his being escorted. We will be working in the center of the yard, and he will be escorted along the track. Murtaugh has informed me that since these lights have been malfunctioning for so long, there is now an owl's nest that has been created among the fixtures. Nelson and Isaac need to be careful when they approach the nest in case the parents are nearby.", says Carmen.

Paul turns to Murtaugh and says, "We appreciate the info, Murtaugh. Have you seen any recent activity among these new residents? Had I known before today, I could have set up a professional removal team but that takes time. We won't disturb the nest if we see hatchlings in it. We will try to repair the six faulty fixtures without going near the nest. You know, they are paying a big fee on this truck and are being leaned on for lights by the Goon Squad or, I mean, Investigative Special Unit Squad." They all laugh.

"That's OK. We call them the Goon Squad here, too.", says Murtaugh. "You know, the State could care less about the owls. Sparrows' nests cover the 3-yard under all of the eaves. They are protected, I believe. I'm not sure about the owls."

"Whether they are or not..." says Carmen, "...we won't disrupt a nest on my watch! Can we make sure that Nelson and Isaac have proper protection, a welder's mask, and leather gloves, just in case... maybe an airhorn to scare away the parents and keep them away?"

"We'll make sure that they are protected. I'm pretty sure that the parents have flown the coop since there has been no activity recently. Either way, as long as we don't touch the hatchlings, they should be fine. The parents will simply fly around or perch and watch from a distance once we go near. They and we will be fine. I won't take any chances. Let's get going, though.", says Paul.

Carmen walks with Paul to the new building, gives him a peck on the cheek, and leaves him to prepare the parts and materials for the day and the tower. Paul takes time to write out a list of tools needed, then adds safety masks and welders' gloves to the list.

He has no air horn, but he adds a sprayer to the list. He is hoping that a simple water spray will scare or deter any aggressive parent owls present. He walks to the materials shelf and pulls out ten H.I.D. rebuild kits containing ballasts and igniter, as well as new 1000-watt lamps, and sets them all in the John Deere cart. While outside by the cart, he sees what seems like three apparitions approaching him along the eerie, fog-enshrouded driveway.

"Hark, who goes there? Friend or foe? They came from the mist!" Paul says jokingly. "Good morning, you two."

"Morning, Paul.", says Stomp.

"Morning, Boss. I hope this fog won't be a problem on the 4-yard, will it?" asks Nelson.

"No. I spoke to Murtaugh already. We are a go. There is an escort planned near ten or so this morning. The time was not spoken of due to security issues, but transports leave here around that time. Early mornings are kept clear for receiving new bodies, but with this transport, it is not being said." informs Paul. "Something else that I was just informed about; it seems that the faulty light tower has been dark for so long that new residents have started a family on top of the tower somewhere, an owl's nest. We aren't sure if it's still occupied, but I have safety masks and leather gloves, just in case. There's also a sprayer to spray a jet of water in case they are still in residence, and we need to coax an eviction temporarily. We won't disrupt their nest if it's occupied. We will work around them. If at any time it seems a danger to you two, we will abort and wait for professional removal. Are we clear on that?" stresses Paul.

"Yes, Boss.", says Nelson.

"One more thing. Stop calling me that, Nelson!" Snaps Paul.

"Yes, Boss!", laughs Nelson.

The three load up their necessary tools from the tool crib, then all four board the John Deere cart and drive to the 4-yard. Murtaugh is at the gate, ready for their arrival. He secures the gate after they drive in and approach the boom truck. All four look through the fog for signs of life, but the top of the tower is still hidden from view. Even the use of binoculars cannot cut through the fog to verify any activity. Murtaugh, with nothing better to do at this time, joins them to watch as a two-hundred-foot-long extension cord is run from the truck generator to the one-inch Milwaukee drive-drill, lying on the ground at the base of the tower. Paul removes the inspection plate to prepare for their work below while Stomp and Nelson are on the lift.

"All right, guys, the fog has almost dissipated or soon will. We can remove the center inspection plate to examine the pulley system at mid-level. After that, we will examine the mid-level plate. We will then move up to the mast plate and inspect the pulley. As you rise up to it, use caution and be on the lookout for any active owl presence. This morning, I did find a couple of pellets on the ground at the tower base. Pellets are regurgitated from birds of prey as a ball of bones, feathers, and whatever else isn't digestible. If you see any sign of the residence of hatchlings or parent owls, use your camp jackets, welders' helmets, and gloves as a precaution. Do not spray the nest or the hatchlings. Spray away from the nest. Use the sprayer to keep any adult owls from perching on the tower. We'd rather that the owls circle in flight than attack from a perched position. If they persist in an attack, we will abort; no argument for that. We are not bird-of-prey experts." Paul explains their rules of engagement. "Here are the Motorola headsets...let's test them out before we begin."

The three don their headsets, set to VOA, and Nelson says, "Testing, one, two, three... can you hear my voice, Stomp? Boss, can you hear me?"

"Confirm, Dan," says Stomp.

"Confirm, Dan. Can you hear me, Dan... can you hear this? Stop calling me Boss!" says Paul.

"Confirm, Boss!" says Nelson, then chuckles, then, "Hey, Boss... uhm...I think I just got shit on by an owl."

Both turn to look at Nelson, and down his back is a huge, white, and green bird turd. All three laugh a little and then they notice the same kind of turds covering the ground all around where Nelson is standing. Turds and pellets are all over the base.

"There is our answer, boys. The parents are, obviously, in town!" says Paul. Then he starts up the truck, "All right, let's check our controls, Nelson." There are two sets of controls, one in the bucket and one on the side of the truck. Both check out.

The lift begins to telescope and rise up to the mid-mast inspection plate. "Removing inspection plate, Boss.", says Nelson.

"You need to have your ears checked, Dan?" says Paul.

"Did you say something, Boss?" asks Nelson.

"Ha-ha, save your stand-up routine for the talent show at Las Colinas, Dan. You know, the one after the dance that I sold you tickets for? I heard that you asked Monique in the yard to go with you." adds Paul.

"Yeah, but she broke my heart by getting engaged to Diaz last week!" laughs Nelson as he removes the inspection plate and peers into the center-cable, pulley retraction system. "Boss, here is the problem. The pulley bracket is twisted, cracked, and torn. I recommend an entirely new pulley bracket and hardware. We will replace the plate and check out the topmast for signs of stress, as well."

"Thank you, Mr. Nelson." jokes Paul.

"Mr....what?" says Nelson.

"Boss...what?" mimics Paul. "What, Boss?" laughing, "All right, moving on up to the penthouse for an aviary eviction process." Another big owl turd hits the platform. "Being bombarded by Mama Bird. She is visible on the nest and I can hear her chicks chirping from here. Removing the top-mast inspection plate."

"Does she seem agitated to you?" asks Paul.

"She tried to shit on me, Boss...uh...I take that as agitated." Nelson looks up, "But she is not moving around, she seems content on her nest. We are still about ten feet from the nest, though, which is situated between two of our non-functioning lights." adds Nelson.

"Got it, Stomp? Can you hear me?" Paul again.

"Yeah, Paul, I hear you."

"Keep the sprayer pumped up for maximum spray, and keep your eyes on the owl. At any sign of her attacking you two... let her have it... try not to hit the hatchlings. It might scare them out of the nest, and they might fall to their deaths. If Mama is aggressive instead of curious, we get out of there. Understood?" asks Paul.

"Yes, Boss!" Nelson and Stomp laugh.

"Oh, brother!" says Paul. "Get serious, you two!"

"Yes, Boss!" together this time.

"Two comedians out of work?" Paul's turn to laugh.

Nelson manipulates the arm of the boom to the opposite side of the tower, away from the nest. He takes it up in 'turtle' mode, slowly. Mama Owl keeps watch on their activity but soon gets used to their non-aggressive presence.

"She sure is a gorgeous bird.", Stomp says. "Her head seems about the size of a volleyball. She is solid white with black ears that look like they could be horns. Her neck swivels almost 360 degrees around. Her bill is the size of my hand, and I think that she could, probably, take off my hand at the wrist if she really wanted to."

"All right, Boss, one light done, moving on to the second one now."

"10-4, Mr. Nelson. Isaac, keep eye contact with the owl. Prove to her that we are not here to harm her or her hatchlings today." Reminds Paul of his previous instructions.

"It seems that she is aware of this. We should have brought a large rat or a rabbit as a gift, although she sure doesn't look to be starving."

The H.I.D. units have spikes attached to the tops of the housings to deter the thousands of seagulls from landing on them; three rows of three spikes, sixteen inches long, riveted to the top of each housing. Their proximity to the salty Pacific Ocean air necessitates that these spikes be made of stainless steel. The weakness here is that the rivets are not.

"All right, Boss, done with light two. Make a note that when we retrofit these housings to L.E.D., we need to include new, stainless-steel hardware to replace the four rivets on three of the gull spikes. The salt air badly damages these. So far, all have the same damage." reports Nelson.

"Great idea, Mr. Nelson. Making a note now.", says Paul, writing on the work order in the 'Suggestions' paragraph.

"Moving the boom to numbers three and four. We will be as close as four feet from the nest, so, now, it gets touchy, but it seems that the owl is O.K. with our presence," confirms Nelson.

"All right, proceed with caution then. Keep all movements slow and talk at a minimum.", says Paul.

Nelson begins by lowering the bucket to clear the nails from the cross-members, then backs the boom away from the mast. He then swings the bucket around to the left so that when he moves the boom to the right, he can position the bucket to face in the proper direction. This way, as he booms up towards the nest, no further movement of the bucket will be needed. At the same time, he notices that eight COs, in full Goon-Squad weaponry, have begun a walk from the gate of 4-Yard down to the track. The owl also notices the presence of extra humans and is swiveling her head between them and the bucket. Nelson decides to wait until the Goon Squad reaches its destination and stops moving.

Marc Sutter is called down to be transferred to Patton and is leg-chained as well as belly-chained. His face card is checked, and he is asked his name for verification. Rettus is surrounded by four huge Goon-Squad escorts and led outside, where four more are waiting on the track. Monster, who has stayed in the background for these last few months, comes out for a breath of fresh air. He figures that once Marc is evaluated, he needs to stay out of sight to convince the doctors that Marc and Rettus actually do not know about the heinous murders that he has committed. After all, he has done this before with Dr. Sullivan and gotten away with murder. He looks up as they begin their track walk. The morning fog is just burning off, and there appears to be a halo around the sun overhead. He sees a truck with a long arm that is telescoped out and up to the top of the light tower, with two men in a bucket and one on the ground, with CO Murtaugh beside him. Murtaugh says something to the man and walks to the gate to where they are going. The men in the bucket begin to rise up higher towards the lights.

Stomp has the sprayer ready as the lift gets closer to the owl's nest. The owl, no longer relaxed, is swiveling her gaze from the men on the ground to Nelson and Stomp. Stomp and the owl make eye contact. The owl seems to wink at Stomp, strange. The owl rises up above her six hatchlings and steps up to the edge of the nest. Stomp can see her talons now; each talon is eight inches long and razor-sharp. The owl stretches her wings to their full, five-foot wing span. He had no idea that owls could be so huge. The bucket is now stopped, and Nelson begins to remove the screws by hand rather than by using his cordless driver. The glass reflector is lowered with a loud, creaking noise, which startles the owl, and she launches herself out and away from the workers. She attempts to perch on one of the triple-spiked, stainless-steel pitchforks, but her weight causes the rivets to snap off.

The owl seems to tumble as she spreads her huge wings, the pitchfork still grasped in her talons. She makes two long flaps of her wings to gain back her altitude and realizes that she is still gripping the metal object. She looks over her shoulder at Stomp and he swears that she winked at him once again. Then she releases her grip, letting the steel pitchfork fall, end-over-end, towards the earth. She makes a lazy, 180-degree turn back towards her hatchlings.

Monster, still being led off the yard, is happy with himself and how he plans to outsmart the courts, with the help of 'their' attorney, Mr. De Santo, and he looks towards the heavens to thank the heavens. As he tilts back his head, he sees a blinding flash of glare as the sun reflects off stainless steel. In an instant, what goes through his mind is that this glare is unnatural. The next thing that goes through his mind is the sixteen-inch, stainless-steel barb of the pitchfork as it penetrates his right eyeball and goes out the back of his neck, killing him instantly. Marc Sutter, Rettus Cram, and the Monster Within all cease to have brain activity in that same instant, and they all collapse on the track in one body.

The owl circles around the bucket, head swiveling. As she passes Stomp and Nelson, she lets out a screech, and again, she gives an obvious wink to Stomp as if a secret is shared between them.

"Did you see that, Isaac? She just screeched and winked at you. What the hell..." Nelson says.

"Boys, better get down here right now! Finish securing that light first to make it safe. Then return to the truck. These gentlemen here have some questions for you." says Paul.

As Nelson rotates the bucket and begins the descent, they notice the commotion on the track. The man being led by an escort is now a crumpled mess and... Oh, my God... is that a pitchfork sticking through his brain? Nelson and Stomp only look at each other; both are amazed by what they see but will never be witness to.

# Epilogue:

"This is Kristy Lyons, flying high above Otay Mesa, coming to you live over R.J. Donovan Prison. In what was determined to be an Act of God or an Act of Nature for our atheist viewers, Marc Sutter has been killed. The murdering culprit, a mother owl of the Great Horned variety, grasping a pitchfork apparatus, which she tore loose from one of the light towers and released in midair. The piece of metal fell end over end until abruptly impaling the high-profile child killer from East County as he was being led to his transport vehicle, leaving for Patton Mental Hospital. We can now close the chapter on this case, ending what was a stalemate for Judge Lazarus of East County Court. Terrence Matt, the District Attorney for East County. Mr. Nicolas De Santo, the defense counsel for Mr. Sutter. As well as all of the Sheriff's Department Deputies and loved ones of the children. God has judged and dished out justice in one fell swoop; pardon the pun. This is Kristy Lyons, saying good night and good riddance!" says Kristy as Don banks the news helicopter back towards Montgomery Field.

Far below on the 3-yard, life is back to normal. The entire facility goes into lockdown for just one day while the Investigation Special Unit (Goon Squad) does their investigation, putting the owl at fault. She and all her hatchlings are given life on the 4-yard for her part in the killing. The boom truck is still sitting there, waiting to be returned after the work is resumed and completed.

There is a small group assembled on the 3-Yard, consisting of Charles 'Carlo' Renovales and Lorenzo 'LoLo' Escoto, representing the South Siders; J.J. Raker and Art Dietrich, representing the Wood Pile; and Douglas 'Pops' Daniels, representing the Blacks and Others on the 3-Yard. Nelson and Stomp are there, as well, with J.J. and Art for an entirely different investigation to be carried out from that by the Goon Squad. This group runs the 3-yard. Some here run all of the yards here at San Diego's R.J. Donovan Prison.

Art begins, "Good afternoon, gentlemen. We appreciate you all agreeing to meet with us. All of us know each other. I am Art. As some know, I am the right hand to J.J. here, who holds the Wood keys to this facility. We apologize for any disruption of programs caused by the unplanned death of the white convict child killer being held in Ad-Seg 17. As you are all aware, our policy to get at any of those protected due to their charges is mandatory and needs no green light. This person was a high-profile, serial child killer named Marc Sutter, impaled by the pitchfork of the Devil himself. Accident, as they claim?... Perhaps. Prison justice dealt out?... Definitely, I have brought these two here to share their first-hand witness experience with all of you without being overly dramatized by being heard ear-to-ear, over and over. We all know Dan Nelson, who has lived with us for the last ten years. Stomp, here, is his cellmate and co-worker. Both were present and were first accused of killing the P.C. convict in transport. Dan?"

"I want to refer this to Stomp here. I was busy with work when this happened. The owl in question was being watched carefully by my co-worker in case she chose to defend her new hatchlings. Stomp?" Dan introduces.

"Good afternoon, gentlemen. I want to say that Dan, my cellmate, and I, although questioned extensively by the Goon Squad, never answered any of their questions when asked. We were suspected, at first, so we refused to speak to them." This is met with nods of approval and praise by all. "It was CO Murtaugh who witnessed the owl's flight and release of the pitchfork, whether the instrument of the Devil or of God. I prefer God. To the Goons, I said nothing. To my fellow convicts, I will explain, in detail, what happened." Stomp informs the group of the circumstances leading to the demise of Marc Sutter, leaving out no details.

When he finishes, Charles 'Carlo' Renovales speaks, "On behalf of La Raza, South Siders, and my good friend, Capone, at the Bay, respects to you, Stomp, and Nelson, as well. Everyone here knows of your actions and work for our communities and families out there where we cannot protect them as you have done. Muchos gracias! Capone also sends his gratitude for your continuing service and friendship. Officially, I am also to let you know, as you do, that the South Siders have your back in every way. We are aware of your and Nelson's refusal to cooperate in their investigation, as well. This takes courage in itself. LoLo, would you like to express your gratitude as well?"

"Por Seguro. Claro que si." says Lorenzo Escoto, "As some of us know, the love of my life is my daughter, Epiphanes Escoto. She is only two years old at the moment, but she is growing quickly, like all of our children are. Our children need us, their fathers, to protect them from these terrible animals who prowl and target innocence. Your work and service, intentional or unintentional, are recognized by us all, here and now. I know Capone as well. His respect is not given lightly, and if I wondered why he would protect one who is not La Raza, I know now. Respectfully, I thank you both." All of those at this important meeting share their gratitude verbally, with thank-you's resounding from all.

The members of the meeting scatter as they draw some attention from the COs in the yard, who begin to stroll their way.

"Stomp..." Nelson begins, "... today we will enjoy in the yard. I'm sure that we will resume our work tomorrow. I can see now that you are going to make our years remaining here, well, an adventure. I have to agree with what LoLo said, 'intentional or unintentional,' I am proud to stand by your side in this adventure. My life, I now know, has a better purpose, a higher calling, being by your side. Sure, I get no signals, stigmata, or winks from wild animals, but I now believe. I believe now when I had forgotten how to believe. I will no longer wonder if you are a religious zealot who imagines his faith. I know now, that what you experienced is a sign of some event to occur because that's what it is. I have no doubt.

"What the hell are you two talking about?" asks Art and J.J. Raker. "I'm not sure that you two would understand and, for now, Nelson and I are plum tired of explaining our experiences. Can we just walk and enjoy a beautiful day?" asks Stomp.

"Sure, Stomp,..." says Art, "... but soon, J.J. and I would love to hear your story from both of you." They all agree that the story will be told but at another time and place.

The End

NO WARNING
SHOT

9 781966 565833